D0966453

Three Minutes' Silence

.

Three Minutes' Silence

GEORGII VLADIMOV

TRANSLATED
BY
MICHAEL GLENNY

Quartet Books
London Melbourne New York

First published in Great Britain by Quartet Books Limited 1985
A member of the Namara Group
27/29 Goodge Street, London W1P 1FD

First published as *Tri Minuty Molchaniya*, in abridged form, 1969, by *Novy Mir*; in
full by Possev-Verlag, V. Gorachek K.G., 1982

Translation copyright © by Michael Glenny

British Library Cataloguing in Publication Data

    Vladimov, Georgii
    Three minutes' silence.
    Rn: Georgii Nikolaievich Volosevich
    I. Title
    891.73'.44[F]   PG3489.3.L29

    ISBN 0-7043-2394-X

Typeset by MC Typeset, Chatham, Kent
Printed and bound in Great Britain
by Mackays of Chatham Ltd, Kent

CONTENTS

ACKNOWLEDGEMENTS

The translator of this book acknowledges with gratitude the generous and invaluable help given to him by Professor A.E. Kennaway, Lieutenant-Commander, RN (retd), and by C.J. Sanders, Esq, formerly Leading Seaman, RN.

'Ye are neither spirit nor spirk,' he said; 'ye are neither book nor brute –
Go, get ye back to the flesh again for the sake of Man's repute.
Go back to Earth with a lip unsealed – go back with an open eye,
And carry my work to the Sons of Men or ever ye come to die:
That the sin they do by two and two they must pay for one by one,
And . . . the God that you took from a printed book be with you,
    Tomlinson!'

from Rudyard Kipling's poem Tomlinson

Part 1

Lilya

1

Once again I was alone on the pier and the fog was for real, not just in my head.

I looked into the harbour at the water, black and smoking, and the mooring warps white with hoar-frost. Below me there was still some visibility, but higher up it was like milk: a little tug was moored about ten paces away and all you could make out was her wheelhouse, the masts not at all. Yet when I'd been walking down to the port I'd been able to see the sky clear and greenish above the hills; but the stars had looked as if they had been swabbed clean, so that I knew it couldn't last long: there would be a frost towards nightfall and the warmth of the Gulf Stream would be cooled. Fog would settle over the harbour and sink down to the water. And tomorrow the trawlers would be quietly putting out and heading for the Atlantic.

This time, though, I wouldn't be going. I'd given up the sea, so I really had no business to be in the fishing port; I had simply dropped in to say goodbye. I was taking my last look at the whole picture, and then I'd let go my lines for the last time and shove off inland to some part of Russia. To somewhere in the south, that is.

It was just then that these two characters showed up, looming out of the fog.

'Ahoy there, mate!' they shouted.

Both of them were scruffy as hell, caps on the backs of their heads, quilted jackets unbuttoned, steaming as if they'd just been run off their feet.

'Hello, mates,' I said. 'Good to see you.'

The fact is, they were no mates of mine. Well, one of them, Vova, had once been a shipmate of mine for a short while; we had twice sailed in the same trawler and had even swapped tattoos. He had my name, Senya, tattooed across his fingers and I had 'Vova' on mine. So what, it was just another tattoo. As for the other one, who was slightly pop-eyed, this was the first time I'd ever clapped eyes on him. He was shouting the louder, and as he came up he sort of couldn't keep his greedy paws off me.

'Look who we've found! Had to get nose to nose to see him in this pea-souper, though. What can it mean, Vova?'

What it means, I thought, is that purple nose of yours can always find whatever you're looking for – and that's most likely to be someone who's in the money. It was obvious what they were – a couple of beachcombers, the kind of sailors who never go to sea but can always spin a yarn about storms and rough trips when it comes to chatting up girls. (Only town girls, of course; they can't fool the port girls.) The only rough trip they ever have is crawling once a day to sign on at the Labour, preferably in the early evening, when all the outbound ships' complements are already made up, then twice a month to join the queue at the cashier's office to pick up their 'legal', the guaranteed seventy-five per cent of the basic seagoing wage. Not much of a life, really. The rest of the time they spend hanging around the quays when the trawlers moor up and the lads come ashore with their pay. This is when they stick to you like limpets, so as you can't shake them off with hand-grenades, and it's: 'Ahoy there, Senya! What's new? Hear the Atlantic water's dropped so low the ships are scraping their keels on the bottom – hey, we ought to drink to that. Are we sailors or aren't we?' You know these bloodsuckers as well as you know your own brothers, yet you buy them food and drink all the same, because when you first come ashore you're glad to see a familiar face and you want to go anywhere but back on board.

'Well, you beachers,' I said, 'where are you going? Don't tell me you're off on a trip?'

'Trip, hell!' shouted Popeye. 'No one's catching anything this year. Seems the fish've learned how to dodge the nets.'

'How would you know?'

'Christ! We were at sea only a week ago.'

The last time he saw the sea was eighteen months ago. In the cinema. Because Murmansk is not on the sea but on an estuary, called the Sound, which is so narrow you can't even catch sight of the sea between the hills on either bank. And only a week ago I had come back from a herring-fishing trip and Vova himself had been on this very same quay to meet me.

Vova looked embarrassed. 'It wasn't a week ago, Askold. More than a month.'

'So what's a month between friends?'

'Or a week for that matter?'

I should have moved on out of harm's way, but you know how it is – it's interesting to find out who's just landed and who's signed on during my last day in the port, and the surest way you'll find out is from the beachers, no need to go and ask at the office.

'OK,' I said, 'let's say it was last week a year ago. Who've you come to meet, Vova?'

'Some pals of mine from Three Brooks,' Vova replied. It was true that he had a woman, a cashier, who lived across the Sound in Three Brooks, so he would have known people from over that way. 'Three-oh-nine has just docked, the *Medusa*.'

This, of course, started off the usual round of seamen's gossip.

'Where's she been?'

'Grand Banks.'

'What was she catching?'

'Perch and silver hake.'

'Good catch?'

'Not too good.'

'Why? Dirty weather?'

''Course not! Flat calm, smooth enough to see your face in the water to shave by. But perch don't catch easy in a calm.'

'So they didn't get their plan target?'

'Hardly caught anything at all, so they didn't make the premium, of course. They'll get their minimum, though, and then there's the foreign-going bonus, which is about nought-point-eight for Canadian waters.'

The beachers know everything: who's been where, what the catch was like, and how much they made. And *they* never come away empty-handed from their little trips to the quayside.

'Some lads had a bit of bad luck,' said Askold, looking suitably glum. 'Came back from the Grand Banks, hadn't had a sniff of the shore for four months, and then they wouldn't let 'em into port. Radar was bust. So they've been standing offshore since yesterday waiting for this muck to clear.'

'So what?' I said. 'At least they're safe from the likes of you out there.'

They pretended not to hear this.

After a few moments of a polite silence Vova asked: 'You sailing today?'

'No,' I said, 'I've finished playing that game.'

'You mean they've put you on the beach?'

'*They* put *me* on the beach? No, I chucked it in myself.'

'How come?'

'Nohow. Just got fed up with it.'

'Picked up your papers yet?'

'That's why I've come down here – to sign off for good.'

'I see,' said Vova. 'And where will you go?'

'A long way away,' I said. 'By train.'

'Some other port? Black Sea? Baltic?'

'People, Vova, don't only work at sea. You can drop anchor on dry land, too, you know.'

'You can. Question is, how.'

'Well, at least I won't do it your stupid way – not at sea and not on land either.'

Askold stood there without saying anything, open-mouthed, as though this wasn't aimed at him, but I could see it had embarrassed Vova. He'd been a seaman for a long time, but he was now so used to being on the beach that if you spat at him he'd just wipe it off.

'Well,' said Vova, 'there's no sense in trying to make a man change his mind once he's made it up. Why don't we get drunk to celebrate it?'

'Don't much fancy getting drunk . . .'

'What's the problem? No more cash left? Look, Askold here can pawn his jacket, you take the pawn ticket and you can redeem it later.'

'Plenty of cash left, Vova. No more *fools* left, that's all,' I said.

Say that to any real sailor and he'd have thumped me, but these two had been beaching for so long they'd forgotten they'd once been real sailors. They just looked at each other when I said I had plenty of cash left; Askold even licked his lips. And I did have all my money on me, pinned to the inside pocket of my jacket – twelve hundred new roubles. All that was left from my last trip. We'd been after herring in the North Sea, off the Shetlands, and we'd had a good catch. Sometimes we had caught three or four hundred barrels a day. We had sweated like slaves, and that way we'd not only earned the premium for reaching our target but the supplementary as well. Plus the thirty per cent due to me – three years' Arctic bonus at ten per cent a year. The only money I'd spent had been on cigarettes and razor blades from the ship's store, a few small debts, and the payments I made direct to my mother by warrant. I had spent some of it on booze, of course, when I landed – maybe fifty roubles. But I never took a single rouble's worth of credit on the factory ships, and none of it went to any of the scrubbers on shore either. So certain people were seeing the end of Senya Shalai: he was signing off for good and wouldn't be asking for an advance!

That's why I said to them: 'Plenty of cash left, Vova. No more *fools* left, that's all.'

'What's he saying, Vova?' Askold had decided to act a bit offended. He went crimson in the face and his big eyes nearly popped out of his head. 'Sounds like he doesn't want to be seen with sailors any more!'

But Vova, my friend, my old mate, only laughed and said: 'He's almost a landlubber now, didn't you hear what he said? He'll go down to the Crimea and try and impress all those daft buggers on the beach with yarns about the dirty weather in the Atlantic.'

I wanted to belt him one for that, but he was an old mate after all, and anyway I hadn't been exactly showering him with compliments myself, so I changed my mind and just walked on. I had just one idea in my head that day – to walk round all the quays, look at the ships and the dockyard, take the ferry over to Cape Abram and go everywhere I'd once been, all the places I'd sailed from or where my ship had been refitted, where I had once been on shorewatch; but now I had suddenly lost interest in it, because I realized I might easily meet someone I knew, get talking and not be able to get away – as was happening now.

'Hey, wait a minute!' Vova shouted after me. They were still standing there on the pier, but by now you couldn't see their faces, only their legs below the blanket of fog. 'So we aren't going to see each other again – is that it, mate? And here's me with nothing to give you for a goodbye present.'

'When you've got something, you can give it to Askold.'

'He's just said we ought to give the fool a present, too. For old times' sake. Wouldn't you like us to get you a nice jacket – cheap?'

'What do I want a jacket for?'

'You can't leave looking like that!'

As they caught up with me, Vova grabbed my overcoat and pulled it open. 'You look a mess! All the girls'll laugh at you in the street. Some sailor you are – couldn't get yourself a gabardine suit or even a decent foreign mackintosh. You've done yourself a bad turn by being so stingy with your money. Where is that man with the jacket?'

'He's here,' Askold waved his hand vaguely. 'Somewhere around these warehouses.'

'Look, there's an engineer from the merchant navy whose flogging this jacket. I tell you, if you dreamed about it and woke up you'd want to go right back to sleep again.'

'It's Norwegian!' roared Popeye. God hadn't given him much else, but He hadn't stinted on his voice. 'Fur-lined, see, with toggles. Sort of grey-like, maybe a bit darker, smokey, you know. You couldn't get one like it on the black market if you tried.'

'Well, isn't he a black marketeer? They all are in the merchant navy.'

'Not this one,' Vova explained. 'He's only asking a hundred for it. Almost giving it away, you might say. You know how it is sometimes – he was unlucky. Bought it on spec and it didn't fit him. But I can tell from here it'd fit you to a tee.'

The fact is, I'd been dreaming of a jacket like that for a long time. I didn't look a mess – though these two beachers did, and that's for sure! – in fact I had on a velour overcoat with a lambswool collar, and a tweed suit, and my cap was OK too, but what I was wearing was all I had. The trouble was that in my outward appearance, as they say, I didn't look anything like a sailor, except for the striped singlet under my shirt. And because I'd put in plenty of sea-time, I wanted something to show for it.

'Why hesitate?' asked Vova. 'He's just been waiting for someone like you, this man with the jacket. Wait right here on the pier, don't go away . . .'

They both clapped me on the shoulders and melted into the fog. I stood and waited a while. Then I thought: Christ, what an idiot I am! Fancy trusting a couple of beachers to get me clothes on the cheap. They'll want twenty-five roubles' commission – that's the going rate with them – because they never do anything for love. And I needed to pay their commission like I needed a hole in the head. Surely I could find this merchant-navy bloke myself, couldn't I? What's more, I looked at my watch and saw it was past two o'clock; at this time of year in Murmansk it would be getting dark soon.

So I set off along the quays, under the cranes and past the warehouses. Then I realized that the whole idea was pointless in this fog. A fine day I'd chosen to say goodbye to the port! The fact is, though, that you don't really *choose* to do a thing like this: you just wake up one morning and you just know – it's today or never. And it's no good asking yourself: 'Why today?', because as soon as you ask that, you change your mind about it.

In any case, I knew the fishing port like the back of my hand. I could've found my way anywhere blindfold, just going by smell or by sound. I could smell something now: that wasn't the smell of salt fish, but frozen fresh fish and ammonia; that meant I was on Quay No. 10, alongside the refrigeration plant. A bit further on it smelt of wet planking, there was the sound of hammers on iron, and truck-drivers swearing: the packing sheds on Quay No. 12, where they filled containers with empty barrels. Further still there was the heady reek of oil and the noise of pumps slurping away: Quay No. 13, where the ships take on fuel and water.

If I'd stayed in the fishing fleet for another five years I would have learned other things too: whose were the hooters calling back and fourth to each other, whose siren was wailing, who was calling for a diver or a welder, the name of the dispatcher whose voice was rasping all over the harbour through the loud-hailer:

'*Ranger*! Switch on your radio, *Ranger* . . . Tug *Sturdy*! Tow factory-ship *Forty Octobers* to Quay No. 26 . . .'

But if anything I had been sailing for too long. A year would have been enough, and I'd have been spared a lot of bad times. I should have just gone somewhere inland and managed without ever seeing the sea again. Or maybe I wouldn't have managed – you never know these things about yourself.

When I reached Central Passage I looked behind me and couldn't see anything. The fog had got so thick that if you stretched out your arm you couldn't see your own fingers. But the two beachers had spotted me. They caught up with me near Central Passage, completely out of breath, poor buggers. With them was this merchant-navy type with a little suitcase. And I'd forgotten all about them.

'Hey, why did you go and stand us up?' Askold shouted. 'We trusted you and you sneaked off. What's the idea, Senya?'

The sailor measured me up for size at one glance. 'Is this him? Let's try it on, then.'

He was a real, straight-up sailor and tiddly in his fur-lined Canadian jacket with a shawl collar, his seaman's cap at the proper angle, the peak two fingers above his eyebrows. More often than not we herring-fishers wear grubby old overcoats or government-issue quilted jackets, but merchant seamen take a pride in their appearance.

We stepped behind some newspaper display-boards, and there he pulled out his jacket.

And what a jacket! It was phenomenal – and then some. White zigzag stitching across the chest, the lilac-coloured lining crisp and new, inside pockets with zip fasteners, two slanting pockets on the outside edged with white fur, a fur-lined hood, a zip all the way down the front, little epaulettes sewn on to the shoulders with the merchant-navy badge on them and none of your anchors – anchors are old hat – and the cuffs edged with fur too. As for the colour, I can hardly describe it – it was like the colour of a big wave in a Force 8 gale when the sun's still shining through the clouds . . .

'It's enough to make you die just looking at it,' said Popeye, with what was almost a sob. 'It's fucking lovely!'

'You pipe down,' Vova said to him sternly. 'It's not fucking lovely just an ordinary, decent jacket. And keep your dirty paws off it, 'cos it's not yours.'

'Well,' said the sailor. 'Isn't it just the ticket?'

I was going to ask him how much he wanted for this treasure, but that's not the way it's done; only peasants in the market haggle like that. I had to try it on first. I took off my overcoat and gave it to Askold to hold, while Vova took my jacket. The new jacket might have been made to measure for me, except that it was a bit loose around the shoulders. But then I was buying something that was going to last, and I would fill out with time.

They buttoned me up, patted it, turned me round to look at it from every side; the sailor took off my old cap and put his navy cap on me instead, in regulation style. Then he opened his little suitcase – there was a mirror fitted inside the lid.

'Don't hurry,' he said. 'Take your time and look at yourself. You need to know what sort of effect it makes. If a shark saw you now, it'd faint.'

It really did make me look like a Norwegian skipper – except that maybe my cheekbones slanted a bit too much, my mouth could have been a shade wider and my eyes shouldn't have been green but grey. And if only my hair didn't have that awful ginger tinge. Still, you can't change your looks.

'How much?' I asked.

'Well, if you like it, let's say a hundred and fifty.'

'A hundred and fifty? I thought you were asking a hundred.'

'For a jacket like that, matey, you don't "ask" anything. They pay the price and say thank you. Who told you I wanted a hundred?'

The two beachers, of course, were looking the other way at this point. 'It's not worth more than that.'

Instantly the sailor whipped his cap of my head and unbuttoned the jacket.

'Suit yourself,' he said. 'Give my regards to the captain.'

'Hang on.' I realized by now I couldn't just part from it like that. 'What's your rock-bottom price?'

'My rock-bottom price is a hundred and fifty. I wanted to ask two hundred, by my conscience wouldn't let me. I can see it suits you.'

I was just reaching for my jacket when I saw Vova had already taken out my wad of money, unwrapped it, and was counting out fifteen pinkies. The sailor recounted them, laid them all one way with the last one folded round the others, the way they do in a bank, and they were gone – stuffed down his shirtfront. Meanwhile Askold had riped a newspaper off the display-board and wrapped up my old jacket in it.

'Well, is that the deal then?' said the sailor. 'Hope you like it.'

'No sir!' Askold smiled at the sailor, with a tug at his forelock. 'No,' he said. 'That's not the whole deal. You don't know our Senya. He's good and generous. Isn't that right, Senya?'

How did this Popeye know whether I was good or bad? He'd never seen me before. 'Good and generous' meant that the whole gang would now go and get pissed at my expense. Yet it was the sailor who had just lined his pockets – with their help.

'Of course,' I said 'No one's more generous than me.'

'And did you notice, Senya . . .' – Popeye wouldn't let up – '. . . we didn't take any commission off you. And they generally do, you know. Did you notice?'

OK, I thought, I'm in it up to my neck now. Well, what could I do, once I'd let myself in for this caper?

'Put your cash away,' Vova reminded me. 'Otherwise you'll lose it.'

I took the wad, already wrapped and pinned up, and shoved it carelessly into the inside pocket of the jacket. I'm surprised that wad didn't start smouldering from the way those two looked at it. How we do love the sight of other people's money!

2

So we all went straight to the nearest restaurant, right there on Central Passage, and sat down at a nice corner table next to a potted palm. Just above us was a notice that read: 'Customers may not bring their own alcoholic beverages and may not consume them here'.

'Pay no attention,' said Vova. 'That notice is for illiterates.' I borrowed a pen from the sailor and blacked out the two 'nots'.

Although we could all read, no one came to serve us and for some time we just sat there. No doubt all the waitresses had gone to a lecture on how to give better service.

'Look , you beachers,' I said, 'Why don't we postpone this meeting until we can hold it at a higher level?'

'I should think not!' Askold jumped to his feet. 'With funds like ours, we don't have to sit and wait anywhere. I'll go and fetch Klavka. She'll fix us up – at the top level.'

Off he went to find this Klavka, while the sailor just looked at Vova and me and grinned. In the merchant marine port they did this with more style, he was thinking; nobody scribbled on notices *there*. Of course they brought their own liquor in there too, but not openly; they would sneak a bottle out of their coat-tails and surreptitiously pour it out under the table, as if they were drinking contraband or stolen goods.

At last Klavka arrived, swept us all with a practised glance and instantly guessed who was playing the host and would be paying. She brushed some invisible crumbs off the clean tablecloth in front of me.

'OK boys,' she said. 'I'll serve you as quick as I can, only keep it quiet, will you? Don't let me down by kicking up a row, OK?'

'How many shall we have?' boomed Askold. He couldn't talk quietly if he tried.

'How many?' I said. 'We'll have four, since it's a sit-down job. It's time you all learned how to live!'

'That's my Senya! You're a good fellow. And why d'you think he's

11

feeling so good tonight, Klavka? He's saying a sweet goodbye to the sea, because he's decided to settle down ashore.'

Klavka was very pleased at this. 'Well, thank God! At least one sailor has come to his senses. Congratulations.'

'But you don't think we're not good and kind too, do you, Klavka? Have you seen the new gear we've just got him?'

'Yes, I'd noticed. Fine, so long as he hasn't flogged the jacket again by this evening and drunk the proceeds.' Klavka flashed me a private smile. 'Don't tie up too close alongside these two, they're just wrecks, beachers. And you're young enough, you might still turn into a human being.'

She was sleek and powerfully built. A smasher, you might even say, with a slightly lazy look about her and eyes that were just a bit puffy, as though she had just woken up. But I knew her sort. When the moment comes they're not lazy at all – and not sleepy, either.

'Who cares,' I asked, 'whether I turn into a human being? Do you?'

She gave me another of her smiles. Her lips were bright from having been bitten, like the colour of poppies. She probably never put lipstick on them.

'Mothers and fathers care,' she said. 'Do you still have yours?'

'I haven't got a father any more, but mother dosn't exactly use the strap on me. Bring us whatever you've got that's best today.'

'Don't rush me, all in good time. Just let me have a look at you, stranger . . .'

The sailor watched her go as she floated away like a little boat – without hurrying, so as to give us more time to stare after her – and he whistled.

'*Very* nice,' he said. 'You seem to have made a definite impression on her already. If I were you I wouldn't let the chance go by – I'd try my luck right away.'

'Why don't *you* try your luck?'

'Got my own one. She'll do for the moment.'

'So have I.'

'Oh well, that's another matter.'

To be honest, I was exaggerating when I said that. I'd had a few, but they had as much 'belonged' to me as to Santa Claus; ever since my days as a recruit in the Navy I'd been chasing girls like this Klavka – powerfully built, good skin, well fed on the ample food to be had in a fishing port like Murmansk. And they were the ones who had aged me quickest.

She brought us a bottle of Riga beer apiece and some snacks that weren't even on the menu – just like the special things they produce for the auditors at the restaurant's annual inspection – roast meat home-style, shrimps, even smoked halibut.

She put down the tray in front of me and asked modestly: 'Will this do?'

I didn't even look at her.

'Aren't we bad-tempered today, Ginger! You said you'd show the others how to live. Tell me, do *you* know how to live?'

She didn't want to know much, did she? And she insisted on calling me Ginger. Well, there is a touch of ginger in my hair, but no one had ever called me that before.

'I know as much as I need,' I said. 'For anything else, the bo'sun gives the orders. As for you, I can tell without looking at you.'

'Oh dear,' she said. 'I do pick 'em . . .'

Askold went out with her, then he came back again, glancing furtively around, with four bottles of vodka under his jacket. He and I pulled the stoppers out with our teeth, poured out a glassful each, mixed with beer. The others decided to drink only half a glass at a time, so as to spin out the chat, but I had nothing to talk about, so I downed mine in one and the others did the same, spurred on by my example.

'You knocked that back all right!' said the sailor.

The drink had brought tears to his eyes, even though he had probably tasted plenty of foreign drinks, like rum and gin, when he was abroad. We started bolting the snacks as if the devil were after us.

'Now Senya . . .' Vova moved his chair close to mine and started preaching at me. Whenever he drinks, he has to preach a sermon about something, a habit of his that bores me. 'See how nice and well-behaved we are? And you didn't want to know us. But I tell you this, Senya: don't turn away from us beachers, we're like your family. There aren't any more real beachers, like me and Askold, the rest are all riff-raff, they'd never lift a finger to help you. Here you are, leaving the fishing fleet for good and there's no one close to you, is there? You were mooning along the quays all on your own. Why should you have to do that, Senya? We'll come and see you off, we'll put you on the train and wave goodbye.'

The sailor winked at me: 'Propaganda!'

But I suddenly felt sorry for Vova. He was turning into an alcoholic and I was doing nothing about it. I wanted to hit him, to try and knock some sense into him, but what was the use? His hands were shaking, he was dribbling down his beard, his eyes were glazed and bloodshot. And I even felt sorry for pop-eyed Askold, too. He was such a fool, and all he could do was shout. He couldn't even close his mouth properly – you've never seen anything so pathetic. I wanted to comfort Vova, comfort Askold – and the sailor too; his life can't have been all roses if he needed to sell that jacket . . .

'Here's some news for you, beachers!' That must have been me, belting it out at the top of my voice, because the place had by now filled up with a lot of people from the port and they were all looking at me. 'I'm giving my farewell party - this evening, in the Arctic! You're all invited!'

My two beachers immediately came to life and cheered up. Askold tottered round and embraced me, almost putting one of my eyes out with his stubble.

'Tell me,' he said, 'why d'you think I liked you as soon as I saw you? You may not believe it, but I'll tell them all: because he's one of the good guys!

There aren't any more left. They've all died out!'

Vova steadied his nerves and said: 'A farewell party – good lad! It's a sacred tradition. How much can you spend on it?'

'Shut up, you lout!' Askold put his hand over Vova's mouth. 'Don't be so tactless. If he hasn't got enough, I'll pawn my jacket. In fact, I'll fetch Klavka and pawn it right now!'

'Don't bother,' I said. 'Keep your jacket on, do me a favour.'

'All right,' said my mate Vova, 'but supposing we want to bring someone else along?'

'Go ahead, bring that woman of yours from Three Brooks. And I'll bring mine.'

'Quite right.' Askold nodded. 'What's a farewell party without women? Who is this girl of yours, by the way? Maybe she's too posh and wouldn't want to be seen in a restaurant with a couple of beachers. Not everyone's like you, Senya.'

'What d'you mean? If she's with me she'll want what I want.'

Vova was obviously very touched. He poured us all another full glass of vodka, this time without diluting it with beer – we'd gone past that stage – and we all tipped it back. Just then I had a feeling it wouldn't be a bad idea to bring this session to an end.

Hastily gobbling some more fish, I stood up. I swayed and my head was spinning, but I stayed upright. 'So long, beachers. See you this evening.'

'Sit down.' Askold wouldn't let me go. 'We haven't had a good heart-to-heart talk yet. And you're an interesting man, there's something about you . . .'

'We'll talk in the Arctic. We'll do everything in the Arctic.'

At this point Klavka put in an appearance, cross because we were making so much noise, so I took her by the shoulders and kissed her on the little downy curls behind her ear.

'And you're invited too, you daft thing.'

She didn't even ask 'Where?', but just nodded and smiled.

'So that's it,' said Vova, starting to add up the bill. 'A double order of drinks for four, that's eight. That'll be twenty for the order and something for the waitress.'

Askold confirmed the amount with an authoritative twitch of his eyebrows. God knows how they arrived at the total. I don't suppose either of them had ever sat down at a restaurant table in the regular way; with their type, waiters always asked for payment in advance. Anyway, I didn't want to haggle with Klavka. I felt embarrassed, because I had wrapped my money in a handkerchief, like some peasant, but Klavka didn't hang around – she just cleared the table and went away while I untied the bundle and counted out the necessary – enough for the drinks, the tip and everything else we'd had.

The sailor got ready to go and put his cap on again, making himself look as neat and spruce as before.

'Wait a moment,' Askold said to me. 'Klavka still has to bring you the change.'

'You can pick it up for me.'

You'll get it anyway, I thought – the pair of you and Klavka are obviously in cahoots. To hell with you, I don't mind. I know for sure that if I was dying of hunger, you two wouldn't toss me so much as a kopeck. But I'll be good to you all the same. Can't help it, that's just the way I am.

The sailor went out with me. 'Look,' he said, 'were you serious about that invitation?'

'Why do you ask?'

'Well, what that girl said was right: you shouldn't let yourself get too tangled up with those beachers.'

'She's a fine one to talk!'

'That's not the point. Good advice is good advice, no matter where it comes from. Hang on to your money by putting it somewhere safe, don't carry it around on you. You worked your guts out at sea to earn it, didn't you?'

'What d'you suppose I worked for? So I could lock myself away and run it through my fingers? I don't care who knows I'm generous.'

'They know it all right, matey. And they'll rip you off so hard you'll have nothing left.'

Listen to him – lecturing me like a professor! Incidentally, *he* had just ripped me off to the tune of 150 roubles, and he didn't seem to be dying of shame.

'And good luck to you, mate,' I said. 'Coming to the Arctic?'

'I may, but I can't promise. Anyway, you've got the jacket to remind you of me for a few years. It'll never wear out. If you get it dirty, rub it with acetone and it'll come up like new.

'I'll remember,' I said. 'Rub it with acetone. So long!'

3

I was still feeling cheerful as I left the port. The cold didn't bother me, only I was now wearing the jacket and my overcoat was a nuisance to carry. Everyone who came towards me grinned: here's a dimwit who's just got himself some new gear and can't wait to wear it! They're all the same, I thought – what will these people remember about me? The sight of a drunken fool lurching along the embankment. Hell, though, so what if they do – I'm never coming back to this place again.

From up above you couldn't see a thing: no water, no quays, nothing but a solid blanket of cloud between the hills. The sky was darkening as night came on and there was a bit more of a breeze, so that as I slogged my way to the Seamen's Hostel – past the station, along by the dockyard – my head started to clear a bit. Then I suddenly remembered about the two beachers and I almost howled out loud. Lord, why the hell did I have to put on that whole stupid performance: 'You're all invited!' I ask you – was there ever such a raving idiot?

What's more, come to think of it, the money wasn't even really mine. I may have been bragging when I said I had my own girl, but in a way it was true. There was a girl, and it was because of her that I'd decided to swallow the anchor and come ashore for good. I had no idea where we might go from here – we'd decide that later – but no one was going to help us over any rough patches, so I was relying entirely on that wad of money to tide us over. And it was getting a lot thinner already – a fact that I could literally feel through my shirt.

I was walking past the Polar Institute intending to go first to the hostel and drop my overcoat there, when I looked at my watch: it was past four, and she finished work at five. Then someone would probably see her home or take her to the cinema – girls in these ports seldom want for company.

The old woman on the door tried to stop me, but I said to her: 'I'm bringing in a marked fish.'

It was like a password. These scientists take a fish that's just been

16

caught, clip a disc on its fin and throw it back in the sea. Then they ask any fisherman who catches one of these fish to bring it back and tell them where it was caught. They've been doing it for years now and the fish mostly stay in the Atlantic – they don't exactly climb up on deck by themselves – so the Polar Institute pays you a rouble for every disc.

The old girl let me pass, telling me to leave my things in the cloakroom. If she'd asked me to show her the disc, I'd have thought up some story – I'm not a sailor for nothing.

On the second-floor landing I ran into a bloke in glasses, who was muttering something into his fist. A real weirdo, he had let his beard grow out northern-style, like a Norwegian, and now he was pulling out the hairs and frowning.

'Excuse me,' I said, 'Could you ask comrade Shchetinina to come out here?'

'Lilya Shchetinina?'

'Uh-huh,' I said, 'that's her.'

This brought Four-eyes to life. He was probably one of the ones who used to see her home and whisper God knows what to her till her mouth dropped open.

'Do you want me to ask her to come and see you?'

'That's right.'

He stared at me suspiciously, but I was holding myself straight and turning aside so that he couldn't smell my breath.

'Impossible, I'm afraid. She's in the laboratory. Sorry, it's working hours.'

'That's a minor detail. Just tell her that her brother from Volokolamsk has come to see her and that he's leaving again today.'

What made me say Volokolamsk? Because our First Officer was from Volokolamsk, I suppose.

'Are you her brother?'

'No, of course not. He's waiting downstairs.'

'Why have you come up instead of him?'

'He's just a country boy, you see. He's shy.'

Still, he went to fetch her. So much for Four-eyes; beard and all, he couldn't guess that a fellow might suddenly need to see a girl very badly. Even if it was in working hours.

At last she came out. Lilya. He looked round the door after her.

'Lilya, I realize it's your brother, but we'll never get the equipment packed at this rate . . .'

Being so polite, he went on hanging around while we stood there like a couple of fools, saying nothing, until he finally slammed a door in the corridor.

Then I asked her: 'Did you guess?'

'No. I thought it might be one of my friends.'

We were standing by the railings. It was quiet as a church, raspberry-red carpet all the way up the stairs, and pictures wherever you looked: pictures of every kind of fish in the wide world and how to catch them – purse-net, trawl, drift-nets, with bait, with lights. For some reason I had never come to see her here before, but some of 'her friends', it seemed, did come here.

'Who are they, these friends of yours? You haven't told me about them before.'

'Two boys I've known for years. From Leningrad. Shades of my forgotten past. They're sailing today on a trip.'

'On the *Perseus*?'

The Institute owns an old tub of a research ship, which never goes out for longer than two weeks at a time.

'No, they're not from the Fisheries Institute. I first knew them at school. They want to go to sea on a seiner, as deckhands.'

'Romance of the sea, I suppose?'

'I don't know. Maybe they just want to make some money.'

'In that case they should go on a DWT – a deepwater trawler. Yet they all want to go on seiners.'

'I told them that. But they seem to like the sound of the word "seiner" better.'

'OK,' I said. 'Want a cigarette?'

I never used to like it when girls smoked, but she managed it well. She held her cigarette like a man, and when she took a drag on it she would tilt her head a little sideways and look past me. I glanced at her out of the corner of my eye and wondered what it was that was attractive about her. Because she was a bit angular, almost as tall as I am, a bit rough – when she shook your hand you really felt it – and she had a shock of hair that looked as if she never had a hair-do. But she had nice eyes – that was it; in fact that was the first thing I noticed about her, and I couldn't remember what sort of eyes any of the others had had. Hers were grey. Yet the main thing wasn't that they were grey, but that they were somehow always calm. And that made me think – she may be angular and tough-like with others, but with me she'll always be as gentle as she can be, she'll always understand me and I'll be the only one who understands her.

'Look, Lilya . . .'

'Yes, Senya?'

'Some people, you know, go to sea. But there are others – certain people, that is – who leave the fishing fleet.'

'Certain people leave it for good, do they?' She gave me a sidelong look and smiled just a little. 'Have you had a lot to drink today?'

'So we had a drink or two. What's wrong with that?'

'Nothing. It can help if you need to pluck up your courage. Is that also why you've got a new jacket?'

I was standing shoulder-on to her, leaning carelessly against the railings as if I'd been wearing the jacket for a year or so. But with her it was pointless to put on an act; I also had a feeling that I wasn't going to manage to tell her what I really wanted to say.

'May I give you a piece of advice?'

'No, you may not.'

'This isn't the first time you've said you were leaving the sea, you know.'

'I've said it before, but now I really am leaving.'

'I suppose that will suit you better, will it?'

That was when I should have asked her: 'How will it suit you?' but I always suffer from an idiotic sort of dumbness whenever I talk to her.

'I've been thinking maybe I should go and study. It's not such a bad idea.' In fact the thought had come into my head for first time that moment. 'The only question is – where?'

'That's one subject I *can't* advise you about, especially as I couldn't make up my own mind about it. When the time came I let my mother decide for me. Mothers do talk sense sometimes. After school I couldn't for the life of me decide which to study – medicine or journalism. For some reason all my girlfriends seemed to be doing either one or the other. But mother said: "Go to the Fisheries Institute." Why the Fisheries? "Because there's no competition." I was furious, I howled and cried into my pillow until I almost made myself ill. Then after a while I got over it and calmed down.'

'And you don't regret it now?'

'What did I lose, after all? I haven't any talents. I'm just very ordinary. Just like all the rest.'

That was all I ever heard from her: 'I don't need anything, Senya. I'm just like all the rest.' The point is that everyone wants something – one wants more money and a less mucky job; another wants people to take orders and salute him; all another wants is a happy family life and he couldn't care less about anything else. With her, though, I could never discover what bugged her, she seemed content with everything. But I could see the sort of life she led: living in a strange part of the world, without a place of her own, without much money, without her mother and father – she missed them badly, and wrote to them almost every day.

'Why are you looking so sad all of a sudden?' She put her hand on my arm. 'You shouldn't ask me for advice. What do I understand about your life?'

My God, if only she would realize that she had already given me all the advice I needed. Starting from when I first saw her. If it weren't for her, I'd still be at sea, still living in the same old way, without a thought in my head. I'd be throwing my money around right and left and getting tangled up with anybody who happened to come my way.

'And you've already taken the most important decision,' she said. 'I envy you, honestly I do. I can sense the blessed state of mind you're in. Maybe the best time of all is when you have no idea of what lies ahead of you.'

It was quite black outside by now. The old porteress switched on the big

19

chandelier and looked up at us, wondering why we were standing there
without saying anything. And I hadn't yet told Lilya why I had come; I
couldn't even think how to get round to the subject. But the party at the
Arctic was still to come, and then tongues loosen. I would tell her then, or
later when I took her home: 'Let's leave this place together!' That's what
I'd say. 'Where to?' she would ask. 'Over the hills and far away.' Just so
long as she didn't ask me why we should go together. But I would think up
a good answer to that one, too.

I asked her:'Will you come to the Arctic this evening?'

'The trouble is, these two school friends of mine want to throw some
kind of farewell party. In my room. They haven't anywhere else to go. I
fixed them up in our hostel, but my God, the rules there are so strict . . .
You can come too, if you like.'

'Thanks . . .'

'But why do you particularly want to go to the Arctic tonight?'

'We could go tomorrow, except that I've already made the arrangements
and some other people will be coming.'

'Just like that, or is this some sort of occasion?'

'I'm giving my farewell party too.'

'Is that a sailors' tradition? In that case I will come. Well, I'll try. Who
else is coming?'

'The usual sort of crowd. Some beachers . . .'

'God, I hear that word "beachers" everywhere, and I've never set eyes
on a real live beacher in my life. You know, I think I really will come. And
what if I persuade my two pals to come too?'

'Please yourself . . . You'll have to pay for them yourself, though.'

'No, in that case I won't. OK, I'll think up something. In fact, all they
need is a roof over their heads.'

'Don't you want to be with them?'

'Well – only up to a point. Anyway, they were vaguely threatening to
bring a couple of ladies of some sort with them. I won't stay long with
them. But don't come and fetch me, I'll make my own way . . .'

Just then Four-eyes poked his head round the door. We were stubbing
out our cigarettes.

'Lilya, I've already asked you . . .'

'Yes, yes Yevgenii – where have you been all this time?'

He flashed his spectacle-lenses in my direction. I gave him the
thumbs-up and ran down the stairs. From below I could hear him
interrogating her: 'Excuse me, but where is this brother of yours? Was that
him?'

She rattled off a string of excuses. One of her gifts was to stop other
people being cross with her.

The old biddy at the desk grumbled at me – marked fish my foot, only
wanted to see your girlfriend, fooling an old woman – but I just felt sorry
for her: she was paid chickenfeed, and any slob could twist her round his

little finger. I stroked her head, but she only hissed and pushed me out into the street.

4

All my room-mates in the Seamen's Hostel were out. I flopped face down on my bed, but I hadn't been lying there for more than a minute when my head began to swim, so I went to the washroom to douse myself under the tap. There something awful happened to me: it was like it wasn't water running down my face but tears. I really did want to cry, to run back to her at the Polar Institute and beg her to come at once, otherwise I'd drink myself to death with those beachcombers and it would all end so badly that it was too frightening to think about. But with her I wasn't afraid of anybody; we'd stay for a while and then leave them, and tomorrow we'd buy our train tickets. The wheels would click, the trees would fly past the window, everything covered in snow . . . I babbled a lot more nonsense, but when she began to answer me, I realized it was all nothing by a load of rubbish. I'd often had imaginary conversations with her before, when my usual dumbness vanished and she seemed to understand me completely, and she had always said exactly what I wanted to hear.

I went back into the room and lay down in the dark. When I turned over on my back, the moon was shining in through the window, throwing a patch of silver, like snow, on the floor, criss-crossed with the black bars of the window frame. My room-mates seemed to have come back and were breathing heavily, asleep on their beds. This meant it must be past midnight, I had overslept and was too late for my party at the Arctic! But I could hear someone walking down the long, long corridor, and I somehow knew it was her, coming to see me. I was terrified – she wasn't allowed to come into the hostel. The others would wake up, and I wouldn't be able to laugh it off . . . Suddenly I heard a shuffling sound – shuffle, shuffle – made by some huge, fifteen-foot creature dragging the soles of its feet along the floor and making an awful noise like the neighing of a horse. She fled from it down the corridor and it went after her, neighing and clattering its hooves, swearing foully as it went . . . no, there were several of them, nightmare monsters, stallion-like creatures; we must stop them and kill them! She shrieked and ran faster, but there was no escaping them, they were catching up with her and would trample her to death with their iron-shod hooves. I wanted to shout to the other lads for help, I could never save her on my own – but I couldn't shout, because I was being smothered by something. And out there they had caught her and were trampling on her, I could hear a snickering horse-laugh and howling, as though a loudspeaker was booming out all over the harbour: 'She's gone! . . . No, not yet! . . . Now she's done for! . . .' I thrashed about and wrenched my head away from the pillow . . .

Lord, it was nothing by the old cleaning woman sweeping under the bedside lockers and putting the stools upside down on the beds. She tried to do me a favour by pulling my sheet over my head.

'It's the limit!' she shouted. 'I've had just about enough of tidying up after you filthy louts!'

'What's all the fuss for, love?'

She leaped at me with her broom at the ready. 'Ah, so you've woken up. Look at it – empty sardine tins shoved under the lockers, fag ends, apple cores . . . Is that any way to carry on? What are the ashtrays for? I'll tell the warden, I will, I'll tell him to move all you lot into the washroom. You can all live in there and make as much mess as you like, only I don't want nothing to do with it!'

'That's not such a bad idea. We're all only passing through here, anyway.'

'Huh! Passing through! I wish I was only passing through too . . . Got a smoke, have you?'

I gave her a Belomor.

'Well that's that,' she said. 'I'm off, I am.'

Away she went. I lay there a while longer, my heart thumping horribly fast. It seemed I was in a really bad way, although I wasn't yet twenty-six. At least, I thought, I could be thankful to the old girl for waking me up at half past seven.

I didn't bother to wait for a bus – they're so crowded, you get taken way out into the suburbs before you've had time to fight your way off – and instead I walked, which cleared my head.

There was a crowd of people around the Arctic, all trying to get in, with a 'FULL' notice hanging on the door, but the cloakroom attendant spotted me right away: 'You can come in, you in the new jacket. He's booked a table.'

He was an expert at his job. It didn't matter that he had only one arm; he knew exactly who to keep out, and he had an instinct for knowing if you were in the money or if you were just sponging. And the man had an amazing memory; no need to give you a numbered tag, he always remembered what you were wearing when you came in. Then when you went out, there was your coat – and not just anybody's but your own.

'I'm expecting a certain person,' I said to him. 'You've seen me with her before. Auburn hair. Wears green eye-shadow.'

He remembered, nodding. I gave him a three-rouble note. He stuffed it into his pocket, took off my cap and unbuttoned the hood of my jacket.

'Nice bit of new gear you've got!' He'd spotted my jacket was new, but if you'd asked him what my name was, he wouldn't have had the faintest idea.

The air in the restaurant was so thick with smoke, you could have cut it with a knife. Up on the little stage four lunatics – a violin, two saxophones and an accordion - were bashing out the music. It wasn't exactly high-grade stuff, but tolerable, sort of souped-up folksongs like 'The Little Birch Tree'. My beachers were over in the corner, hanging on to their double table like grim death. Though they still looked scruffy, they were at least wearing suits, and Vova had even put on a tie. With them were Vova's girl from Three Brooks, called Lidka, and Klavka. This Lidka, I can tell you, was really bad news: thin and scrawny, she seemed to be forever irritable, or maybe just nervous. She kept fiddling with her permanent wave and rolling her eyes upwards. Klavka, though, was stitting there like a queen, wearing a big loose cardigan with mother-of-pearl buttons, and gold earrings dangling from her ears. She looked all pink and glossy and was fanning herself with a folded-up headscarf.

The beachers waved to me and I was just about to move in their direction when I suddenly saw the Chief.

The Chief – he'd been Chief Engineer on one of my ships – was alone at a table and had probably been there for some time; three of the four buttons on his tunic were undone. The chair beside him was tilted to lean against the table; the Chief was either expecting someone or didn't want anyone else to join him. He had aged noticeably since I last saw him. The wrinkles on his face had deepened and there were definite bags under his eyes, but his shoulders were still the same, still in good shape if a bit slumped.

The Chief saw me too, and without even saying 'hello' or 'ahoy, there', he straightened up the chair and smiled. 'Sit down, Senya. How come you're looking so smart?'

A waitress appeared at once, as if she'd been sent for by some big boss.

'Same again, please, my dear,' the Chief said to her. 'Three hundred grammes. Better still – make it four hundred. And set a place for Senya here. He hasn't yet learned to order for himself, so I'm ordering for him and you can chalk it up to me.'

He raised the menu almost to his eyes and started running his finger along it.

'Look Chief . . . The fact is, I'm here with some friends.' I pointed to the beachers.

The Chief glared at them and pulled a face. 'Are *those* your friends?'

The waitress pulled a face too. I laughed; somehow they can always spot beachers, even when they're wearing suits. 'I picked them up without meaning to, and I had to invite them.'

'Can't get out of it, eh? All right, order for them, only don't be too generous, then come back here. After all you and I haven't seen each other for six months.'

'More than that, Chief. Eight months.'

I went over to the beachers, told them to order whatever they wanted on my account and to keep two places free, as we'd agreed. Klavka wasn't too pleased at this, but I didn't care; she had come with Askold, so she could be Askold's girl for the evening.

When I returned to the Chief, the waitress brought him a decanter of brandy, which he poured out then and there.

'Let's drink to your arrival, Senya. When did you get in?'

'A week ago.'

I could have bitten off my tongue: why hadn't I seen him in all that time?

'Well, I'm casting off tomorrow. Don't blush, I've been hard to find. Been over at Cape Abram for a whole fortnight, day and night. We were in floating dock.'

'What were you in dock for, Chief?'

'They were welding a patch on the hull. Let's drink to that, too.'

'What ship are you on now, Chief?'

'No. 815, the *Galloper*.'

Once he and I had sailed together on the *Orpheus*, then the Chief had gone sick, I had a bust-up with the skipper – I forget why – and after that we'd been assigned to different ships.

'Just a minute,' I said. 'It was your *Galloper* that handed over her nets to us in the North Sea when she was heading back to port. And I didn't know you were on board her.'

'Yes, I remember we gave our nets to someone or other. Still, how was I to know who it was? Didn't even come up on deck, otherwise we might have hailed each other.'

'How was the patch? Was it a big job?'

'Above the waterline. But it was a long one, two ribs long. All eaten up with rust.'

'But did they weld it properly? Was it passed seaworthy by the registry?'

The Chief grinned. 'Which interests you more – the quality of the welding or whether it was passed seaworthy? Yes, we have our certificate. We're covered if it starts to leak, and what more can you expect to have? If anything happens out at sea, no angel's going to come flying to your rescue, not even a seagull.'

I didn't like it when he joked like that. I knew what happened when a repair was inspected for a certificate of seaworthiness: three types would come on board, prod the new plating with their fingers and frown, while everyone tried to hustle them into the cabin and offer them vodka or brandy. This wasn't the way the Chief usually did things, but it sounded as if this time he had lowered his standards a good deal. In the past he would lean on a captain until his vessel was in as good shape as when she first came down the slipway.

'Come on, Chief, let's drink to your patch.'

'OK.' He ruffled my hair and said reassuringly: 'If you replaced all the plating the result would be the same . . .'

No, he was still the old Chief. He was, in fact, already well tanked up, although you couldn't tell it – anybody else would have been under the table by now. I looked at him: he had livened up, even seemed to have grown a bit younger from meeting me; I knew he liked me, and I liked him. Then I found myself thinking: How am I going to tell him about my decision? The Chief was someone I would have to tell it to.

'Well, how are you, Senya? Taking shore leave for a month or so?'

'Maybe longer.'

'No point in taking any longer. Now if it was summer . . .'

'No, I can't wait till summer.'

The Chief glanced at me suspiciously. 'You're hiding something. You've never done that with me.'

'And I'm not doing it now. I've simply signed off, that's all.'

'For long?'

'I don't know. Right now, I feel like signing off for good.'

The Chief said nothing, staring into his glass.

'The fact, is I've had all I want. I put in three years' sea-time in the Navy, and three years in this game. Soon I'll forget how to walk on dry land, nothing but decks all the time. And, well, you know, life's passing me by.'

'Mm' yes.' The Chief sighed. Then he smiled, as if remembering something. 'Maybe you and I might sail together again, Senya.'

'Sail with you? Sure, why not?'

'We're leaving tomorrow.'

I shook my head. He hadn't understood.

'Another time, Chief.'

'There won't be another time. I'm being pensioned off.'

'You? Pensioned off? You're joking.'

'Why shouldn't I joke? You joke too. But to be honest, I won't pass the next routine medical.'

'Come off it, Chief . . . You'll still be at it when all us herring-fishermen have been put on the beach.'

'Look, Senya, I hear the ship's complement isn't made up yet. They need a warpman. I know, because the trawlmaster and his mate had to stow the trawl-warp in the hold themselves. So you go and sign on as warpman. I'll fix it with the captain.'

I thought to myself it wasn't going to be much fun for him on that damned *Galloper*, when all the crew knew he was sailing his last trip.

'Chief, we won't be saying goodbye for ever. You go and come back again. And make sure nothing happens to you.'

The Chief suddenly frowned and lowered his glance. I hadn't noticed the two men approaching, who were standing behind my back. One was no less than Grakov in person, the big boss of the herring fleet; the other was my former captain, or rather one of my former captains – there were seven of them – also a famous personality in his time, but now just one of the parasitic sucker-fish who hung around Grakov.

They were on their way to their own reserved table and had seemingly just stopped here by chance.

Now I wonder what's the matter with Sergei Andreyich?' The tone of Grakov's voice was cheerful, but also slightly concerned. 'Greetings, Sergei Andreyich.'

The Chief grunted someting in reply, which I didn't hear.

'By the way, how did it go with the repairs to No. 815? Are you sailing tomorrow? Sorry, maybe I'm talking out of turn . . .'

'We're all the same,' said the Chief, 'at work we talk about football and at football we talk about work.'

'What's that? Interesting thought!'

Grakov came half a pace nearer to us. His sucker-fish was positively gurgling with sycophantic excitement, and even the bald patches on his head gleamed brighter.

'It should be the other way round,' said the Chief, 'but that's human nature.'

'That's human nature for sure!' Grakov then immediately became concerned again. 'But I hear reports that in the end everything was smoothed over.'

'Well, since you've heard reports, then . . .'

'Yes, but I know you well enough, and I don't need to check on *you*. So your old *Galloper* can canter round the course once more and then off to the knacker's yard, eh?'

'That's right. Off to the scrapyard,' said the Chief.

And that, you might think, was the end of their talk. But Grakov swept the room with a glance, and the sucker-fish instantly ran off to fetch two chairs. And we, if you please, had not invited them to join us.

'I suppose you and I are probably off to the scrapyard, too. What do you think?'

On this point the Chief did not think anything.

'Spending your last evening ashore?'

'That's right.'

As I thought he would, the sucker-fish returned with a couple of chairs, followed by a waitress with a bottle of Ararat, one of the best Armenian brandies. The Arctic kept a special supply of it for Grakov, who wouldn't drink any other sort. She was just about to pull the foil off the top when the sucker-fish took the bottle from her.

'No, no, give it to me'.

He removed the cork by using the palm of his hand, pulling off the old trick very effectively – after twisting it and twisting it he banged the bottom with his hand, and out flew the cork. He handed the bottle to Grakov, who had sat down – not straight-on to the table, but turned slightly to one side – and was now waving the bottle around, as if to ask whose glass he should fill first.

The Chief covered his glass with his hand, as it was still half full.

'But it's Ararat!' said Grakov in astonishment.

'All the more reason not to mix it.'

'In that case, with your permission, let's help this young beacher to get merry.'

He filled my glass up with a movement so quick that I didn't have time to cover it with my hand. To be honest, I hadn't the heart to do it anyway. After all, he was God. I only said : 'Not a beacher but a working fisherman. Please don't confuse the two.'

'Of course not, of course not!' laughed God, going so far as to lay a hand on my shoulder. Even the sucker-fish, who was just pouring himself some brandy, gave me an affectionate look. Obviously he'd forgotten how he had once yelled at me in the wheelhouse. 'But they're cheeky, the young, these days!'

At once the sucker-fish's expression changed from affection to disapproval.

'He's not being cheeky,' said the Chief. 'He has some self-respect, that's all.'

'Yes, all right. Self-respect comes first nowadays, and *then* respect for your elders.'

The waitress was still standing there. Grakov turned round to her, pointed at the table with his finger and described a little circle in the air, which meant: Put all this on my bill.'

This started off a little scene. The Chief grunted and said: 'But we've been sitting here for a long time.'

I'd better explain the finer points of all this. In the Arctic, nobody pays for himself alone. If a party of sailors are sitting together, each one tries to be the first to pay for all the others. If they all lay out their money at once, then the waitress decides who to take it from. But when people have been sitting together and pay separately, it means they're enemies, it's an insult. And whichever way you looked at it, we had been sitting together.

Grakov almost broke out in a sweat all over, but he didn't keep his tame sucker-fish for nothing, and it was the sucker-fish who saved the situation: 'Dmitry Rodionych,' by which he meant Grakov – 'just wanted to order a snack for us two to have with the brandy. One of your special salads. Then you can serve the main course on our table, we'll be going over there later.'

The waitress wrote it down and went away.

'Well, now . . . will you let me drink to you?' asked Grakov.

I looked at the Chief and he looked at me. He picked up his glass. I picked up mine. The sucker-fish was gazing at Grakov with something like devotion in his little eyes, like bear's eyes, with his button nose and lips forever pressed tightly together. His whole expression made it seem as if he was about to say something very, very important – the sort of thing *you* would never think of in a lifetime, that you would never hear from your father or mother, that you would never even read in a book.

'Sergei Andreyich . . . Firstly, here's wishing you a hundred feet of water under your keel. Please accept that. It's meant sincerely.'

The Chief nodded. At once the sucker-fish's brow cleared.

'And secondly . . . Look here, we're not living in the stone age! You know what I'm talking about. We're all human, we all make mistakes, we don't deserve to go on being punished for twenty years. You're a prehistoric relic, you obstinate old cuss! It's time to forgive and forget. The times – think what times those were. There's this young man sitting here – I don't suppose he can even imagine what those times were like, can he?'

The sucker-fish was looking back and forth at the Chief and Grakov with such a sad look on his face, meaning – please stop punishing him, forget your old scores, if only you two would embrace and make up. The Chief just sat there in silence, frowning. Grakov put his hand over the Chief's hand; I could see it annoyed him, but he didn't take his hand away.

I gazed quickly around. No one was looking at us. The Chief shot a glance at me, realized that no one was looking at us and I could see this made him feel better.

'Listen, Rodionych,' said the Chief. 'Why did you start this up? I haven't said anything to offend you. Maybe I did once, but that's all in the past. Only I can't for the life of me see what there is to drink to.'

Again Grakov's eyes swivelled around the room. 'Why hasn't she brought us anything? Even some mineral water would do . . .'

The sucker-fish leaped to his feet and strode off between the tables.

'Ah, now *that* I can tell you right away.' Grakov flashed a golden smile. 'As I understand it, this is your last year at sea, isn't it? And that's sad.'

'Sad? Who for? For you?'

'For the fishing fleet, Sergei Andreyich. The fleet is going to be lost without you.'

'Well, it will just have to lump it.'

'You ought to know your own worth, Sergei Andreyich. You can still give so much to the younger men in the fleet. An engineer of your calibre – are there any "Chiefs" nowadays who can compare with you? Those twenty-five-year-olds? I just don't want to let you leave the fleet on a pension yet. I very much don't want to do that.'

Meanwhile the sucker-fish had brought a bottle of mineral water. He opened it with a fork and poured the bubbling stuff into all our glasses.

'What do you say, Ignatych? Can we allow Babilov to leave the fleet?'

'No we cannot, Dmitry Rodionych, we most certainly cannot!'

'That's what I think too.' Grakov was now holding the Chief's hand in both of his own. 'I suppose they won't let you work on trawlers any longer because of your eyesight, is that it?'

'You're well informed, I see,' said the Chief.

'But what if you were made Group Chief Engineer? How about that? You'd by my right-hand man on the technical side. You'd be in charge of a whole flotilla – twelve, fifteen vessels. Based on the factory ship, with a de luxe cabin. It's getting tough on a DWT at your age, you want a bit of peace and comfort. And power, if it comes to that. So – how's that for a toast? To the new Group Engineer, Sergei Andreyich Babilov!'

'Yes,' said the Chief, 'it's tempting. But wait a moment.'

'Well, what's bothering you?'

'Just this – if I'm going to be your right-hand man, will you make me go and fetch you mineral water for you?'

I didn't mean to look at the sucker-fish, my one-time skipper, but I couldn't help seeing him break out in a sweat, even though he didn't stop smiling. Yet the man had all the looks of a guardsman, the very type that's given the regimental colours to carry on parade or to command a guard of honour. It's terrible to see what they can bring a man to.

'What's that got to do with anything?' Grakov frowned. 'I'm making you a serious offer.'

'I just want to know in advance. What my place would be. Otherwise, out of ignorance, I might get the wrong idea.' The Chief took away his hand and stared hard at the sucker-fish. 'Tell me, Ignatych, don't you miss being on the bridge?'

Just imagine – all he did was to look at the Chief and smile.

'Well, as for me,' said the Chief, 'I think I'd probably die without my stinking engine-room. So pretty soon they'd carry me out of my de luxe cabin feet first. What's the idea, Rodionych, do you want me to die?'

With an effort, Grakov smiled. 'So my toast was no good?'

'Not that one,' said the Chief. 'Think up another one, then come and see me.'

Grakov pushed away his brandy and stood up, at which the sucker-fish also jumped to his feet. Right now he didn't know whether to smile or to frown.

The Chief reminded them: 'Don't forget your Ararat.'

'A pity,' said Grakov. 'You didn't understand me, Sergei Andreyich. I came to you with the best intentions, yet you still bear me a grudge. As you have made very obvious.'

And suddenly – know what he did? He bent right down to the Chief, clasped him round the shoulders and said very sincerely: 'All right, old man. We'll talk again. You're obviously in the wrong mood at the moment . . .'

I watched them go. They left their brandy behind, of course. They weren't such fools as to walk right across the restaurant carrying a bottle. But I was wrong when I'd thought no one was looking at us. The whole of the Arctic was looking at us, and they had all seen Grakov embrace the Chief. I suddenly had a funny feeling – had it really all happened? It can't have done! But that was probably because I was starting to go muzzy in the head. I turned to the Chief, who had cut himself a slice of meat and was chewing it slowly. He had bad teeth – we all do because of the water on board ship – and for some reason I felt very sorry for him.

'But Chief – he got what he wanted. Why did you let him?'

He gave me a glum look and pushed my glass towards me. 'Drink that up, and then that's your lot for today.'

'Look, you know why you're sitting alone, don't you? It's not everyone who'll sit at your table when *he's* around.'

'I'm sitting with you, Senya. And if you're going to say damn' fool things like that, you can go and sit somewhere else. Got it?'

'OK,' I nodded. 'Are you going to stay here any longer?'

'Maybe ten minutes, no more.'

'Why the hurry?'

'Marya Vasilievna has been packing my things and she must be getting bored on her own. I must go and spend some time with her before I leave.'

'The fact is, there's a girl coming to join me this evening, and she asked to meet you.'

The Chief smiled. 'It's a long time since girls asked that!'

'Well, to be honest she didn't ask, but I want her to meet you. Will you wait for her?'

I went out to the lobby. The cloakroom attendant had put a bar across the doors and was looking out of the window into the street.

'She hasn't come yet. Don't worry, I won't make a mistake.'

I offered him a three-rouble note.

'No need for that. I haven't earned the other one yet. Go back into the restaurant.'

The mad musicians on the stage were now swinging away in the dark, still busting their guts as though somebody might be listening to them. The hubbub of voices was as noisy as a bazaar. When the Chief had settled his bill with the waitress, he handed her the bottle of Ararat and pointed out Grakov's table to her. She nodded, but instead of taking it over there she put it away in a little cupboard.

'Is she late?' asked the Chief. 'She'll be putting that stuff on her face. It takes them a long time.'

'No,' I slumped down in a chair. 'She won't be coming at all.'

'How do you know?'

'Because . . . she's a bitch.'

'That's a nice way to talk! Maybe she's changed her mind about meeting me.' The Chief glanced at his watch. 'Like to come outside with me for a breath of fresh air?'

'I'll stay here a bit longer.' I felt horribly ashamed of myself; why had I called her that? 'I'll wait just in case. Don't worry, I'm OK. Honestly, I'm OK.'

'Promise me not to swear at her?'

I promised. We had one more drink – to all those at sea – then the Chief buttoned up his tunic, stood up and carefully pushed the chair back under the table.

'Come to the quayside tomorrow and say goodbye.'

I shook his hand with both of mine as if we were parting for ever, and watched him go out. The Chief was heavily built, and there wasn't much space between the tables, but he didn't bump anyone. Then I turned round and just sat there, staring like an idiot at the back of Grakov's neck. OK, I thought, I'll get even with you. I'm not a man if I don't get even with you.

I heard the waitress clearing away the crockery.

'Bring me another hundred and fifty grammes.'

'I'm not bringing you anything more.'

'I suppose you think I'm broke? I'll show you!' I unzipped the jacket and fingered my wad of money. 'See that? I sweated my guts out at sea to earn this, OK? All of you ought to be falling at my feet!'

'I'll fall at your feet if you like, but I won't bring you anything. You've been told not to have any more.'

'Who said so?'

'The man who was sitting here with you. You've forgotten already. I can bring you a soft drink.'

'Take it to that hog over there. Look, the one with the shiny bald head.'

'You little fool,' she said. 'Keep your voice down. You don't want fifteen days in the police cells for drunk and disorderly, do you?'

She took my hand with the money and shoved it into the inside pocket of my jacket. They're tough, the old bags who work at the Arctic. They have to be, so no one wants to start a fight with them, and if necessary they'll throw you out.

Then the whole room somehow spun around – chandeliers, tobacco smoke, music and all – and I found myself sitting with the beachers, drinking out of someone's glass. Everything would have been fine if that stupid cow from Three Brooks hadn't been there, frowning, fiddling with her perm and sneering at me so that it really got on my wick.

'Why d'you keep pulling at you hair?' I asked her. 'If you don't look out, you'll go bald. As it is you've only got enough hair to go round three curlers.

'Ugh!' she said. 'How I hate drunks!'

'Look, my love, it's better for you I am drunk. If I was sober, I wouldn't exactly mistake you for Sophia Loren, would I? As it is, you're in luck.'

She didn't quite catch my drift, but shrugged her shoulders. 'I'm not your love!'

'No, someone else is his love,' Klavka said to her. She was sitting directly opposite me, fanning herself with a headscarf and smiling all over her face. 'He's missing her, so he takes it out on us for no reason at all. As a rule she's his true love, only tonight she seems to have let him down.'

'Rubbish,' I said. 'My true love never lets me down!'

'You saw him, didn't you? He was talking to those old men, then he had to run out into the lobby just to see if she hadn't relented and turned up after all.'

'What d'you mean – "old men"? The Chief's not an old man! You don't know what he's been through in his time . . . Right now he could knock your Popeye out cold with one finger. I'll have you know he once swam eleven miles and he didn't conk out. Do you know what that is – eleven miles?'

Klavka waved her hand and laughed. 'So what – miles-shmiles!'

I started to laugh too, though I don't know why. She hadn't said anything very funny.

'You really messed things up tonight, Ginger,' Klavka said to me. 'You invite me, and then you go and sit at another table. I'm surprised you aren't more pleased to see me. Aren't I pretty enough for you?'

'Too pretty,' I said.

'Wouldn't you like to have someone like me?'

'No,' I said, laughing. 'I'll do better to steer clear of you. I've had a boatload of your sort in my time, and that's enough for me.'

Vova's woman snorted, but Klavka didn't seem to mind at all.

'Well, at least we've given you a bad fright!' she said. 'Have you taken a good look at me, though? Why am I so terrible?'

'God knows what you do to men, but it's not human.'

'So far, it seems, that's just what your girl has done to *you*. Just decided not to come. And she was right – it's the only way to treat your sort!'

Vova's woman pulled a face as if she was chewing a lemon. 'Don't hurt his self-esteem,' she said. 'You can see the condition he's in.'

And she stared at me sort of pityingly, as if I was – well, as if I'd been ruined in my prime. She had little eyes like a mouse, set close, so close together it made me feel a bit sick to look at them. And a feeling of utter misery came over me. So this was all my life amounted to – sitting around with boozers like these and girls like these two. Never a decent word out of them – 'Self-esteem', 'condition' – I ask you! Bloody cashier. What was her name, anyway? Miss Senseless?

'The trouble with you, Miss Senseless,' I said to her sweetly, 'is you can't sense the subtle movements of my soul.'

'Very witty!' she hissed. Why she was so full of spite and who it was aimed at, I had no idea.

'I could show you a girl who'd made you want to go and hang yourself just because there *are* women like her.'

Klavka burst out laughing again. 'You should have gone after her and brought her here. I'd be interested just to see with my own eyes how you cope with her.'

In the lobby the cloakroom attendant rushed at me, but I sent him reeling back three paces. I pulled at the door, but it was closed with an iron bar, and when I started to pull that out I felt someone gripping me round the shoulders.

'Get off, you one-armed bugger!'

But it wasn't the attendant at all – there were two arms around me. It turned out to be Askold, who had run after me.

'What d'you want, you pop-eyed owl?'

'What do you think?' His big, thick lips were wide open. 'You're going – and they'll bring us the bill!'

'I told you – I'm coming back.'

'How do I know that, Senya?'

'Ah, scared you, did I, pussycat? There you are, put that in your dirty paw, go back to that Klavka of yours and order her a vermouth.'

'What about the cake? Lidka wants some chocolate cake.'

I shoved a bunch of five-rouble notes at him, dropping several of them, which he picked up and put note by note into a neat pile. The cloakroom attendant, looking grim, stood to one side and counted how many notes Askold took from me.

'Watch it,' he said. 'I'm a witness.'

Askold showed him what he had taken and stuffed the rest back into my pocket. The attendant jammed my cap on to my head, then reached behind the counter and stuffed something down the front of my jacket. 'Don't loose your hood.'

I wanted to weep for having treated him so badly. 'Sorry, dad. Let's kiss and be friends.'

'Bugger off,' he said, 'and stop being such a damn' nuisance'.

At last he pulled out that stupid iron bar, and I went out into the street without looking at him.

5

As I walked through the snow it crunched underfoot and the cold burned my face. I didn't bother to button on the hood, because that would have meant taking off my jacket and gloves and I was freezing anyway. One lunatic I knew, once when he was drunk, got the crazy idea of stopping in the street to rewind his foot-cloths – then fell asleep barefoot in the wicked frost, and they had to cut off half his leg. I just stuck my nose into my collar and walked almost half a block with my eyes shut. In fact I could have gone the whole distance like that without loosing the way.

She rented a room on the courtyard side of a huge block on Volodarsky Street; you went under the archway and immediately turned left, and it was the corner window on the fourth floor. I'd been there four times before. Almost nothing in the room was hers, except for the bedspread, a little mat, and some knick-knacks on the bedside table, yet you felt she'd been living there for ever. 'The chief thing is not to want anything,' she used to say to me, 'then at least you can be more or less happy. Today these are my things, but tomorrow, who knows, we may not be here.'

The light was on in the window

I stood down below for a while – didn't want to go up straight away, better let my head clear a bit – and saw someone come to the window. It was her, looking down into the courtyard. Everything around was white, not a bench, not a bush showing up; I was the only black object to be seen. No, she hadn't noticed me. She turned back into the room, and all I could see was her dark shock of hair. Then she moved away.

Some lad came over, turned his back to the window, jumped up on to the sill and was joined by another one. It was so high up, I couldn't see what they looked like but they seemed to be laughing. And why not laugh – if you're in the warm, there are drinks on the table, a nice girl with you, and she's telling you how I invited her to the Arctic and she didn't go but stayed with you instead? Christ, I thought, so what if she didn't come? I'm not the only pebble on the beach. Only why did she have to lie about it?

There was once a girl called Nina, a dishwasher on the factory ship, I had a typical sailor's love affair with her – afloat and ashore – and I behaved like a pig to her, not showing up for months on end, yet even so she had never played any tricks on me like this. If she'd tried to throw me out, I'd have left her without a second thought. Because this life of ours turns you into a brute.

I suddenly realized I was standing there like an idiot and counting the floors. From bottom to top, then from top to bottom. Why, I wondered, was I counting them? Well, obviously because I had to get up there somehow! As for what I'd do when I got there, we would see; the main thing was to go on up. But just as I was heading for the entrance, some man came out – all in black, you couldn't see his face. He took two paces, then seemed to change his mind and stopped. Why should he be afraid of me, I wondered? Ah, that was probably his car, a Moskvich, parked beside the ground-floor windows under a tarpaulin, and he'd decided I was planning to hijack it or pinch the wheels. Serve him right for thinking such nasty thoughts!

'Go on,' I said to him, 'go back home to bed. I don't want your wheels.'

He made a dash to one side and stopped again. Completely off his rocker. 'Who are you?' he asked. His voice sounded like it was coming from the bottom of a barrel. 'Where have you sprung from?'

'Same place as I'm going back to now. You go to bed.'

I didn't want to worry the poor dolt. He'd probably stay and guard his wretched Moskvich till morning, and either freeze to death or oversleep and be late for work and get a bollocking. By the time I was out on the street again, he was standing under the archway and watching me, looking so sad and miserable. To hell with you – and your wheels – I thought. And you up there with your farewell party, you can go to hell too. I'm going back to where I came from, take my word for it.

There was no end to that street. I went on and on, thinking what a bad business this was. If only I could get back to somewhere warm – to the hostel, or to the Arctic. But I was going in the opposite direction from the hostel, so there was no point in wearing out my shoe leather more than necessary; in the Arctic, though, there were those two beachers, and Klavka would laugh at me: 'What did I tell you, Ginger? Didn't she come after all?' 'So she didn't come,' I'd say. 'I can do without her, anyway. And I can do without you too, you sleek, pink-faced, fluffy–haired slut. I'd do better to go to Nina. It's warm at Nina's place, she'll put me to bed and she won't rob me, she's nice and kind, is Nina, she always looks after me, not like some people who are only after my money. She loves me, does Nina.'

I finally reached the terminal, from where the ferry boats go across the Sound, and flopped down, stiff with cold, only just able to wrench my hands out of my pockets. The stove in the building made it nice and warm, and it was packed with maybe a thousand people – some going to the docks on night shift, some going home from work – but they all looked surly and glum, miserable bastards, no good trying to talk to them. I squeezed in beside somebody and started telling him I was going to Cape Abram to see Nina, because I hadn't forgotten her, and he said to me: 'Shove off, then, and go and see your Nina!'

'How can I?' I said. 'There's still a fog out there and the ferries can't sail without radar.'

'The fog's in your head and *you* haven't got any radar.'

'That's just the trouble,' I said. 'Well, I'll have a bit of a kip, give me a prod when . . .'

I'd just slumped on his shoulder when they started shouting: 'Ferry's in! Anyone for Cape Abram?'

He grabbed me by the jacket, hauled me to my feet and ran off. Everyone was galloping somewhere, so I went with them, trying not to get left behind. We seemed to be running for an awful long time.

6

As the old ferry boat was chugging away to itself at the landing-stage, the passengers all tumbled aboard and went below; but there was nowhere to sit down there, so I stayed on deck and sat on a bollard. The man was right – the fog had lifted. The last wisps of it had been blown away by an onshore wind from the Barents Sea. No longer smoking, the water was black and calm, without a ripple, dotted with lights: red, green and white. From the far shore shone lights from the docks, from ships, and from houses away up the hillside. Somewhere up there lived Nina. One of those lights was hers. Whenever I came back from the sea, I always knew whether she was at home, and the lads used to say to me: 'Your Nina's lit her lamp.' I liked it that she didn't come down to the pier, but waited till I came up in my own time.

We were soon under way, and the wind burned first one cheek then the other. That was because we were doing a circuit, passing under the bows and sterns of ships. Work on ships was going on round the clock, sparks falling into the water and hissing; some gangs were welding, some sitting on cradles, scraping the sides and painting while jazz blared out from the loudspeakers.

But before long the passengers were pouring out on deck, then tearing down the landing-stage hoping to catch a bus or hitch a ride, so to avoid being trampled in the rush I stayed put and went ashore last of all. Then I started to climb up to Nina's place – by the short cut, across the hills. You can go by road, only the bugger twists and turns and it takes two hours that way, so I always used to go straight up the hillside. The houses here are stuck to the slopes, one above the other like swallows' nests, and the little plots of land around them are like a ship's deck with a heavy list – one foot's always higher than the other. They all try to grow something on that land – potatoes, carrots – but not a damn thing grows there and never will. We took that land from the seagulls, so for that we must live there like seagulls too.

It took me a long time to climb up, and I was soaking wet under my jacket. At the top I was hit by a wind that turned me to ice, and I began to think this was the end; I could easily fall off that steep hillside and no one would even hear me shout. Then I spotted Nina's wattle fence and pulled a stave out of it, which I leaned on like a shepherd's crook to help keep me upright on that slope. The light was on in Nina's window. I pressed my face against it but couldn't see a thing, because it was covered in hoar-frost. I knocked on the window, went round to the door and slumped against it, where I waited until Nina opened it.

Nina got a fright when I collapsed on to her. Without saying a word, she held me up. But she didn't hug me, like she always used to do.

'Don't I get a kiss, Nina? It is you I've come to see, you know.'

My lips were trembling with cold. Nina leaned me up against the wall like a log of wood, while she locked the outer door. Then she put her arms around me and burst into tears.

'Oh, you poor thing,' Nina said to me. 'You must be dying.'

And so on and so on. I almost started crying myself. I hugged her tighter and kissed her on the forehead. If I was dying, I might as well make the most of it.

'Wait a moment – I've arrived, but I'm still in the porch. Why are you keeping me out here?'

She started crying even harder. I couldn't stop her. But she still wouldn't let me into her room.

'Nina, have you got someone in there?'

I couldn't pull her arms away.

'I can tell you've got someone,' I said. 'OK, but even so can't I just come in and pay you a visit? What d'you think, Nina?'

Personally, I thought I ought to go. But I wanted to know what Nina would say. She stepped back, but the porch was so small that I quickly found Nina's shoulders in the dark. It seemed she was standing in front of the door into her room and blocking my way.

'What's the matter, Nina?'

Her face was all wet.

'I won't let you in. You'll start a fight.'

Hell, I thought, as if I'd come all this way to see her just for that.

'OK. Let me go!'

'Will you start a fight?'

'Let me out, I mean. I'm going back.'

'What? You won't get as far as the landing-stage. You'll freeze to death.

'So you see the problem. What are we going to do now?'

Nina opened the door and I went in after her.

He was sitting at the table, wearing singlet and breeches, a fresh-faced clean young soldier, sturdily built, his hair cropped in a crew-cut, all pink and glowing as though he had just stepped out of a bath. And he was smiling at me. Nina was standing between us. His tunic was lying on the bed, on top of the red quilt; I remember when Nina bought it. Before that she had a patchwork bedspread, sewn out of scraps. She really loved to be warm and always had the stove burning so hot that if it had been me sitting at that table I'd have been wearing nothing but a singlet too. She was sewing on some buttons for him, or the collar-lining of his tunic, I don't know which; I simply noticed that her scissors were not hanging on their usual nail on the wall but lying on the quilt, with a needle and thread alongside them. She had put his canvas boots by the door; I didn't notice them and knocked them over. Not on purpose, but just because I didn't notice them. He realized that, and kept on smiling.

There was some food and vodka on the table. They had already drunk half the bottle, which was why he was looking so good and bright, a sight for sore eyes. He wasn't very tall, though, which was unlucky for Nina. Well, come to think of it, so much the better for me.

'Don't just stand there, Nina. Why don't you introduce me to the comrade from the military? Soldiers and sailors,' I said, 'are friends and helpers to each other. Co-operation and mutual assistance.'

Nina did not move but stood between us, facing him, her back turned to me. He jumped up as if he was on springs, hand outstretched.

'Sergeant Lubentsov. But most people call me Arkady.'

Pushing his arm aside, I went over to his tunic, which I straightened out so that I could see the stripes on his shoulder-boards. I didn't give him my hand at once, but first wiped it on my trousers.

'I'm Senya.'

'Glad to meet you. Is that short for Semyon?'

'Oh, come on!' I said 'Semyon's for when you're sober. Otherwise it's Senya.'

'So shall we be pals?'

This little soldier with his high, prominent cheekbones was very determined to keep things sweet.

'Not just pals,' I said. 'Even relatives, in a manner of speaking. After all, we have Nina in common.'

Sergeant Cheekbones frowned. I went over to the table and poured myself a drink in Nina's glass. He watched, blinking his ash-blond eyelashes. Well, I thought, are you going to wade right in and hit me? It would be easy enough; I would keel straight over. Except that wouldn't be the end of it. I'd fall, but I'd get up again. And then it'd be no holds barred: a bottle's a bottle and a stool's a stool. And whose side would Nina take? Would she help you to show me the door?

'Sit down and join us.'

Cheekbones was saying this to me and pointing at the table. But I had already poured myself a drink. There was a situation for you.

'No, thanks all the same,' I said. 'I've just had supper.'

And I stuck a fork into the sprats. At that he started smiling again. This soldier's defences were impregnable. Sorry – this *sergeant's* defences.

'How's life at sea, sailor?'

This was him, a landlubber and an army type, asking me!

'What's a sailor's life?' I said. 'Nothing but trouble.'

'That can't be true!'

'Well, for instance, there was this mate of mine . . . you don't know him, Nina . . . came ashore one day. Belted off to his woman, all sails set. And what d'you think? There was another man with her. The old story. She'd get bored with waiting. But two's company, three's a crowd. So the third one ought to go, as it says in the song. My mate said to him: "Do I see you or do I not?" He was a stern man, was my mate. He's dead now, lost at sea. Died in the unequal battle with the codfish. Well, it can happen to anyone. And believe it or not, this other man winked and wouldn't go. Seems he was shy of going. Then d'you know what my mate did . . .?'

At that moment I looked at Nina and stopped. She was now sitting on the bed, legs crossed, with her hands resting on her knees. She was looking at me and biting her lips. Though I wasn't looking at her lips but at her hands.

Did I tell you, or didn't I, that she used to be a dishwasher on a factory-ship? At sea or at home, she used to take in washing, too; there was always a tub full of it in her kitchen. Just think how much laundering she must have done in her life and what her hands must have been like! She probably wasn't thirty yet – I never did ask – but her hands were about thirty years older than she was, honest to God. It was as if they'd flayed the skin off someone else's hands and pulled it over hers like a pair of gloves – only the graft had never taken, so that the skin stayed dead, damp, pale pink, all wrinkled and baggy. Whenever I made love to her I used to think: she mustn't touch me with those hands, or I'll go flop. It used to drive me out of my mind, and made me want to run away from her. She sensed it, too, and hid her hands from me. Now I saw them and everything went clean out of my head. Why had I come here? What was I talking to Cheekbones about?

'What was I saying?'

'About this mate of yours,' Nina reminded me. Her lips trembling. 'What did he do? Kill them?'

The soldier looked embarrassed, but I shook his hand and clinked glasses with him.

'Why feel embarrassed?' I said. 'You know what Nina's like. You can't go wrong with her. She'll do all your washing and mending for you. With her you'll always get your fill of food, your booze and your smokes. Only don't ever hit her. Any fool can do that. But if anything's not right, just tell her so, firmly – but then I don't suppose I need to teach you that – and she'll do as you say . . .'

Nothing like this had ever happened before: I was drinking and getting more and more sober. And honestly, I suddenly thought – maybe this is it for Nina and she's going to be happy. Who knows, maybe he's really the one she needs. In that case, what am I doing here, why don't I go? With her and me it'll never be serious, I'll just keep on spinning her yarns and getting her all mixed up. Perhaps with him it'll be for real.

'By the way, pal, your ears must be burning,' Cheekbones said to me.

I finished my drink and looked at him. There was a bright look in his eyes now, though with a hint of worry behind it. He probably couldn't believe it was all going to end well and he'd be staying with Nina tonight.

'That's a fine thing! What were you saying about me?'

'Nothing about you personally. It was when Nina dropped a knife just now. She said we must knock on the table, otherwise a man will come and see us. And I said: "Superstition's a bad habit. If someone does come, it'll hardly be because of that."'

'Well said, Arkady . . . What's the rest of your name?'

'Vasilievich. Personally I don't believe thirteen's an unlucky number, or any of that silly stuff about black cats. Man is master of nature and everything else, so he ought to take a firm line and not bother about things that don't matter. If you want to commit suicide, for instance, you should go ahead and do it. Don't you agree?'

'Why ask me? Ask her.'

'No, I was thinking of something else. I've got a friend, too, you see. Changeable, forever getting some new idea in his head. I'm always trying to make him see sense. And it's definitely having some effect, too. Nina knows him . . .'

Nina looked at me and sighed. What was Cheekbones aiming at? For today, his aim was to get under her quilt. Then when his army service was finished he'd go home, where another girl, his real intended, would be waiting for him. And Nina would still be perched on the slopes of Cape Abram like a seagull, her window lighting the way for the latest slob to chat her up. But what could I do for her?

I took off my jacket – to button in the fur lining – and saw the inside pocket, zipped up and still nicely bulging. Maybe this was all I could offer – that is, providing she would take it.

'Come outside with me, Nina. I've something to tell you.'

That made him freeze to his chair. He kept on smiling, though; of course I wasn't going to take her away with me.

'What's the hurry, sailor?'

'Got to go on watch,' I replied

'A good watch keeps itself!'

Ah, Cheekbones, what do you know about sailors? But he didn't try to make me stay. He shook my hand – as hard as he could, of course – but I somehow had a feeling that their thing was not going to last long.

Nina followed me. I let her out into the porch, waved my hand to him and shut the door behind me. In the darkness I took her by the shoulders and pulled her to me.

'Senya!' Of her own accord she pressed herself against me, but now it meant nothing; that wasn't why I'd asked her to come out here. 'Shall I send him away? You only have to say . . .'

No point in it, I thought. It won't do her much harm even if the affair with him doesn't last long.

'Forget it, Nina, put the idea out of your head . . . It'll all work out nicely between you two. He's the steady type, I can see that, and he'll play it straight if you do. You'll never be able to depend on me, but he's reliable – you'll see.'

'Did you ask me out here to tell me that?'

'No, it wasn't for that . . . Nina, take my cash, will you?'

'What for?'

'For safe-keeping, otherwise I'll blow the lot.'

I offered her half my wad of money. She gripped my hands – with those hands of hers! – so that I twitched and dropped it all on to the floor. Nina bent down and started scrabbling around in the dark. I helped her to pick it up, she stuffed it into my hand but I dropped it again. She pushed me back against the wall and began picking it up herself, then crammed all of it at once into the inside pocket of my jacket. I reached for it again, but she gripped my hands to stop me.

'Go away! Go away for ever. I don't want anything from you. You're a pig, an obstinate pig!'

She wasn't holding me any longer. Only her voice, coming through her tears out of that pitch darkness, kept pounding at my ears: 'Pig . . . obstinate pig . . . brute . . .'

'You don't have to kick me out, I'm going anyway.'

'Get out! I never want to see you again! And I hope you freeze to death . . .'

As I fumbled for the latch, Nina shouldered me aside and opened the door herself. The wind burned our faces with stinging snow. Nina cooled down at once – no doubt she hadn't really wanted to throw me out, but there was no way the three of us could have spent the night there, even though she had a separate little kitchen in that tiny shack of hers.

Nina asked: 'How are you going to get back in your state?'

I patted her on the shoulder and set off downhill. By the time I'd gone twenty paces I heard the latch click.

On the ferry I kept trying to make out the light from her window, but I couldn't see it; it was lost among all the others. So that's my whole evening, I thought to myself – a complete washout. But it wasn't over yet, that evening . . .

When we docked at the ferry terminal, the duty deckhand made a boss shot and couldn't get the eye of the warp over the bollard; I went to help him pull it out of the water – and the bugger elbowed me aside!

'Out of the way, lover boy, if you don't want your face bashed in.'

OK, I thought; seems like today's my day for getting thumped.

7

No sooner had I stepped on to the landing-stage than those two – black as two wolves of the night-time steppes – came running up to me.

'Senya!' they shouted. 'Hi, what are your plans now?'

I didn't know – or care – what the two beachers had in mind, but my plans were to get back to the hostel and kip down.

'What did I tell you?' said Vova to Askold. 'There's us flogging all round town, just going to ring the police in case he was freezing to death – and he wants to go to bed!'

'What's the matter with you, Senya? Have you suddenly got old, or don't you want to know us any more?'

Now there's a couple of mates for you. I was so upset I actually sat down on a bollard. They were right – I might easily have frozen to death.

'Get up, Senya, don't sit down there, it's bad for you.' They lifted me up by the elbows. 'Let's go and warm ourselves up.'

Vova ambled along on one side of me, breathing into his collar, and Askold trotted on ahead for a bit then stopped, his teeth flashing as he told their story: 'I said to him, "Vova," I said, "this is a bad business, it's a sin if we don't try and find him." And he said, "Sin, my foot, he's just gone off to his woman and forgotten us." "No," I said, "he's a decent bloke, something's wrong, people can die in this cold." Well, we took the bus to your hostel, thought we'd have to turn the place upside down, but they know you there, Senya, you're a famous man. "Look for him at Cape Abram," they said, "he often goes over there."'

'Who said that? Tolya? Sort of baldish?'

'Doesn't matter who it was, Senya. Point is, we've found you – alive and well!'

There's a couple of good mates, I'm telling you!

We reached the Arctic. There they were throwing the last people out and two policemen were standing guard alongside the cloakroom attendant. One lad, tall as the doorway itself, was pushing his way through to them and trying to wheedle them in a hoarse voice: 'Look, dad, let a stoker in, my kid's ill.'

Askold barged in to support him: 'Let us in, our girls are sitting there without us.'

'No they're not.' The attendant cut him off sharply. 'They've gone.'

'What? Gone? Without us?'

The four of us started trying to force the door. It was just beginnning to give way when a fur-jacketed comrade from the police stuck his head out: 'What's all this carry-on?' he said. 'Looks like someone is going to be spending the night in our cells. OK, Sevastianov, get that one in the jacket.'

I knew that trick. He couldn't fool me with that 'Sevastianov', just because he didn't want to come out into the cold. So I stuck my foot in the door, expecting help from right and left of me. But Vova and Askold had lost heart, and pulled me away. Then the door closed. The humiliation of it!

'Doesn't matter,' Popeye yelled at me. 'I've got another plan. Let's push off to Rosta, we'll find some booze at Klavka's place. Specially as she fancies you, Senya!'

Aha, I thought, so we're going visiting. And Klavka probably likes her bit of fun, too.

'Will she have anything to drink?'

'You won't find Klavka without a good drop or two! Wait here, I'll nip along to the station for a taxi.'

All right, I thought, let him go, he's got long legs and the station's only about a couple of hundred metres away. But I noticed that Vova was swaying slightly, so I held him up. And he supported me. It's a fact, you've got to stick together. We were mates, weren't we?

I don't remember how long we were clinging together, but eventually a taxi hooted, and there was Askold waving at us out of the window. As Vova and I climbed in, we found two other people inside, with luggage and all. Vova squeezed in somehow, and I ended up with my legs hanging out of the window. We'd get there somehow, anyway.

'If you want it that way, you can walk.' This was the taxi-driver having his say. He got out and replaced my legs inside the cab. Seems he'd found a little space for them. 'OK, you capitalists, where to?'

'Take us to Rosta,' roared Popeye. 'Number seventeen, Initsiativnaya Street.'

Remembered that address all right, didn't you, pussycat! And he was pretty well tanked up, too.

'I can't go all the way out to Rosta. My shift's nearly finished.'

'That's no way to talk, chief!' yelled Popeye. 'Switch the meter off, and then we'll do a deal. Turn left!'

And he reached out to turn the steering-wheel himself.

'Hey, I don't need your help, thanks.'

'We all love you, chief. We'd die for you.'

'No need, stay alive a bit longer. Only I've got these other passengers going to Gorka, and it's nearer.'

'Nearer or farther, that's not the point – we got in first, after all.'

This came from the woman sitting behind me. Seems I'd fallen back on her. At least it was something soft for me to sit on. I turned round to her to apologize for our behaviour, but for some reason she put her hands on my chest and pushed me away.

'Sit still,' I said. 'You don't need to do any of that stuff. I know your husband's riding with us.'

I wanted to look at her husband too, but my neck wouldn't turn that far. At this point the husband spoke up: 'Really,' he said, 'seeing that we've made room for you, at least you might not behave like hooligans. Otherwise we may have to call the police.'

'Huh!' said the driver. 'Some hope of finding any police at this time of night!'

And he drove off, bless him. Just as we were pulling away, someone pressed his nose against the window.

'Hey, boys, take a stoker with you, my kid's sick.'

The driver braked hard.

'Will you push off, you pest?'

'Drive on,' boomed Popeye, 'and he'll have to let go.'

'How can I drive on? He's hanging on to the door handle.'

They started to argue out in the cold, and stood there a long time waving their arms. Then the driver got in again and roared off. The stoker hopped alongside for a bit, then fell back.

'Listen,' the woman said suddenly, 'have you really switched off the meter? It must have clocked up a bit already.'

'Now look,' said her husband's baritone, 'we'll go where we're going, then you lot can make your own arrangements.'

'Who asked you?' Askold said to him. 'Who are you? You're from out of town, aren't you? Well, you sit still, Mr Outsider, and don't shoot your mouth off. If you want to know, we can pay for you too. See this fellow in the new jacket? Any idea who he is? He's the senior captain of the whole herring fleet. The biggest capitalist of the lot!'

'Rockefeller!' shouted Vova.

'The papers print interviews with him every day. He supplies the whole country with fish. And sends it abroad, too. Why, we could buy you up – you and all your luggage too, Mr Outsider. Show him how much capital you've got there!'

I laughed, put my hand into my jacket and pulled out the whole wad. Though it wasn't a wad any longer but a messy bundle – when Nina and I had picked the money up in the dark we had simply shoved it back any old how. I showed the bundle to the woman and her husband, and to the driver too, in case he was afraid we were broke.

'Put it away,' said Vova. 'They're dazzling me. They shine in the dark.'

'Got it, Mr Outsider?' Askold asked. 'You're travelling with three patriots of the Soviet Arctic. Patriots, but modest with it. If I had a guitar I'd sing for you . . . "We love our frozen northern climes, far more than palms or southern vines!"'

And Vova joined in: '"Our stern and rocky northern soil – a home of peace and honesl toil!"'

He was a lad, that Popeye. And Vova was pure gold too! The taxi didn't drive – it flew along the streets, the tyres not touching the snow, and I felt so good, the movement began to rock me to sleep . . . Then the out-of-towners let the cold air in as they pulled out their luggage. The husband tried to pay, but Popeye yelled to the driver: 'You don't want their chicken-feed, you're a patriot too! We don't take tips in this town of ours!'

Literally only a minute after we'd set out again Askold was waking me up: 'Had a good sleep, comrade senior captain? Time to pay.'

I laughed, and unfastened the zipper on my jacket.

'Go ahead and pay.'

Vova shoved his hand inside, pulled out some of what was in there and gave it to the driver.

'Look, lads, I won't take more than a tenner from a bloke who's drunk.'

'You're soft in the head, chief!' Popeye shouted. 'You don't know when you're in luck. The captain's giving you a bonus as compensation. Senya, tell him that's right!'

'Uh-huh,' I confirmed. 'I'm the generous kind.'

It was true – I felt so good and so happy because they all loved me and I loved them like they were my family . . .

When I woke up completely, it was from the cold: a motorbike engine was sputtering and I wasn't in a taxi any longer but in a sidecar. How on earth had I moved from one to the other? The mind boggled.

'Hey, you artist!' A fur coated comrade from the police leaned over me. He was sitting on the pillion-seat. 'Want me to hold on to you? You won't fall out, will you?'

'He's a hooligan, not an artist!' some voices shouted.

The motorbike was moving slowly out of a courtyard and a whole crowd of people was seeing us off the premises.

'Lord, when are we going to clean them out of this town? . . . I'll have you know, lieutenant, that we're all prepared to sign a collective statement!'

'Go home and go to bed, citizens,' said the lieutenant, trying to calm them down. 'Collective statements aren't necessary, but anybody who has had a window broken can make a specific complaint.'

Popeye was walking alongside and whispering to me in a hoarse voice: 'They're not going to touch us, Senya. Just remember the fun we had, Senya!'

What fun? Scraps of memory started coming back to me . . . There was a flight of steps, and then I charged head down and smashed both halves of a double glass door, which was maybe why my head was splitting. And my face was smarting, as if it had been punched. Yes, that's right, it had been punched, because before butting the door I'd been fighting with someone . . . I ran my hand over my face and saw blood on it. God, yes – I'd been fighting my two mates, who else could it have been? Vova had punched me in the face while Popeye held my elbows from behind.

I remembered all that fun, and started to clamber out of the sidecar. Askold jumped back. Somehow Vova, my friend, my old shipmate, was nowhere to be seen.

'Sit down,' said the lieutenant, pressing hard on my shoulder. 'And what are you up to?' he asked Askold. 'Want to come with us as witness?'

Popeye was gone in a flash.

'Right then. OK, Makarychev, back to the station. Go to bed, citizens!'

Makarychev looked down at me from the height of his saddle.

'What an artist!' he said, as he opened the throttle.

8

My eyes were weeping from the fumes of ammonia, my face was stinging and lymph was oozing from the fingers of my right hand. The lieutenant gave me a piece of wadding to put on them, sat me on a bench in the duty-room, and then he and Makarychev drove off again.

I made myself as comfortable as I could, while the desk officer, not looking at me, busied himself with writing. I was just wondering if maybe I could sneak out, when in came a sergeant wearing a sheepskin jerkin, tough-looking with a brick-red face, and leaned against the doorpost. There was also another door with a grille in it, where a curly-haired woman was standing and inspecting me through the bars. I don't know what she'd done to deserve being put behind bars, while I was allowed to sit on the bench. No doubt the desk officer had his reasons.

He was a middle-aged man who had made it to major, losing a lot of his hair in the process, though he was still able to cheat a bit with an 'internal loan' – brushing the hair from the sides over the top. I stared at him and laughed. At this the pen stopped scratching the paper.

'Thought of something funny? Tell me about it, then I can have a laugh too.'

'With pleasure,' I said. 'Only I need a little time to remember what it was.'

'That we most certainly can give you. You'll have plenty of time – fifteen days, in fact. You don't mind, do you?'

'No, why should I? Nobody dies from it, after all.'

'What's your name?'

'Ah,' I said, 'and if I didn't have a name, would you not be able to put me in the cells?'

'Nyrkin, were there any papers on him?'

The sergeant shifted his weight from one foot to the other. 'No'.

Quite correct; I'd left them all in my jacket in the hostel.

'What did he have on him?'

'Some money. Forty kopecks.'

'What!!!' I jumped up from the bench and stode over to the barrier. 'What d'you mean – forty kopecks? I had twelve hundred new roubles, I'd just been paid off after a trip.'

The Major looked at me and bit his fountain pen. 'Are you telling the truth?'

'Well, maybe a bit less. I bought this jacket, went to a restaurant and spent something on a taxi. But I couldn't have blued a thousand!'

The Major looked at the sergeant, who only spread his hands.

'I don't know . . . what's your name? . . .'

'Shalai.'

'Right now, let's get acquainted. I'm Major Zapylaev. So this is the situation, Shalai. We didn't pinch your money. You know that very well.'

I went back to the bench. So when had my cash been nicked? Fragments came floating back . . . Askold, with his back to a door, was hammering on it with his foot, while Vova put his finger on the bell and kept it there until Klavka opened it on the chain: 'What the hell do you want now?'

'Open up, Klavka, we've brought Senya to see you specially. He can't live without you!'

She was laughing, standing there in a dressing-gown patterned with red and green flowers. 'And what am I going to do with you three idiots?' The woman from Three Brooks, in curlers, was standing behind her and whispering something. 'Don't you stick you oar in!' – that was Askold shouting at her. Then he was sitting on the sofa strumming a guitar: 'Another's come, but I am not to blame for growing tired of waiting for your love . . .' I laughed at this. Vova was cuddling his Lidka, while she slapped his hands and hissed: 'Stop tickling! I mustn't laugh, can't you see I've put all this cream on my face? . . .' I was sitting on the floor by the radiator. Klavka brought me a glass of vodka and something to eat, and wanted to clink glasses with me. I could only see her beautiful legs with their nicely rounded knees, so I clinked my glass against her knee. I loved her so much, this Klavka, I'd never loved anyone so much in my life! Then I was in the kitchen, with my arms around her . . . I'd gone there to put my head under the tap . . . I asked her to go away with me, because these beachers would rob me and only she could save me . . . 'Oh Ginger, I'm not made of wood either, I can lose my head too. And what if your true love threw acid in my eyes?' I mumbled some more nonsense to her. Then she pulled herself away, wrapped her dressing-gown around herself and went out of the kitchen . . .

'Look,' said Major Zapylaev, 'can't you remember anything?'

'Not a thing.'

'Who were you with in the restaurant?'

'Some friends.'

'You don't suppose they could have done it?

I didn't answer.

'Where did you go in the taxi? Can you remember?'

'To a woman.'

'What sort of woman?'

I found her in the other room with Askold, practically making love. Or so I thought. I threw him on the floor, sat down beside her and began to kiss her, on the neck, on the breasts. She didn't pull herself away but only laughed and blew in my face. Suddenly Popeye was trying to strangle me. Vova came over, seemingly to separate us, but it was he who first hit me. They dragged me out into the passage to beat me up, but there I wrenched myself free and gave them each a hefty punch. With the third one, though, I hit the wall and did myself a lot of harm. After that I couldn't stop them beating me up. Askold held my arms, while Vova took aim and hit. 'That's not enough for him. He'll remember this one, though. And this one.' This went on until Klavka came running. 'Stop it, you brutes! Or I'll shop the lot of you!' But it was useless to threaten them when they'd tasted blood. They opened the door and kicked me head-first down the stairs . . .

Suddenly the old girl behind the bars piped up: 'Try hard to remember, lad. The police are all right, they don't pinch other people's things.'

'Go and sit down, Kutuzova,' the sergeant said. 'Nobody asked you.'

'All right, sergeant. I'm sorry for the boy, that's all.'

'We're sorry for him too. So you just shut up.'

Major Zapylaev gave a sigh and said: 'So what about it, Shalai? Are you going to help? You see, it's my duty to find your money.'

'No it's not. At any rate, I'm not asking you to find it.'

'You're wrong to say that. The people who did it should really get it in the neck, and you're shielding them. Can't you even remember the woman's surname?'

. . . When I started throwing bricks at her window, I hit someone else's window, and a whole bunch of them came pouring out to grab me, and some bloke from above shouted out: 'He's been with Perevoshchikova, her place is always full of riff-raff. I've had my eye on her flat for a long time!' And Klavka shouted from the doorway: 'You mind you own business! Been watching who comes to see me, have you? Well, I'm a free woman. Maybe I want to live my own life.' Some voice my lady-love had!

But then I remembered about Nina. The beachers knew I'd been to Cape Abram, the police would investigate, and maybe some of the money was still lying around in her porch, in fact it was bound to be; they might easily arrest Nina and then even I couldn't get her out of trouble. And if they picked up the beachers and Klavka . . . well, villains they might be, but that money wasn't worth anyone going to prison for. When I was in the Navy I only spent twenty days in the cooler, but that was long enough for me to know that no money was worth that. It would be better for them if I grabbed them by the throat next time I met them.

'Where are you from, Shalai? From the trawler fleet?'

'Trawler yourself!'

'Go on, be rude to me. It's all going down in the report.'

'I'm not in the trawler fleet. I'm a herring fisher.'

'Right, then answer properly. I'm writing an official report on your case. Where do you live?'

'On land and sea,'

'All right, I'll be more precise. Where is your official place of residence?'

'On the ship.'

'OK . . . so you're in the hostel. Well, you're going to spend the next fortnight with us. In the circumstances, we won't charge you for the drying-out treatment.'

'Thank you.'

'Nyrkin, give him a set of bedding. We'll question him tomorrow.'

Nyrkin was just about to go, when the old woman behind the bars started whining: 'When are you going to take me to the toilet?'

'We took you,' said Nyrkin, 'less than an hour ago. You can wait a little longer.'

'I can't wait. Any minute now I'll piss on the floor.'

Nyrkin said in a good-natured sort of tone: 'If you piss on the floor you'll have to wipe it up with your skirt.'

'I will not! My skirt's woollen!'

Lord, I thought, what an old bag! To think there are woman like her in this day and age! And I'll be stuck in there with her, there's no one else in the cells.

I stood up and went over to the barrier again. 'I don't fancy it here with you, I'd better go back to the hostel.'

'I'm afraid, my friend, it's for me to decide where you'd better be. If you've been disturbing the peace, that means you'll be better off with us.'

'I can't stay, Major. I'm at the end of my shore leave. I've been back from the sea a week.'

'What else can we do, Shalai? It wasn't Sergeant Nyrkin and I who smashed windows and disturbed the sleep of honest citizens, was it?'

'But I have to go to sea again tomorrow. We're sailing in the morning. No. 815 – you can check it.'

Major Zapylaev stopped writing his report and sighed. 'Nyrkin, which vessels are sailing tomorrow?'

'Who knows? We'll have to ring up the despatcher's office.'

'Mm' yes . . . Even so, the despatcher won't know whether Shalai's signed on or not. Who's your captain?'

I shrugged. I hadn't yet managed to think up the captain's name.

'We'll meet,' I said, 'at sea.'

'He's lying,' said Nyrkin. 'And then again, maybe he's not.'

'Well, can you remember anyone's name? The First Officer? The trawlmaster?'

'Any of the mates?' said the woman from behind the bars. 'The engineer officers?'

'Yes! I remember the name of the chief engineer. Babilov.'

'Sergei Andreyich?'

'That's him.'

Zapylaev sighed again. 'I expect he's got a telephone, hasn't he?'

It was true, the Chief was on the phone. Three years ago he'd been elected a deputy to the District Soviet. Only I didn't want him to know about all my adventures.

'He's asleep,' I said.

'Dosn't matter, we'll have to wake him up. It's your fault.'

'I was only joking. I'm not sailing tomorrow at all.'

'So you were lying, is that it?'

'Uh-huh.' I went back to the bench. 'Sergeant, give me my bedding, I want to go to sleep.'

All the same, Major Zapylaev dialled the number. In my mind's eye I saw that long, long corridor lined with trunks, tin wash basins and refrigerators, and bicycles hanging on the walls; I heard the phone bell ringing and ringing until someone, the most nervous of the tenants, jumped out of bed, rubbed his eyes, fumbled for the light switch, and padded all the way to the telephone at the far end of the corridor. Then back again to knock up the Chief – also a major expedition down to the other end. No question of not waking up the Chief; they swear at him, but they respect him. So now the Chief gets up, wheezing, throws on a pea-jacket, shoves his feet into a pair of warm galoshes and goes out, while all the other tenants strain their ears at the doors – who can want him at this late hour? Funny, funny – 'Major Zapylaev of the police'; the Chief was staggering a bit when he came home. Oh no, it's nothing to do with the Chief himself, just a sailor from his crew who's been kicking up a bit of a shindy – 'in a state of insobriety, of course'. Just think, he's managed to lose a thousand roubles and can't remember where. These sailors! What relation is he to the Chief – a son, a nephew? Ah yes, it's that one who comes to see him so often, sort of like a foundling. Much joy he's had of *that* foundling. And the old man's pleading for him, abasing himself, and all for that no-good. Lord, now Marya Vasilievna's come out too; they're too kind for their own good, taking all this trouble over that hulking, grown-up lout, never think of themselves . . . Then they both walk back again, between the rows of keyholes, in silence. They shut themselves in their own little room without a word to each other.

Major Zapylaev put down the receiver, stroked the hair combed across his head and frowned: what was he going to do with his report now?

'Well, I'll leave it on file, just in case. The tenants of those flats will be complaining, anyway. You'll have to pay for their broken window panes to be replaced. Agreed?'

I nodded. All was well, the earth hadn't swallowed me up, although my face seemed to have broken out in blotches.

'Can I go?'

'Push off! Wait a moment, though. Lunev and Makarychev can drive you to the hostel, otherwise you may get into trouble somewhere else and we'll have to wake up Babilov again.'

At that moment Lunev and Makarychev came back from patrol, both in a filthy temper. Makarychev was pressing a handkerchief to a bruise on his cheek, and Lunev tipped four empty cartridge-cases from his pistol on to Zapylaev's desk – apparently they'd had to intervene in a conflict between foreigners, when some British and Canadian sailors had started fighting each other near the International Seamen's Club.

'What a night!' said Major Zapylaev. 'Now you'll have to go out again, Makarychev, and take this beacher back to the hostel.'

Lunev glared at me in fury. 'So that's how we work, is it? We arrest him and you let him go.'

'Look, Lunev, it's like this: how are you proposing to reform him when he's in custody? Give him a broom and make him sweep the streets? For him that's a rest cure. He's going to sea tomorrow at 8 a.m. I've checked it out. You won't think up any better form of corrective labour than that. And you and I are not catching fish for the good of the country, Lunev . . .'

'Let Makarychev have a rest,' said Lunev. 'I'll drive him myself.'

On the way, I asked Lunev to stop outside a certain familiar courtyard, went in and craned my neck upwards. The light was out in the window on the fourth floor. I came back and got into the sidecar.

Lunev took me to the hostel, woke up the duty supervisor and waved goodbye to me. 'It's damn' bad luck, but don't fret about it.'

'Thanks,' I said.

'Have a good trip!'

I went in, took off my jacket only and flopped face down on the bed. Like a child I fell into a dreamless, mindless sleep.

9

The supervisor knew her job. If you were due to go to sea, she might turn the hostel inside out but she'd make sure, even if you were dead, that you were on your feet. You'd stand there, swaying – and you'd come to life. Of course, your room-mates wouldn't sleep through it either. All my four room-mates woke up, saw it was still dark outside and started smoking. They were sympathetic. It was hard to believe we'd lived together for a whole week, especially since we'd never managed to get together in one party. Later today someone else would come in my place, like in the famous story: 'Sleep faster, comrade, we need your pillow.'

They smoked in silence while I packed. My suitcase was crammed pretty tight with two changes of underwear, three shirts, a tie and a fur hat; my gold watch, overcoat and suit I decided to leave for safe keeping, so I borrowed a needle and an indelible pencil from my neighbour, sewed up my extra gear in a piece of sacking and wrote on it: 'Shalai, S.A. Keep till April. DWT No. 815 *Galloper*'. That was all my possessions together with my new jacket, which luckily had come to no harm. The blood had washed off completely, without leaving any traces. Oh yes, and half a packet of Belomor; that would do for today, and tomorrow I could get some more cigarettes on credit from the ship's store. If I really was going to sail today, money was no use to me anyway. Of course, if I'd had the money that would have been another matter; still, least said soonest mended.

'So long, slaves!'

'So long.'

'See you at sea. Off the Faroes.'

We sat for a minute in silence, as the custom is, then I shook their hands, still warm and soft from sleep.

I've lost count of the number of times I've left this place. Well, not this very room, but they're all furnished exactly alike: five beds with bedside lockers, a table covered with sheets of newspaper, cracked mirror on the wall, and a picture of some shipwrecked sailors clinging to a broken mast with a wave rolling towards them in a gale of about Force 10 – some hope they have! On the other wall, a patrol of Frontier Guards on a cliff-top is gazing out at a grey sea, the sergeant shading his eyes with his hand – no doubt because he's dropped his binoculars into the water. We can't get away from the sea even when we're ashore, so the pictures may as well hang there. And I went on my way.

The supervisor stopped me just as I was going out of the front door. 'Wait a moment, son, you haven't paid for seven days lodging.'

This was something I hadn't taken into account. Seven days – that was seventy kopecks. I produced my forty kopecks.

She looked at me over the tops of her glasses and sighed. 'Couldn't you borrow the rest from you room-mates?'

'No sailor borrows less than a tenner.'

'All right, I'll pay it for you myself. Will you remember?'

'No, I'll forget. You remember for me, please.'

'Just a minute, I'll write you a pass.'

I showed her what was in my suitcase, tore up the pass and threw it into the spittoon. Who would I be showing it to? Only to the same supervisor when I came back.

'So long, love.'

'Off you go, and have a good trip.'

It was still night and the sky full of stars as I stepped out. I walked down the path to the embankment. Lights were twinkling all over the port as far as the most distant docks, the water gleaming in the mooring-bays; the whole place was alive, seething and groaning as sirens and hooters called back and forth, while people hurried towards the port from all directions – in crowds, in ones and twos, from the streets and from the buses.

On the corner near the Polar Institute I stopped. It was a quarter past nine. She was either there already or would be arriving any minute now. And not because she was coming to see me off. I had no coins for the phone box, but I knew the trick of ringing up without paying.

A man answered. 'Impossible,' he said. 'She's in the lab. Personal calls are not . . .'

'What a pity! And her brother's come . . .'

'From Volokolamsk?'

It was him – the creep in glasses.

'Well, if it can't be done, then don't call her. Just tell her the same person rang. He's going to sea today and asks her to come to the quay-side.' I told him the name of the ship and how to find the quay. 'Will you remember that?'

He whispered something to someone else, then said: 'Very well, I'll try.'

'Don't you try; she's the one who should try.'

'She . . . I expect she'll come. If she can. Nothing else?'

'No, thanks.'

And that was the limit of my contact with her.

I still had to go to the personnel office. It was nearby, on the hill – a little single-storey shack. Inside it were peeling, blue-painted walls, scribbled all over in pencil, and hung with posters: 'Fishermen! Never be without a knife when the nets are cast.' – 'Don't just gaze hopefully into the water. Act confidently, make use of the echo-sounder!' – 'We will over-fulfil the year's planned target for cod by umpteen per cent!' There are five or six little windows along the corridor, windows so small you can't see a face on the other side and can only push your handful of papers through them. Morning to night, the place is so crowded with people attacking those little windows that there seems no chance of ever being attended to. But it only *seems* that way.

I barged my way in and shouted:

'Hey, beachers! Gangway for a volunteer!'

They stepped aside, and a girl even poked her head out of a window.

'Are you a volunteer?'

'Uh-huh. Give me a boarding-pass. It's urgent!'

'Take any one you like. Which ship d'you fancy?'

'Number eight-fifteen.'

'Try again! She's already sailed.'

'Impossible,' I said. 'She's not due to sail till eight o'clock tonight, and it's only half past nine in the morning. Look, there's her nominal roll lying on your desk.'

'Oh dear!' She got busy. 'Can I really have forgotten to hand it in?'

The other beachers were breathing down my neck and watching as she registered me on the roll.

'Hey, look!' said one to another. 'They're going to catch herring off Norway.'

'Hoping to, that is.'

'You're joking! Who ever caught herring in January?'

'*I'm* not going. They're going.'

The girl tossed me a boarding-pass and shut her window. The beachers sighed and went off for a smoke, while I had to carry on with the rest of the paper-chase. It was nearly an hour before I'd bashed my way through it and got all my papers stamped.

Outside, people were streaming down the hill on the raised wooden walkways. I wedged myself into the crowd and moved off, like a fish in a shoal. The snow and the planking creaked underfoot and a cloud made by our breath floated along with us; it was like walking in a fog. At the dock gates we split up into three streams to pass the three police checkpoints. The port workers weren't carrying anything and so went straight through, but with my suitcase I was stopped.

I had no spirits with me.

The policeman was amazed: 'I suppose you passed it to someone over the wire?'

'Yes, from on high,' I said, 'like the Holy Ghost.'

'How much?' the policeman laughed.

'Maybe three bottles.'

'That's not much. Just now we stopped a stoker who was carrying eighteen bottles of vodka in his trousers.'

'You're joking,' I said. 'Did you confiscate them?'

'Well, if they fell out it's his own fault. He shouldn't have let 'em fall out.'

'Quite right,' I said.

'Have a good trip!'

The crowd was fanning out to the quays, the workshops and the warehouses. People I knew hailed me – an engine driver, dockyard fitters, girls from the smoking-sheds and the refrigeration plant; I smiled back, waved and went on my way without stopping until I reached Pier No. 16. There was my *Galloper*, covered in hoar-frost like sugar icing. Stevedores were loading empty barrels into the hold. A dockside crane swung over with a net full of them, the net dangled over the hold and was released, sending the barrels crashing into the hold.

A bored-looking character at the head of the gangway, wearing the watchkeeper's armband – two blue stripes with a white stripe between them – was staring at the stevedores and spitting into the water. He didn't like the job. I handed him my boarding-pass and my seaman's paybook. He added them to a pile, then took a look at my jacket.

'Are you sailing as a deckhand?'

'Yes.'

'Fine.' I don't know what was particularly fine about it, but that's what they always say. 'And I'm the Third Mate.'

'That's fine too.'

'Passed your medical?'

'Don't need one this year.'

'What about VD? Haven't caught a dose, have you?'

'My guardian angel saved me.'

The Third Mate was a little shorter than me, with a nasty quarrelsome look to him. Somehow he had acquired a scar right across his cheek. When he smiled his scar turned white, and this made him look so grim that his smile was completely cancelled out.

'Are we sailing today?' I asked.

'At three o'clock, probably. Or maybe tomorrow. The captain hasn't arrived yet. And why are you late?'

'They took a long time to do my papers.'

'Excuses! There must be discipline. You don't want to sell your jacket, do you?'

'No, I don't.'

'OK. Since you're late, you can take over the watch. Put on the armband.'

He handed me his armband and immediately cheered up.

'I'll just nip ashore to the office. Got to fetch the medicine chest.'

'If anybody asks, I'll tell them that.'

'And keep your eyes open! Watch those stevedores. See how they're flinging those barrels in – they'll smash all the staves at this rate. Shout and tell them to put a fender down.'

'I'll do that.'

'At least shout at them.'

We understood each other. If you put down a fender or a mat, such as the tarpaulin from a lorry, you have to drop in each barrel separately. That way we wouldn't be sailing for a week.

'When you get bored,' said the Third Mate, 'there's a dog in the galley and you can play with it. Clever little beast.'

'I certainly will.'

'Sure you don't want to sell your jacket?'

'Quite sure.'

He ran down the gangway and disappeared. I went off to find myself a berth. The crews quarters in a DWT are in the foc's'le. The trawlmaster and the bo'sun get a tiny cabin apiece; for the rest of the deck-crew there are two bigger cabins, one for four and one for eight men. I had no hope of a bunk in the four-berth cabin; that's reserved for the fish-packer, the trawlmaster's mate, the cooper and one other senior hand, a 'veteran' of that ship. Somehow I always seem to be the junior on any vessel, so I belong in the eight-berth cabin. I ran down the companion-way and pushed open the door, to be met by wreaths of tobacco smoke, a cloud of steam from the stove and a pleasant aroma from the table, where three members of the crew were sitting with their ladies.

'Hello, savages!'

'Hello, nigger! Sailing with us? Take a seat.'

'Can't. I'm on watch.'

'What's there to do on watch? Say your prayers?'

I looked around – not one familiar face. And all the bunks were occupied for the present. Some were piled up with gear, others had couples on them, locked in each other's arms and whispering – four feet poking out under the curtain, two in men's shoes, two in women's. That farewell whispering goes on until we get to Tyuva. Because when you leave the port, that's not departure: the point of departure is Tyuva. There we take on board the tackle – nets, hawsers, floats – we take on fuel oil and coal for the galley, check the compass, and stretch our legs on land for the last time. Then we move out into the middle of the Sound and the Frontier Guard launch moors up alongside us. We are all mustered in the saloon, the lieutenant takes our passports and calls out each man's surname, which we answer by giving our first name and patronymic. We know the drill; it's not our first foreign-going trip. Meanwhile soldiers search the whole vessel, bring the women up on deck and take them back to port. It will be night-time by then. Although we usually finish at Tyuva in four hours or less, we spend as much of the time as possible in relaxing and loafing about. This is where we see these women for the last time, and in the glare of the searchlight we shout to them over the ship's side: 'Watch it, Vera – or Nadya or Tamara – if you're a bad girl I'm bound to find out. Rumours fly around at sea, you know, just like on land! I'll stop your allowance in a flash and that'll be that!' And she shouts up from below: 'Don't be silly, Senya – (or Vasya or Seryozha) – and talk sense. When have I ever cheated you? I do have some self-respect, you know!' And the launch plunges into the darkness, its masthead light bobbing, carrying away our ever-faithful wives and girlfriends. I can vouch for this; I've said goodbye to enough of them like this in my time.

As I was saying, I couldn't find myself a bunk straight away, and that's a bad business, believe me, because at sea your bunk is your refuge. You don't only sleep in it: you read and you write letters in it, you ride out storms in it - and that's why it's better if your bunk lies fore-and-aft and not athwartships. But I seem to be born unlucky. I took what I could get, threw my suitcase on to the upper bunk by the door, and went out.

Just as I emerged from the doghouse at the head of the companion-way I was hailed by some long streak of piss in a sleeveless jerkin, no cap, and slippers on his bare feet: 'Watchkeeper! Why haven't you hauled up the flag?'

'Maybe it's already up?'

'No, it isn't. The dispatcher just called me to say so. Better go and haul it up.'

I climbed up to the boat-deck, made my way astern past the lifeboats and hauled up the flag – all greasy, discoloured and sooty. Would the dispatcher be able to see it with his binoculars now? I made fast the halyard and went back to the main deck, where the long streak was waiting for me, hopping from foot to foot in his thin slippers in the freezing cold. He looked the kind who can survive anything: boyish face, ruddy glow all over his cheeks, and no doubt a lot of latent strength in his well-covered shoulders.

'You've just joined – want to make out a pay warrant to anyone?'

'Yes. To my mother in Oryol.'

'No wife or girlfriend?'

'No.'

'Not paying any alimony? What sort of sailor are you with no ties?'

'I'm just – myself . . .'

'Well, I'm the same.' He offered me his large, pink, freckled hand. 'Come and see me in your own time. Nozhov's the name. Zhora Nozhov. Second Mate.'

'Fine.'

'So that's that. We'll get along well, I can see that. Keep a good watch and no skiving.'

He hopped off back to his quarters, just as someone hailed me from the shore: 'Watchkeeper!'

A little man with a full beard was standing on the pier, waving the nozzle of a hose: 'Are you going to take on water or not?'

'OK, dad.'

'Well, look sharp and uncap the tanks, What d'you mean – "dad"? I'm younger than you are.'

I must have looked terrible after last night's caper.

'Is that drinking water?'

For some reason he looked into the nozzle of his hose. 'No, I think it's washing water.'

I unscrewed the cap, positioned the hose nozzle and waved to him. He waved to his mate, bearded like him, who waved to someone else, and so on all the way to the water-tower.

'Watchkeeper!'

It was the ship's cook, calling from the galley. A lorry had brought food supplies. I swung a derrick over the side, looped a runing hitch around a cow's leg and pulled it tight.

'Haul away!'

Solemnly, like a flag, a frozen cow's leg slowly floated up from the quayside to the galley. Then we loaded some sacks of potatoes, dried fruit, vermicelli and God knows what else.

No sooner had I dealt with this than another voice came from the shore:

'Watchkeeper! Who took on that water?'

'What d'you mean – "who"? The ship took it on.'

'Who was personally responsible? Name? Shalai? Then why, Seaman Shalai, did you fill the washing-water tanks with drinking water? It costs extra money to purify it. The state's money. The people's money. Abroad they charge you gold for it. Foreign currency.'

'But we're not abroad.'

'Worse still: that means we're robbing ourselves. Who gave the order?'

'The man who passed me the hose said it was washing water.'

'Who was it? You don't remember. How did it happen then?'

God knows how it happened. Nobody knew.

'What do we do now?' I asked. 'Pump it back? That costs money too. The state's money. The people's money. On the other hand, we'll be able to wash ourselves cleaner. Some problem!'

The man in the hat looked perplexed. 'Well, I don't know, really . . . But if they all start taking on drinking water . . . Inefficiency. That's what we'll call it.'

He waved his hand and went away. A minute later someone else shouted:

'Watchkeeper!'

It was the First Mate calling from the wheelhouse; his job was to be on watch when we sailed. He was standing in the window like a portrait in a frame, looking down at me on the deck. And there was someone else standing there, near the hold, someone wearing a beaver-fur hat, scarf, overcoat and warmly lined galoshes, with his hands behind his back as he watched the way the stevedores were chucking the barrels about. Ah, I thought, any minute now he'll start yelling about putting down fenders.

'Are you the watchkeeper?'

He was looking at me with a cold stare, and frowning.

It was the captain, of course – who else? Captains always stop in the middle of the deck and take their time before they say anything. At sea a captain has plenty to say, but when he comes aboard for the first time he's in no hurry, and he has to say something that people are going to remember. Something that will make an impression.

'The deck's slippery, watchkeeper. Someone could fall and break a leg.'

So he's afraid people may break their legs. And I thought he'd be worried about the fenders.

'I'll sprinkle something on it,' I said, 'right away.'

'Very good. And what will you sprinkle on it? Salt?'

'No,' I said, 'That's against regulations. It has to be sand.'

'Have you got any sand?'

'No, but I'll find some.'

'You're new, I see, but you seem to know what to do. Well, get on with it.'

So the captain said his say, and with a slightly rolling gait he went off to his cabin. I took a shovel, went to a locker full of salt and started strewing it over the deck. I was new, but I knew what to do. And he knew too. Some genius had written in the newspaper that salt rots the planking. They printed his article, only they forgot to ask him one thing: what is it that's washing all over the deck when a ship's at sea, if not salt? They didn't ask this because the man who wrote the article was waging an economy campaign. If I sprinkled sand, it was supposedly cheaper. Except that in winter sand costs more than salt. And in summer there's no need to sprinkle anything on the deck.

When I'd finished doing that no one else seemed to want me, so I sat down on the hatch-coaming for a smoke. A man came clambering out of the foc's'le, staggered a bit in the doghouse, came over to the hold and stood looking into it. I jumped up and pushed him back half a pace.

'Push me, would you? You in charge around here?'

'I'm not in charge, but I'm the watchkeeper. If you fall in, I'm responsible.'

At that moment a barrel fell out of the net while it was still high up and crashed down, breaking all the staves. I don't know why it broke, when other barrels fell too and didn't break up; probably because the hoops were over-tempered and therefore brittle.

He grinned lazily, then suddenly grabbed hold of my jacket and breathed right into my face. It smelled of rotten teeth and alcohol fumes.

'I'm responsible for the casks, got it? Because I'm the cooper.'

'Let go,' I said, 'or you'll tear it.'

Even though he was drunk, he had an iron grip and was obviously stronger than me, sober as I was. Like an angry bear, he glared at me from under his grey eyebrows as if he could kill me.

One of the stevedores, who was stowing barrels down below, said to us: 'You two ought to be ashamed of yourselves. If you're going to sea together, you ought to be like brothers to each other.'

'You shut up,' the cooper barked at him. He let go of my jacket but shook his fist in my face: 'Brothers like this need to be killed.'

And he went back into the foc's'le. The stevedores stopped work and watched him go. The one who was down in the hold said: 'Listen, watchkeeper. Was all that row really about barrels? It isn't worth it, you know. Maybe you and he have fallen out over something. If that's so, then it's better not to go to sea together.'

'Us? Fall out? First time I've ever seen him.'

'That makes it worse!'

That, I thought, really does make it worse. Because there's nothing worse than when two people are shipmates and they don't like each other. Not just because of an argument over some barrels, of course, but when they simply can't stand the sight of each other. When you're at sea, you end by getting fed up with the people you *like*, without even being able to find a reason for it. So maybe he was right; perhaps I shouldn't go to sea with the cooper.

'Look here, watchkeeper,' said the man from the hold, 'forget it. After all, the man was drunk.'

'That's right. Listen – how about having a poke around in the galley to see if there's a crust of bread to spare? We're starving.'

God, these stevedores. They're always trying to scrounge something from us sailors. They seem to imagine there's a bottomless store of good things aboard a trawler.

'OK, I'll have a hunt around,' I said.

'Maybe you could even find a scrap of meat? Or some chicken?'

In the galley a saucepan was bubbling on the stove, and two of the cook's assistants were peeling potatoes. The cook himself was feeding a dog out of a bowl – a fluffy, gingery little mutt with slightly pop eyes and a scratch on its forehead. It wasn't eating properly, just sniffing at the food with its ears pricked up and one paw curled back. It couldn't believe its luck.

'Go on, Wavey, eat up, there's a good dog,' said the cook encouragingly. 'You'll be going on watch soon.'

All port mongrels are called 'Wavey' if they're bitches, and 'Surf' if they're dogs. This one would go ashore at Tyuva, of course; these port dogs are not such fools as to go to sea with us. They have a fixed plan: they can tell who's a sailor, they chum up with him, live on board for a few days in the warm and eat their fill, but at Tyuva they nip ashore and go back to the port on inbound ships. I never could understand how they tell the difference between ships going out to sea and those coming into port – after all, they all moor up at the same quay. Probably it's by smel!; the sailors are sober when they're returning. And their mood is quite different.

I asked the cook if he had anything to spare for the stevedores. He groaned, but fished a piece of meat out of the saucepan and wrapped it up, along with a loaf of black bread, in a sheet of newspaper.

'Don't you want a bite to eat yourself?'

I hadn't eaten since yesterday, but somehow I didn't feel like it.

'Well, at least have some stewed fruit.' He gave me a half-full saucepan and a ladle. 'Finish it, I've got to make some more anyway.'

The cook himself, a skinny man with a wrinkled, pain-wracked face, was chain-smoking cigarettes. He probably had an ulcer from working in ships' galleys.

I ate without much appetite, watching his assistants peeling potatoes. They cut out every single eye. At that rate, the potatoes still wouldn't be ready tomorrow. They were doing their best, of course, but they were slow. We seamen do everything fast, because peeling potatoes or rolling barrels, for instance, is not much fun. Tying knots, though – that's another matter; I like doing that. Even then, all the pleasure is in doing it quickly. But peeling potatoes, that – as our First Mate from Volokolamsk used to say – 'isn't white man's work'.

One of them noticed I was watching him, gave me an embarrassed smile and pushed back a shock of blond hair from his forehead. He was a good-looking lad, but still a kid, with puffy lips.

'What's the matter? Hand gone numb?'

'No, it's nothing.'

I saw at once they were apprentices. An old hand would have admitted he'd hurt himself. It's nothing to be ashamed of.

I dropped the ladle into the saucepan, took the knife from him and showed him how to peel a potato: snick down one side, snick down the other – and into the pan.

'But you take off so much like that.'

'All right, do it your way.'

The other one – dark-skinned and slit-eyed like a Mongol – smiled, but only with his lips.

'Alik, my friend, all knowledge is valuable. Say thank you.'

'Thanks,' said Alik.

A man in a little cap and a greasy ski-jacket came in from the saloon, took a poker and shoved it into the glowing coals of the stove. Then he counted how many of us were in the galley.

'Shura!' he bawled into the saloon. 'Make that four.'

'Count me out,' I said, 'I'm on watch.'

'Don't listen to him, Shura! The watchkeeper gets a ration and a half.'

His glum, wrinkled face unbroken by a smile, he thrust his open hand at me: 'My name's Firstov. Seryozha. Leave that stewed fruit, we can have it to eat while we're drinking.'

Alik seemed to be wriggling with embarrassment.

'Count me out, too, please . . . I don't drink that stuff. I've never drunk it before.'

Again Slit-eyes smiled with just his lips. 'He prefers champagne.'

'Sort it out between yourselves, kids, as to who drinks what!' said Seryozha.

The poker was now red-hot. He lit a cigarette with it, went into the saloon and we followed him. Shura had unpacked a crate of eau-de-cologne, which he was pouring out of the bottles into a clean mess-tin. Twenty-four 100-gramme bottles. It was meant as after-shave lotion for the crew, but no one ever used it for shaving; the deckhands drank it all on the day we sailed. The mates didn't touch it; they had their own perks – the spirit from the compass, three-and-a-bit litres per trip, and then all the way they'd be shouting down to the engine-room: 'Stoke her up, or the compass'll freeze!'

As Shura watched the process in the mess-tin with glee, the cook was opening a box of ships' biscuits from the lifeboat rations.

A young, rather sullen-looking girl was standing beside Shura and holding him by the shoulder.

'Shura,' she begged, 'when are you going to talk to me?'

He only twitched his shoulder. She didn't even notice us. Shura was the only one she could see. If I'd been in her place I wouldn't have looked at anyone else either, the lad was so good-looking, an absolute winner: big eyes, dark eyebrows, teeth like pearls. I don't think he had any idea how handsome he was; if he had, the girls would have been following him from quay to quay in hordes. But perhaps they did. Anyway, our lads never know their own worth. Although you couldn't compare him with Shura, Seryozha was a fine specimen too, with pitch-black hair and blue eyes, a combination you don't often find, but he had a way of twisting his face into such a grim look that you'd say he was ten years older than he really was.

Shura poured the drink out of the mess-tin into mugs, and for some reason gave me mine first.

'Take yours, mate.'

I didn't take it until all the others had theirs. Shura looked at me with a cheerful grin. You and I will get along all right – and Seryozha too, I've no doubt. I can't explain why I felt that.

'Where are you from?'

'Oryol.'

'You don't say! We're almost neighbours, I'm from Mtsensk. Let's drink to that, neighbour.'

Even his girlfriend gave me a kind look. Then we tossed it down; she sipped some out of his mug too, and pulled a face, waving her hand in front of her mouth. The stuff made us feel a bit queasy, so we quickly ate the dried fruit and reached for the ships' biscuits. The apprentices took a long time to pluck up courage, looking at us and wondering if we would live or die, then Slit-eyes gulped down his mugful all at once, clutched his stomach and breathed out upwards to the deckhead. Alik, on the other hand, drank in convulsive gulps and seemed to melt, tears pouring from his eyes .

'They'll survive,' said Shura. 'That's made sailors of 'em.'

Despite the heroic smile on his face, Alik was feeling sick. The cook jumped up and led him back to the galley. It was time for me to go too.

'Sit down, neighbour,' said Shura. 'No one's going to steal the ship.'

His girlfriend glared at me: 'Let him go, if he has to . . . When you're at sea you can talk to him as much as you like.'

I picked up the food wrapped in newspaper and went out.

The stevedores had stopped working, needless to say, and were waiting for me. They sat down at once and started eating.

'Come into the saloon, lads,' I said to them. 'It's warm in there and there's a drop to drink, too.'

They thought it over and refused.

'No point in us drinking, we'll breath it all out in this cold. You go ahead, though. After all, you're going to be on the wagon for three months.'

'That's true. Three and a half, in fact.'

I went up on the foredeck, sat down on a barrel, smoked and stared at the quayside. I still hadn't lost hope that she would come. Last time she'd been late too, and had only arrived just as we were sailing. Suppose the bloke in glasses hadn't told her I rang? But if I was leaving, what reason would he have for not telling her? And who was he whispering to while I was phoning him?

It wouldn't take long to run to the Polar Institute or to ring her up from the harbourmaster's office, but I was tied hand and foot by this damned armband. No one would want to take it over; for everyone on board, these were their last few minutes. Should I just go and to hell with it? Nobody would make a big fuss; they'd just shout a bit and then find someone else to keep watch. But that wasn't the point. This is just an obsession of mine that I can't explain. It's fate, I suppose: some are born to live in the warm, others to freeze and get wet. I was born to freeze and get wet. And not to leave my watch. I chose this myself, no one else is to blame.

It had already started to get dark when I was hailed again: 'Watchkeeper!'

It was just after three o'clock and no one had come to the quayside; I'd have seen them from a long way off.

10

It was the Chief calling me. He was rummaging about below the wheelhouse, getting some hosepipes and a dipstick from behind the derrick – preparing to take on fuel. Without turning round he said to me: 'The flood tide's just starting. Don't forget to slacken off the mooring-warps, otherwise they'll break.'

'I never have forgotten so far.'

The Chief turned around and looked me up and down: 'They told me the watchkeeper was a new man. Let's dip the tank and see how much there is left.'

He unscrewed the filler-cap; I put in the dipstick, made sure that it touched the bottom and pulled it out again.

The Chief was bending over to look at it. 'How much?'

He couldn't even see the markings. I could see them from where I was standing, and it wasn't very dark yet either. I squatted down and felt where it was wet with fuel-oil.

'About thirty-five . . .'

'That's what I thought. Screw the cap on again.'

'Why do you dip the tank yourself, Chief? You could have sent a greaser to do it.'

'I'm not doing it myself,' said the Chief. 'You're helping me. Don't worry, I'll get a grip on them when we're at sea. Did they bring you home all right?'

'Yes, thanks to you.'

'Why thank me? Don't be upset about the money, no money's worth worrying about. I expect you'll be more careful in future.'

I laughed. This was all the Chief's ticking-off amounted to. And that was why I liked him.

'Coming to my cabin?' asked the Chief. 'Got a drop of something to cheer you up.'

'Well, I've already . . .'

'I can tell. You smell like a ballerina.'

'I'll come.'

On a DWT only three people have separate cabins: the captain, the chief engineer, and the radio operator. Even the mates have to share a three-berth cabin. But 'Marconi' – that's what we call the radio operator – keeps all his apparatus in his, so it's not so much his cabin as his place of work. In fact, then, it's only the two of them who have single cabins, one opposite the other. The Chief is, as they say, 'the second power on the vessel', and nobody goes into his cabin. People go to see the captain for various reasons, but I was the only person who went into the Chief's cabin, and some even looked askance at me for that – and at him too, but we didn't give a damn.

By the time I arrived, the Chief had poured brandy into a couple of mugs and was slicing a sausage on a sheet of newspaper.

'My wife got this for you and me,' he explained. 'She felt very sorry for you last night.'

'I'm sorry I didn't get a chance to meet Marya Vasilievna this time. Is she coming to see you off?'

'She knows the best place to say goodbye. It only upsets her on the quayside. Well, down the hatch.'

I felt warmer at once; only now did I realize just how cold I'd grown from being on deck since morning.

'Have you met any of them yet?' asked the Chief.

'The skipper. Didn't care for him too much.'

'He's OK. I've sailed with him before. You only got a superficial impression.'

'Who cares, anyway, as long as he's good at catching fish.'

'On the whole, though, are they a decent bunch?'

I shrugged my shoulders.

'Don't you want to go to sea?' asked the Chief. 'Are you only doing it for the money?'

I didn't answer. The Chief poured out some more brandy and sighed.

'I'll tell you what I've decided. Senya. You're a handy seaman. I've seen you – you're a good deckhand. But you don't love your work, it doesn't satisfy you. That's why you're so restless, can't settle down. In any case, it's no good getting too fond of the job, soon you'll all be replaced by a machine – machines will cast the nets and salt the fish.'

'That's fine by me! Only I'll never be able to make sense of that machine of yours.'

'I'll show you how to! But that's not the point; it's not enough to make sense of it, you've got to love what you're doing. I can't teach you how to live, I'm not much good at it myself, but you *can* learn to love your job. If you can do that, everything else will fall into place. You'll feel yourself a different person. Because people cheat you and let you down, but a machine is like nature – it gives you back exactly as much as you put into it and it never holds back.'

I smiled at the Chief. You could feel a deep, rhythmic thumping under the deck, and the mugs on the table were sliding about from the vibration. We hadn't switched on the light, and we had no need to; in the Chief's cabin you could reach anything without getting up from the table, but I could see his face in the half-light. He must have felt good in his cabin, with the engine humming away underneath him night and day.

'Listen to me,' said the Chief, as if he could hear what I was thinking. 'When I landed in Gulag, at a time when normal human values were being destroyed, I only came to life when they put me in charge of a machine.'

'What did it do, that machine?'

The Chief pushed my mug towards me and said sternly:

'It did no harm, Senya. It laid as asphalt road through the Siberian tundra.'

I felt sorry for the Chief, so very sorry for him. I really decided that I would learn his trade from him. Maybe I could make something of myself after all.

Just then someone called from on deck.

'Off you go,' said the Chief.

As I went out, he was sitting hunched over the table in the dark and looking out of the porthole. Then he cleared away the unfinished bottle and the mugs.

'Where have you been, watchkeeper?' It was the First Mate, standing at one of the wheelhouse windows. He no doubt came from the coastal region around the White Sea – high cheekbones, broad nose and white eyebrows. He was a big-head, very much aware of his position. 'I've been calling you for an hour and you don't answer.'

An hour – than meant he had called me twice. I didn't argue. It's better that way.

'Don't go away, we'll be casting off soon. Is everyone on board?'

'Those who've come are on board.'

'That's not an answer to my question.'

What else was I supposed to say? He wasn't going to send me off into town to find any latecomers. They'd catch us up at Tyuva, anyway.

Two more men bounded aboard from the quayside, carrying suitcases, and disappeared into the crew's quarters. Then came the Third Mate, with a sack over his back – or rather not a sack but a pillow-case. No doubt it held the contents of the medicine chest, because on a DWT the Third Mate acts as doctor. He has every kind of medicine you could want, but all he ever prescribes is green liniment or aspirin – he doesn't know anything else. Green liniment if you're hurt, aspirin if you've got the glooms. We never get sick with anything else at sea.

The Third Mate had a woman in tow, who was wearing a hat and an overcoat trimmed with fox fur, and they started hugging each other right there at the foot of the gangway. The woman was big, and the mate was a little fellow. He put his arms around her waist, while she clasped him round the neck. She threw herself at him like a tigress, and he must have been more dead than alive when she let him go. The Third Mate ran up on deck and gave her a big sailor's wave. His eyes glistened with emotion.

'Off you go now,' he said to her tenderly, ' or you'll catch cold.'

For a minute she stood there like a statue, then went.

'All right, eh?' said the mate. 'Big enough for one and a half blokes wouldn't you say?'

'Big enough for two.'

'Her name's Sashka. We met yesterday.'

I nodded.

'Heard the latest? We've been recalled, we're not sailing on this trip. It's true, a reliable man in Personnel told me.'

'Why are they recalling us?'

' 'Cause the herring aren't catching.'

'They were catching a week ago.'

'A week ago! Anything can happen in a week! An earthquake, or God knows what else. I'm telling you – they'll recall us.'

Very reliable news, of course. My old auntie heard it and my pal in the bar confirmed it. Mysterious rumours always start circulating just before a ship's due to sail: the trip's cancelled, we won't do a full trip, we're going to come back twenty days early. Sometimes, it's true; they do cancel a trip. But on any trip that I've sailed, we've always done a full stint and we've always come back dead on the hundred-and-sixth day.

'Well, well,' I said, 'that's nice to know.'

'I'm telling you! Don't argue with me. Changed you mind about that jacket?'

'No.'

'You're making a mistake. Take this sack to the mate's cabin.'

'No, I won't. That's your job. I can't leave the deck.'

'And cheeky with it!'

He turned up the collar of his greatcoat, slung the pillow-case over his shoulder and ran off, bent half double.

'Watchkeeper!' The First Mate called from the wheelhouse.

'What?'

'Not "What", but "aye, aye". Haul up the gangway.'

A little man on shore, his cap on one side of his head, passed the gangway to me. There was no one else on the pier. The loud-hailer boomed out all over the harbour: 'Number eight-one-five – departure! Eight-one-five – cast off moorings!'

In the wheelhouse the First Officer was standing proudly at the wheel. He was glad the skipper had entrusted him with the job of casting off.

'Watchkeeper! Cast off astern!'

The same little man threw me the warp, then I went back for'ard and stood under the wheelhouse, waiting for the ships's side to move away from the pier.

'Why don't you say something?' asked the First Mate. 'Have you cast off?'

'Sure,' I said. 'You can get under way.'

'You're supposed to say: "All clear astern"!'

'I know what I'm supposed to say.'

Amazing thing, a ship. It was as if I was the only one getting her away. Not counting the First Mate, of course.

The engine shook the deck, the screw snorted away under the stern and churned up the black water. The ship's side began to move away and I went up to the foc's'le.

The First Mate shouted after me: 'Cast off for'ard.'

Again I met the little old man. He did his job, then slapped his chest and thighs with his mittened hands and said: 'Have a good trip lad.'

'Uh-huh. Take care, old man.'

We were already a metre away from the shore. In the faint light I could see the oily water frothing between the ship and the quayside, chips of wood and rubbish floating in it. I went to make fast the line across the gap where the gangway had been.

Suddenly I was pushed aside: weeping and moaning, a girl jumped ashore from the deck. She only just made it, landing on the pier with the tips of her toes. She was terrified, and burst into floods of tears.

Shura came running after her, in his shirt and no cap. He shouted to her: 'I'll hear all about you, don't think you can keep anything a secret!'

'Shura!' She walked along the quayside, her hands pressed to her chest, half her face covered by a headscarf. 'How can you say such things! I'd rather die than sleep with him!'

'I love you, d'you see, but if I hear anything about you and your Venya – I'll turn nasty, and that'll be the end of it all!'

'Shura!'

She dropped astern, floated away and was hidden behind the wheelhouse. I made the line fast. Shura was standing beside me, swearing terribly and shaking his head.

'Your wife?' I asked.

'We've only just got married.'

'You shouldn't go on at her like that, the girl loves you.'

'She loves me all right! . . . Anyhow, what's it to do with you? Mind your own business!' Then he calmed down, and even smiled. 'Don't worry, it won't make her love me less. She'll come to Tyuva tomorrow all the same. And if she doesn't, that's no bad thing either. We said goodbye with a bang. She'll remember it.'

The pier vanished astern into the distance, other piers and ships' hulls approached and slid away. The water, black as pitch, sparkled with points of light. Our siren above the wheelhouse gave three blasts, low and long-drawn-out. From far away someone sent out an answering boom – a shipyard, probably, or the harbourmaster.

'It wasn't like this in the old days, remember?' said Shura. 'Then the whole port would answer you. They'd give you a send-off from over the hills.'

He shivered with cold, but stayed there, looking at the port.

'Why didn't anyone come to see you off? Couldn't she find the time?'

'She couldn't make it.'

'Killing's not good enough for her. Go below and get warm. I'll stand watch for you.'

'Don't bother.'

'OK, have it your own way!' He went into the foc's'le.

We sailed past the town, passing the Arctic abeam, then Volodarsky Street, lights glittering, like an arrow aimed at our side, until it too swung away astern. We passed Cape Abram on the other side; somewhere up on the hillside Nina's little window was blinking. Then came Rosta.

'Ahoy, watchkeeper,' the First Mate called out. 'There's a Force 8 gale reported in the Barents Sea. We're in luck. We'll be sailing for an extra day before we have to start fishing.'

'We're always lucky. The worse the weather, the better for us.'

'Why are you so snotty? Had trouble with your woman too?'

'I'm not snotty. You've just got a superficial impression.'

'Listen to him! Don't worry, we'll rub off the rough edges. You can go and sleep now, you won't be needed till we get to Tyuva.'

I didn't go below right away, but sat smoking on a bollard in the stern. Here the water was thrashing noisily from the ships's screw, glinting with cold flashes of light and frothing away into the darkness. My face turned stiff with cold. The wind was from the north – no doubt it really was blowing a gale in the Barents Sea. But we wouldn't be going out into it tomorrow; we should be at Tyuva all the next day. If I badly wanted to, I could still come back from there.

We butted our way against the flood-tide, tacking between the dark hillsides until finally one hill shut off the port, the town and the lights of Cape Abram from sight.

Coming towards us was a little tug, panting with the effort as it hurried home. Fenders were hanging all around its sides, like so many ears. I could have even gone back on the tug, if I'd badly wanted to.

Her stern went past us, and I could just make out a sailor wearing ear-flaps and a black quilted jacket. Like me, he was sitting on a bollard and shielding his roll-your-own cigarette from the wind. He saw me and waved.

'Have a good-trip, lads!'

I threw my dog-end overboard and waved back to him. Then I went below.

Part 2

Senya Shalai

1

The good old Gulf Stream! . . . As soon as we come out of the Sound and turn towards the North Cape, the Gulf Stream hits us head-on and the ship starts to yaw so much that it's hellish hard to keep her on course. According to schedule we're supposed to take seven days' sailing time to reach the fishing grounds, but the Gulf Stream won't let us; it holds us back and the passage takes eight days – that's to let us get our sea-legs, to come to our senses after being ashore. But when we're coming home from fishing, it's the Gulf Stream that hurries us along, helping the engine and giving us an extra puff in the sail, so that the trip home takes six days instead of seven and we reach port a day early. What's more, it's pleasanter sailing in the Gulf Stream; in fine weather it can be as warm in winter as in April, the water's a blue you won't even see in the Black Sea, and all kinds of sea creatures swim along with us: killer whales, sharks, porpoises – and birds settle on our yards and shrouds . . .

On the other hand, we also have to pass through the Barents Sea, and there in winter it's almost always blowing a gale. All that night the barrels were rattling and banging in the hold and we were tossed about in our bunks, so that no one got any sleep before dawn.

The porthole in our cabin is in the deckhead, and it had only just started to show a little light when the First Mate bellowed: 'Wakey, wakey! Show a leg there!'

He banged his fist on the doors of the neighbouring cabins, then came into our cabin and sat down on the bench in his wet oilskins. 'As from today, lads, we start living like seamen.'

No one moved, but lay listening to the waves slapping against the side. Only Shura Chmyrev answered him in a sleepy voice: 'Go ahead, then, no one's stopping you.'

'There's work to be done on deck, got it?'

'What work? We've only just left port. Is there an emergency?'

'Get up and you'll find out.'

'No,' said Shura. 'First you tell us what's going on out there, then we'll know whether we need to get up.'

'What's going on? The float-caboose is damaged.'

'You don't say! Has the net broken, or what?'

'Not the net – a stanchion.'

'A steel stanchion?'

'That's right.'

Vasya Burov, the ship's storeman, turned over in the lower bunk beneath me. He's the oldest one among us, and bald. As senior hand, he is automatically nominated to run the ship's store.

'Call yourself a first mate?' he said. 'Fancy waking up the whole crew because of one lousy stanchion. There's one of us here you didn't need to wake up.'

'You, for example?'

'Not necessarily me. Anyone. You're a fool, not a first mate.'

The First Mate's face went mottled with anger. 'It's not my doing, you know that. The skipper said to me: "There's work to be done, wake them up and don't let them idle in their bunks."'

'And I say you're a fool. You say the skipper told you, but there isn't any work. Yet you go calling all hands on deck.'

The First Mate soon disappeared, but we didn't lie in. Wheezing and grunting, we went up on deck. On a ship, nothing can be left till later; everything should be dealt with at once, even though that float-caboose wouldn't be needed until we started fishing.

There was no horizon to be seen, only blue-grey murk. The waves were lead-coloured, with white crests. The sea was rolling at us from the north, hitting the bows and surging up in a pillar of yellowish spray, which would slowly break and run down the deck as far as the wheelhouse, where all the windows were splashed with foam; then it spilled unhurriedly out of the scuppers with a long-drawn out rumbling noise. The seagulls were gliding overhead in slanting circles, giving sad cries and every now and again settling on the waves: a gale is the time they long for, because the fish go crazy and come to the surface. The birds gulp them down as though stuffing themselves for a week ahead – as soon as the tail of one herring is seen wriggling in their beak, they're pouncing on another one. It's sickening to watch.

We jostled each other as we came out of the doghouse and ran aft to the float-caboose. Nothing serious had happened to it; the stanchion simply needed to be sawn off a metre and a half from the top, smoothed down and lashed up. It was maybe twenty minutes' work for one man, even in a gale – but nine of us had come to do it! That meant it would take us at least an hour, because it was deck-work – and whose job was it to do it? One man wouldn't do it alone if the other eight were sitting in the foc's'le; he'd shout: 'I'm working for you lot, and you're just kipping!' And there'd be an argument.

In the end it took us a bit less than an hour and a half by the time we'd fixed it and gone below again to get dry. Some of us caught up on a bit of sleep, because the cook hadn't yet called us to tea. Near the doghouse we saw our apprentices – Alik and Dima – who hadn't been with us on the job. Alik, green as death, was leaning over the gunwale and puking into the sea. With one hand Dima was holding him by the shoulder, and with the other clinging on to one of the shrouds.

The trawlmaster, whose job is to oversee everything we do, said to Dima: 'You can be forgiven as this is the first time. But from now on, remember – when your mates have a job to do, you must go and help them.'

Dima turned his sarcastic, slit-eyed look on him: 'And I'm helping my mate now.'

'Helping him to puke? That's not work!'

Dima spat on the deck and turned away. He was right: there was nothing more to be said. But the trawlmaster was all wound up; he hadn't yet cooled off after the float-caboose job.

'You don't turn your back when you're being spoken to, got it?'

'I'm not being spoken to, I'm being shouted at,' Dima replied over his shoulder. 'And when that happens I answer in a different way . . . You can be forgiven as this is the first time.'

The trawlmaster froze, his two little eyes popping out on stalks like a crayfish's eyes. His neck actually turned red. In fact he hadn't shouted at the lad; his voice just sounded like that. Because of his job, he had to shout a lot on deck. Even so, the apprentice was in the right, and the trawlmaster would have done better to shut up. On the whole I rather liked this lad. I'd first taken a liking to him at Tyuva, when we were loading the nets. He sniffed at the nets and said to Alik: 'It smells of ski-wax.' I'd been humping nets for years, without being able to put my finger on it – it was true, they smelled of ski-wax.

'For a start, take your hand off that shroud!' Now the trawlmaster really was shouting, and standing over him with clenched fists. Bo'suns often show us the rough side of their tongue, too, but a trawlmaster has to keep a firm grip on the whole deck-crew, so his fists are something to be reckoned with. 'Or else you'll be standing on the deck with three legs!'

'Certainly,' said Dima, and took his hand away.

Then one of us, it may have been Shura Chmyrev or Seryozha Firstov, had a word with the trawlmaster and took him below, after which we all crowded down the companion-way to our quarters. There we sat down to play cards until the cook called us. Seryozha produced a greasy pack and dealt us six cards each. We'd been joined by our bo'sun Kesha Strashnoi; though the name means 'fearsome', in fact he wasn't fearsome at all but a really decent bloke. On top of a solid, peasant's build he had clear, regular features that gave him the look of a figure on an ikon, the more so as he had started to grow a beard. He'd enjoy having a beard until we got back to port, and then his wife would make him shave it off.

What did we talk about? Oh yes, the bo'sun started to give us a moral lecture: why were we wasting precious time on cards? It was early morning and we already had the cards out; we'd do better to be reading books.

'We get the message,' Shura said to him. 'Now sit down with us, or we won't have a proper game.'

'If the skipper catches you at it, he'll give you cards,' The bo'sun picked up his cards, sorted them out and sighed. 'We shouldn't really be doing this on board ship. It's a family game.'

'Well, aren't we a family?' asked the trawlmaster. 'A family's what we are.'

At that moment Dima came in, picked up a towel from his bunk, and making sure we could all hear him, said: 'A family! More like a lot of spiders in a tin can than a family!'

We put our cards face down and looked at him. He was scowling and flushed with anger.

'Now what's he up to?' asked the trawlmaster. 'Still trying to tease the tiger?'

'I don't understand jokes,' said Dima. 'A man's sick, and all you can do is rant and snarl. That's a pretty scummy way to behave.'

Just between us, the trawlmaster had asked his question in a genuinely friendly spirit. He had already clean forgotten having shouted at Dima on deck, and the reason why he had been shouting, because the deck is one thing and the cabin another. People may have their arguments up there, but once they come below it's all forgotten and we sit down to play 'six up'. But the apprentice didn't know that.

'Have you gone crazy? Again the trawlmaster's eyes were popping out of his head. 'Have I offended you?'

'All's well, forget it. It was I who offended you. If it doesn't happen again I'll take back what I said.'

Dima threw the towel over his shoulder and went out.

'They're recruiting mental defectives into the fleet!' said the trawlmaster. 'We have to put up with their problems *and* they shoot their mouths off. Lumps of shit.'

I put my cards face down again and said to him: 'Haven't you got it into your head yet, trawly, that you're a lump of shit yourself? Didn't you realize that up on deck just now? Then let me explain it to you here in the cabin.'

'Oh, lay off, will you?' Shura frowned. 'Don't get all wound up.'

But I was already wound up. The way we behave to each other really makes me mad.

'That apprentice taught you a lesson, and anyone else would have died of shame. But not you – oh no! With that great thick head of yours you just laugh it off and carry on as if nothing had happened.'

'All right, but those two lads won't exactly die from it, will they?' said the bo'sun. 'They'll only kick themselves a bit harder.'

'Why should they kick themselves, bo'sun?'

'Why? For coming on a DWT. They'll find it's not a kindergarten.'

'Oh, go to hell! What's the use of talking to you lot?'

'No, let's go on talking, Senya,' said the trawlmaster. His face had gone white and his nostrils were flaring. 'You were going to explain something to me, and you haven't. All you've done is swear. I'd better do some explaining to you. You see, Senya, on this job we earn the sort of money you won't get anywhere else – not in a factory, not on a collective farm. That means we've got to work flat out. So have we also got to play nanny to the apprentices, teach them how to work on deck? And did *they* think they'd come on board a trawler and be able to act as our assistants straight away? No, Senya, they didn't think that. And what, d'you suppose, is the way to make seamen and shipmates out of them? They'll become seamen when we take on our last load of fish and get back to port to count our money. *That's* where we'll get some help from them! Meanwhile they're millstones round our necks. They must realize that. And learn not to shoot their mouths off whenever someone tries to teach them some sense.'

'You – teach them?! You should bow down and thank that lad for the lesson he taught you.'

'Go and teach them yourself, then. If you're so good and kind.'

His shoulders were working visibly under his shirt, and he kept boring into me with those little eyes of his. I was tired of talking to him.

'Work flat out, trawly? How? Do we all hammer in one nail together? And if someone doesn't come and join us, do we all go for him in a bunch? Not on this ship!'

The bo'sun laughed and said as he looked at his cards 'How do you know what it's going to be like on this ship, Senya? How it has to be – that's what it'll be like.'

Vasya Burov, who was lying on his bunk, sighed and turned his face to the bulkhead. 'How can you bark at each other like that on an empty stomach? Let's have our breakfast first – then you can bark away till lunch. As it is, you're a pain in the arse.'

'You're right.' Seryozha began to collect up the cards. 'Seems like our cooky's a bit behindhand this morning.'

There was one other man in the cabin, called Kolya Mitrokhin. A very doleful character. I'd noticed one thing about him – he could sleep with his eyes open. He could even answer you while he was asleep; it was his special talent. There was nothing worse, though, than when he was on watch after you. You'd wake him up in the night: 'Kolya, time for your trick at the wheel!' – 'OK, coming.' You'd go back to the wheelhouse and stand watch for another fifteen minutes, then you'd hand the wheel over to the mate and go and wake him again: 'Kolya, are you crazy? You're not asleep, damn you!' – 'No,' he'd say, 'I'm coming.' And all the time he was sound asleep.

Well, now he was sitting there and listening, wrinkling his forehead, and he announced: 'You know, lads, I reckon this trip's not going to work out.'

The trawlmaster turned to Kolya and his eyes began boring into him this time: 'What d'you mean – not going to work out?'

'Things won't go smoothly. It'll all go cockeyed, somehow. Or there won't be any fish. At any rate, we won't make out target.'

'Irresponsible bullshit! Tell me – can you see into the future?'

'I don't know. I can't say exactly.'

'You don't know, and you're talking crap.'

Mitrokhin went back to his own thoughts, frowning. Maybe he really did have some kind of second sight; I tend to believe in people like him who are a bit touched. Suddenly a kind of gloom fell on everybody.

I got up and went out of the cabin. Up in the heads Alik was leaning over a washbasin and Dima, one foot braced against the coaming, was holding him by the shoulders to keep him from hitting the bulkhead.

'Feeling better?'

Alik raised his wet face and smiled with an effort. He wasn't green any longer, just a bit pale, and the colour would soon be coming back into his cheeks. 'God, all this fuss about me! It happens to everyone, after all.'

'Yes, it does. Sooner to some, later to others.'

'Did it happen to you?'

'Yes, to me too.'

He looked out of the doorway at the heaving, bluish-grey sea and turned almost the same colour himself.

'Don't look out there,' I told him. 'As a general rule, learn not to look at the sea.'

'That's interesting.' Alik smiled again. 'What's the point of going to sea, then?'

'I don't know why you went to sea. If you'd have asked me on shore, I'd have advised you not to.'

'Somehow we didn't meet you when we were ashore,' said Dima.

Alik wiped himself with a towel and said bravely: 'You have to experience everything. Now I know what it's like.'

'Yes,' I said, 'you were lucky.'

At last the cook called out: 'Tea's up!'

In the saloon we all watched to see how our apprentices would manage. Everything came easily to Dima; he acted like any old sea-dog. He at once grasped how to stop the tea from slopping out of his mug in dirty weather – he filled it less than half-full. Alik frowned and frowned, and eventually started eating. But that wasn't the real test; now if someone were to start smoking . . .

The trawlmaster opened his cigarette-case and offered it to Alik. Shura produced a match.

'Thanks,' said Alik, astonished, 'but I've got my own.'

'Yours are the kind that make you feel seasick,' said the trawlmaster. 'I recommend mine. They contain anti-stormine.'

Alik looked at him suspiciously, expecting some trick. Then he lit up all the same, and we all broke into smiles. It's always good to see: another one cured of sea-sickness and turning into a sailor.

'Now you'll have to do your skiving under me, my lad,' said the bo'sun. 'You'll be taking the wheel today, like a good boy.'

'Have I refused to?' asked Alik.

Dima understood it all and laughed. But he didn't take back what he'd said.

2

Beyond the North Cape the weather improved and we began gradually to prepare for trawling: the nets were taken out of the net-hold, spread out on deck and rolled up in readiness along the port side, while a long sisal warp was uncoiled and cut up into twenty-metre lengths for the standing lines. This is usually done on the third and fourth day out, to make sure everything is ready to start fishing, but if the weather's good it's better to start doing it right away, because it won't stay fine for ever and there's nothing worse than having to fumble around in dirty weather.

From early morning it was sunny and a flat calm – really calm, so that you could have seen your face in the water to shave by – and we sailed past the Lofotens, close enough to see all the islands in detail, only faintly veiled in a bluish haze. The water was deep blue with a hint of green. The seagulls were not settling on it – the fish had gone down deeper again – and only the occasional albatross would dive in after them. Screaming wildly, their white bodies would hurtle down from a great height and it was a long time before they surfaced; you thought they'd never come up again, but no – they'd appear with a fish in their beak, their eyes all bloodshot: these poor old birds really have to work for their food! Usually when you're fishing you never see any of this – there's not even time to scratch your head – but preparing the trawl is steady work; you can smoke and spin a yarn or two, and you can admire the beautiful shoreline.

We had just sat down on the nets and were having a smoke when the bo'sun brought Alik and Dima to see me.

'This,' he said, 'is our Senya. Seaman first class. A learned man. He's the man who can teach you what's what. Obey him as you'd obey me.'

And off he went with a satisfied look, stroking his little beard. Well, what could I do? I'd as good as asked for it myself. The other seamen looked up, expecting some fun. It's an essential ritual, and I enjoy it myself. The apprentices stood in front of me, shifting from foot to foot as if they were facing some captain-instructor.

OK, so I sat down again and said to Alik and Dima: 'Let's begin,' I said, 'with a bit of theory, which, as you know, comes before practice.'

'Not quite correct,' Alik smiled, 'it also summarizes practice.'

'Who's going to do the talking – you or me?'

'Beg pardon,' said Dima. 'Go ahead, chief.'

'First question. What should a seaman be?'

By now the other sailors were quietly sniggering to themselves.

'Well, that's a matter on which everyone has his own ideas,' said Alik.

'Do you know or don't you?'

'No,' said Dima. His cheekbones had tautened, stone-hard.

'A seaman should always be polite, clean-shaven and slightly drunk. Second. What must he be able to do?'

'We're ignoramuses,' said Dima. 'Please enlighten us.'

'That's just what I'm doing. A seaman must know the right way to approach . . . a table, a woman and a mooring.'

Corny old stuff, I agree, but that's just the start of it. The apprentices even liked it; Alik's face positively lit up.

'Now,' I said, 'for the practice. Familiarization with shipboard occupations.'

'Beg pardon, chief,' said Dima, 'we know that you don't drink tea at the masthead.'

They were, as the saying goes, very rewarding material. It's no fun playing these games with absolute blockheads.

'And I'm not going to send you up to the masthead,' I said. 'I'm giving you proper jobs to do. You, Alik, can go aft and look over the stern to see if the propellor's making the water boil. In other words, is steam coming from it or not?'

'Does that happen?'

'Someone has to keep an eye on it to see it doesn't happen.'

He shrugged his shoulders, but went. Dima looked at me with a frown – he sensed a practical joke, but didn't quite know what it was.

'And you, Dima, this is what you can do: fetch a sledgehammer from the trawlmaster's locker. You must knock in the bollards. Look how they're sticking out.'

And off he went too. The whole thing bored me to death, but the deck-hands, of course, were splitting their sides – especially when he spat on his hands and hit the bollard a couple of times; this produced gales of laughter.

'What, won't the bollards go in?' I asked. 'You'd better order up a sack of steam from the engine-room to soften them up a bit.'

At that moment Alik appeared from the stern.

'No,' he said, 'it's not boiling. At least, not as far as I could see.'

By this time the other sailors were rolling about all over the nets. 'Ah, Alik, you crafty bugger! So it's not boiling, eh?' Alik looked at them and laughed too. Dima gripped the sledgehammer and went for me. He wasn't going to catch me, though. While he was taking a swing, I nipped up on to the float-caboose. Then when he did let fly, he hit a float. Luckily the float was only partly inflated, otherwise the hammer would have bounced back off it and hit him in the forehead.

'Hey, don't play the fool, lad. You don't know how to hold it properly.'

'Oh yes I do, as you can see. I could chase you up aloft.'

'OK, playtime's over, go and put it back. We've plenty more work to do.'

'What sort of work, chief?'

He looked at me like I was Public Enemy No. 1. God knows what's on little Slit-Eyes' mind, I thought. There was no joking with him, this flat-faced Buddha.

'All sorts,' I said. 'We've got to raise the deck with a derrick otherwise there's not enough room for the barrels in the hold.'

'No, chief, that's a lot of crap.'

'Blow up the floats.'

'What with? Our lungs?'

'What else?'

'That's crap too.'

It would have served him right if I'd made him blow up a float himself instead of using the compressor. But it was a job that had to be done.

'All right, we've had our fun . . .'

I jumped down and took the sledgehammer from him. He was a tough lad, after all, and the sailors were beginning to respect him. Alik, on the other hand, was a slacker by nature and work on board was likely to wear him out.

'Shall we go on with the practical, chief?'

'Right, let's go on.' I trod on his toes, then on Alik's. They, of course, were expecting another practical joke. 'First thing, ask the bo'sun to give you each a pair of sea-boots that are one size bigger. Then if you do happen to fall overboard, you can kick 'em off. After all, it gives you one more chance of survival.'

'By the way, just between us girls,' asked Alik, 'what are those chances?'

'Just between us girls, let's make an agreement: don't fall overboard.'

'Fair enough, chief,' said Dima.

'Second thing: don't let me ever see you on deck without a knife. If something gets fouled up, there's never time to untangle it.'

'Will this one do?' Dima pulled a little flick-knife out of his pocket, pressed it and the blade sprang out like a little devil. 'Click – and it's ready.'

'Put it away,' I said, 'and don't show it again. That sort looks fine in films, but it's no good on board ship.'

'Why not, chief?'

'Because you waste time making an extra movement. Get a gutting-knife and sharpen the blade on both sides.'

There was plenty more that I had to teach them: how to tie knots, how to whip the end of a warp so that it doesn't fray, how to lay out the nets. All sorts of things. No one ever taught me any of this. Well, admittedly I came straight from the Navy into the fishing fleet, but here there's a whole lot of special fisherman's know-how, and I was certainly never taught any of that; I was just bawled at until I picked it up on my own.

They weren't stupid, these two, and they learned well enough: in any case, you don't need to rack your brains for long if someone explains things sensibly. The only real problem is to find someone who's able and willing to explain them. Believe me, you get a funny feeling when you part with some of your secrets. Something dies inside you, some of your pride. Is that really all I know, you think, all I can do? No more than that? In any case they won't pick up all the tricks of the trade in one trip, and they probably won't be going on a second trip.

'So my lads,' I said, 'what the hell made you go to sea anyway? Romance of the sea, and all that stuff?'

Dima just grinned with the corners of his mouth, but Alik hesitated like a shy girl.

'People do go to sea for that, don't they?'

'They don't only *go* for that,' I said, 'they find it too. You'll be taught a whole lot of new swear-words, that's for sure.'

'Well, chief,' said Dima, 'we know them already.'

'Yes, it does help to blow off steam. But tell me honestly – was it the money that attracted you?'

'That did have something to do with it.'

'What's more,' said Alik, 'it's interesting to find out how they catch herring, which are so good to eat with some vinegar and sunflower oil.'

He looked embarrassed as he said this.

'I see. And what did you do back there, on shore?'

Again Alik hesitated and looked at Dima, who said quickly: 'Drivers. Lorry-drivers. If you're interested, we can tell you about it sometime, chief. We'll have a chat about carburettors and distributors.'

'Like hell we will! I never did understand a damn' thing about all that.'

We were paying out a hawser from the winch and smearing it with axle-grease against rust. I sent Alik for an adjustable wrench, then gave it to Dima to unscrew the cotter-pin.

'How's the work?' I asked. 'Did you like it?'

'Not too mucky,' said Dima. 'Get's a bit boring at times.'

'What's the money like?'

'Enough to keep you in vodka. On public holidays.'

'And on Saturdays?'

'Why not, chief?'

I laughed. 'No,' I said, 'it wasn't enough for Saturdays.'

Now it was Dima's turn to look embarrassed: 'Sorry, chief. I don't get you.'

'Because you never did work as lorry-drivers.'

'What makes you say that?'

'Simple. When you unscrewed that nut, you first tried turning it to the right, then to the left. A driver wouldn't do that.'

'Come on, chief, that's no sort of proof.'

'OK,' I said, 'don't get steamed up. If you don't want to tell me, you don't have to. I'm not asking you to fill in some official form. And cut out all this "chief" this and "chief" that.'

I went to reel in the hawser at the winch, where they thought I couldn't hear them.

'He's right,' Alik said to Dima, 'what's the point in being dodgy?'

'All right, then tell him, big-mouth. Who your family are, where you're from. Then you'll be one of them.'

To hell with them, young fools, I thought; you can't keep secrets for long on shipboard. People find out everything about you sooner or later.

By the fourth and fifth day out they were beginning to learn the ropes a bit, starting to discover what's what. They pretended to know more than they really did, but it was obvious from watching them – they were still in the dark: with a hundred different lines strung all over the place, they had no idea which one to take hold of. Once I heard Dima shout to Alik: 'Drop that rope, we're both coiling the same one. Take that one, under my boot.'

Alik picked up that 'rope' and started coiling it round his elbow using only his left hand, with his right hand in his pocket. I called him over and said quietly: 'Whatever you do, lad, don't work like that with just one hand. They'll give you hell, even bash your face in if they catch you at it.'

'What does it matter to anyone,' he asked, 'if I can do it with one hand?'

'Because you can do it all the better with two. Both hands should be occupied. And tell that to Dima.'

'That's interesting!'

'I don't know whether it's interesting or not. But that's my advice to you.'

They paid no heed. But there's always work on deck for a spare pair of hands. Admittedly nobody tried chasing Dima too hard because he had a sharp tongue in his head and gave as good as he got, but the other one was always willing to do as he was told.

'Alik!' Someone would shout at him. 'What are you standing there for? You've got fuck-all to do, go and get me a needle and a reel of twine.'

Alik wasn't just standing there, he was waiting for someone else to pass him a line that he was to make fast to a shroud, but he ran and fetched the needle and twine.

'Alik! Come and give me a hand to take off the hatch-cover. I've got to nip down into the hold.'

'But I'm already . . .'

'They'll manage without you!'

Alik pulled off the tarpaulin hatch-cover.

'Alik, where are you? What are these lines hanging there?'

'I don't know.'

'You're here to find out.'

He finally sorted out the lines and wiped his brow. Then the cooper gave him an order. 'Alik! Come here. Ram down these hoops.'

The cooper had planned to prepare thirty barrels in readiness for the first trawl and Shura and I were helping him. We were managing perfectly well and we didn't need an apprentice. I lost my patience.

'Go back,' I said to Alik, 'and stay where you were. You don't have to obey every big-head.'

The cooper grinned but said nothing, continuing to bang away at the hoop with his hammer. He had bared his arms to the elbow – sinewy as a gorilla's, covered in red hair. He and I had somehow managed to avoid coming into contact and I thought he'd forgotten me. But no – I had stuck in his memory.

'Are you still alive, shit-bag?'

He gave me a slow, affectionate smile. His watery eyes were half-shaded by his eyelids.

'There you are.' I rolled him a prepared barrel.

'And is your jacket still alive?'

'It's fine. Are you trying to pick a quarrel with me?'

'Are you looking for promotion?'

I laughed. 'You fool. What promotion? In charge of the apprentices?'

'But it's nice when those two young puppies obey you, isn't it? Try hard enough and you'll make it to bo'sun. Then you can chase me too.'

'Some hope I'd have of chasing you!'

All this time we were banging away at the hoops. Shura listened to us for a while, then asked: 'What are you two beachers shooting off about? Doesn't make any sense to me.'

'Do you suppose,' I asked, 'it makes any sense to us either?'

He stared at both of us suspiciously, then spat overboard into the sea. A seagull immediately dived down and shot upwards again with an insulted squawk.

'If you're going to carry on like this, one of you ought to sign off. That's my advice.'

'Let him sign off,' I said.

The cooper grinned and said nothing.

Later on, when I came up on deck, the two apprentices were standing on their own, and they couldn't see me behind the mast. Dima was lecturing Alik: 'When nature created us bipeds she didn't take into account that one day we'd be sailors. But there's a secret: the chief was talking sense when he told you not to look at the sea. Watch how they walk about on deck. It's their horizon. They never look at the real horizon, only at the deck, They lean over with it and they straighten up with it. But *your* balance in your inner ear gets exhausted. And all the time you keep wanting to grab hold of something.'

'I see,' said Alik. 'And the fresh breeze of the trade winds cools our skin.'

They went away, pleased with themselves, although they still kept on grabbing hold of something. Meanwhile I put myself in their place; it would be interesting to see exactly how I walked along the deck and where I looked as I did so – was it at the deck or at the horizon? I looked at the horizon and suddenly I found myself clutching the derrick-boom. To hell with them – this way I'd forget how to walk properly.

3

'They're looking for the meaning of life, no less,' I said to the Chief.

It was late evening and we were in his cabin, finishing off the bottle.

'Is that so?' said the Chief. 'And what about you – have you given up looking for it?'

'I've stopped for the time being. During the catch.'

'That's all right. But there's something about you that I don't like. You don't so much tell me about these apprentices as grumble about them. Are you getting old, or what?'

'Maybe I am getting old. But I can take just so much fooling about. This isn't their real job, is it? They've read a few books, had enough of it, and thought they'd like to go to sea for a change . . .'

'But that's what's splendid about them, Senya! They've had enough of reading books – and they've gone to sea. There are plenty of others who read their books and *don't* go to sea. No, you're wrong to grumble about them. Right now the best young people want to go out and do things and see for themselves. I'm pinning all my hopes on them. As for my generation, it's terrible to think of how many were killed, how many left an arm or a leg on the battlefield, how many lost fifteen years of their lives in the camps – like I did. Even the ones who came through it untouched are not exactly to be envied: when you meet some of them and look in their eyes, you see a sheer cripple. But there's something obstinate about young people today, they want to find out everything for themselves. They take nothing on trust. At least "fooling about" like this, as you call it, is better than knocking up girls.'

I smiled. Neither of us wanted to get on to the subject of morality; he wasn't very strong in that department and nor was I.

'And what's wrong with that? If the chance comes along I'll be in there like a shot!'

'That's enough of that. Come on – down the hatch.'

We drank up and stared into our empty mugs. Grunting with seeming irritation, the Chief lowered the window and threw out the bottle, which for an instant flashed red from the navigation light as it flew over the gunwale and vanished in a splash of foam.

'Now the plan says we must be sober,' said the Chief, 'until April.'

Leaning on the window-frame, he stared out into the darkness, his old hairs ruffled by the breeze. Now and again there would come a bang from an unclosed door on the bridge or some piece of loose metal; the engine was thumping away beneath the deck and you could hear the screw, rumbling steadily when it was solidly under water, then whining and thrashing when the blade broke surface. I suddenly found myself missing Lilya. Each turn of that screw was taking me further away from her, and we had already put 2,000 kilometres behind us. Not that I resented her any longer; after all, there are plenty of good reasons why people can't come to see ships off. Maybe she's been suddenly taken ill or Four-eyes didn't tell her that I rang. And why did I imagine she'd overheard that phone call? He'd probably been whispering to some secretary.

'Hasn't it worked out with you and . . . that girl?' the Chief suddenly asked. I almost jumped. 'The one you were waiting for at the Arctic.'

'Why d'you say "hasn't it worked out"?'

'I was just asking. I think you were looking out for her at the pier, weren't you? Maybe I only got that impression.'

'Of course I wasn't looking out for her.'

The Chief didn't reply. But I wanted him to go on asking; I was sorry for cutting him off so sharply.

'You see, Chief, she's not a local girl, and she's bound not to know all our habits and customs. Anyway, one of the good things about a bit of skirt is when she's not like the others. Wouldn't you say so?'

The wind was making the Chief frown as he listened to me. Then he said: 'You need a woman, Senya, and not a bit of skirt.'

'Is there a difference?'

'Can't you tell? All that rubbish people talk, like: "she promoised – she didn't promise", "she must – she mustn't"; it's peasant women's talk, if you'll forgive me saying so.'

'Wait a moment. When you own wife and family were waiting for you to come out of the camps – and that was long enough – didn't you think it was right and proper she should keep on waiting for you?'

'No, I didn't.'

'But all the same you hoped she would, didn't you?'

He shook his head, still staring out into the darkness: 'That's also peasant women's talk: "hoped – didn't hope".'

'You're an old dinosaur, Chief, an extinct species. But you're interesting to talk to. Pity we've finished the bottle.'

'Just be patient,' said the Chief. 'I'll get some more on the factory-ship. We're not monks, are we?'

'I think I'll go now, Chief.'

He bustled around, found a book on the little bookshelf and gave it to me, then took it back again and put on his steel-framed glasses. The book was called *Marine Engines*.

'We talked about this last time,' said the Chief, looking somehow embarrassed as he turned over a few pages. 'If you can cope with the first chapter, the rest is easy. If there's anything you don't understand, I'll explain it to you on our diesel.'

'Good.' I pushed it inside my jacket. 'I'll definitely read it.'

'You can easily finish the whole course by the time we get back to port. You won't even notice you've done it. Then you can sit the exam on shore and next trip you'll come as my assistant engineer.'

'Next trip? I thought you were being pensioned off.'

'Well, perhaps I won't be. Nothing's certain in this life.'

I went out and stood under the wheelhouse. Flashes of many colours, like fish-scales, glittered in the water from the bow-wave, and in the far distance lights winked on the Lofotens. The air was alive, as heady as spirit. How is one to know when that day comes, I wondered, that day when you suddenly realize it's all too late and you've frittered your life away? If only one could be aware of it a year in advance. The Chief probably won't be around when I realize it; soon he'll be an old man, a grandad, even though he hasn't any grandchildren. Or any sons, either. Not counting me, still footloose. Once he said to me: 'When we were young, we didn't think about it. We didn't know that before two years were out everything would come crashing about our ears. Then – we were suddenly old. And even *then* we didn't think about it.' So even he had come up against this borderline – and what a line it was! But where would my borderline be?

The end window in the wheelhouse was lowered and the mate on watch – the Third Mate – was humming to himself, wrapped in his fur-lined jacket and looking up at the stars. I couldn't recognize the man at the wheel, because his face was lit from below by the binnacle-light shining on his chin and nostrils.

Suddenly I stamped my boots on the deck – God knows why – and started singing in a nasal whine:

> 'Though a ship's leaving port on a journey,
> A cry follows her like a dove!
> For love knows no frontiers, no boundary,
> There's no parting for true hearts in love!'

The mate swore, switched on the searchlight and shone it on my back until I disappeared down the companion-way. Still, I'd done a bit to cheer him up; now he'd have something to talk about with the helmsman.

No one was asleep yet in the crew's quarters. In the next-door cabin someone was vamping an old tune on an accordion: 'For you, for you alone are to blame . . .' I was just about to go in, then I remembered that Rebrov, the cooper, was in there and it would be wiser not to enter his territory, so I went straight into our cabin. There more serious matters were in hand: Shura Chmyrev and Seryozha Firstov were playing cards. The trawlmaster was heaving his torso back and forth along the bench, looking first at one player's cards then at the other's and slapping himself on the thighs. He was getting worn out by the strain of a split personality: the game was still even, and he was always on the side of whoever was winning.

When he saw me, he stretched out his nose and sniffed.

'Ah!' he said. 'I smell brandy. Come in quickly, Senya, and shut the door, otherwise it'll blow away and that would be a shame.'

Shura and Seryozha raised their heads, looked at me vacantly and turned back to their cards.

'How many stars were there on the brandy bottle?' asked the trawlmaster.

'Three or five?'

'None at all now.'

He sighed mournfully.

'What a pity I haven't palled up with the skipper. It must be nice to be invited to drink with the officers.'

As I took off my jacket, the book fell out. I'd forgotten that I'd tucked it into my belt. He pounced on it at once.

'*Marine Engines*, eh? So you've decided to requalify, Senya. Was this when you were drunk, or are you serious?'

'Give it here.'

I grabbed at the book, but he had already hidden it behind his back. I climbed into my bunk, lit the deckhead light and drew the little curtain. He immediately pulled it open again, breathing hard just above my ear.

'Breathe on me, Senya. Why are you being so selfish and anti-social?'

It was impossible to get annoyed with him. I breathed out and he purred, screwing up his eyes.

'Ah, happy days! And who was paying for the drink, Senya? Were you offering it to the Chief or was he giving it to you? I was just wondering why he might want to get a beacher like you drunk.'

'Shove off!' Shura said to him. 'You're such a nosey parker that no one's ever going to offer you so much as a half-bottle of vodka. Don't be shy, Senya – give him one round the chops.'

'Play,' said Seryozha.

The trawlmaster had got bored by now and gave me back the book.

'Read, Senya, stuff your head with knowledge. And then just think – you'll wear a tie and lie in your cabin with your feet up while the engine does all the work for you!'

'Engineers have to stand watch too, you know,' said Shura.

'Of course they do, we haven't reached the stage of pure communism yet. They still have to lift a finger now and then. Pour in a drop of oil, watch the pressure-gauge. But that's only what's called "maintenance", that's not "work".'

Shura laughed.

'And to hear engineers talk, you'd think deck-work was the best job on board. What do deckies breathe? Fresh sea air. And what do engineers breathe? Diesel fumes, hot oil . . . '

'Now the cook has a cushy job. And his cabin-boy,' said Vasya Burov. 'They've got the stove to keep them warm, and they can scoff at any time of day.'

'The radio operator has it even better,' said Mitrokhin. 'He has his own cabin up there on the boat-deck, and there's no one to check whether he's working or skiving.'

The trawlmaster disagreed: 'He has to know the Morse Code, doesn't he? Have you ever tried learning the damn' thing? Or finding out how a transmitter works? No, the mate's got the best job of all. Stand your watch and kip down, that's all.'

'In that case the skipper is the best off of the lot,' said Shura.

'Use your loaf! The skipper carries the can for everything – for the catch and for immoral behaviour. And for you falling overboard "at your own request". The skipper finds the fish. But the engineers and the mates – they're the idle ones, that's for sure.'

'Some brain you've got!' said Shura. 'I can't understand why you want to be a trawlmaster. Why aren't you an engineer?'

The trawlmaster scratched the back of his head. 'I like it better this way. I'm a working sort of man.'

'But I thought . . . '

'Don't think,' said Seryozha, 'play.'

The trawlmaster sat down with them again. I opened my book: 'Marine engines serve as the main or auxiliary means . . . They are subdivided into . . . Their fuels are . . . '

'Quiet,' whispered the trawlmaster, 'he's reading!'

But I wasn't reading any longer; I was staring at the deckhead immediately above my face. Then I carefully shut the book, put it under my pillow and took out another one: *Short Stories* by Richard Aldington. I read one and started another, but somehow this Richard Aldington didn't grab me. It was all arguments and no action. I'd been a fool to pick the book. There are about eighty books in the ship's library, and everyone naturally grabs the thickest one he can find, so that he reads just one book for the whole trip. They don't like books with plots that jump all over the place, either; you get in a complete muddle about who's married to who, and so on.

I put down Aldington's *Short Stories* too. Then I turned and poked my head over the side of the bunk. Underneath me Vasya Burov was buried in some thick tome, with only his beard sticking out and twitching.

'What's that you're reading, Vasya?'

'Don't know, Senya. The title page has been torn off.'

'Is it a good read?'

'I should say so!' He gave me a beatific smile, showing all his few teeth. 'It's worth it for the heroine alone – she's called Oxana.'

Having kicked off their boots, the apprentices were sitting on Dima's bunk, the lower of the two, practising a knot. As far as I could see it was what's called a 'seaman's love-affair', a complicated slip-knot. No doubt the trawlmaster had shown it to them, as a way of making peace. You tie it by making twenty or thirty turns – there are several different versions – and you think you could never unravel it in a lifetime, but when you pull on both ends the whole thing unties itself. Well, it's something to do.

And what was our nut-case, Mitrokhin, doing? He was plaiting a shopping-bag out of grey twine, without using any sort of hook or knitting-needles, just with his fingers. He had started pretty early; on the return trip, when we're nearer to port, other people start plaiting them too. Why, you may ask? I don't know; he has learned to make doormats and to plait ropes, too – but what does he do with them? Back in port he'll give that shopping-bag to his wife or his mother-in-law, then next day they'll throw it away and buy one made of coloured nylon that costs about ten kopecks.

Dima said as much in his sarcastic tone: 'All that performance just for ten kopecks!'

But the trawlmaster took it, inspected it under the light and asked Dima: 'Do you know why soldiers in the trenches whittle themselves spoons out of maple wood?'

'Well,' said Dima, 'why do they?'

'They don't know themselves. Each one of them's got a government-issue aluminium spoon tucked in his boot.'

Shura and Seryozha were finishing their last hand. They were cheating desperately, but they didn't hold it against each other; we never do play cards without cheating. When it comes to paying up, you must put your cards on the table and hold your nose out like a bowsprit so that it's easy to slap it from both sides. This time Seryozha had lost; he's no worse at playing but he's bad at cheating – he doesn't have that 'freedom from conscience', as our First Mate from Volokolamsk used to say. When they had totted up the score, the result was that Seryozha was due to be slapped eleven times on the nose with six cards. With a malicious smile Shura laid the cards firmly together and settled himself in a suitable position, while Seryozha wiped his nose and held it out to receive his shameful punishment.

This gave the trawlmaster great pleasure. Now, of course, he was on Shura's side for life.

'Twenty-eight!' he counted aloud. 'Twenty-nine! . . . Watch him take a beating!'

It was worth watching. After the fifth slap Seryozha's nostrils were burning, after the eighth the burning had spread upwards towards his eyebrows. He took it all like a martyr, only his cheekbones standing out sharper and his eyes glistening.

Then he rapidly started to deal a new hand.

'Don't hurry,' Shura said to him affectionately. 'Give yourself time to cool off.'

With a careless air Shura sorted out his hand.

'Well, it's hardly worth wasting time playing with you. I've got so many trumps in my hand, I might as well prepare the six cards already.'

'Play!' said Seryozha. 'I'll give you trumps!'

Shura waited a little longer, to give Seryozha time to get even more steamed-up. This good-looking lad was lucky – lucky at cards and lucky in love.

Our cabin was the liveliest and the most cheerful; the others couldn't resist coming in. The noise brought in the bo'sun, who was carrying a thick book in which he had stuck one finger to mark his place.

'So that's it!' he sighed. 'What's to be done with you? You hopeless bunch! Will I have to use force to make you read books?'

'We've done enough reading,' Seryozha replied. 'Got to give our grey cells a rest.'

'If only you had any!'

'I did have,' said Seryozha, 'but I stuffed them full with all sorts of trash. Writers all write the same: what nice people they are, how well things are going for them.'

'They're only trying to do their best for fools like you. So you can have an aim in life. So that you, don't you see, have something to compare yourself with. Something to strive for.'

'For truth, bo'sun,' said Dima, 'for that and nothing else.'

The bo'sun turned to face him. 'Shut up! Not everyone can tell what the truth is, you know.'

'Oh really? That's a new idea.'

'For instance, there's the sort who'll sit down in mud up to the top of his head – and he'll tell you that's how it has to be.'

'Comrade bo'sun, you're a very learned man!'

The bo'sun snorted and said: 'Sweep up in this cabin. I don't want to see a single fag-end.'

'Whose job is it to clean up? There's no roster.'

'The roster starts with you.'

Grinning, Dima said: 'What's more, bo'sun, it seems you're also a voluntarist.'

'Get the broom, lad. That's an order.'

'Aye, aye sir!'

'Right, then. You're a hopeless bunch, you are!'

When the bo'sun had gone, Dima crawled back into his bunk. He was beginning to catch on.

I lay there listening to the water hissing on the other side of the bulkhead, almost above my ear. I was being gently rocked by the ship's motion and I was flying away somewhere over those terrible, solid depths while I stayed warm and dry. I had almost dropped off to sleep when they started talking again.

The eighth man in our cabin was Vanya Obod. I haven't told you about him yet; in any case, I hardly even noticed him. He was all boot and cap, his little wrinkled face barely peering out under his cap. Always silent and gloomy, whenever he came into the cabin he would flop straight on to his bunk, with only his boots hanging over the edge. Vanya had been lying there all this time, swinging his boots, when he suddenly spoke: 'So you can have an aim in life, eh? Well I've got one. A gypsy woman told my fortune once and she said: "You, my darling, will die in prison when you're thirty-seven years old." So what have I got to worry about?'

Shura half stood up, holding his cards, but he probably couldn't see Vanya's face, hidden behind his legs in their wide sea-boots: 'What was that you said, Vanya?'

'Nothing. Questions! Questions!'

'What is your aim in life?'

'To do in my old woman. About time, too. I know who she's with right now. And I made out a pay warrant to her, fool that I am.

'Come off it, Vanya,' said Shura with a grin. 'Can you see her all the way across the sea?'

'Uh-huh. Across the seas and over the oceans. Did the same thing myself once. Had a bash with a married woman in Nagornoye. She and I had a whale of a time living off her old man's pay warrant. He was a second mate. That was the life! Drunk all the time, we were. What a cow!'

'Happy memories, eh?'

'What do you think? Then she met him on the quayside: "Oh Vitya, it's been no life without you, I've been pining away." She said that: pining away. Well, when I get home – God if I find them together! I'll stop her little game with a hatchet.'

'You mean the one you had a bash with?' asked Shura.

'Why her? No, I mean my own wife.'

'But how will you catch them together? She'll find out from the despatcher when your ship's due in.'

At that Vanya stopped and thought for a while. We couldn't tell whether he was fooling or being serious. Then his voice came again from behind his boot-legs: 'But she won't find out. I won't stick it out for the whole trip; I'm going to sign off the first time we reach the factory-ship. Or the second time. I know a woman doctor. She's an understanding woman – Sophia Davydovna. Stupid, but she can't help it. She always used to write me a sick note as soon as I asked: "I've got a slipped disc," I'd say, "it's hereditary." She never checked up on it. "Quite right, dear, take a rest, you must be sensible about your health." And there's an axe stashed away in the porch at home. I'll walk in with that axe.'

'Just a minute,' said Shura. 'Supposing she's alone?'

Vanya stopped to think again, but not for long.

'If she's alone, then of course there's no point. Anyway, she can't be alone. A woman gets bored being alone.'

Alik suddenly spoke up: 'Why "can't" she be alone? What if she loves you?'

'Did I say,' said Vanya, 'that she doesn't love me?'

'In that case, she'll wait for you . . .'

The boot-top shook – with Vanya's laughter. It shook for a long time. Vanya laughed openly and heartily, even though his voice was cracked and hoarse. Then he sat up on his bunk and his cap was shaking too, his ears sort of jumping up and down (he often didn't take his cap off when he flopped on his bunk).

'Are you a little kid? Or are you loopy? Don't you know who women love? They love the man who's to hand, got it? And when he's not there, they love another one. The one who's to hand at the moment. You're as green as grass. Have you ever slept with women or just with your mother's pillow?'

'And are there no exceptions?' asked Dima, with his characteristic hint of sarcasm.

Vanya dropped back on to his bunk. 'Exceptions! A mate of mine wrote to me about her, during my last trip. A real mate, wouldn't tell a lie. He saw her with this scum, coming out of a shop arm in arm together. And d'you know what sort of a shop it was?'

'No,' said Dima, 'what sort of a shop was it?'

'A fancy goods shop. Where they sell perfume. And stockings. And those . . . brasseers. So now he's pawing her, like the villain he is.'

Vasya Burov stopped reading his thick book and turned over. 'Listen, beachers, stop talking all this crap. It's so boring, it'll stop me from going to sleep.'

'Come on, you,' said the trawlmaster, 'join in the conversation. It's not crap, Vasya, it's a family problem.'

'I've solved all my family problems long ago. And yours are no business of mine.'

'Then tell us how these problems are solved.'

'They solve themselves. Get yourself some kids and be glad of them.'

The trawlmaster actually bounced up and down on the bench. 'So that's it! Be glad of them, eh? I've got four myself. It gets so crowded, we almost have to sleep out on the porch.'

Shura and Seryozha roared with laughter.

'And a good thing too,' said Vasya. 'Now no one's going to seduce your old woman. And even if they do, it doesn't matter much. The main thing is your kids. Are yours all boys?'

'Yes, four little recruits for the Navy.'

Vasya sighed with envy: 'I wish I had at least one boy. Both of mine are girls. Good ones, but girls.'

'You're no good at the job, Vasya. If you haven't improved by next trip we won't choose you as ship's storeman any more.'

'I suppose I should ask you to do the job for me.'

'Vasya, I'm always ready to help out a mate.'

'Of course you are. You've got just about enough brains to have kids, but no more . . .'

The trawlmaster was offended, but roared with laughter because everyone else did. Vasya turned over with his face to the bulkhead, but the trawlmaster wouldn't let up on him: 'Hey, Vasya!'

'What is it?'

'Don't play the fool, we're not going to let you go to sleep anyway. What have you called them, these girls of yours – Sashka and Mashka? or Sonya and Tanya?'

'D'you think I had them for fun?'

'What for then, Vasya?'

'You're a fool. They have their lives to live. You give them their names for life, not just the way you give a nickname to a cow.'

'Well then, what have you called them, Vasya?'

'If you must know . . . one's called Nedda.'

'Phew! You ought to be swallowed by a striped whale. And the other one, Vasya?'

'The other one's . . . Zemfira.'

I thought they would all laugh till they cried.

'No, Vasya, don't take offence. You're not much good on the job, but you're very good at naming. Nedda and Zemfira, eh? Those are gypsy names. Ah, you old gypsy!'

Vasya was silent for a while, then sighed a deep sigh: 'No, beachers, I see you're not going to shut up . . . All right then, I'll tell you a story.'

The trawlmaster jumped again, making the bench creak.

'Go on, Vasya, spin us a good creepy yarn about wolves.'

'So once upon a time there was a king. In days of old. Young and very handsome.'

'Where was it?' asked Shura.

'Where? In Turkey.'

'They don't have a king there, they have a sultan. With a harem.'

'Pipe down!' shouted the trawlmaster. 'You only went to primary school but you think you know everything – where there's a king, where there's a sultan. Listen to the story.'

'So there was this king. Now his cook was a beacher, who was deformed from childhood. He had a hump on his back.'

Shura didn't like this and said: 'Couldn't we do without the hump?'

'No, we couldn't. The whole point is in the hump. This cook had his job under one condition – he had to cook a new dish for the king every day. He must never repeat himself, otherwise it would be . . . off with his head. So this beacher really bust his guts at the job, and the king liked him a lot for this. As soon as he came in from hunting, he would go straight to the cook: "What have you cooked up for me today?" – "Venison soup, Mr King" – "Wasn't it venison soup yesterday?" – "No sir, Mr King, sir, yesterday it was wild boar soup" – "And what about tomorrow?" – "It'll be . . . what d'you call it? . . . bear soup" – "OK, off you go, but if you ever dish me up the same stuff as I've eaten before, you swab, I'll slice your head off with my sharp sword and order my courtiers to eat it." And that was how this sea-cook lived. His name, by the way, was Little Muk. One day three witches arrived. Dreadful hags, with fangs sticking out of their noses. They went to this cook in the kitchen . . .'

'Where were the guards?' asked Shura, who had been in the army.

'Where were they? They'd all ridden off with the king to hunt bear. But witches can get past any guard. So they said to the cook: "Listen, cook – would you like us to straighten out your hump?" – "How will you do that?" – "That's our affair. We'll straighten it, and that's that. You'll be handsome as a prince, and the king's daughter will fall head over heels in love with you. She'll bear you twelve kids and she'll always be faithful to you. For example, you may go away to sea to search for diamonds in distant lands, and even if she has to make do with black bread, she'll stay faithful to you." – "But what must I do for this?" – "Just this: make him some venison soup." – "But he's already had venison soup." – "Doesn't matter – make it."'

'Ah, the slags!' The trawlmaster was fidgeting again.

'"Hey," said the cook, "that way I'll not only lose my hump but my head as well." – "Take it or leave it," said the witches, "we're offering you the easiest way out." – "But suppose the king notices? What excuse shall I make then?" – "Ah", they said, "that's the whole point! We can't give you a guarantee, otherwise you won't be a hero, will you? And to get the king's daughter you have to show you're a hero, don't you?"'

'Yes, I can see that,' Shura nodded. He wasn't looking at his cards any longer.

'Well, the cook scratched his hump and thought: Come what may, I'll make him some venison soup. I think there's some left over from yesterday. Maybe he won't notice. The king came back from the hunt: "I could polish off at least eight plates of soup right now!" – "Help yourself, Mr King, we've cooked a whole tubful." The King sat down to eat. "What's this I'm eating?" – "What's the matter, isn't it tasty?" – "It's tasty all right," says he, "in fact I'm sorry I'll never have any more in my life." This gave the cook some hope. Maybe the king would pardon him. Because he was an honest man, this cook, and had never once told a lie, he fell down at the king's feet and banged his forehead on the ground. "Why do you do that, my faithful Muk?" – "I'm sorry, Mr King, but you ate that soup yesterday." The king immediately threw down his spoon. "Ah, you villain, where's my favourite sword?" All the men of his guard rushed forward: "Here, Mr King, take mine!" – "No, I'd rather use my own . . ." The king lost his temper with the guard: "I told you to give me my favourite sword! All my life I've longed to chop off someone's head with that sword, but I've never had the chance . . ." So away they ran, to find his favourite sword . . .'

Here Vasya fell silent.

'What happened next?' asked the trawlmaster. 'Hey, don't go to sleep! Finish the story. They brought the sword – and what then?'

'Who said they brought it?'

'They ran off to get it, didn't they?'

'That's it. They ran off sure enough. But they couldn't find the sword.'

The trawlmaster was almost moved to tears.

'They'd pinched it, the slags – it was those witches, wasn't it?'

'Uh–huh,' said Vasya. 'It was the witches.'

By now he was quite drowsy.

'But didn't the king want another sword, instead of his favourite one?'

'No, he didn't.'

'Vasya, don't go to sleep. Vasya!'

Vasya only grunted.

'Vasya, none of us will be able to sleep now. What happened next?'

'I don't know. I haven't thought it up yet.'

'Why did you start a story when you hadn't finished thinking it up? That's no way to carry on.'

'I'll think it up tomorrow and then I'll tell you the rest.'

The trawlmaster was so offended that he almost pulled the door off its hinges when he went back to his own cabin. The other men quietened down anyway, as it was late, and they turned in. Only Shura and Seryozha finished playing their last hand, after which they settled the score: 'Thirty-six, thirty-seven, thirty-eight . . .'

As I guessed, Seryozha had lost again. Finally he too simmered down, stretched out on his bunk and lulled himself to sleep by staring at the deckhead and the bulkhead in front of him. Whenever he took over a bunk, he covered it with pin-ups. Some were from magazines, some were snaps he'd taken himself – waitresses and hairdressers, in sweaters or in their birthday suits in the bosom of nature; you could feel the goose-pimples. He had even removed the standard list of alarm warnings and distress signals to make room for his collection . . . Then Seryozha, too, switched off his deckhead lamp.

Pitch darkness and silence descended, except for the rustle of water above my head, while somewhere deep in the warm bowels of the ship the engine thumped away. And I was flying, alone, floating above those terrible liquid depths. All fairy tales had come to an end as far as I was concerned. They had, in fact, come to an end long ago. On this trip I had the feeling I was sailing for the first time; my eyes and ears had been opened all over again, and I was seeing and hearing everything as if I was standing aside from it all – even aside from myself. Strange. Who had done this to me? Perhaps it was Lilya? No, she had appeared later; it had started before that, when I myself had suddenly wanted a completely different life, where there were none of those things: things like female gossip, stupid mistakes, and nagging worries over what's happening at home and what you're going to be doing tomorrow. Then she had appeared. We met at a dance in the International Club. I was to entertain some visiting English merchant seamen, or they may have been Norwegians, I can't remember now, but I do remember how it happened . . . Well, you can imagine what it was like, the room full and the air so thick with smoke you could cut it with a knife, and everyone behaving like lunatics – drinking, shouting themselves hoarse, exchanging all kinds of buttons and badges, someone already asleep in a corner on several chairs pushed together. The official hostess was still doing her stuff, even though she could hardly stand by now and she was as hoarse as a bo'sun calling for 'all hands'. She wanted us to join in some 'international' dance: 'Attention!' she called, clapping her hands: 'Ettenshen pliiz! Everybody look at me. Do as I do. And – one! And – two! Now all join hands in a circle.' Then some girl's hand was in mine. Hot, holding tight. Later I took her to the bar – 'Pliiz, ledi, pliiz.' There I got us drinks and we sat down at a table, where some mulatto had laid down his head to sleep, waking now and again to wink at us. What an atmosphere it was! For some reason I was talking with a sort of 'foreign' accent, either as a stupid joke or to cover up a sudden shyness, and she kept trying to find out who I was: 'You English? No, you're a Norwegian!' until I gave the game away: 'I'm just a local lad, don't be shy.' How she laughed! . . . She was wearing a green dress with a plunge neck line, a kerchief tucked in her sleeve, and . . . a shock of hair. Later I saw her home. I still knew nothing about her – who she was, what she did – but I suddenly had the feeling this was it: I could junk all the rest, I had all I needed . . . And now I had tripped and fallen into the first ditch. Seems like I'm made of the same stuff as everyone else, after all.

4

We were lying fully dressed on our bunks, waiting to be called out to cast the trawl.

It was the tenth day out and we had started searching for fish that morning. The water was the same, blue and green. Thirty-odd miles away was the same shoreline, a row of snow-topped mountains, and we could just see the Norwegian warships patrolling the limit of their territorial waters.* But there was still no elbow-room, because there was such a concentration of foreign fishing vessels – British, French, Norwegian, Faroese – all of them roaming about the sea like so many balls on a billiard-table, zigzagging back and forth under each other's noses. They're a sight for sore eyes, these foreigners; although their trawlers are smaller than ours, they're clean and smart, their sides gleaming with paint – blue, orange, green and red – their wheelhouses snow-white, their motorized lifeboats neatly slung from davits. Then along comes one of ours, black and rusty, and the others scatter from her in all directions. On the other hand, none of the foreigners stay at sea for longer than three weeks; they're all near home, so there's no excuse for not keeping a vessel looking shipshape. Ours, though, after a hundred and five days at sea, get so shabby that we feel ashamed to go into port, as if they'd chase us out like mangy dogs.

And those foreigners catch plenty of fish, too, especially the Norwegians; they know their own waters. They use purse-nets, which they carry outboard on a motor boat and then haul the purse back – always full. Half an hour's work, and there's a ton of fish on board. Then they go and watch television. One Russian told me – he fell overboard, our people didn't see him and some Norwegians rescued him – there were three TV sets in their saloon and you couldn't decide which one to watch. On one of them there were cowboys galloping across the screen, on another there was a cartoon

---

* Since this was written, Norway, in common with many other states, has extended her 'zone of economic interest' to a distance of 200 nautical miles from the shore. (Author's note.)

that made you split your sides, and on the third girls were dancing with so little on it was indecent. And their oilskins! Black and glistening, fringed with white fur at the cuffs and round the face; in oilskins like that you could walk around the streets and people would think you were some kind of fashion model.

At first we only watched the others fishing, the mates staring at them through their binoculars. Then we started to search, but we had no luck all day; the echo-sounder only picked up small quantities and thin concentrations, so by suppertime we hadn't yet cast our nets. Now all we could do was lie down and wait – till midnight, maybe, or even till two o'clock in the morning – but we must not sleep; no one could fall asleep, anyway.

We're always silent at times like this. Even the two apprentices, normally always whispering to each other, held their peace. They had caught our mood. I doubt if I could tell you just what that mood is like before the first cast. The ship steers a zig-zag course, swinging from tack to tack, while at any moment they may call us out. Have you ever seen athletes before the start of a cross-country race? They don't seem to want to run. Yet no one is making them do it. We're all the same, except that everything up till now – the passage out, preparing the trawl, rubbing the rough edges off each other – was just fun and games; this is the real thing.

A wave hit the ship's side, broke, and ran hissing over the deck; the bulkheads shook with the vibration. Then all at once it went quiet. We could even hear the wind whistling in the shrouds. Then the engine began to rumble and thrash and the cabin shuddered again – we were going astern.

'We seem to be going backwards for some reason,' said Alik.

Grudgingly, Vanya Obod explained from behind his boot-tops: 'You wouldn't understand. We were drifting by inertia, and now we've stopped. They've found it.'

'You think they've found some fish?'

'Think? Now's the time to cast the trawl, not to think.'

Vasya Burov put on his cap and sighed a long sigh. 'Happy days are here again. Fish for the country, money for the wife, and for us – noses into the water.'

At that moment there was a crackling in the loudspeaker and the First Mate's voice boomed out: 'Deck-crew, stand by to cast the nets.'

The door banged in the bo'sun's cabin, the trawlmaster clumped noisily up the companion-way. We began picking up our oilskins, first pulling on our quilted jerkins and trousers, pushing our feet into the wide-topped sea-boots and putting on our sou'westers.

Shura pushed his way past us into the cabin, coming from the wheelhouse, where the mate on watch had taken over the wheel for him. Someone said to Shura: 'OK, Shura, let's go and have a look and see what sort of fish you've found.'

That's what they always say to the helmsman: 'Let's go and have a look at your fish,' although he, of course, doesn't do any searching; he just obeys orders.

Shura replied, almost apologetically: 'The echo-sounder is really squealing, lads – you'd think the paper was going to start smoking. Still, who knows – maybe it's only recording plankton.'

Maybe it is only plankton. We'll find out tomorrow. Meanwhile both searchlights have been switched on and the whole deck is lit up. Over the side it's pitch-black, spray lashing us from the wave-tops. We disperse to our stations, yawning, shivering, hunching our necks into our collars. My place is right near the doghouse. I have to open the round hatch-cover over the warp-hold, place the roller in its grooves, pass the end of the warp over it and pay it out to the trawlmaster; he splices it into one end of a line lying coiled at his feet under the port gunwale. The other end has to be made fast around the drum of the winch. Then I have to watch the warp coming out of the hold and shout: 'Mark! . . . Splice! . . . Mark! . . .' The warp is marked at intervals of thirty metres, and it's my job to warn the trawly in advance so that he knows when he has to tie a line to the warp at the mark and when to keep his hands clear of a splice.

The lamp was switched on in the hold and for the first time I saw my warp – yellow sisal, made in Japan. A boa-constrictor as thick as your arm, this brute had cost a lot of hard currency. It still had a silky look to it, never having been in the sea and still smelling of ski-wax. Tomorrow, though, it would come back to me grey and smelling of salt, seaweed and fish. The nets, too, would be smelling of the sea, their green colour would darken and they'd be torn in more than one place; we would have to mend them and mend them over and over again.

Marconi, the radio operator, had switched on some music for us in the loudspeaker – not too loud, so we wouldn't miss hearing the orders, but just enough to raise our morale. The trawlmaster stuck his knife in the deck and pulled on a pair of white gloves. Nobody would believe us if we told them that we prepared to cast the trawl to the sound of jazz and wearing white gloves; but this work can be delicate, and you could never do it in canvas mittens. These gloves are simply undyed cotton, and they tear so easily that he wears out about forty pairs in a trip.

The skipper came out of the wheelhouse on to the wing of the bridge. He was in no hurry, but waiting for the right moment. No doubt he felt cold standing out there – not from the wind, but because everyone on deck was staring at him. The mate, leaning his chest against the wheel, was also looking at him.

'Skorodumov!' the skipper shouted. The trawlmaster cupped his hand to his ear. 'What standing lines have you prepared?'

'Sixty metres!'

The skipper thought for a moment and waved his hand: OK, sixty metres will do.

That's about the average. The nets are usually kept at depths of between forty and eighty metres. The echo-sounder is no help at this point: it has pinpointed the fish ahead of us, but we have to move forwards, and there is no way of telling whether the shoal will rise up or drop down before it reaches our nets. You can't cover the whole depth of water from the surface to the seabed; the net from its top to the bottom edge only measures twelve metres, so for the fish to be caught in those twelve metres it's a question of guessing how far down to position the nets.

'Bo'sun!' he shouted again. 'Hoist the forestay-light!'

A lamp and a black ball rose up the forestay to the truck of the foremast, the ball to be seen by day, the lamp by night. This signals that we have staked out a shoal and are requesting others to stay clear. Whatever fish there may be there, they are now ours and we are going to catch them. The helm was put hard over and the ship was sailing with a heavy list, almost shipping it green. She described a circle. One second, another second, and the skipper shouted: 'Let go!'

And then it all began. The trawlmaster bent down, scooped up the whole coil at once and heaved it over the gunwale. After it, three standing-line floats flew overboard, hit the water, settled on the surface, then bounced up on a pitch–black wave and vanished from sight. Then my warp started to crawl out – at first like a lifeless thing, then faster, growling and making the roller creak. It was all yellow so far, then out came the first mark, painted on in black.

The trawlmaster, already squatting down with a standing line in his hands, lashed it to the warp with a rope-ladder knot. When it reached the mark he pulled it tight with one jerk, keeping his hands clear. The first marks are always easy, both for him and for me. To begin with I can spot them standing up, but then they come faster and flash past you because the warp is moving flat out, and I have to squat down too, to be able to see them by the light of the little lamp in the warp-hold while the devilish thing uncoils itself in heavy, snake-like rings and flies out with a rumbling noise.

'Mark! . . . Another mark!'

Seryozha was taking down the standing lines from the shrouds, where they had been hung in readiness, and handing them one by one to the trawlmaster. It wasn't difficult work. None of our work is difficult at this stage, except for the trawlmaster, who has the main job on his hands. Just try tying on those lines when the warp is moving at full speed. You can't stop it then, even if you set all hands to it. If it gets fouled up, it can wrench the fairlead out of its seating – and that's made of cast iron.

'Splice coming up . . . Past . . . Mark! . . . Another mark! . . .'

I am the only one of the deck-crew to speak. Even the skipper is silent. He's done his bit: 'Let go!' – and then it's too late to change anything. He stood there for a while and then went away. The skipper isn't the only one who doesn't want to see the end of the cast. There's nothing to look at now; tomorrow we shall see.

The floats danced on the waves and bobbed away past the wheelhouse.

The nets streamed over the gunwale, three kilometres of them – all of which we had tied and laid out. We watched them proudly as they went, like warships sailing past in review, as if we and all our foolishness, fears and worries were going away with them too. I know what every one of us feels at this moment, because I've done every job on board in my time; now I'm acting as warpman and shouting: 'Mark! Splice! Another mark! Another! . . .'

I've been in the float-caboose, too, throwing floats out on to the deck; Alik's doing it now. As Dima is handing them out now, I once handed them to the trawlmaster's mate, who makes them fast to the top end of each standing line. Like Vasya Burov and Shura, I've straightened out the nets and watched over them to make sure they go overboard without getting fouled up. Only I've never been warpman before. Big change in my life – a real thrill, I can tell you!

From my position, I suppose I can see them all better than anyone. They're standing either with their backs to me or sideways-on, looking out to sea where the nets are floating away. Staring, unable to take their eyes off them. Standing with their legs spread wide on the heaving deck, the points of their knives rammed into the planking. Bathed in artificial light, we gleam like green ghosts – strangers to this sea, landsmen from Oryol, from Ryazan, from Kaluga, from Vologda – we fly on the blackness above a bottomless mass, leaving only the yellow floats behind us.

But it's a job like any other, and it'll be finished before too long. There are fewer and fewer nets on the deck, and the coil of warp in the hold is getting lower and lower.

'Much left?' asked the trawlmaster. He was soaked in sweat; he had tied nearly a hundred knots.

'You can knock off soon.'

Everyone started to move about and talk again. The last mark flew out, at which everyone whose job was over crowded down below into the cabin. I still had a bit more work to do – close the hatch-cover, go down to the main deck and check that the lead-hawser was lying on the 'scotchman' – a canvas sleeve lashed over the guardrail – so that it wouldn't chafe the rail. When I came back, Alik and Dima were standing amidships, and the cooper was dousing the barrels with seawater from a hose. Everything was quiet, the wind had dropped – we were already lying-to.

'Is that all?' asked Dima.

They thought the cast would take an hour. But it had lasted perhaps ten minutes.

5

Now we could see that all the others had cast their nets too – Englishmen, Norwegians, Frenchmen, Faroese, Soviet fishermen from Tallin and Kaliningrad in the Baltic. They were all now drifting, not one ship's light moving. A scattering of motionless lights. And music coming from every vessel.

I ran below to change into my jacket and came back up again to 'walk down the avenue' until all the others had turned in.

Alik came up to join me on the foc's'le and sat down beside me on a coil of rope. There were three coils there, lashed down for dirty weather, but he sat on mine. He too had come out for a breath of fresh air. We relaxed in silence – the best of all.

'Beautiful!' he said to me

'Uh-huh.'

It really was a beautiful sight, with the searchlights switched off and the stars and masthead lights shining brighter as a result. But it's boring to talk about it. He laughed.

'Some people talk too much, don't they?'

'And how.'

'But I didn't mean this,' he nodded at the sea and the lights. 'I was meaning the cast. Now that really is something beautiful. I was watching it from above, from the float-caboose. It was splendid. Everyone looked like Vikings . . . It'll be a let-down if we don't catch anything tomorrow.'

For him, of course, it was the first cast. I've seen all I ever want to. But the first one is always exciting.

'I shouldn't count too much on a good catch tomorrow,' I said to him. 'Right now is not a good catching season. We'll do better later, towards March, when the fish are heading for the fjords, full of roe. Then the problem is to catch them in time.'

'So is there any point in fishing in winter? Wouldn't it be better to go in March?'

'Yes. Provided the fish don't stuff themselves with krill. Then we have to gut them. Disembowel them.'

'Is that difficult?'

'Make it a rule not to ask that question on board ship. Nothing's easy. Have you ever gutted a fish at home?'

'A couple of times, to have as a snack with vodka.'

'Ever tried gutting a ton of them? In the cold, wearing mittens? If you don't cut off a finger, you can think yourself lucky.'

'What is krill?'

'A sort of tiny shrimp. When the fish eat krill, their innards won't absorb salt, so they'll rot if you don't first gut them.'

'Don't they eat it in summer?'

'In summer they don't shoal. They swim out of the fjords singly, on their own.'

'Yes, that must be like trying to fish over the whole Atlantic.' For some reason he sighed. 'Thanks.'

'What for?'

'Well, just because . . . now I know something. Smoke?'

He offered me a packet and lit a match in his cupped hands. As I was lighting my cigarette he suddenly said: 'By the way, old man, the water does boil around the screw.'

'You don't say?'

'Yes. It's called "cavitation". It's a bad thing, because it ruins the propellor. When the number of revolutions exceeds a critical figure, little air bubbles form on the reverse, sucking side of the blade. No steam is given off, but it has all the characteristics of boiling.'

'You know plenty!'

He shrugged his shoulders and sighed again. 'We all managed to pick up a bit . . . I used to experiment with outboard motors.'

'Why did you go, then, when I told you to?'

'To the stern? I didn't go. I went to the heads. But I did provide you with a little fun, didn't I?'

I looked at him: he was a good-looking, strapping boy. No doubt the girls loved him. I wondered why he always played the role of junior to Dima. But there was, in fact, something about him – how shall I put it? – which made everyone want to take care of him, look after him: to make sure that he kept clear of the winch, or a taut hawser, or that he didn't unthinkingly make a move where he might fall overboard. No one ever thought of keeping an eye on Dima.

'Do you find it tough at sea?'

'My God, no!' He smiled. 'I've never felt like this before. The tougher the better.'

'Good for you!'

'It's the truth. Sooner or later you have to make yourself. Change your face.'

'What do you mean?'

'Don't you remember – in Alexander Green? Have you ever read him? It's in *Scarlet Sails*, I think. Or maybe *Scudding over the Waves*.'

'Well, let's suppose I have.'

In fact, I hadn't read this man Green. On the whole I don't like reading books about sailors. Jack London is the only one I respect. He wrote the truth: 'Man will never become accustomed to cold.' He knew what he was talking about.

'Green describes it very powerfully. How callouses grew on his hands and how his face changed . . . I expect I've done too much reading. But when you come to think of it, my lot in life has been terrible.'

'In what way?'

'Not in the way you might think. No one in my family was ever in prison or the camps. They're all alive and well, thank God. But it was all so easy and comfortable for me – ten years back and forth along the same path to school, two blocks there and two blocks back. Then along another path to university. Then to another institute. You're positively choking on the amount of information pumped into you, yet you'll never see . . the Paumotu Archipelago, for instance . . . Easter Island . . . or Tahitian girls dancing. Except in the cinema. And you'll never sit down wearing a garland round your neck that the chief's daughter has woven for you.'

'I shall die without having seen any of that either.'

'Ah, but that's not the point.' He spat his fag-end overboard. 'Because you're really living. At least one day every week is going to imprint itself on your memory. Because a person remembers the times when things were tough for him. When he was starving. When he was crouching in a trench. When they divided a home-made cigarette into three and he got the butt-end with no tabacco in it. But when you're living in a warm flat with a bathroom and lavatory, it's all very nice, for heaven's sake, but there's nothing to remember . . .'

A nice little tune came floating over to us from a Danish trawler. Alik picked it up and began to whistle.

'You mustn't do that,' I said to him. 'You'll frighten the fish away.'

'Yes, sorry. That's one of your famous superstitions. In the old days, I suppose, the bo'sun would have given me a taste of the rope's end, wouldn't he?' Then he forgot, and started whistling again, but soon stopped. 'Got that tune on the brain . . . Let's have another cigarette. Got to have something to keep your mouth occupied.'

I asked him: 'What will you do after the trip? Go back to the institute?'

'Of course. Where else? We've taken what's called sabbatical leave . . . A great way of doing absolutely nothing at all. Even so, we have done something, even if it's only going to sea on a seiner.'

'What seiner?! You're sailing on a DWT.'

'Well, yes, but it doesn't sound so good.'

Smiling, he looked out at the sea and the lights. And I suddenly remembered where I'd heard about a trip on a 'seiner' before. Was this the lad I'd seen in the lighted window on Volodarsky Street? Was that him sitting on Lilya's window-ledge having his farewell party? I hadn't been able to recognize him from down below, and my eyes had been watering from the cold.

'Listen,' I said, 'tell me something . . . When girls and boys get together at one of your student parties, say, do the girls swear too?'

'How do you mean?'

'You know – four-letter words. Like the boys do.'

My question amazed him. 'Yes, it happens. Quite a lot.'

'But why? If there's no one to get angry with . . .'

'They don't do it out of anger. It's . . . how can I explain it? What you'd call a complex, I suppose. All according to Freud. It's sort of . . . as if she was undressing in front of everyone. I suppose it gives her some sort of pleasure.'

'You don't say! And the boys – do they like it?'

'It all depends; some do. Though I personally don't much like it.'

'Would it be better if she really did undress?'

'Do a striptease? Well, that's another matter altogether. Not every girl would dare.'

'But if she did, you wouldn't respect her afterwards, would you?'

He smiled, embarrassed.

'Apart from that they're perfectly decent.'

'The ones who undress in public?'

'As I say – that's quite another matter. On the whole, though, you're right, there is something rather nasty about a girl swearing. But you get used to it. It's even hard to imagine some girls without it. But if you come to think to it – what do they like us for? It's also for something a little nasty. I agree with you.'

'I'm not saying anything more. You should turn in and sleep.'

This surprised him even more, but I was suddenly sickened by him. Because she had been at a party with him – well, might have been – and had wanted to undress in front of him. I even pictured it to myself. No, she hadn't used any four-letter words – although I once heard her do so – but she had done the other thing. And he had watched her, laughing, and everyone had great fun, and she let them touch her, too. God, the things you can think up if you let youself! Well, maybe they hadn't done everything quite as I had imagined it, but why shouldn't she love him? After all, he's a good-looking, well built boy with a clever tongue in his head. And the fact that his fate had been a 'terrible' one – well, he and his fate fitted hers exactly.

'You ought to turn in, otherwise you won't get enough sleep. They'll be getting us up at six tomorrow.'

'I'll stay here a little longer. It's a pity to miss such a beautiful sight.'

Christ, I thought he'd said his piece on that one.

'Well, please yourself.'
I got up and left him.

6

I would have gone to see the Chief, but there was no light on in his cabin. He's probably gone to the engine-room, I thought; it was his assistant's turn on watch, and this greaser of his, Yurka, was a crazy type and the Chief didn't trust him to do the job on his own, especially as the engine was now running slowly to keep the ship under just enough way to straighten out the trawl.

I peered down the skylight into the engine-room. Yurka, stripped to the waist, was sitting at the workbench and grinding something on the carborundum wheel, while the Chief walked up and down the duckboards with an oilcan – doing Yurka's work for him, in fact.

I ran down the companion-way.

Yurka saw me and waved. 'Hello, Mr Jacket!'

'Hello, Mr Bodybuilder!'

'Shall we have a talk, Senya?'

'Let's have a talk.'

'What about – women or politics?'

'We talked about politics yesterday. So today it's women.'

'OK then, Senya, Let's discuss the question of sex. Let's face it, it's an obstacle to living and creative work.'

This was a sort of ritual greeting between us, and that was the end of the conversation, because Yurka is as stupid as a frozen codfish and I have no wish to talk to him about women or politics or anything else. He was making a knife – his latest craze. Last trip, so I was told, he made about twenty cigarette-lighters as presents for his mates. He doesn't smoke himself, because he's careful about his health. Although he has developed the most enormous biceps, he's the idlest bugger you're ever likely to meet.

Meanwhile the Chief was oiling the engine. I have no idea where he was pouring his oil; I could never make head nor tail of that machine in three hundred years – there are too many little taps, nuts and bolts. I simply like watching him do it. Now Yurka hardly ever touches the engine, yet he is always filthy and there's so much oil on his beret you could squeeze it out; but the Chief is dressed in tunic, shirt and tie and there's not a drop of oil on him. As he walked around the engine it was panting and spitting like a mad thing, but not at the Chief. That was the problem: I could never be someone like the Chief, and to be like Yurka the greaser – well, was it worth wasting your grey matter to take the qualifying exams?

The Chief noticed me, but gave no sign of it. He liked it when I looked at his engine; it was as if I'd decided to learn all about it.

'Senya! Come over here.' He had finished oiling and was wiping his hands with tow. 'Listen.'

I couldn't hear anything special. The engine was banging away like three machine-guns. Valves were poppng up and down on springs and spitting at me.

The Chief leaned right over to my ear: 'That's the noise a normal engine should make.'

'Ah!'

Yurka looked at us, laughed, and went back to grinding his knife-blade.

The Chief walked along the duckboards down the whole length of the engine. He was telling me something about it, but I could hardly hear him. I didn't even try to hear. And then, d'you know what I did? I turned around and climbed back up the companion-way. I didn't mean to offend him. I simply couldn't stand the heat, noise and stuffiness. I had also forgotten that he wouldn't be coming back again to his nuts and bolts, where he'd spent all his life. Remembering it now, I feel ashamed of my stupidity, but that's what I did: turned round and climbed back up the companion-way.

In the saloon Vasya the cook, in his 'whites' and chef's cap, was playing chess with the cabin-boy. The Third Mate, who had just come off watch, was eating stewed fruit with a fork and giving advice to both sides. Also sitting there was the cooper, reading the newspapers we had brought with us from port. He reads all the bound sets of papers and magazines from cover to cover, and he knows about anything you care to name – all about Vietnam, all about Laos. Yet he's always as filthy as a dog and sleeps in his clothes. His cabin-mates complain about him. He's as bad-tempered as a dog, too – with everybody, but with me in paticular. As soon as I came in he looked at me as if I'd just seduced his wife. Or the other way round – as if I'd dumped my ex-wife on him. Then he stuck his nose back into the newspapers.

Staring at the chessboard, Vasya the cook asked me: 'Want some stewed fruit?'

'No, thanks.'

'What would you like?'

'Nothing, thanks.'

The Third Mate had grown bored with prompting the chess players and turned his attention to me: 'Why are you mooning around like a lunatic? You just throw your jacket on and walk. You could lead yourself into crime this way.'

'Maybe I want to sell you my jacket at a higher price.'

'Crap!' He immediately came alive and grinned, making his scar turn white. 'In that case, don't wear it on this trip. It'd be safer hanging in my locker.'

Suppose, I thought, I just took the jacket off and gave it to him? Just like that, not for money. At least I'd be making someone else happy!

'I'll be thinking about it till we get back to port. Maybe I'll give it to you as a present.'

'Get away! I don't want that. I'm making you a serious offer . . .'

'In that case, it seriously cost me twelve hundred. Honestly. Do you want me to tell you about it?'

'Go ahead.'

I went out on deck again. At least there was music playing out there. Marconi had turned on the loudspeakers and switched to some variety programme, Danish or Norwegian. Someone called Max was arguing with someone called Sybilla. It's a sad thing, I can tell you, to listen to music pouring out over the sea at night, even when it's cheerful music. Music is one thing but the sea is something else; you can hear it all the time, even when it's only a tiny little wave slapping against the ship's plating.

Then I remembered: Marconi had a certain little song on tape. In fact it wasn't even a song, just a tune played on a flute with a drum tapping quietly in the background, almost out of time, it sometimes seemed. It was called 'Expectation', and it gave me a lump in my throat to listen to it.

Marconi had the topmost cabin in the after superstructure, even higher than the captain and the Chief, alongside the wheelhouse. There's no room to turn around, because it's so full of radio equipment; being so high up it rolls much worse than our cabin below decks, and people are always crowding into it. I wouldn't mind his life, though; at least you're alone at night, you can see other ships' lights through the porthole, and if the mate is humming to himself on watch or talking to the helmsman, you don't have to listen, you can always drown it with music.

It was dark in Marconi's cabin, and he was asleep face-down on the blanket. The tape in the tape-recorder had finished, but he seemed to know this in his sleep, and as he crawled over to change the spool, still only half awake, he bumped into me.

'Who's that? . . . Are we going somewhere?'

'No, drifting. We're only straightening out the trawl.'

He scratched the back of his neck.

'Oh, that's right, you cast the nets today. I'd completely forgotten. Sit down.'

I sat down on his bunk. Marconi rewound the spool and started it off again. The receiver in the corner was buzzing softly to itself and giving off a faint light from its little green eye.

'Are you expecting a call?' I asked.

'They're going to send a confirmation of the weather report.'

'What's the forecast?'

'Force 2. From 2 to 3.'

'Why do you need confirmation when it's not a gale warning?'

'No need, really, but the skipper will come and ask. He's very meticulous – I have to put everything in the log for him: what's forecast, what's confirmed. Have you brought a radio-telegram to send?'

'No. There's a song I'd like you to play.'

'An Icelandic song?'

'I don't know where it's from.'

'Well, I know which one you like. It'll be on this tape.'

We lit up. His face went first red from the glow as he drew on his cigarette, then green from the light on the transmitter.

Suddenly he asked: 'Listen, have you and I sailed together before or not?'

'I don't remember.'

'No, nor do I.'

'My name's Senya. Senya Shalai.'

'I know. I transmitted your pay-warrent request. My name's Andrei Linkov.'

I thought I had perhaps seen him briefly once before. He had a big head and high forehead; he smiled easily and frowned easily, but the wrinkles never completely left his brow. The hairline was receding at his forehead and temples, his hair was thin and the baldness had spread quite far back; he must have been nearer forty than thirty-five. No, all my previous Marconis had been younger.

'Did you ever sail with Captain Vatagin?'

'One trip to the Barents Sea.'

'Ye-es,' he sighed. 'That proves nothing. Who hasn't sailed with Vatagin? He was a beast, eh? A beast, not a skipper!'

'A beast in the best sense.'

'In the very best! Which trip did you go on? It wasn't the one when he swam ashore carrying the mooring-warp and almost drowned, was it?'

'No, that wasn't on my trip.'

The radio in the corner started squeaking; Marconi slid over to the other side of the bunk, put on his earphones and began taking it down. Then the little green light went out.

'Between Force 1 and Force 2. That'll make it easier for you to haul in.'

'Do you want to sleep now?'

'Stay where you are, let's talk a bit more. Sleep! Huh! I've still got to transmit all these radio-telegrams. Your mates have been writing whole novels.' He lit the light in the deckhead over his desk. There lay a whole pile of sheets torn from notebooks, scribbled all over in indelible pencil.

'Read them if you like. Just between ourselves.'

'I oughtn't to.'

'Go on – have some fun! All right, I'll read them to you myself.'

Oh those radio-telegrams of ours! Vasya Burov spent pages on greetings to his relatives and close friends, instructing his wife to take good care of little Nedda and Zemfira: 'Keep them fit and well, and daddy will bring them back some presents from the ocean and he'll tell them a story about the wonders of the sea.' Shura Chmyrev addressed his Valentina in stern tones: 'Remember what I told you, and if you can't put up with my jealousy and my character in general, then it would be better to split up before it's too late. Also I borrowed ten roubles from Garik, so give the money back to him from my pay-warrant and write to me more often. Your husband Alexander.' Mitrokhin sent a message to his brother, who was sailing on another ship: 'Hello Petya! I know you've started fishing by now. Our working routine has begun too. First cast today! We have a good crew. Tell me how things are with you. Petya, try as hard as you can, and I'll try from my side, to make sure that we meet at sea . . .'

'I don't know how to cut these messages down,' said Marconi. 'It all seems essential. It's no good telling them I'm not allowed to transmit more than twenty words per person. But the Third Mate – there's a real man of the sea for you: "Dear Alexandra. I am unworthy of you. Cherpakov."'

'Leave them, it's none of our business.'

He put the messages aside, lay down and folded his bare arms behind his head. On his elbows and on his chest, where his lumberjack shirt was unbuttoned, could be seen tattooed letters, mermaids and anchors, swords entwined with snakes.

'So what d'you think, Senya? Have you and I sailed together before?'

'What difference does it make? We both breathe the same air.'

'But surely we ought to be able to find out? Oh, listen! You must know a girl called Lenka. Lenka the "cabin-boy" . . .'

'I've heard of her, but I never sailed with her. There have never been any women on trawlers in my time.'

Three years before I made my first trip, the fishermen's wives started sending a heap of protests to the management of the fishing fleet, demanding that all women sailing as 'cabin-boys' aboard DWTs should be removed: their family life was being ruined because of these women. So they were all replaced by men.

'They haven't been forgotten, though,' said Marconi with a wink. 'Lenka was a famous woman. They made up legends about her – about how she was always going to the crew's quarters, ready and willing for anybody who wanted it. And when they got back to port and the skipper was paying the men, she would be sitting at his left hand and the trade-union representative at his right. The union man collected his dues and she collected hers.'

'Sounds fun,' I said. 'Did you ever see this?'

'Well, Senya, you can't see everything, but I was told about it. Probably more talk than fact. I did see something, though. She and Vatagin had an affair. Everybody on board knew about it. The deckies used to go straight to her if they wanted anything: "Lenka put in a good word for us up on the bridge and see to it that we don't cast the nets today. It's dirty weather and we need a rest." Well, she always had the deckies' interests at heart, so she would tell the skipper: "Vatagin, we're not casting the nets today, the deckies are tired." And they didn't cast, but watched films instead. What a woman! I don't know what eventually became of her. It was as if she'd simply fallen into the water and disappeared.'

'She did fall into the water.'

'You're joking!'

'No. Although I never sailed with her, I know about it.'

'How did it happen? Come on, tell us.'

I told him what I'd been told. On one trip, late in the evening, Lenka went out on to the stern to throw away a bucketful of rubbish. It was half an hour before the cook missed her. Well, in the time it took to stop the ship, turn back on her course and look for her with the searchlight, she had already gone stiff with cold; she was only wearing a quilted jerkin. They tell me she was fished out alive, but she lived for less than ten minutes, even though they did all they could to warm her up and give her spirit to drink. They sailed to the factory-ship to refrigerate the body; it had to be taken back to port, because we don't bury people at sea any more as they used to in the old days. But because there was a gale of more than Force 7, the factory-ship wouldn't let them come near or moor up, so they had to carry on sailing with poor dead Lenka wrapped in a tarpaulin in one of the lifeboats. They all went nearly out of their minds.

'Listen, though,' said Marconi, 'didn't they tell you why she did it?'

'People fall overboard accidentally.'

'No, Senya, it's not as simple as that. After all, she was an experienced "cabin-boy". She'd done plenty of trips. Would she suddenly go out at night with a bucket, and in a gale too? She could have asked the cook to do the job anyway. Maybe she was really in love with Vatagin? Men don't die for love, but with women, you know, it does happen.'

'I don't know. Perhaps it was because people made up so many legends about her.'

'Think so? Who ever commits suicide for *that*, Senya? Most probably it was a combination of all those things.'

Then he started talking about Lenka in a quite different tone.

'If you want to know,' he said, 'her fate was decided as soon as she first set foot on a trawler: she was the only creature in a skirt on board a ship, surrounded by twenty-three healthy full-blooded sailors – and in those days the trips lasted six months, remember. She shared a cabin with the ship's engineers and the only concession to maidenly modesty was a sheet drawn round her bunk. There are any number of dark corners where men could paw her, squeeze up against her and then slobber all over her. And she didn't manage to hold out. At first, probably, she gave them hand-jobs and mouth-jobs, then she started drinking, until one day Vatagin seduced her. Yes . . . Lenka! What you've told me about her has upset me a lot. She was a splendid girl.'

'I wouldn't know.'

'Splendid girl! But you're right – people talked about her too much. Vatagin had any number of mates, and they all wanted their little bit of happiness. Maybe she made *him* happy, too. Who can tell. It's not so easy to cheat on your wife without everyone in the crew knowing about it. And not just the crew; plenty of people throughout the fleet became involved, persuaded him to give her up and go back to his family. I can tell you – when other people begin sticking their noses . . . into your intimate, delicate affairs, it always ends badly. The same thing happened to me. When were you in the Navy, where did your serve? In the Northern Fleet?'

'Yes.'

'I was in the Far East, torpedo boats. Well, I met this girl – just a kid, knew none of the tricks, nothing. You could see through her like glass. One Saturday they didn't let us ashore, and we couldn't go on liberty till Sunday morning; she waited for me on the pier all night, till she was soaked with dew. The watchmen chased her away, but she hid in some warehouse. You have to admire that, Senya! I was seriously thinking of going off with her for good when I was demobbed. Why not? But the Devil tricked me into asking my mates for advice. We split a bottle, and they gave me their advice: "Are you in your right mind, Andrei?" they said. "Why bother with this little girl from Sakhalin? When you get back to Russia, the girls will be fighting over you!" Well, that's as may be, but then came the clincher: "She's so devoted to you, it's suspicious! Women aren't like that, Andrei old man, that's a fact of female nature, you ought to read the books about it. You only see her on Saturdays, but what d'you suppose she does the rest of the week?" – "She waits for me," I said, "and she studies, what else is there for her to do?" – "You don't know anything! But just you wait – when you're due for demob, she'll go to the authorities waving a paternity order. And no one will ever be able to tell who was the real father." D'you think all of that didn't give me a shock? It did, and it made me think. I didn't even go and say goodbye to her when I was demobbed. I just sent her a telegram: "Recalled urgently. Aunt sick." And there was nothing she could do.'

'What about going back to her?' I asked.

'Go back to her? When I've already got three kids? The eldest is going to school already. I even used to dream that when he was old enough I'd tell him all about the girl on Sakhalin. Maybe he might understand and let me go back to her. We're both men; surely he'd understand?'

'He may understand, but she won't wait.'

'You know – she will wait. Last trip I got a letter from her, at sea. I hadn't told her about my kids . . . At first sight there was nothing important in her letter – it was just about her everyday life – but between the lines you could feel she'd gladly take me back any day. Well, for some reason the letters stopped – maybe she sent them to my address on shore and my wife got her hands on them.'

'Write and tell her to send them to the post office.'

Marconi laughed, almost cheerfully. 'Ah, Senya! When do we have time to go to the post office?'

Until then we hadn't noticed that the engine had stopped, the helmsman had gone below to sleep and all was quiet in the wheelhouse. Then that song 'Expectation' started to play. Some things have a bad effect on me, like the first drink on an alcoholic. I just knew I would start telling Marconi everything – about Lilya, about how I went to see Nina, and how Klavka and the beachers robbed me – although this was the first time I'd even seen or talked to him and I'd noticed, of course, that he was a blabber-mouth. I might regret it later and curse myself, but given the opportunity I would do the same stupid thing all over again.

Marconi listened, asked no questions, only sighed and nodded. Then he said: 'Yes, Senya . . . We should be drinking with this sort of conversation but there's nothing to drink. But I say to you, as if we were drinking – we're good people, Senya! If only things always went well for us, we could move mountains. And if only someone could teach us to know which people will make us winners and which will make us losers . . . why, we'd load that person with gold, Senya!'

And so on and so on in that vein. Then he asked: 'What are you going to do with yourself after this trip?'

'I don't know. Go on another trip.'

'Well, I've had enough. A mate of mine in air-freight has been persuading me to join him in their summertime crews. They use the same transmitters. Of course the money's not so good, but I thought – to hell with the money. We'll send the kids to their grandmother for a while and my wife can work and earn a bit. And to make up for it, the trips in air–freight last hours instead of months. Why don't you come with me?'

'What would I do?'

'Oh, you can fix yourself up with something. And if you can't, I'll take you along as a radio operator.'

'I suppose I could be a radio operator.'

'No.' He sighed. 'If it's just a case of "suppose I could", then you'd better not. You wouldn't be happy. I hear our Chief is trying to make an engineer out of you, but you don't want to. And you're right, if your heart's not in it. What does a person's happiness rest on? It rests on three whales – your work, your mates and a woman. A lieutenant back in my topedo-boat days made me see that. If those three are in good shape, all the rest comes by itself. Agreed?'

'So all I lack is those three whales, is that it?'

Marconi thought for a while, scratching his forehead.

'It's a bad business, Senya. Why did you and I become sailors, eh? Were we attracted by the naval uniform?'

'I think I was.'

'Dreamed about it since childhood, I suppose?'

'Since I was quite a kid, anyway.'

'But oughtn't we to come to our senses at some point? When I finish this trip I'll go and get a job as a driver.'

'But I thought you wanted to go into civil aviation?'

He laughed. 'Go and get some sleep, brother. They'll be getting you up before dawn tomorrow.'

I came into the cabin at exactly the right time, when they had all quietened down. The door was shut and the stove was giving off enough heat for a blast furnace. How we northerners love heat! We'd die without it.

I lay down but couldn't sleep, either because of the heat or because Marconi and I had managed to get each other all wound up.

It was true, you see, that I had been attracted to the sea by the naval uniform, although it wasn't quite true when I said I had felt this since I was a kid. As a boy I never played sailors or thought about the sea. Anyway, how could I have thought about it? The only water at Oryol is the piddling little River Orlik which is so shallow in places that you can't even float all the way to the big River Oka on a raft.

So when these three sailors on leave appeared in Sacco-and-Vanzetti Street, where I lived, I gave them no more thought than if they'd been dummies, although they were splendid lads – straight–backed, smart and shipshape, their bell-bottoms not too wide. They always went everywhere as a trio, taking up the whole pavement – like three destroyers steaming in 'line abreast' – and they never looked to either side but always straight ahead with a stern expression, and gradually our local riff-raff began to respect them. Later, though, the local lads started to get worried when the sailors each got themselves a nice girl and the trio turned into six – three couples in 'line astern'. This didn't worry me, though; they hadn't pinched my girl, and in any case I had no time to think about such things. That summer my father, an engine driver, had been killed in a train crash, and I was having to support my mother and young sister. I'd had to leave school at fourteen and go to a trade school; there you at least got a student grant, and in the evenings I earned a bit extra by working as a brake-fitter in the locomotive depot. All I did was to replace worn-out brake shoes with new ones. But as a railwayman I too had a black uniform greatcoat and a peaked cap, which I wore two fingers above the eyebrows, so that I too had the right, no less than those sailors, to look straight ahead with a stern expression and not step aside for anyone.

Then these sailors did something that amazed me. It happened in Sacco-and-Vanzetti Street one Sunday in summer. I was out for a walk with my sister when I suddenly saw a crowd gathered beside a tramcar.

Well, you know how it is when something like that happens – when someone gets run over or falls under a car: everybody finds it interesting, you feel good because it didn't happen to you, and everybody starts shouting indignantly: 'Disgraceful – they should be taken to court! . . . Why doesn't someone call an ambulance? . . .' And what did I do when I came along? I yelled my head off at the conductress: 'Where were you looking, you fool, ringing the bell before all the people had got on.' While I was telling her off like this, she was speechless and simply sat, white and silent, on the step. I yelled at the driver, too, so that for the rest of his life he'd remember not to start off without first looking in his mirror. I didn't look under the tramcar, of course. Just before this happened, I'd been told in detail how my father had been picked up in pieces at the foot of the railway embankment. I don't say that as an excuse – it's no sort of excuse – but you can't just walk away, and yelling at somebody is at least some relief to you, if not to the other person. Meanwhile the victim was lying silent and invisible, just like a switched-off television set. Nobody had any idea of what had happened to him.

Then the three sailors came past – or rather the six of them, but they left their girls on the pavement (it never occurred to me to leave my little sister there) – and they barged into the crowd, slicing it apart like three destroyers cutting through the waves in a turn. Grasping the situation at once, two of them pulled off their greatcoats and crawled under the tramcar with them, while the third held back the crowd to stop people from blocking the light. They put the victim on one greatcoat, covered him with the other and pulled him out between the wheels. He wasn't seriously hurt, only slightly bruised, and the flange of a wheel had sliced the sole off one shoe together with some of the skin of his foot. He was bleeding a bit, but a cut like that is hardly fatal. He was simply in shock, which was why he was silent. While we all moaned and groaned over him, they tied a tourniquet round his leg – some kind-hearted girl sacrificed her headscarf for this – slapped his cheeks and gave him the kiss of life. The third sailor had already stopped a taxi and was sitting on its radiator. The taxi-driver didn't object; he recognized the man as a friend of his with whom he'd been drinking the night before, crossed himself, and drove like the wind to the hospital. Then the sailors cleaned themselves up, put on their greatcoats and went back to their girlfriends. And that was that . . . But we all, like so many boiled lobsters, stared after them as they calmly walked away up Sacco-and-Vanzetti Street, and the reason was – they hadn't said a single word the whole time!

One day, perhaps we'll realize that all really good deeds are done in silence, and though we may, even if by chance, do some good to our neighbour by using our hands, we'll never do it by wagging out tongues. I know I'm preaching a sermon now, yet personally I've long since had it up to here with sermons and gossip; they make me furious whenever I hear them. That's why, for me, those three sailors will always be the three best people I've ever met. And that's why I asked to join the Navy when I got my call-up papers. I even hoped to meet them, because I thought – the sea makes people like that. I was a romantic young man.

Later, of course, when I went to sea I met men who were the biggest chatterboxes you're ever likely to find. The most kind-hearted ones were the worst, because they, you see, want you to be happy, so their tongues never get tired. And if, on top of that, they all start yapping in chorus, then you'd better run for your life, and anyone who doesn't can reckon himself a goner. Than man Vatagin, for instance, is as dead as Lenka, even though he didn't fall into the water but lived on. I sailed with him on his last trip. Nothing of the legendary character was left of him, just a bundle of nerves, because of what people might be saying about him after the Lenka affair. And what did they say? What had Marconi told me about Lenka? He could at least have dreamed up some new piece of gossip, but all he did was repeat like a parrot what those fishermen's wives had written in their letters of protest: 'She goes into the crew's quarters, gives it to anyone who wants it, then deducts her fees from their pay . . .' Yet for all that he called her a 'splendid girl'. Was that because she had been *his* girl? Well, the closer someone's been to us the more we like to throw shit at them.

After all, I thought to myself, she did go to sea with us. That says a lot for her, doesn't it? A girl like Klavka Perevoshchikova would never go to sea; she does things differently. She'll meet you on the quayside, will Klavka, waggle her hips, and you'll follow her like a bull with a ring through its nose. Provided you're not too stingy and you throw your money around to your heart's content, you won't be disappointed, because for all the fifteen or seventeen days of your shore leave she'll make sure you live well – warmth and comfort, drink and the best food, a TV set, and true love. If there's no vodka in the shops, she'll get some: she'll run down to the 'Polar Arrow' express at the station, where she knows a waitress in the restaurant car, and buy a crate of vodka. She'll buy fish, of the sort you can never normally buy in this fishing port of ours. She'll wash and iron all your clothes, knock herself out for you, bust a gut for you. Then just as you're beginning to get a taste for all this, one morning she'll wake you up and say: 'Are you awake, darling? Don't forget – you're going to sea today. There, have something to eat, it'll help you get rid of your hangover . . .'

When you're past the North Cape you suddenly realize you haven't got a kopeck in your pocket; but then you don't need money at sea, and instead you have such sweet memories! And her bright image shines over the water. It floats there for three months, I'm telling you from experience, and in that time she's knocking herself out for someone else. When you come back, you may meet her again, or you may meet another woman, who'll be no worse than her. Any number of them carry on this trade in the port, make themselves a nice little pile and then head off for warmer parts – never once having been to sea.

But Lenka went to sea. I don't know why she did it. On shore she could have got away with murder, but at sea gossip spreads at once, like ripples when you throw a stone into water. At sea, we're all supposed to be 'brothers', and you might think there was no point in tongue-wagging if you happen not to like one of your mates. Yet even the soberest ones are apt to lose their heads, and Vatagin wasn't one of the soberest. He must have known all about Lenka when he shacked up with her: what she'd really done, what other people had invented about her – so what changed and made him ditch her? Simply that the ripples had spread from a stone thrown into the water. They all pulled together to get him out of trouble: they talked to him and to Lenka, and at the same time they encouraged his wife, whom he was planning to divorce anyway, to write letters to the fleet management. So Vatagin caved in and personally struck Lenka's name off the ship's nominal roll. And 'they', of course, did not fail to tell her this, too.

After it was all over, these same nice people showed themselves. It was quite amazing to see how quickly they went into reverse. Yesterday they had 'saved' him – today they wouldn't shake hands with him; they demanded a Party committee meeting, condemned him for immoral conduct without making any allowances for his professional skill and success, and proposed he should be dismissed from the fleet. And who saved him then? Grakov! He literally pulled Vatagin out of that meeting by his ears and stopped all the accusing speeches in mid-sentence. How did he do it? By taking him off the list of seagoing personnel, giving him a job in his own office and making him effectively his right-hand man in charge of the operational side of the fleet management. So all the people who'd tried to ruin Vatagin became his subordinates! Well, as you can imagine, no one dared utter a squeak of objection . . .

What, you may ask, became of Vatagin then? You remember the former captain of mine who came up to our table in the Arctic with Grakov? And who ran off like a good little boy to fetch a bottle of mineral water? That was him – Vatagin.

7

In the morning came news. During the night our First Mate had distinguished himself by setting a course that would have taken the ship across dry land. It was the helmsman who brought us this tit-bit; all news from the wheelhouse comes from the helmsman. The First Mate had got the impression that the current was making our trawl swing inwards, so he decided to extend it by manoeuvring. He consulted the stars – but the wrong ones – and ordered the helmsman to keep on such-and-such a course. Well, the man at the wheel changed to that course and kept to it; his was not to reason why. Fortunately the skipper came into the wheelhouse, glanced at the compass and realized that on this course, in half an hour's time, we would sail into Norwegian territorial waters with our nets out, where a Norwegian warship would be bound to pounce on us. Then it would have been goodbye to our nets, because the Norwegians would have confiscated them. As a result, there had been a fine old row in the wheelhouse.

I wondered what sort of shape the First Mate would be in when he came to wake us, but the incident had made no difference – his voice was none the worse for it.

'Wakey, wakey!'

Dima and Alik stirred themselves and began to dress. Well, let them; they think if they're first to start they'll be the first to finish. Obviously they've never been in the Navy. All our old hands stayed in their bunks.

The First Mate sat down on the bench and tried to hurry us up: 'Look lively, boys. There's a big load of fish in the nets today.'

'Don't bullshit,' said Shura Chmyrev from behind the curtain around his bunk. 'There's maybe ten herring there, enough for the cats' breakfast, and you'll scare *them* away by talking like that.'

The First Mate's oilskins squeaked audibly as he turned towards Shura. He didn't like it, of course, when people were rude to him, but although he was offended he didn't dare answer back; Shura was, after all, a senior and experienced seaman, and this was the mate's first trip as First Mate. Coming from Archangel, what sort of authority could he wield? And we already knew about his navigational feat of last night.

'What d'you mean, "bullshit"? You should see the seagulls circling over the trawl. They know what's what.'

'They may know,' said Shura lazily, 'but you don't.'

At this point Mitrokhin decided to put his oar in. 'I had a dream last night, lads I dreamed a seagull flew straight into the wheelhouse. He settled on my head, pecked at the deckhead light and said in a human voice: "Beachers!" . . .'

'Just like that? "Beachers"?' said Vasya Burov, turning over from his back on to his stomach.

'Yes, he said "beachers". "You'll get twenty barrels from your first trawl," he said, "and after that everything will go wrong for you." Then he pecked the deckhead light again and flew out.'

The apprentices giggled, but we were silent. Dreams are a serious matter.

Then Shura swung his legs over. 'Out of the way, First Mate, or I'll kick you out.'

The mate was already out of the door and yelling at them in the next cabin: 'Wakey, wakey! Show a leg!'

I started to get dressed, knowing that Shura didn't get up for nothing; he'd been in the Navy too. The apprentices had only managed to pull on their shirts and trousers by the time Shura's boots were thumping up the companion-way. They'll have to put in more sea-time before they can catch up with us; and they'll never overtake us.

Vasya Burov lay on his bunk a bit longer. He's been at sea longest of all, which is why he's so devilish lazy – so lazy, in fact, that no one else can be bothered to try and make him buck himself up.

I won't try and describe what the sea was like. It was a good sea. Not absolutely calm – wind Force 1 to 2. It's no fun in a flat calm, because there's no wind to cool your face. The seagulls were hovering over the trawl in clouds – a good sign.

Over tea in the saloon the talk was all about the hopeful prospects for this, the first cast. We seemed to have struck a good patch; with any luck it might be like that all the time – and then we'd spit three times over the left shoulder in order not to tempt fate.

Then we heard the winch start running, and we gradually got up and went on deck. The trawlmaster and his mate were already hauling in the lead-hawser, and we all took up our positions.

I started on my job – unclip the hatch-cover, push it back, place the roller in its grooves – but I didn't go down into the warp-hold yet.

The trawlmaster wasn't hurrying. None of us were hurrying, but just looking at the blue sky and green sea, our eyelids still sticky from sleep. The lead-hawser had already come to an end; then out of the sea came the warp, looking as if it were plaited out of silk, the water on it sparkling with all the colours of the rainbow. The seagulls settled on it, taking a ride towards the winch, but the winch was jerking and the tautened warp was twanging like a mandolin, so no bird managed to stay on for long. The trawlmaster was hauling it in slowly – that's to say he wasn't hauling but only pressing the turns of the hawser against the winch-drum to prevent them from slipping – but it looked as if it was he who was hauling in the trawl: floats, lines, nets and fish. Though of course we couldn't see the fish yet. No doubt the trawlmaster wasn't thinking about the fish – no one can think about that and nothing else – but was probably thinking about the seagulls (which we call boobies, blackmugs or soldiers), wondering whether they were happier or unhappier than us. Or maybe he wasn't thinking about anything at all but simply staring at the water, fascinated, overcome by a incomprehensible joy.

I went over to him.

'Just the weather, Senya!'

'Just the weather, trawly.'

'If it was always like this, I'd stay all the time on deck and never go away.'

'No point, trawly.'

'But the work has to be done, Senya.'

'No question of it, trawly.'

'Because – why?'

'Because the country needs fish.'

'Correct, Senya, you know your stuff. Well, that being so, unshackle the lead-hawser.'

Without further words I unscrewed the shackle-pin and dropped down into the warp-hold, carrying the first length of warp. Goodbye, deck!

Down there it reeked of stale fish, carbolic, the ski-wax smell, the black paint used to put the marks on the warp, and rotting timber – from the barrels in the main hold that I could see through the gaps in a thin bulkhead.

While I was looking around and sniffing, the warp, like a great boa-constrictor, was sliding through the fairlead and down on to me from above in curls that weigh half a hundredweight. I had to coil it – and smartish, before it smothered me.

'Haul in!'

That was the trawlmaster calling to me from somewhere up above, from the blue sky.

The warp-hold is a metre and a bit wide by eight metres long, so there's not much space for running. But the work has to be done at a run. I'd never been near the job before, except for a passing glance from the deck to watch it being done by someone else, who would afterwards lie flat on his back for hours staring up at the deckhead. I only knew that the warp had to be coiled clockwise and from the outside inwards. Why not anti-clockwise?

And why not from inside outwards? God knows; probably because of the lay of the rope. Anyway, it wasn't worth worrying about.

This was how it went: seven paces forward along the bulkhead, turn right clockwise, back all the way along the skirting-board; you bump into the bulkhead and it's clockwise to the right again, seven paces forward again, turn clockwise, then a new length slides down into the hold, you turn, along the bulkhead again . . . Have you ever seen a horse going round and round in circles to drive a threshing-machine?

'Haul in!'

That damned warp isn't coming from just anywhere but out of the sea. And the sea is wet. Gradually the water started trickling down inside my collar, my canvas mitts were sodden in a moment and the salt water made my eyes sting. I'd just paused for a moment to draw breath and wipe my eyes when it suddenly went dark – someone was looking down into the hold at me.

The First Mate was blocking up the whole hatchway with his big wide nose. No doubt the skipper had sent him to check up on me: it was my first day on the warp, after all.

'Look lively down there in the hold! The warp's lying around all over the deck . . .'

I'd like to see him running in this hold – he wouldn't be looking so lively. I just spat and went on running, or rather loping along, bent double. It was tolerable as long as I running on duckboards, but by now I'd laid down the first layer, so I had to run on the coiled warp, and that's no parquet floor – at any moment you can slip and sprain an ankle. What would it be like when I'd coiled almost all of it and there'd hardly be room for me between it and the deckhead? Then I'd have to do it on all fours. Better not think about it. Got to put down the second layer.

'Haul in!'

By now the trawlmaster wasn't shouting in an official tone but with fire in his voice. No doubt he could be heard on all the foreign ships. They must have thought we used the loudspeaker when we hauled in our nets.

It was probably true that the warp had piled up on deck; it was becoming difficult to haul on it, and somebody ought to have been untangling it for me.

'Hey there, on deck! Someone sort out that warp!'

They probably couldn't even hear him, what with the winch screaming and sea-boots clumping around. Then someone came over to the warp and started kicking it clear, but that made it even worse for me, because the coils fell on my head and shoulders all at once.

'Come on, look lively, Senya! Move your ears!'

Aha, it was the trawlmaster helping me. His voice sounded slightly kinder too. He's a human being after all, and understands what it means to be unfamiliar with a job. I just spat and started running again. Not bent double but straight up, like a madman. So what if my legs buckled under me? I didn't care if my heart jumped out my mouth: I might die but I'd sort the thing out! I'd coil the damn' thing down, the sodden, salt-soaked bastard . . . Now there were only two coils left, maybe three, and that would be it, I could take a rest. As long as it doesn't snarl up again on deck. I hauled on it again. It wouldn't give a centimetre. Was it fouled again, or what? Who was going to keep untangling it for me? I was literally hanging on it.

At that moment I was given such a jerk that I was flung violently to one side, hitting my chest against the bulkhead.

'What the hell are you pulling for, down there? The net's coming in. They're shaking the net!'

So that was it! It hadn't got fouled up at all. The coils had slipped loose on the drum, which gets polished so smooth you can see your face in it. I had simply pulled the warp off the winch and it was a wave that had jerked me. The trawlmaster might have warned me and told me to stop hauling for the time being – but who has time to think of the warpman?

I leaned against the bulkhead to catch my breath and looked up through the hatchway. There I suddenly saw a star, blue, swaying right over my head. I thought I was going crazy. Finally I realized that it wasn't the star swaying: it was standing still and *we* were being rocked from side to side. No one could see it except me – from this dark hold. Where had I read that at high noon you can see a star from the bottom of a well? I didn't believe it then. Now I was in that well myself.

I stood there looking at it, though I was on my guard in case I was jerked again. I could hear the winch working – they never switch it off while the nets are being hauled in – but the trawlmaster had probably taken one turn off the drum to let the warp slip a bit. And I could sense that when he put it back on again, it would take that much warp away from me and there'd be nothing to haul on.

Now they were shaking the first net – crash! – and the fish were pouring out of it. They hadn't caught all that much, I could tell from the sound, but still it was a catch. I couldn't wait to see it, so I climbed up the Jacob's ladder to have a look, and suddenly something wet and slippery hit me on the neck. A socking great fish slithered down my sleeve and flopped on to the coiled warp. It was a big, strong herring, twitching and wriggling furiously, trying to push its way under the coils, which were still saturated with water. When I hauled it out and held it in my mitts it was so furious at having been caught that its gills were squeaking. What a beauty – straight out of the sea. It wasn't grey or lead–coloured or rusty, as they are in the shops; this fellow was all blue, green, raspberry-red and mother-of-pearl, shimmering like shot silk, every moment a new colour.

After that one, another fish flopped down, but without a head; it had been knocked off when they were shaking the net. Then another, bleeding with torn gills. Several more plopped down from the deck all damaged, but the fish I was holding was completely intact, no gills or fins torn, not a scale missing. I gripped it firmly, climbed up the ladder and threw it as hard as I could over the gunwale. A seagull dived for it, but my fish was lucky – the gull missed it, and it swam away.

I could hear them roaring with laughter on deck.

The trawlmaster looked down at me. 'What's this, Senya? Throwing our fish away? We catch 'em and you chuck 'em back!'

'Let the poor bugger live.'

'What sort of life will it have? It'll just go straight back into a net.'

'No it won't. It's learned its lesson now.'

'Yes, but what if this clever fish teaches the other, stupid ones to keep out of the nets? There'll be no brandy for us then. You're too kind to dumb animals, Senya!'

They laughed a long time. I caught any fish without heads and gills and threw them back on deck. There's nothing worse than a dead fish getting lodged somewhere below decks – the stink's enough to kill you. Up on deck it was crash, crash, crash as the nets were shaken, and every so often a fish would come flying my way. If it was damaged I would chuck it back on deck, but if it was whole – into the sea. Let them laugh. It was something to keep the deckies amused.

I'd forgotten all about the warp. I hadn't noticed the trawlmaster had pulled a length away from me and taken another turn round the winch-drum, and a lot more had come down into the hold while I'd been waiting. So it was seven paces forward again, turn clockwise, and another layer was laid. When I looked up through the hatch, the star was still there, swaying. My hands were ruined, my mitts were sodden and my whole body felt as if it was stuck with needles. But things were going well: fish flying all over the place meant they were being caught, so the nets had to be shaken and the warp had to be stopped each time; but if the nets had been empty the warp would have kept on coming all the time, and I would've passed out with exhaustion.

The trawlmaster looked down at me again. 'Getting used to it, Senya?'

'Yes, I'm getting the hang of it,' I said, 'but couldn't they think up some way of making the warp coil itself?'

'What do you suggest, Senya?'

'How do I know? Some kind of drum driven by a motor.'

'It wouldn't fit into the hold. And it's cheaper to have you coiling it.'

'So the idea's impossible?'

The trawlmaster said: 'Stop inventing, got it? Your job's to haul in.'

But was it really impossible? Of course they'll invent something sooner or later. And when they do, I'll be mightily offended, after all the time I've spent getting the knack of coiling it by hand. There's nothing shameful, I can tell you, about swabbing out the heads by hand, because there's no machine to do that yet. But shaking the nets by hand, for instance, is stupid, when several ships already have net-shaking machines. They're not much good, and they only replace one seaman, but they do exist. It's like being a tram-conductor: one day he's punching tickets, and the next day bang! – they've put a money-box and ticket machine in his place. Then he's pretty sore at being replaced by a tin box.

No doubt I had got the hang of the warp, as I now had time to think about other things. Before, I could only think of how to stay on my feet, but now the job seemed to do itself and my mind was miles away. OK, I thought, so we'll survive this after all. Then came a splice, big and thick, which had to be stowed in a special way, otherwise it would upset my system – God, that meant I'd only completed the first coil. There were still six more to come. Or was it seven? I ought to ask the trawlmaster, but there was no time to crawl out of the hold.

Up on deck they were roaring with laughter again.

'Chuck it down to Senya the warpman,' I heard, 'he's so fond of dumb animals.'

'Hey, Senya – catch!'

Something flopped on to me – something grey, white, black and fluffy. Struggling and screaming, it went straight into a corner and huddled there, only its eyes gleaming like two little buttons.

A seagull, what else? Blue-grey, with a white breast and black wingtips. He pressed one wing against the bulkhead and held the other one in front of himself like a shield, fluttering back and forth along the warp. I tried to pick him up, but he only flapped even worse, screamed, and pecked at my mitten. Then I took off my mittens, held my bare hand out to him, and he came to me. Well, any animal will come into my hands. I took him over to the light: one wing was hanging down unnaturally, the wing-feathers were all torn, and if you touched it he immediately screamed and pecked you.

The deckies looked down at me through the hatch: 'Feed him up with fish, Senya, then we'll get the cook to roast him.'

The gull was quiet now, except that I could feel his little heart thumping away. The greedy little fool had flown into a net and got caught up in it.

In a corner of the hold, behind a partition, was the place where the trawlmaster kept his tackle – spare coils of line, hemp, reels of twine – and I put Tommy there. I'd christened him Tommy; you have to give an animal a name if it's going to live with people. I threw him a herring. Catching it in his beak, he didn't swallow it but pulled it under him and covered it with his wing.

Then the warp started coming in again. The catch in the nets was getting thinner and it took less time to shake them out. The work got easier for the hands on deck and harder for me.

The trawlmaster yelled again: 'Haul in! You gone to sleep, warpman?'

And I forgot about everything – not just Tommy but about everything else. I started running like a maniac. And the warp kept coming and coming. Now, of course, everyone was furious with the warpman for coiling it so slowly.

'Haul in, you mother-fucker . . . Move your ears!'

I was just going to lean against the bulkhead, to wipe my forehead and stop the sweat running into my eyes, when the damn' thing came tumbling down in loops, right on top of the lengths I'd already laid down. To coil it now I had to throw all that back up on deck, otherwise it would get in a hopeless mess. I pushed it out with my feet, my elbows, my head but it kept on coming and I became hopelessly entangled in its coils.

The trawlmaster came clumping over to me, bent down and said: 'Are you going to haul in or not?'

'What d'you think I'm doing?'

'I don't know, Senya. I don't know what you're doing, but you're not hauling in. Look how much warp there is on the deck. You've cocked it up, Senya. We'll capsize with a warpman like you.'

'Can you do it better? Well, get going and show how it's done.'

He actually broke out in a sweat from the way I was answering him back.

'Come on out!'

'Why?' I said, although to be honest I was longing to climb out.

'Come out. And get a marline-spike.'

I fetched a spike from his store and clambered out. He was standing, legs spread wide, and watching me. I stuck my head out of the hatch and screwed up my eyes. The sun was so bright, the sea so blue it dazzled you.

I sat down on the deck, my legs dangling into the hold. The warp, I must admit, was heaped up all over the place, but by now I didn't give a damn how much it had piled up. I very much wanted to look at the sea.

'Give it here,' said the trawlmaster.

'What?'

'Give me the spike.'

'There you are. Now get off my back.'

He swung his arm and drove the spike into the deck. It must have gone in two fingers deep; there was no denying he was strong.

'Right. Let's leave it sticking in there.'

'Let's,' I said. 'What's it to do with me?'

'If you don't haul in, I'll stick this spike into your head.'

And he walked over to the winch. From down below he had seemed to me taller than the mast. Now, hands hanging below his knees, he looked just like a bear in oilskins.

Like in a dream I wrenched the spike out of the deck and hurled it at his back. Right at his green back. I didn't want to kill him. I didn't care about anything. But I missed him. The spike buried itself in the planking of the ship's gunwale. You can't get a proper swing when you're sitting down.

Nobody said a word – none of the deckies, nor the mate on watch, who of course had seen it all from the wheelhouse. Also without a word, the trawlmaster went over to the spike and twisted it out of the planking.

He measured how far it had gone in.

'One and half fingers, Senya.'

'Not much. I thought it would be two.'

'Not much, you say?' He came over to me. 'And what if it had hit me? Eh, Senya?'

'Nothing much. You'd be lying there and not twitching.'

His face was a pale purple. He squatted down on his haunches beside me.

'What shall we do with it, Senya? Shall we throw it into the sea?'

'Why? It'll always come in handy.'

'You idiot. Did you really think I'd stick it into your head? I just said that for effect.'

'Well, I just threw it for effect.'

He clicked his tongue and put the spike down beside the hatch-cover.

'Why are we so touchy, Senya? Who made us like this? Khrushchev – that's who. He's always thinking up something new. But in Stalin's day remember ? – there was good order. And every year on the first of April, prices were lowered . . . Those were the days . . . But still you'd better haul in Senya. Don't overdo it, but haul in.'

Then his voice went sharp again.

'Why are you lot standing around like a lot of spare pricks? Come on, help him.'

Seryozha Firstov and Shura rushed over to us. I climbed back into the hold. They gradually passed the warp down to me, length by length, until I had coiled it all.

The trawlmaster said from up above:

'Shall we drink to this, Senya, when we get home?'

I didn't answer. He stood there, clicking his tongue, then went back to the winch. My whole face was burning my hands were shaking.

The nets came inboard – sometimes fast, sometimes slowly, because the shoal was uneven in density, so that I was alternately run off my feet or able to get my breath back. If the warp did start to pile up on deck, the trawlmaster came over to help with it. He would say in a kindly voice: 'The warp's piling up again. Will you haul it in a bit, Senya?'

Or: 'Our warpman seems to have fallen asleep. Will he be cross if we wake him up?'

I said nothing. The layers of warp were building up under my feet and bringing me nearer and nearer to the deckhead. First my cap touched it, then I had to turn my head. The last coil was the hardest of all – it turned out there were altogether eight and not seven – and I was coiling it almost on all fours. Then came the lead-hawser – made of steel. It had a hellish number of kinks that had to be straightened out, and you had to watch out lest a frayed metal strand got driven into the palm of your hand. When the final length whipped through the air, I couldn't believe it was the end. I just held it in my hand – no, there was nothing else fastened to it. The end.

'That's the lot, Senya. Come out into the fresh air.'

The trawlmaster was standing over me and smiling as I climbed up to the deck and almost fell backwards into the hold. He gripped me under the armpits and heaved me out.

I went up to the foc's'le and leaned over the rail, staring into the water. Now I understood why warpmen spent hours staring at the deckhead after coiling a complete warp.

The water was splashing gently against the side, with fish–scales floating in it. Blue water and silvery scales – it's really beautiful, say what you like. I couldn't think of anything more.

'Tired?' asked the trawlmaster.

I only sighed. My tongue wouldn't move to answer him.

The fish-scales circled faster, floated aft, and the water began to stream past the ship's side . . . We were off on the search for more fish.

I replaced the hatch-cover and screwed it down . . . Sooner or later, I thought, I would have to go and help the other deckies. I didn't want to get the reputation of being a skiver; anyway, it's not fair on your shipmates.

The trawlmaster reminded me of it: 'Rest a minute, then go and give the deckies a hand. There's still work to be done on deck.'

8

I knew they hadn't forgotten about me and the marline-spike. The cooper hadn't at least. He was only waiting for an excuse to bring it up.

'Who wants a hand?' I asked, although my hands were not exactly itching to get to work again.

'No need for you to help, Senya,' said the cooper with fake concern. 'You've swung your arm enough for today. A spike's a heavy thing.'

'All depends who you're throwing it at.'

He grinned into his whiskers, sealed a barrel with three hammer-blows and rolled it away.

'If you'd thrown it at me, you'd be lying on the bottom by now.'

'No, I wouldn't. If I'd thrown it at you, I wouldn't have missed.'

After this exchange of pleasantries none of the other deckies said anything more about it. The subject was closed.

The others were no less tired than I was, and they were a lot filthier. At least my work in the hold was clean, but they were covered in fish-scales, slime and blood from head to foot and half a hundredweight of muck was stuck to their boots.

'You're lucky, Senya!' said Vasya Burov enviously. 'Thank your lucky stars. And when it gets cold, you'll be warmer than all of us.'

I looked around – the whole deck was at work, alive with movement. The nets had already been stowed and weighted down with an iron bar, the last fish had been scooped out of them and dumped on the gutting-table, where the fishmaster and the bo'sun, wearing big rubber gauntlets, were salting them and dropping them into barrels at their feet.

The apprentices had begun swabbing down the decks. One swabbed, while the other watered the swab with a hose. It's a job that can be done by one man, so Vasya Burov took Alik by the shoulder and put him on to something else. Vasya has eyes like a hawk and always sees when someone has less than his fair share of work.

The trawlmaster and his mate were busy dealing with the net-winch, which had got jammed. It jams because it was designed on shore, where the deck doesn't roll and the netting doesn't get caught in the ratchet and torn to bits. They dismantled the winch, inspected it, and began putting it together again. Everything seemed to be in order. Tomorrow it would jam once more, and they would dismantle it and check it all over again.

All the others, of course, were at work shifting the barrels. What a job, those barrels! You have to get them out of the hold, knock out their bottoms, hammer down the hoops and douse them with water, so that the wood swells up by next morning. Then they have to be stowed in such a way that they don't upset the ship's trim, and so that they don't fall over and roll around the deck. Even so they do upset the trim, they do make the ship list and they do roll about, because the deck's small, there are a hellish number of barrels, and you never know how many you will need the next day. Seventy barrels are put out in readiness and there isn't room for any more. If there's a good catch, that means a bit of juggling: we have to take out an extra ten empty ones and put ten full of fish in their places – and so on until you're blue in the face. And while we're heaving them about, the ship is under way and the motion wrenches the barrels out of your hands, but the skipper can't wait for a moment: he's looking for tomorrow's fish.

So Alik had a tough time when Vasya landed him with the job of rolling the full barrels into position to be winched down into the hold. Vasya himself took charge of the winch, where you don't need any strength – you just fasten the hooks on to the rims of the barrels and wave your mitt. Rolling full barrels is the worst job of all. You have to grasp the horrible thing with both arms and edge it on its rim out of a narrow space, after which you must then tip it on to its side and roll it over to the hold. Somehow the apprentice managed to edge it out and tip it over, but then it rolled away out of control, first having knocked him off his feet. I was only just able to catch and stop it.

'Did you work in a circus,' I asked, 'or are you just tired of life?'

He was just sitting there, eyes goggling. He hadn't even had time to be frightened, not realizing how it would have ended if the barrel had rolled back on him when the deck tilted. He jumped up and seized another barrel.

'Wait a moment,' I said 'and watch how it's done.'

'Why coddle him?' Shura Chmyrev yelled at me. 'If he gets a few black eyes, he'll learn. Whoever showed me how to do it?

'That's why you're a fool and always will be. Look,' I said to Alik, 'I can roll it with one finger. See? It rolls by itself. Got it?'

He nodded, then tried to do it himself but it tore itself out of his hands.

'Alik!' Dima shouted at him. 'Don't disgrace the basketball team!'

'What the fuck does it matter if he's a basketball-player? You've got to use your head here. You're working on board ship, where everything's a hundred times more difficult, but you make use of the way the ship rolls. You didn't notice you were trying to roll it against the tilt of the deck, which made it harder for you. But I wait, and then the barrel rolls by itself and all you have to do is hold it by the edges. The deck is tilting towards me now, in a moment the barrel will roll back, but I'm standing in its way to see the bugger doesn't go anywhere. And that's the whole course of study.'

He seemed to understand, tried it himself and it worked. He beamed with joy. 'Thanks,' he said.

'Forget it. I don't need your thanks. I just want to make sure you get back home alive.'

Together we quickly rolled all the barrels, and he got so enthusiastic that he wanted to do more work on deck.

'Is that all?' he asked.

I was suprised; he'd been shown how to do one job, but with any other he'd be useless. He could see the hold was not covered with the hatch-planks, and the tarpaulin was lying alongside.

'So are we going to go on sailing with an open hatch?' I asked.

His ears burned.

We laid all the hatch-planks, covered them with the tarpaulin, and he started wedging it into position.

'Have you ever held a beetle?'

'What's a beetle?'

'What's in your hand.'

'Ah! A hammer?'

'Give it here. And go below to the cabin.'

Zhora the mate shouted to me from the wheelhouse: 'Tell him to bugger off and do it yourself.'

Alik looked at me and I felt very bad. There were almost tears in his eyes. Yes – why was I giving him such a hard time?

'Go and get washed, I'll manage without you.'

He stood there with his hands in his pockets but didn't go away. He watched me driving in the wedges. Beside him was another beetle and some wedges – yet it never occurred to him to pick them up.

'What are you standing there for, like a dummy?'

'Listen,' he said to me, 'I used to think you were different from the others. Or so I thought. But you're just as much a brute as they are. It's a pity, chief. Spare your nerves, at least. What pleasure is there in yelling at someone?'

I stood up too: 'Not much. But it's no bad thing if I shout. Because when I'm well and truly fed up with you, I won't say a word to you – will that be better?'

'You ought to know – yes, I suppose it will.'

He bit his lip and went. Honestly, I felt sorry for him. At the same time I hated him – since yesterday evening. Well, OK, so I am a brute. But why does a man have to try and take on a job that's not his?

Everyone else had gone below. Thanks to this apprentice, I was the only one left. And it's fatal to stay behind on deck.

'Hey, what's your name? Shalai?' It was Zhora the mate shouting at me. 'Who left that hose lying there?'

'Who left it? Whoever was watering the barrels.'

'Ah, that thick-headed apprentice. Stow it away, will you?'

I went and stowed it away. While I was doing this, he found me something else to do.

'Look at that barrel over there on the port side, the sixth in the row.'

'Well?'

'Lash it down, to be on the safe side, otherwise it may roll.'

That was Vasya Burov's little gift, the idle bugger.

'And they haven't lashed down the gutting–table.'

Everyone else had galloped off to their dinner and here was I, still hard at work. So much for Alik's 'Is that all?' Finally I begged: 'Zhora, there's no end to this deck-work. And I'm due for my trick at the wheel.'

He waved his hand. 'Got and eat. Tell the bo'sun to come and see me.'

While I was taking my oilskins off and washing, the saloon filled to bursting. It happens quickly; nobody wants to crowd up along the bulkhead, so there's only room for eight people at the table. On top of that, there always has to be one of the mates or engineers taking his time over his meal – as if they couldn't find some other time to eat.

This time it was the Third Mate who was sitting there. He was finishing his stewed fruit in a leisurely fashion, spitting the pips into his spoon – no doubt they taught him that at Nautical Academy. They get special lectures there on how to behave in society.

There he sat, while we squeezed ourselves up against the bulkhead.

To cap it all he said: 'You lot shouldn't get any dinner today, you've caught so little fish. Eleven barrels – call that a catch?'

'And who was looking for it?' asked Shura. 'You were on watch.'

'The echo-sounder looks for it, not me.'

All said in fun, of course. Only you shouldn't try to be funny when everyone's fed up with slaving over a catch that turns out to be a thin one.

'That's true enough,' the trawlmaster said to him. 'But the echo-sounder also needs brains to use it.'

The mate froze with his spoon in mid-air and slowly began to turn pale.

'I don't get you. Say that again, please.'

The trawlmaster repeated what he had said, and added something about some people on board taking the bread out of other people's mouths.

'Yours, do you mean?'

'Mine, among others.'

'Please, do me a favour. In front of witnesses. Exactly who are you referring to?'

With an effort, the trawlmaster kept silent. Someone was squeezing his elbow and treading on his toes to shut him up.

The cooper, though, had to say his piece: 'You shouldn't blow your top like that, Sergeyich. You can see people have just come in from a catch and they're dog-tired. It's easy enough for someone to let slip an unnecessary remark, without meaning it for anyone in particular. And you have to take it personally.'

Some peacemaker, our cooper. There's a snake inside him with enough venom to poison us all, and as soon as he sniffs a row brewing he sticks his oar in with that fake-kindly grin on his face.

The Third Mate went to the door and said: 'Well, I won't add any more unnecessary remarks. But I regard it as my duty to bring what was said here to the attention of the captain.'

'Go ahead, split on us.' Again the trawlmaster couldn't restrain himself. 'You're good at it.'

As soon as the door slammed behind the mate, Vasya Burov added: 'What can you expect from Sergeyich the Jackal? He's sailing on someone else's mate's ticket.'

And off they went on that subject.

'What d'you mean – on someone else's ticket?'

'He stole it, I suppose.'

'No he didn't steal it, he bought it on the black market, all signed and sealed. All he had to do was write in his own name.'

Dima had been listening to all this, smiling and exchanging looks with Alik. Then he said: 'What a charming bunch you are, you beachers! You fascinate me, because I can't understand what binds you all together. It's not friendship, it's not affection, it's not even because you're simply used to each other. Nothing but backbiting. And you expend all your energy on it. Suppose something made you all join forces against someone else – would you have enough energy left?'

They were all looking at him with angry looks. And saying nothing.

'That's enough.' Vasya the cook intervened. 'Go and fight somewhere else.'

He lugged in a whole panful of fried cod and tipped it on to sheets of newspaper on the table. We'd caught four codfish that day, and while we were working on the catch he had kept them overboard on a length of twine. Only now had he tossed them alive into the frying-pan – because, as our First Mate from Volokolamsk used to say: 'Your damned codfish ought to be eaten when it's in a state of clinical death.' And at that, of course, all arguments ceased. What happened afterwards I don't know, because it was time for me to take the wheel.

9

I relieved Gesha, the trawlmaster's mate. Gesha has a gold wrist-watch
that he doesn't even take off when the catch is being hauled in, and he
always thinks he's standing watch too long.

'Why didn't you come in a hour's time?' he asked. 'You're too early.'

'I know I'm early,' I said, 'but the cook has fried some cod, and I was
afraid there might not be any left for you.'

'Course seventy degrees. Wheel handed over.'

'Seventy degrees it is. Wheel taken over.'

I stood there for some time before anyone came to relieve Zhora the
mate. The Third Mate was due to come on watch with me and he's never
late, because he's afraid of Zhora. He's afraid of both Zhora and the
captain. Well, he's not exactly afraid of them, but he's always trying to find
out why he isn't sailing as First Mate instead of Flat-Nose.

The Third Mate arrived – frowning, red in the face, with only his scar
showing white.

'Dead on time, Konstantin Sergeyich.' Zhora always addresses him
formally, although the Third Mate is younger than him and junior in rank.
'Course seventy degrees, the herring have all gone to a dance. If you see a
shark, give it my love. Adieu!'

The Third Mate walked across the wheelhouse and went into the
chart–room – the echo-sounder was making a pinging noise – and from
there he asked: 'What's your course?'

'Seventy degrees.'

'Alter course to seventy-five.'

'All right.'

'Not "all right", but "Seventy-five it is". I'll never teach you peasants.
Can't expect any seamanlike efficiency from you lot.'

He came back on to the bridge and lowered a window. Just then the
trawlmaster was walking past on deck – hands in his belt, the backs of his
oilskin trousers gleaming, the top of one sea boot turned inside out to show

the yellow lining and a knife stuck in it. Fisherman's chic.

The Third Mate spat on the deck and turned to me 'How do you feel about him threatening you with a marline-spike?'

'Who threatened anybody?'

'Don't be dodgy. Did he threaten you with a spike or didn't he?'

'I threatened him too. I even threw it at him.'

'That's nothing to be proud of, either. But he started it. Everyone saw him.'

'OK. It's forgotten now.'

'Ha! D'you think he's forgotten you?'

'How do I know? I've forgotten what he did.'

'Well, you're a fool. These things always have consequences.'

'His job makes him tense.'

'And is your job all peace and calm? He's paid more for his work than you are.'

I didn't want to get drawn into their quarrel. It wasn't going to end here. Like my quarrel with the cooper. We'd taken a dislike to each other – so the best thing to do was to transfer to different ships and not to bring it all into the open.

'Listen, Sergeyich, I'm not going to complain to the skipper. I prefer my own method.'

'It's the wrong method, you know. You only untie his hands. It fosters the wrong sort of relationships in the fleet, don't you see? Did you hear how he shot his mouth off in the saloon?'

I said nothing. If I let him, he would keep harping on his argument for the whole watch.

'What course are you keeping?'

'Eighty degrees.'

'And what course did I give you?'

'Seventy-five.'

'What are you up to? Get back on the right course!'

He watched as I adjusted the course. Why did he have to bother? We were on search, combing the sea. Then he got bored with watching. He obviously wanted to talk.

'How many years' schooling did you have?'

'Seven.'

'You see? And our friend Fishface only had four. Yet he bawls at you and threatens you.'

I said nothing.

'Why the hell are you wasting your time as a deckie? You should go to the Nautical Academy.'

I nodded. If that's what pleased him, I would agree.

'I'm serious. Do you really like sitting around in the foc's'le with seven others and listening to their illiterate twaddle? The trawlmaster, the bo'sun – they're all the same. But you've got a bright head on your shoulders.'

I laughed. Wherever did he get that idea from?

'Why do you laugh? You should be crying. You'll suffocate to death in that cabin. I predict that for certain.'

'The Chief's been telling me the same thing. Only he says I'll end my days in a ditch. And he wants me to qualify as a ship's engineer.'

'Don't listen to the Chief. The Chief, well . . . Although in general he's right. But you'd do better to work for your mate's ticket. You know all your stuff already. And when you've got your ticket, there's nothing more to do – understand?'

'No.'

'But don't you see? All you do is stand watch, and the other sixteen hours out of the twenty-four are your own, you can spit on everyone from the masthead. When you buy yourself an officer's mackintosh and put on a peaked cap, you feel you're somebody. I can see you want to better yourself – that's why you bought that jacket. So imagine you're a mate: you wear a naval mackintosh, and a white scarf, you take taxis, you go to restaurants and you enjoy yourself like a gentleman. People respect you. It's no good dithering and havering in life. You have to be a hard man, got it?'

'Ah.'

'What's your course?'

'Seventy-two.'

'Back on course! And all those other clowns – you despise them, see? They're not worth more. You have to put them in their place. Coldly and sharply, see?'

'I see. Got to be a hard man.'

'That's it! Now hold that course.'

The echo-sounder began squealing again. The Third Mate ran out, then came back and spat on the deck. He had a way of spitting slowly that was very impressive.

'Are you married?'

'Not yet.'

'You don't say? You're worth your weight in gold. Footloose and fancy free. I'm paying one slag twenty-five per cent of my pay-warrant, I'm just breaking loose from another, and I'm having a row with a third – but there's a kid from her, you see. What a kid – he's a knockout! "My daddy's a fird mate," he says. He's just like me in character, I don't even mind paying maintenance for him. He'll be a hard man. As long as she doesn't spoil him. That's what I'm afraid of.'

The door banged and the skipper came in, wearing a cap, a quilted jerkin and those little soft, thin leather boots that Caucasian dancers wear. You can't walk about the deck in those things – but captains sometimes don't go down on deck for weeks on end. In his peaked cap he had a determined look, a real seaman; like that, you couldn't tell he was as bald as an egg. First he glanced at the echo-sounder, then at the compass. He frowned.

'What course is he steering? Looks as if you're a destroyer zigzagging to depth-charge a submarine.'

'Keep on course!' said the Third Mate. 'What's the matter with you – pissed?'

It was useless to argue. They knew as well as I did that the compass-card never stays still for a second. You can only keep roughly on course. But he has to grumble about something.

'Stop zigzagging,' the skipper said to me.

'I'm not.'

'I know you're not – the ship is.'

'No zigzagging it is.'

Thank God the echo-sounder squealed again. Both of them rushed to look at it.

'Might be worth a cast,' said the Third Mate.

'What about the depth, though? The weather's light at the moment, and the fish, you can see, are keeping to the bottom. But by tonight, God knows how far up they'll come.'

They came back to the bridge.

'That Norwegian over there is trawling,' the mate remarked. 'Should we ask him how deep his nets are?'

'I'll give you "ask"! Think up something better.'

'What – won't they answer?'

'It's not done, that's all.'

The Norwegian was all orange and gold, with a snow–white wheelhouse. The lifeboats and doghouses were painted the same colour as the sides. On deck, two men in gleaming black oilskins were leaning on the rail and watching us sail past them. Why not ask them, anyway? I've asked them before and they always answer. All you have to do is go out on to the flying bridge, point downwards and make a question-mark in the air. Every Norwegian will immediately show you, by holding up his fingers, how deep their nets are. It's no skin off his nose, it it?

'Let's check for ourselves,' said the skipper.

'It's embarrassing, skipper. I'd feel awkward.'

'It's awkward putting your trousers on over your head.'

The mate reduced speed to 'slow' on the engine-room telegraph and went to watch the echo-sounder. Off to starboard the Norwegian's floats were bobbing on the wave-tops, a red chain stretching for half a mile. They have shorter trawls than ours, but then their ships are smaller too.

'More to starboard,' said the skipper. 'Can you steer between their floats?'

'I'll try.'

'You won't just "try": you must not hit them.'

It's always done like this when you have to pass over someone else's trawl, but I was certain the Norwegians realized we were doing it to check the depth of the nets. Why else had we altered course? The two men on deck exchanged amused glances. Even the skipper was embarrassed.

The echo-sounder squealed and then was silent. That meant we had passed over their nets.

'Eighty,' said the Third Mate.

'There you are, you see,' said the skipper. 'There was no need to ask them.'

The Norwegians looked at us and grinned.

'Give her full ahead,' said the skipper.

The mate pushed the handle of the telegraph, but someone was already overhauling us to starboard as if we were standing still. White letters on a blue side flashed past. The mate was reading the name:

'"Girl Peggy. Scotland."'

'A Scotsman, you mean,' said the skipper. 'And you said "Scotland". You can tell your mate's ticket's not your own.'

The Third Mate's face went blotchy.

'She's moving fast enough,' the skipper said enviously. 'And she's only got a car-engine.'

'But she has a good tackle.'

'That tackle's a dream.'

The Scottish vessel overtook us – proud and graceful as a swan. We watched her stern with its lifeboats hanging in davits, painted the same glossy blue as her sides. Out of her galley came the cook, wearing white hat and apron, and carrying a bucket. He looked at us, shouted back to someone through the door and threw his garbage over the stern, right in our path.'Cheeky,' said the skipper. 'Cheeky devils. And you wanted to ask them.'

'Not them. The Norwegians.'

'They're all the same. Stinking aristocrats.'

Marconi came out of the radio cabin on to the bridge. With a crafty smile on his face he watched the Scots ship moving away, then said casually: 'Radio signal for you, Nikolayich.'

The skipper glared at him. 'From that one? From *Peggy*?'

'Uh-huh.'

'Why did you take it?'

'Just happened to.'

The skipper took it with two fingers, as if it was a razor blade.

'They're playing kids' games; "IVAN. NO HERRING HERE. CALL A KOMSOMOL MEETING." They might at least think up something new.'

He crumpled it up and threw it overboard out of the window.

'Don't give me any more of those. I suppose you've nothing better to do.'

'What could I do?' Marconi winked at me. 'They tuned in on the Soviet captains' conference, they know the wavelength.'

'That's a lie. You tuned in to *their* wavelength.'

'You can check that.'

The skipper glanced at his watch. Sure enough, it was five o'clock, the start of the captains' radio conference. He went into the radio cabin, where he could be heard booming away: 'This is number eight-one-five calling. Good evening, comrades. Today we made our first cast. Thin catch, eleven barrels. Depth sixty metres. Today I'm thinking of casting to eighty. I have a suggestion . . .'

He came out looking gloomy, paced up and down the wheelhouse, then took another glance at the echo-sounder: 'It's still registering . . . Nothing but small stuff, though. Or plankton. OK, I'm going back to my cabin. Call me when anything worthwhile shows up. And mind you keep a proper eye on it, instead of spending all your time lecturing him . . .'

How had he heard our conversation? No doubt through the speaking-tube to his cabin. Although it's plugged up with a whistle, you can hear through that if you put your ear close to it.

'I'm not the one who's lecturing him,' said the mate. 'It's the Chief – trying to persuade him to become an engineer.'

The skipper tapped his forehead with his finger – I could see him out of the corner of my eye.

'Anything to keep the kiddies happy . . .'

He was about to go, then turned back, scratching his cheek: 'By the way, that Scotsman has given me an idea – we *should* call a meeting. There are a few questions to discuss.'

'So was there some point in my giving you that signal after all?' asked Marconi.

The skipper lost his temper: 'You stick to your job, Linkov. Study your apparatus, raise your qualifications. You're just playing kids' games too.'

Later I asked: 'Why doesn't he like the Chief?'

'Who likes anybody?' said Marconi.

'Keep on course,' said the mate. 'You've veered off to starboard. Don't.'

We spoke no more.

Then I was relieved, and went to see my seagull. He'd managed to eat his herring, and had crapped a bit, of course. I cleaned him up and scrounged him a few more herring out of the scuppers; some fish always end up there and no amount of hosing-down will wash them out.

Tommy looked at this feast, swallowed one at once and covered the rest with his wing. He was no longer afraid of me at all, didn't bury his head in his feathers when I stretched out my hand to him. But his wing was still bad; when I brushed it slightly by mistake, he screamed and tried to back away. Then he glared at me angrily, just waiting for me to go. Our friendship was shattered . . .

10

We held a meeting that same day. Not a Komsomol meeting, but an all-hands ship's meeting. We still couldn't find any fish, and the skipper decided not to waste the time.

We assembled in the saloon – where else? Well, on a fine day in summer meetings can be held on deck, but otherwise the saloon is the biggest space on board. It's almost completely taken up by the table and two benches; at one end is a film projector and facing it a sheet stretched out as a screen. In the door into the galley there's a little hatch, through which the cook passes bowls and mugs to the cabin-boy, and the galley crew watch the films through it.

We crammed ourselves in, everyone except the men on watch. The skipper read us his report: this trip would last a hundred and five days, during which time we would go to the factory-ship five times, discharge five loads and the sixth load we would take back to port. Our overall target figure was three hundred tons; for reaching the target, the premium would be twenty per cent, for each ton over target – two per cent of the premium . . . On every trip we listen to this very carefully.

'Well now, men, it's up to you to say – how much tonnage over target shall we aim for?'

We were silent. Deeply silent. Then Shura spoke up; he was sitting beside the film-projector and twiddling the reel. On the other side, Seryozha was also playing with the reel.

'Depends on what the catches are like,' said Shura.

'But we must undertake to aim for a specific figure.'

Silence again. Vasya Burov asked to speak, and plunged straight in, as if diving into the water: 'Three hundred and one tons!'

The skipper grinned.

'Only one ton over target? Well, Burov, you're not planning to give the country much fish!'

'All right, if that's too little, then say four hundred. Only we won't catch that much.'

Zhora the mate, who'd been elected secretary, resolved our doubts: 'What are we arguing about? Last trip we undertook to make it three hundred and twenty, and we caught three hundred and five. So what? We're the same men we were before, we haven't got any thinner.'

So we voted for three hundred and five. The skipper didn't argue and it was written into the minutes.

'Kindly note, however,' said the skipper, 'that if we continue to get catches like today's, it's obvious that we'll end up with figures well below target.'

This was just what the trawlmaster was waiting for. 'It doesn't depend on us. We, for our part, put our backs into it. But who searches for our fish? The mates. And they should use the latest scientific methods of searching, so that we don't cast for practically nothing, as happened yesterday.'

The Third Mate was fidgeting on the bench and his scar had turned white. 'We staked out exactly as much as we found. Therefore there were no bigger shoals.'

The trawlmaster didn't look at him. 'I have a question on that point.'

'Put your question,' said the skipper.

The trawlmaster beamed, his face positively glowing: 'Some mates here are sailing without mates' tickets. Can I trust them when they're on the bridge? Can I trust them with my own life – or with the fish?'

'Do you have someone in mind?'

'Let him speak and the meeting will listen.'

Everyone looked at the Third Mate. He stood up, red in the face. 'Who told you, you bumpkin, that I haven't got a certificate? I can show it to you.'

'I don't want someone else's, I want to see yours.'

'Cherpakov,' the skipper said, 'what's all this about your certificate?'

'Yes,' said the trawlmaster, 'explain it to the meeting.'

'I have a certificate. Only I don't have the record of my exam results.'

'Have you lost it?' asked the trawlmaster.

'I haven't lost it. I left it in port.'

The trawlmaster roared: 'I ask for that to be put in the minutes! He hasn't got his exam results with him.'

'Stop nit-picking. I only have two more exams to take.'

'Please put that in the minutes! Two exams not taken. How did you pass out if you hadn't taken them?'

'Well, they did pass me out. I promised to take the exams later. I had to leave to go on a trip, so they allowed me to pass.'

'How much did you give them? A litre? Or a litre and a half?'

'Mind your own business, peasant.'

'Cherpakov,' said the skipper to the Third Mate. 'You will kindly take those exams as a matter of urgency. Which subjects haven't you taken?'

'Russian literature essay. And maritime practice. As soon as we get back to port, I'll take them.'

The trawlmaster hit out again: 'No, not in port. We've all got to sail with you before we reach port, and entrust our lives to you. You can take the exams on the factory-ship. There are instructors on board.'

'I have to prepare for them.'

'Well then, prepare. You can get down to it after you've stood your watch. And no kipping and no watching films. Resist all temptations, take your exams, and the whole crew will be glad.'

The skipper said: 'You must do it, Cherpakov. Which one will you take first?'

'The harder one. The literature essay.'

The trawlmaster burst out: 'Please enter that in the minutes! On our first call at the factory–ship he will take the literature essay, on the second call – maritime practice.'

All this was entered in the minutes. Sitting there like a beaten man, the Third Mate said to the trawlmaster: 'So you've got your way, you peasant.'

'I'm not doing this for myself. It's for the good of the whole crew.'

'All right,' said the skipper. 'Who's next? Shipboard living conditions? Well, on the question of living conditions . . . I must honestly say that some aspects of life on board are terrible . . . I came into the saloon today, and there was Chmyrev telling Burov some story and mixing in more four-letter words than a pre-revolutionary cab-driver. This is our saloon, after all, there are certain portraits on the bulkheads; it's not a cobbler's workshop.'

'So what?' said Shura. 'It's more expressive!'

'All right – but without *those* expressions. Just because we have no women on board, we forget how to control our behaviour. I make a personal suggestion – that we refrain from using obscene language.'

Another deep silence.

'Captain,' said the trawlmaster, 'even you yourself sometimes, on the bridge . . .'

'And you must stop me when I do. Anyway, that's on the bridge and not in the saloon.'

'I have a proposal.' Vasya Burov held up his hand. 'Write in the minutes: in order to create a healthier atmosphere, we won't swear out of working hours.'

'Why only "out of working hours"?'

'It won't work anyway, captain, so why pass a useless resolution?'

The skipper brushed him aside. 'We will not put that in the minutes. Write in the minutes: "No swearing at all." We really must keep our tongues in check.'

We voted in favour of this.

'Now about the ship's wall-newspaper,' said Zhora. 'We must produce one, even if only a few times.'

Seryozha said glumly, still turning the reel of the projector: 'Give that job to the apprentices. They've had more schooling that the rest of us.'

'Well?' said the skipper. 'That's reasonable. Only they're not apprentices but young seamen. Do they agree?'

'We'll do it,' said Dima. 'Alik here is good at writing slogans.'

'Good. Design a better masthead for the paper than usual. And we must think up a suitable title, something that sounds good.'

'I know,' said Shura, '"For a Good Catch!"'

The skipper frowned. 'Couldn't we have something a bit more original? Any suggestions?'

'"For a Good Catch!"' Shura insisted. 'It's what we go to sea for, isn't it?'

We voted: 'For a Good Catch!' it was. At that the meeting peacefully broke up.

11

'It's blowing a gale, boys,' the First Mate announced to cheer us up next morning. 'And it's up with the nets.'

We in the foc's'le already knew about the gale; we'd been tossed from side to side in our bunks for half the night. No doubt there had been a long dicussion with the skipper about hauling in, because for some reason they hadn't woken us before first light, as they usually did.

My apprentices wanted to know how strong the gale was. Officially it was Force 7½, but you could count on that meaning Force 8.

'When I signed on,' Alik recalled with a smile, 'I was made to sign an undertaking that I wouldn't go on deck in anything over Force 6. It's simply forbidden.'

'That's right,' said Dima in confirmation. 'Why do they make such strict rules, I wonder?'

We were all silent as we got dressed. How could I answer their question? We all sign that undertaking before each trip, yet sometimes we work in a Force 9 gale. The cook is not supposed to prepare hot meals in anything above Force 6, but only to issue dry rations instead; yet he does cook. No one ever thinks of those bits of paper when we're at sea, otherwise we'd never reach our target figure – because the fish don't sign those forms, but they catch like fury in a gale. Come to think of it, the fish are right, too – otherwise our job wouldn't be work but a piece of cake. And it's supposed to be like hard labour in Siberia.

The horizon was completely covered with streaky cloud like strips of muslin, the other ships could hardly be seen, and even our own was half invisible behind a curtain of spray. I looked out of the warp-hold; like green toy soldiers, the others were all standing at their posts, shoulders hunched like condemned men, only their oilskins gleaming. You couldn't recognize them under their sou'westers; they all looked alike, with exactly the same expression on all their faces – they'd rather be dead.

This time my work was a bit easier, because the nets were heavy, it took a long time to shake them out and the warp moved slowly. I remembered what Vasya Burov had said: 'You're warmer than anyone else down in your hold.' Except when water came over the hatch and down the back of my neck. But with the fourth net the trawlmaster looked down at me and said:'Come on out, Senya, and help with the shaking.'

That was fair enough – when you're working on deck there's nothing worse than seeing someone else sitting down having a smoke. Even if he's done his job, the mere sight of him makes you wild. So it was an extra irritation that just then Marconi, the First Mate and the engineers were going on 'watch below'. Not that they can be much help; they can only scoop up the fish we kick in their direction, then carry them in nets over to the gutting-table, and none of them ever lends a hand with the shaking. And shaking is the toughest work of all.

I was standing by the net-winch. The net came out of the sea like a wide strip full of fish, all silver and twitching. Seryozha and the trawlmaster's mate made it fast to the ratchets on the winch-drums by the edge-line, at the same time pulling it inboard from the middle with the fluted roller; then with all the fish-heads pointing upwards the net was hauled inboard across the roller and straight into our arms.

You grip the net by the edge-line or by some other part of it where there aren't any fish, using both hands, and then – up with it above your head, your whole body strains and aches with the weight of it, the wind blows fish-scales and slime into your face and makes your eyes sting: then over and down in one jerk, and the fish crash down around your feet, their fins and heads get torn off, their blood spurts all over you. You never shake them all out at once, but that's not your concern – you only have two shakes and there's no time for a third; you lower it half a metre or so then grip it again with both hands, and – up, and – over and down. First your shoulders go numb and your back burns as if it's on fire, you're almost glad when water spills down the back of your neck. Then your hands start to lose feeling. By now you're up to your knees in fish, there's no time to push them away, and when you do manage to do it, a wave comes and washes the whole lot from the gunwale to the hold-coaming, and takes us with it, throwing us against the net-winch, against each other, and there's no foothold because you're standing in something like a quagmire. And if the fish are in roe, you slip on it like soap and there's nothing to hold on to except the net.

We were covered in fish-scales up to the eyebrows, our oilskins were no longer green but greyish-pink, our boots silvered and bloodstained. Most amazing of all, at such times we still managed to grab a smoke – one or two drags, then you put your Belomor into your mitten and passed it on to someone else, otherwise it got wet and sticky – and we even chatted about this and that. I could hear Vasya Burov telling one of his fairy stories: 'Once upon a time there lived a handsome prince and he loved a beautiful fisher-girl . . .'

The bo'sun was telling a joke (I won't repeat it), which Gesha, the trawlmaster's mate took a long time to catch; he only started laughing when everyone else had finished, so they laughed all over again at him.

Later they got me up on deck to help with the final shake. This job seems like pure paradise after the big shaking – the net by now is much lighter, with only five or six herring to the square metre still caught in it, together with a few severed fish-heads. These are easy enough to remove by shaking or picking them out by hand, and there's plenty of time for it. Then the net passes over the roller under the derrick-boom and is laid in folds on the port side of the deck. There three men roll it up – one in the middle, holding it with his feet, and two at each end gripping it by the edge-lines. This is not so much work as a sheer rest-cure, just as it is for those whose job it is to untie the standing-lines and hang them on the shrouds; you can even sit down on the net while they bring you the next one. They put you on this work when you're worn out from shaking. Everyone, that is, except the warpman; he has to go back into the hold.

By lunchtime we had only hauled in twenty nets. And there are ninety-six of them. Or ninety-eight. It's never an odd number. I don't know why. They say the fish like even numbers and keep away from odd numbers; some kind of superstition, I suppose. We have lots of superstitions. They also say the fish don't like a round hundred, so it has to be a hundred and two or a hundred and four.

The deck was crammed with barrels. How many would we fill today – three hundred, four hundred? We had long since lost count. All we could do was shake the nets till we were numb and all wet under our oilskins – until the cook hailed us from the galley: 'Crew to dinner!'

We shook and scooped fish and rolled out barrels for another five minutes before the message sank in.

The trawlmaster stopped us: 'Stand fast, lads, don't take your oilskins off. We'll eat in shifts, in the stern-sheets. Otherwise we won't get it all in before nightfall.'

In fact, if we went on till it was time for the 'watch below', we wouldn't get it all in either. Four men went to eat, while we stayed behind to carry on salting, sealing barrels and stowing them in the hold. Our feet and hands had lost all feeling, and we were just angry at everything and everybody, so angry that we were silent. Once only, when I rolled a barrel over the toe of his boot, did the cooper say to me: 'When are you going to die?'

He asked it in an indifferent monotone, as though without malice. I knew, though, that when people ask that sort of question in that kind of voice the most terrible things can happen.

'On the day after your funeral,' I said.

That at least shut him up.

Then the other four returned and relieved us. We didn't even wipe ourselves down, didn't wash our hands or boots – but clambered over the barrels towards the stern-sheets. We sat down on bollards – Vanya Obod, the apprentices and myself. There you don't get sprayed or dripped on, but you have to sit tight in order not to fall off. The cook brought us *borshch* in bowls, which we put on our knees and ate in silence, looking at the sea.

A killer whale was skimming through the waves, its grey belly flashing right under the stern and breathing noisily through its black blowhole. The cook threw it a loaf of black bread – to tempt it away from our herring. Otherwise, if it took fright it might easily tear our nets to shreds until it got free.

As we watched it our minds somehow wandered with it. The cook poured *kasha* and salt beef into our bowls, then brought us each a mug of stewed fruit. And that was it; time to go back on deck again.

The apprentices wanted to stop a while longer for a smoke. Alik said: 'Just give us time for a breather.'

'You can rest when you get back to mother,' was Vanya's answer.

'What sort of job is it where you can't take a smoke-break? It's a sacred custom.'

'It's this job,' I told him. 'Our job – fishing. And there's nothing sacred about a smoke-break. The sooner you get that into your head, the easier life will be for you.'

Dima said: 'Come on, Alik, let's go. There is something sacred – the word of our good chief.'

He seemed to have understood. You can, of course, find ways to sneak a bit of time off work, but afterwards you'll find it a hundred times harder, because you get out of the rhythm. It's better to drive yourself on until you're half-dead, then collapse on your bunk, rather than break the work up with smoke-breaks.

The fish had all been scooped up and the decks cleaned, and the others were waiting for us.

'OK, back to your places,' said the trawlmaster, 'and let's start hauling in another one.'

Nobody noticed when he had found time to eat.

After the meal, Zhora the mate was relieved and the Third Mate came on watch. Before long a row started between him and the trawlmaster.

It began with the shark. Five or six of the buggers were cruising round us; they could smell the mass of fish. They don't just grab fish out of the nets; they bite huge chunks out of the mesh itself and make holes so big you can't patch them. Herring-sharks are only a bit over a metre in length, but they're hellish greedy and nothing will stop them.

The Third Mate came out on to the flying bridge and began shooting at them with a rocket-pistol. A rocket hit one of them right in the mouth – you could see it explode between his teeth. The shark only blinked, dived, and surfaced again, alive and well.

While the Third Mate was shooting ineffectually at the sharks, the trawlmaster was watching him and getting hot under the collar. Then he asked: 'Are we going to keep shooting, or get under way and straighten out the trawl?'

Straightening out the trawl would have been useful, because wind and wave tend to bunch it up. This is even worse than sharks, because it then takes an age to pull it apart and disentangle it.

For some reason the Third Mate turned obstinate. 'Who is the mate on watch? You or me?'

'I'm saying we need to go astern for a while.'

'And I say you're interfering in matters outside you competence.'

The trawlmaster came and stood amidships, facing the wheelhouse. 'I'm asking you nicely – get under way!'

In fact, he wasn't asking but bawling, his mouth as wide open as the shark's. For a moment I though the mate might shoot a rocket into it.

'And I'm telling *you* nicely – you're sailing too close to the wind, got it?'

'Will you get under way or not?' Now the trawlmaster was yelling like a madman. 'Otherwise I'll send the whole fucking crew below!'

'Who are you shouting at, blockhead? Who are you talking to like that in front of the whole crew? You're talking to the mate!'

'I don't see a mate. I see an idle bugger. You've got one scar already – watch out, or I'll give you another one in a moment just to even it up.'

'You'll regret that!'

'I'll say what I like!'

'The captain will make you change your tune!'

'I'll sing the same tune to the captain!'

All of us had stopped work and were watching them as they barked in the freshening wind. It was beginning to blow up a storm and they were being lashed with spray, but the row was only just starting to hot up. It was a welcome breather for us deckies, and a sort of entertainment, too, in a way. We had lit up, and a trickle of smoke was coming out of each man's sleeve.

They might have kept up this slanging match for a long time if the skipper hadn't come into the wheelhouse. At once both of them shut up, there was peace and calm again on board. The trawlmaster went back to his winch and the mate, of course, started to get the ship under way to straighten out the trawl.

The trawlmaster said hoarsely: 'Keep slaving, lads, till teatime. We've taken a hell of a lot of fish on board today.'

We had tea in shifts, too, sitting on bollards, then we went on hauling in till dinner, and it kept on and on, net after net, each one solid as a silvery fur coat. Darkness fell, the searchlights were switched on, but there was still no end to the damn' thing . . .

When it did finish, it seemed to happen suddenly, when no one was expecting it. The warp came to an end, the last net, the last barrel was stowed in the hold.

I don't know what hour of the night it was when I finally closed the hatch over the hold. As I wedged the tarpaulin fast, I kept hitting my fingers with the beetle, but I felt no pain, as if even the pain in me was exhausted.

Then, I remember, as I was going into the doghouse, a wave hit me. I held on to the bolt of the door and stood on one leg to empty the water out of my boot. I must have poured out a gallon, then the same amount out of the other one. Another wave caught my first boot, and I had to run after it barefoot. I picked it up and threw both boots down the companion-way, not even thinking I might hit somebody with them.

In the cabin they were already asleep, having just dropped their oilskins on the deck. I took off my own and crawled into my bunk wearing my quilted jerkin. Then I saw that Dima was struggling to pull the oilskin trousers and boots off the sleeping Alik. I climbed down again to help Dima, but I don't remember whether we pulled off those oilskins or not.

An hour later we were woken up – to cast the nets again.

It went on like that for four days, those damn' fish – three hundred and fifty, four hundred barrels per trawl. Every day it blew a gale tossing us about in our bunks so that we slept badly. Then it suddenly stopped; we didn't haul in empty nets, but the catch just wasn't anything like those four days. The echo-sounder was picking them up, big cigar shaped shoals were passing under our keel, but somehow they didn't go into the nets.

At about two o'clock in the afternoon I finished coiling the last length of warp and climbed out. The deck was all wet and grey, and then suddenly it turned yellow from a burst of sunlight. Feathery clouds were sailing overhead, against the wind, pointing to a change in the weather, and the sea was just a little choppy, blue-green with white horses. You could survive this.

And I could survive the warp, too. It wasn't that I'd got used to it – you never get used to it – but simply that I was getting the knack: when to 'move my ears'; when to take care that it didn't knock you over as it flew off the winch; when to hold it back; to listen out in time for the next net being hauled it; and when you could come up on deck for a smoke in full view of others without getting yelled at.

'Well, how's it going, Senya?' asked the trawlmaster. 'Have you got on top of that warp?'

'More or less.'

'When we're heading for home, you'll have plenty of time to coil it – all the way from the fishing-grounds to port.'

He was right – I reckoned I'd have a passage of two thousand miles in which to do the job.

I spat and went to work on the barrels. At least it made a change.

12

That day our mail and some films were delivered by the *Medusa*, another DWT of our flotilla; she had left port a week after us.

The cooper prepared an empty barrel, while Seryozha stood by with a boathook. He had acquired the job of projectionist and, when necessary, of salvageman, his job being to pick up the mail or things like a lost float, which would be put in the so-called 'Komsomol moneybox' – a locker reserved for objects fished out of the water.

The *Medusa* hove-to about fifteen metres away from us and the two skippers did a little bartering: 'How are things?' – that was from the *Medusa*.

'OK, thanks, and how are things with you?' our skipper replied. 'We've got two spy films and that other one . . . what d'you call it? . . .'

The trawlmaster cupped his hands into the megaphone: '*Beware Automobile!*'

A short conference ensued on the other ship. The *Medusa* answered: 'We'll take what you've got.'

'And what have *you* got?'

'One spy film, but it's a double-length feature. And a foreign film about a carnival. With music and singing.'

The skipper looked at us. I thought I'd seen that film in port, and said: 'It's not bad. Good fun.'

The skipper put the megaphone to his mouth: 'OK, let's swap!'

They sealed their barrel, threw it overboard, and stood off. We moved over, grabbed the barrel with a boathook and threw our own into the water. While the two ships were manoeuvring like this, everyone on board yelled his head off, exchanging remarks with people on the other ship.

Seryozha took the cans of film and last week's newspapers out of the barrel. And a thin bundle of letters – our folks on shore had not yet had time to do much letter-writing.

The cooper, standing near me, was saying to Seryozha: 'Good ship, that. I've sailed in her.'

'What's the skipper like?'

'Same as this one.'

'And the trawly?'

'Just the same.'

'And the bo'sun?'

'No difference.'

I looked, and it was true: the ship was exactly like ours; she might have been our reflection in a mirror – the same skipper standing on the bridge in cap and quilted jerkin, the same loud-mouthed trawlmaster, a bo'sun sporting the same little beard, the seamen looking like frogs in their green oilskins. There was even someone standing, just as I was, holding on to a stanchion of the float-caboose and looking out for friends on the other ship. It was exactly what we must have looked like, seen from the other vessel.

Somebody jogged my elbow. It was the cooper, glaring at me like he was spoiling for a fight. In fact he was handing me some letters. 'There you are, you foreigner.'

I wasn't expecting any letters. My mother didn't yet know which ship I was sailing on, but there was a letter from her – forwarded from the Seamen's Hostel.

'Why do you call me a foreigner?'

'You don't seem one of us. And you don't dress like a Russian.'

So that was the cause of the rift between us: it was all the fault of my jacket.

'You should wear boots and a proper coat, like everybody else. As it is, only whores will go for you, with names like Lilya.'

Aha – he'd already looked to see who my letters were from. The second one was from Lilya. The third was from some old mate of mine, whose surname I'd forgotten.

The *Medusa* gave three blasts on her siren; we answered her and the two ships parted. She went on her way to the Orkney Islands, with more than twenty-four hours passage-time still ahead of her, while we continued to search for fish.

I went up to the foc's'le, where I sat down on a coil of rope. I wanted to read Lilya's letter first, but put it aside. Instead I opened the letter from my mother.

Senya, my dearest, why didn't you come home for New Year as you promised? Svetlana and I were longing to see you and we got everything ready, but you never came. Since I wrote to the minister asking for your military service to be shortened by a year because you're the family's sole breadwinner, a lot of time has passed but you're still at sea and you've only been to see us twice, and even then you were always just passing through – here today and gone tomorrow. Do at least come here this spring and spend a bit longer with us.

Svetlana is a big girl now, old enough to get married, and boys see her home from school. She remembers you every day – she says, 'Our Senya has forgotten us.' You write so few letters and they always seem to come at funny times – first I had a letter you wrote in December, then after that came one from November. You're upsetting your old mother. At Christmas I went to your father's grave, had a bit of a cry and weeded the path. The wooden pyramid, which the railway put on his grave, has got all marked with rust from the bolts holding it together, I'll clean it up in the spring. Well my dearest, we bought some wood for twenty roubles which will probably do for some bookshelves, you like reading so much, so write and tell me what to do about these planks – should we leave them plain and not stain them or varnish them, perhaps that would look more abstract? [*sic*]

I met Lusya the other day. She's still unmarried and as pretty as ever, she remembers you and sends her regards. And Tamara remembers you, although she's going round with a big belly, I don't know who from, she's unmarried too. She once lived opposite us and the two of you used to walk to school together.

We had some actors from Moscow in a show at the Palace of Culture, oh how good they were, they did it all so beautifully, and I enjoyed it so much. I was sitting in row forty, but I could see and hear everything.

My dearest, it worries me that you don't seem to hold on to your money, even though you're earning well. When I looked at you last time you were here, I wondered why you hadn't bought anything more for yourself than a suit and a winter overcoat. You should send it all to me, I wouldn't spend any of it on myself. Write, dearest, and tell me how you are, your nerves and your moods. I very much want you to be content, not to worry and to be healthy, that's all I want.

Your mama, Alevtina Shalai

PS I'm quite well on the whole, sometimes I get a tight feeling in my throat, but then it goes.

A.S.

It's good to read letters like this at sea. Then and there I swore a hundred oaths that I'd go back to Oryol for the whole summer. And I refused to believe that when we did get back to port, I would have quite different plans.

How had it all happened? When I was demobbed from the Navy – a year ahead of the others – I made a vow that I'd never go to sea again, not even as a passenger. Yet a week later I went – on a trawler. It just had to happen that I read an advertisement on the station, put there by the fishing fleet management. They were having a big recruiting drive at the time, and the money they were promising looked very good. How could I go home with nothing but ten roubles in my pocket? So I decided to sail on a trawler for just one trip. I wasn't mistaken: I came back with more money than I'd ever had before in my life. But in the train, near Apatitov, I was robbed of the whole lot. Cleaned out, including all my gear and my suitcase. I fell in with what seemed a decent crowd in the dining car, and I was fool enough to invite them back to my compartment: why should they sit on wooden seats in the third class, when I had room to spare? One, I remember, sang quite well, another played the guitar – ideal travelling companions, in fact . . . Luckily for me, some shipmates of mine were travelling in the same carriage, and they passed the hat round so that I had enough for the return journey. I'd already met the Chief by then, and it was he who bailed me out, so at least I was able to spend three weeks in Yalta and soak up enough sun to get the Atlantic chill out of my bones. So that was why I had to sail on a second trip, though I thought that would be the last time and nothing would induce me to go again . . .

I remembered Lusya, too. She wasn't all that pretty, but she was the first girl I ever kissed and I think we were in love. When I left school, though, we saw each other less and less. Even so she came to see me off when I was called up into the Navy and promised to wait for me – four whole years. And apparently she's still waiting for me to this day. Then again maybe she's not waiting, we were just not destined for each other. I also remembered Tamara. We didn't walk to school together, but went on opposite sides of the street as if we didn't know each other. Then one day she came to me in the railway depot and said: 'From now on you mean nothing to Lusya see? And you mean everything to me.' Maybe there was a kind of love between us, too; she also came to see me off at the station, although I hadn't asked her to, and she watched from a distance as I kissed Lusya – staring hard at us with such angry little eyes.

But all that was just childhood, and there was no going back to it. I began reading Lilya's letter:

Dear Senya,
This time I'm writing you a short letter. Don't be offended that I didn't come. No doubt I broke a very important tradition by not waving my handkerchief to you from the pier, and this has caused me serious pangs of conscience, but you'll forgive me, I know – especially as there is a chance we shall see each other very soon. And what's more – at sea. I can see your astonished look. It's true, it's true. Because there is a certain influential person, comrade Grakov, head of the operational division of the fishery management, who is very, very insistent on the need for research and production to get closer together. He says we're not worth a damn until we've seen at first hand how it's caught – the herring, that is, that's so good to eat with some onion and sunflower oil. He didn't say this, of course – I've just made it up and put my words into

the mouth of the big boss. He has decided to take several young scientists with him on a trip. Just imagine: not on the *Perseus* but on a real factory-ship. We are to spend a couple of weeks on board, and we shall, of course, get a hundred and five per cent closer to the actual job of production. I don't know yet which factory-ship we are going on, but it's bound to be somewhere near you, so you can look out for me. That is, of course, if you want to. We're leaving the day after tomorrow, and I haven't got anything ready yet. I still have to write a heap of letters and at the very least have my hair done. So I'll finish off now, with a firm clasp of your manly hand that is helping bring home untold quantities of fish! See you at sea!

Lilya

She hadn't put a date on the letter, but I was able to work it out: the *Medusa* had been sailing for seven days, but the factory-ship sails faster, so she would already be there. Which ship was she on, though? Two are allocated to each fishing-ground, but then the question was – which ship would we go to? '. . . it's bound to be somewhere near you . . . That is, . . . if you want to . . .'

I put it away under my oilskins and inside my jerkin.

13

I transferred Lilya's letter to a secret pocket inside my jacket. Then I did a trick at the wheel and thought about it all the time: the letter was there in the cabin, I'd soon be relieved and I'd read it again. Perhaps, too, I might read something more between the lines that I hadn't noticed the first time.

For the whole watch the Third Mate was nagging on at me about the same thing as before: 'You're bright, Shalai, you ought to go to the Nautical Academy . . . how can you live in that cabin with seven blockheads? . . . buy yourself an officer's mackintosh . . . got to be a hard man . . .' He asked me how many items should be kept in a lifeboat (this was part of his preparation for the exam on maritime practice); it turned out to be ninety-six items. I could hardly wait to be relieved.

I forced myself not to go straight to the cabin. It would be better after dinner, when everyone flops on to his bunk. Then I'd read it ten times or so behind my drawn curtain before going to sleep. Meanwhile I went below to feed Tommy and clean up his little nest.

At dinner in the saloon I just sat there like a dimwit, still thinking about that letter. Then I heard people laughing. At first I didn't realize it was me they were laughing at, until the cooper said: 'Our warpman's crazy about some tart called Lilya.'

I looked up. The cooper was smirking into his whiskers, watching with interest to see what I would do. I sensed now was the time to settle things with him – to get up, lean across the table and belt him one. Let him say just one more word about her.

Shura asked: 'Is she pretty, this Lilya?'

'I don't know whether she's pretty or not. I only know she's sharing herself between three. Him and the two apprentices. The same Lilya Shetinina is writing to all three of them.'

I looked at Alik and Dima, they looked at me. But we didn't say a word. I got up and left the saloon.

That evening I didn't read the letter behind my curtain before going to sleep.

Next day we finished work by noon, and I went to pay out the lead-hawser in readiness for casting the nets, so that I wouldn't get it snarled up later in the dark.

'Don't bother.' The trawlmaster stopped me. 'We're not going to cast today.'

'Why not?'

'We've got a full load. We're going to the factory-ship now.'

He was right; I'd forgotten. Yesterday we had filled our last barrel.

'Which ship are we going to, do you know?'

'There's only one in the Norwegian fishing ground, the *Fyodor*.'

'The *Fyodor Dostoyevsky*?'

'That's right. The skipper's asking for permission right now.'

Around five o'clock we got permission and set off. The last of the fish, a couple of tons or so, was still lying on the deck, until another DWT from our flotilla took pity on us and chucked twenty barrels into the water for us to pick up. In exchange we passed her two hoses and through them pumped fuel oil and fresh water.

Evening was setting in by the time we'd finished everything. The ships who were staying on to fish hooted to us in farewell and we answered them. Even though we weren't going home to port, it was goodbye all the same. From the factory-ship we might be ordered to the North Sea, to the Shetlands and Orkneys, or maybe to the Grand Banks. It would all depend on where the fish were catching best.

We still had some fresh water left over, and the First Mate announced that we could have a bath and do our laundry. After all, we had to be looking clean when we arrived at the factory-ship, and all our clothes were soaked in sweat and reeked of fish.

I washed my underwear when I took my shower, but it was absolute murder. The little cubicle is like a lethal chamber and you don't know what to grab first – to prevent your naked body from hitting the rusty partition or to stop your tub of washing from slopping over. So I didn't even bother to try laundering my other clothes, and as for my trousers and tunic I decided to use an old sailors' method of washing them. I tied the sleeves and trousers-legs together with a thin line and trailed them overboard. When a ship's making good speed, there won't be a spot left on your clothes by next morning. and we were going flat out – about twelve knots. We're always in a hurry to get to the factory-ship, almost as much as if we were heading for port.

It was then that Alik and Dima came over. They each held on to a shroud and watched me throw my things into the water.

'Brilliant,' said Alik. 'Does it get them clean?'

'You'll see tomorow.'

'Wouldn't it be better to hang them from the stern?'

'Yes it would, but there's always a chance of the line fouling the propellor.'

'Yes, of course.'

I sensed that they really wanted to talk about something else. Alik stood there for a while and then went away, but Dima stayed to watch my clothes bobbing in the stream and the line slapping against the ship's plating.

'Have you known her for a long time, chief?'

'Who?'

'Come on, chief – why pretend you don't understand?'

'All right, let's not pretend. Why do you want to know?'

'Listen.' He took me by the elbow, but I pulled away. 'Please don't be coy. The fact is I've known her since I was a kid. We went to school together.'

Well, my guess had been roughly right. The only thing that interested me was: for whose sake – Alik or Dima's – had she failed to come to the quayside?

Dima asked 'Was there anything between you? I simply want to know how deeply involved you are.'

I shrugged my shoulders. That was exactly what I *didn't* want to talk about.

'There wasn't,' said Dima. 'You can be thankful. And there won't be.'

'Why are you so sure?'

'Chief, I'm not talking about sleeping together. With someone like you she would actually find it good and worthwhile. Don't think I'm saying that out of male solidarity; my feelings about her are exactly the same as I feel about you. But I *know* that an affair between you two would just never work out. The only difference is that on her it would leave no trace at all – but on you it would. I was watching you in the saloon, and I realized it would.'

'Who's is she? Yours or his?'

'Nobody's, chief. Our relationships are just what you'd call comradely. It's such an age-old platonic friendship that it wouldn't even be interesting to turn it into something else. Chief . . . I'm sorry, old man, that I keep calling you that. Just got into the habit. Anyway, there's no harm in it.'

'Call me anything you like.'

'OK, chief. I don't want to upset you. You're a great guy, and I don't want to see you hurt and disappointed.'

'You mean – she's a scrubber?'

He laughed. 'Oh, no! That would make it all too simple!'

'Well, perhaps she's some sort of . . .'

'Chief, she's no sort of anything – that's the point.'

This gave me a funny feeling. 'I can't believe that. She must be something. You simply don't know her well enough.'

'I'll tell you why I think I *do* know her well enough, chief: it's because I'm exactly the same myself. You see, I think we're probably all seriously ill. I'm talking about myself and about Alik, and about all our fine friends who've stayed behind in Leningrad and belong to our set. All nice, decent people: wouldn't shit in their own nest, don't make careers at each other's expense. And that's a big plus-point, chief. But in actual fact you can't depend on them. Because they're nothing-people. I'm sure that when they say one thing for a long time and later they say something quite different, it's bound to affect them in some way. Taken all in all, a generation is growing up that doesn't know the difference between good and bad.'

'What kind of things did they say to *you*?'

'Well, not to us but to our parents. We're still very close to our parents' generation . . . It all started in Stalin's time – they were taught to denounce their father and mother if they suspected them of anything, to forget any "rotten" feelings of family loyalty. Then they were told the opposite: you must believe the promptings of your heart and ignore any false slanders. So now what are we to believe? During the war – so my father used to tell me – there was a poster stuck on the wall of our house which read: "Citizens! Don't believe false rumours!" And nobody laughed, although the whole thing was absurd – how were they to know which rumours were false and which weren't? OK, so what if the slanders *weren't* false? After all, there really were some things about the system that their parents disliked. In that case, could you denounce them? In that case, was it actually a virtue to sneak on them to the authorities? You may say that state of affairs has gone for good now. Yet haven't you heard it said that we shouldn't harbour any "false feelings of comradely loyalty"? That we should be prepared to speak up in front of the collective if necessary and denounce our best friend? In other words, that state of affairs hasn't quite gone for good, has it? So there you are, chief. First we're told one thing, then quite the opposite, then the first thing again. And each time it's dinned into us with such conviction, for Christ's sake! How are we to discover who was right – our fathers or our grandfathers? Somehow or other we have to find a way of living our lives without acting like shits.'

'That's as maybe – but what about Lilya?'

'Chief, that's what I respect about you. You stick to essentials. A child of nature. You just want to know – is she good or bad? Have you ever heard of a philosophical system called "Yesnoism"? A pal of mine, Vadik Sosnitsky, thinks he's the founder of that system. He's a great man, is Vadik. Maybe as great as Aristotle – he was an ancient philosopher, the tutor of Alexander the Great, who was the first fascist. According to some sources, it was Aristotle who invented the dialectic. Anyway, "yesnoism" is the ultimate development of the dialectic, its flowering, beyond which it can't be developed any further. You see, the Russian language contains the word "yes" and the word "no". But the word "yesno" is missing, which is a disaster. Vadik Sosnitsky believes that it simply must be introduced, because with every decade that passes mankind will need it more and more. He and I used to play a game like this: "Vadik, do you love your girlfriend, Alla?" "Yesno." – "Do you want to marry her?" – "Yesno." –

"Do you want her to go away and not come back again?" – "Yesno." If for a joke you asked him: "But do you want to come and have a drink with us?" – even then Vadik would remain true to his philosophy: "Yesno!"'

'So you end up by never doing anything!'

'Now, chief, I'll tell you about Lilya. As I understand, it was you who invited her to the Arctic that night. Well, she spent the whole evening talking about it. How she must, must, must go. How her conscience was causing her agony, agony, agony. Alik and I got thoroughly bored with this, we were ready to throw her out. She kept vowing she would go – but she stayed, and kept talking to us. I don't know about you, but as far as I'm concerned it's better if someone gives you the elbow straight away and makes a clean break, instead of having all these boring attacks of conscience about you. Does she like you? Yesno. She's as much of a yesnoist as Vadik Sosnitsky. Well, there you are, chief. If you've managed to understand even just a bit, I'm happy. Have I upset you very much?'

'Don't worry, I'll survive.'

'In that case I can turn in with my mind at rest and sleep the sleep of the just. *Ciao!*'

He went below, while I went up to the boat-deck and sat under one of the lifeboats. It was windy there, the loudspeaker was belting out jazz right by my ear, and soot was dropping on me from the funnel, but at least it was a place where a person could be alone and think things over. One thing, at least, I realized: there was no point in rereading her letter, because I wouldn't find anything between the lines. I needed, instead, to meet her and look at her – hard, in a way I had probably never looked at her before.

The wind was carrying the black clouds astern and the other ships' lights were moving away from us – masthead lights, navigation lights and lights in the shrouds. The Englishmen were celebrating some holiday, and all their masts and stays on their trawlers were outlined with lights.

Part 3

Grakov

1

The first thing I saw next morning was the factory-ship. I'd gone up on deck to see how my clothes were, and it hit you in the eyes – a huge grey-green ship's side, white upper works, yellow masts and derricks. She was lying about a quarter of a mile to westward of us, and floating in the haze behind her were the Faroe Islands: white cliffs like pyramids, with lilac-coloured streaks in them, and peaks that were orange from the rising sun – a simply fabulous sight. The base of the cliffs couldn't be seen, and with the factory-ship standing still it looked as if those cliffs were floating in mid-air.

There were about eight trawlers ahead of us, waiting to moor up alongside the factory-ship, all of them watching each other like hawks to see that no one tried to jump the queue.

It was quiet all around, only occasionally broken by the mate on watch calling out from the factory-ship through the loud-hailer: 'Number eight hundred and twelve – come alongside and make fast to my third mooring.'

Or: 'Departure! Cast off springs, cast off bow and stern lines!'

I pulled my tunic and trousers out of the water and hung them out on the derrick-boom. A window was lowered in the wheelhouse, and the skipper and the First Mate looked out.

'What's happening in the foc's'le?' asked the skipper. 'Are they still asleep?'

'They're waking up.'

'Tell them to get a move on. We'll soon be given permission to go alongside, and the barrels have to be shifted.'

The barrels need to be shifted in order to correct the ship's list before we moor up. Why she lists at all is a mystery, but on old fishing-tubs like ours there always is a list for some reason. After counting up the queue in front of us, though, I reckoned we wouldn't be coming alongside for at least two hours.

The sound of someone whistling into the speaking-tube came from the wheelhouse. The skipper went over to the tube and listened.

'What is it?' asked the First Mate.

'It's the Chief reminding us not to moor up on the port side. He's worried about the plating that was repaired on that side.'

'It all depends on which side they order us to tie up.'

'OK,' said the skipper. 'We'll ask permission to moor up on the starboard side.'

Gradually the sailors came up on deck to have a look at the factory-ship, where practically everyone had a mate or a girlfriend. A lot of women sail aboard her – waitresses, doctors, fish-processors, laundresses. My Nina used to sail on her once. In any case, the morning was fine enough to bring everyone out on deck. The smooth, calm water gleamed like oil, the sky was clear with just a few feathery clouds floating along in the wind. This weather wouldn't last long, of course; the windsock on the backstay was pointing north-west, and by noon the sea would probably turn choppy.

In honour of our visit to the factory ship, Vasya the cook had baked a cake and iced it; there's always a certain feeling of solemnity about such occasions, although to be honest there's not much to be solemn about, while there is plenty of work – and the most back-breaking sort of work, too, that lasts two days and nights without a breather and without sleep. For that reason we drank our tea in silence and no one even praised the cook for his cake, although he hovered around us all the time, hoping for a compliment.

Then we heard: 'Number eight hundred and fifteen! You have number two mooring! You may come alongside!'

The skipper called through the megaphone: 'We'd like to moor up on our starboard side, if possible.'

'Why are you so choosy?'

'We're just like that!'

They thought for a while and then replied: 'OK, moor up on number seven, you wretched people!'

'Thanks!'

It wasn't clear what he was thanking them for – for the mooring or for the 'wretched people'.

The engine started running at a more cheerful rate, and the bo'sun stuck his head through the doorway to call for a crew to man the mooring-lines – four each on the foc's'le and in the stern. Immediately the cake was forgotten, the side of the factory-ship could already be seen through the porthole, so high that it blotted out half the sky. It drew closer until it covered the whole sky, and out we went, our tea unfinished.

I was in the stern with Vanya Obod and the two apprentices. We cleared a space around the bollards, where it was cluttered up with a barrelful of cabbages and some sacks of coal. The side of the factory-ship loomed above us – streaked with rust, the outlet-ports giving out a slight hiss as they dribbled slops and a trickle of the brown 'juice' produced by salted herrings. Finally the officer of the watch came in sight, wearing a quilted jerkin and a cap with dangling earflaps.

'*Fyodor*, ahoy!' said Vanya. 'Is there a doctor on board?'

The officer didn't hear him properly and cupped his mittened hand to his ear.

'They're all deaf,' said Vanya, waving a hand in irritation.

There was no time for talk now; orders were coming from the factory-ship and from our own bridge, and the *Fyodor*'s officer of the watch threw us a line. Then we had to pass it back again, because our ship had made a faulty approach to the mooring, making it impossible for our bow to come alongside in the correct position.

'Let's go and finish our tea,' said Vanya.

Surprised, the apprentices objected: 'But we'll be coming alongside again in a minute.'

'In a minute!? That's another lesson you need to learn. When we do come alongside, there won't be any time for drinking tea.'

They stayed at the bollards, while Vanya and I went back into the saloon.

'Are you really going to sign off?' I asked.

He had a dazed look about him, as though he still hadn't quite woken up.

'When I decide on something, I do it, see? I just have to think up a symptom. There has to be a symptom. Look – is my ear twitching?'

His ear wasn't exactly twitching, though it was moving. That didn't suit Vanya.

'We know too little about our minds. OK, I'll dream up something; it works better when you do it off the top of your head. When I do that, my eye sort of swivels.'

'I though that was all a joke – about the axe.'

'Some joke! I tell you, I've had it up to here.' He drew his hand across his throat. 'But I'll do my share of unloading fish before I go. That's a sacred law of the sea.'

We had time to drink a mug of tea and eat a slice of cake before they called us out again. This time we seemed to have made a proper approach.

'*Fyodor*, ahoy!' Vanya started again. 'When does your woman doctor see patients?'

'You mean the dentist?'

'No, the doctor. It's my nerves.'

The officer of the watch tapped his forehead with his mitten.

'Something wrong in the top storey?'

'Just a bit. I'm sleeping badly, in fact I'm not sleeping at all. My chest feels tight all the time. My knees tremble. And I keep on drinking water, can't get enough of it. I don't even feel thirsty, but I keep drinking.'

'It happens to me, too,' said the officer, 'only with me it's vodka. All right, I'll put you on the sick-list to see the doctor.'

'Thanks. My name's Obod.'

'Obod. OK. Only it's not a woman doctor but a man. He's very tough.'

'Is it Volodya?'

'Yes!'

'How can he be tough when he's a saint? He'll just write me out a sick-note.'

The officer passed us a line. The apprentices kept trying to help us, but they only got in the way.

'Bugger off!' Vanya said to them. 'It scares me, having you around here. If one of you gets a limb crushed between the ships, it'll be our fault. And we have enough problems as it is.'

The line dangled in the air and we slowly hauled on it.

'Why do you call him "saint"? Is that his surname?'

' 'Course not! His surname's . . . well, I've forgotten it. No, that's his nickname. They even made up a song about him.'

He started singing in an awful, tuneless voice.

'Volodya, our ship's doctor, he really is unique,
Just qualified, as new and fresh as paint:
He loves the girls on Sunday, and even in the week,
And he's earned himself the nickname of "The Saint".'

The officer laughed: 'You really *are* barmy. Just a bit.'

'Just as much as necessary.'

We made the lines fast and left the stern-sheets.

A derrick-boom had been swung out from the factory-ship, with a large net dangling from it. This wasn't the freight-sling, but a net for hauling up people. It's just the same, made of steel hawser, but newer than the kind used for freight, so that when you grab hold of it you don't injure you hands on loose strands.

A queue of people waiting to go up in the net had already formed. Each of them had some job to do on the factory-ship. The radio operator needed to change his tapes or hand in equipment for repair; the fishmaster had to make sure they didn't cheat us when they calculated the amount of our catch; the trawlmaster needed some new nets; the engineers required spare parts; the cook had to get more food; the bo'sun wanted to give in worn-out tackle for scrap. Only the slaves, the deckies, have no business on the factory-ship; they're allowed on board last of all, if there chances to be some delay. This seldom happens, as there are always so many trawlers waiting for their turn and still more coming all the time. You never know if you'll have a chance to go aboard the factory-ship or not.

Five men grabbed themselves a place in the net, planting their feet on the mesh. The First Mate shouted from the wheelhouse to the Third Mate: 'Don't stay there too long. Just take you exam and come straight back – I want to go too.'

'That all depends on my results. If I pass, I'll come back at one. But if I fail, I'll have to do it all again.'

'Big deal!'

'OK, don't fret. I'll stand two watches for you when we're fishing.'

'That won't make up for missing my spell on the factory-ship!'

'Don't worry.'

The net was hoisted up and swung over the side of the big ship, where the derrickman caught it. The First Mate was still looking out of the wheelhouse.

'Mind you don't fail! I'm trusting you.'

Another five climbed into the next net. When it was lowered again, only four men got into it, at which Vasya Burov ran up to jump in.

'Hey, where d'you think you're going?' Seryozha yelled at him. 'What have you got to do there, you skiver?'

'I'm the storeman, so I have to collect supplies – apples, tangerines, cigarettes.'

'The cook'll get those!'

Seryozha caught up with Vasya to pull him back, but the net had already started to rise and he only succeeded in grabbing one of Vasya's boots.

'But I'm the storeman, why d'you suppose I'm paid an extra ten roubles?'

'To make working on deck more fun for you.'

The boot was left in Seryozha's hands. As Vasya flew upwards, twitching his foot, his foot-cloth unwound itself. Then he looked down over the ship's rail and began pleading: 'Hey, beachers, give me back my boot, or my foot's going to freeze.'

'Come down and you can get it.'

'Come down! If I do, you won't let me up again. You can't let the senior seaman appear on the factory-ship without his boot! It'll disgrace the whole ship.'

'OK,' said Seryozha, 'lower a line.'

Vasya ran off, found a line and let it down. Seryozha tied the boot to the end of it.

'Haul away, skiver.'

'Thanks, beachers. For that I'll pick out the very best apples and tangerines . . .'

Someone hailed us from the big ship: 'Sling coming down!'

Fastened to a heavy-duty hawser by one corner, the sling – square, made of steel mesh – was lowered to us. We spread it out and began loading the barrels on to it: one after another, each man rolling his barrel on the heels of the man in front, with no stopping. You tip a barrel on to its side, roll it across the deck, push it into the sling and turn it upright with one jerk. And it has to be in exactly the right spot, like a billiard-ball dropping into a pocket, not an inch to right or left, because nine of them have to fit in the sling. They don't count our fish by the barrel but by the sling; if there are only eight, the derrickman will spot it and make us reload the sling.

Now there are nine of them, three rows of three, the dear pot-bellied things. Two men pull the corners together, each with a noose that is clipped into the hook – and then they scatter and stand clear, for the derrickman can't wait. He has work to do on both sides of the ship, because there's a trawler unloading on the other side too. He just waves his mitt and vanishes, while the sling with our potbellies flies skywards and swings between the masts. If just one noose isn't fastened as it should be, then there's trouble: the whole sling can fall apart, the barrels drop out and smash like water–melons.

All was well, though. The first sling went up safely and disappeared over the side, and while they were unloading it we ran back to the hold to get nine more barrels ready. If we prepare them in time, we keep on putting more ready in reserve until the shout comes from up above: 'Sling coming!'

After an hour of this our backs were ready to break. Now and again one of us would stop to rub the small of his back, just as if he'd slipped a disc. Alik the apprentice was the first to give in. He spent a long time rolling a barrel, positioned it badly, then tipped it back on its side again and we all waited for him, stooping and ready to run – you must never let go of a barrel on deck when it's on its side, because it can roll anywhere.

Soon he gave up the ghost altogether and was unable to turn the barrel upright, even though he strained at it with all his might. Admittedly it's harder to turn them upright on the sling, because your boots can get caught up in the hawser-mesh and in any loose steel strands. First I had to up-end my own barrel, then go over to Alik and turn his upright for him.

'Weakling!' the others yelled at him. 'Cripple!'

'He's healthier than you, Senya. He's just too idle to move his muscles.'

In fact he was no weaker than, say Vanya Obod. It was just that tiredness had caused him to lose the knack, and he hadn't noticed one crafty little trick – you must roll it over the hawser-mesh along the middle of its side, so that it moves like it's on rollers, then you tilt it over to one side, swing it back the *other* way and it pops upright on its own, like one of those dolls that always stand up again whenever you push them over. I was showing this to Alik when the cooper shouted at him: 'So is the warpman going to stand all your barrels up for you? While you just roll them?'

'Shut up,' I said to him. 'I don't know why *you* suddenly feel so sorry for me.'

Alik had gone quite red in the face. He wrenched the next barrel so hard it almost started to spin, but he failed again because it's not brute strength that's needed. Dima came over and took the barrel away from him.

'Take a rest, Alik. Miss your turn.'

'But I'm not tired.'

'But I'm telling you – take a rest. And watch carefully.'

Shura, of course, immediately shouted: 'Can I take a rest too?'

'You can.'

'In that case you can do my work as well, while I sit down and relax for a bit.'

'And you can shut up, too,' said Dima, 'or I might belt someone in the teeth.'

Shura liked this reply so much that he didn't even answer, but sat down on his barrel and lit a cigarette.

Dima showed Alik several times how to do it, in fact he filled a sling himself, while Alik merely nodded.

Again Shura couldn't bear it: 'Why only one sling? You can load one for me now.'

The result was that Dima not only gave Alik a breather, but the rest of us too. And he also gave us a little lesson . . .

We hadn't noticed that the weather was changing; the deck was no longer yellow with sunlight, but grey, and the waves were cresting. We had only unloaded the first, upper layer of barrels – and in each of the two holds there were four layers.

We hadn't noticed, either, what was happening around us – which of the other trawlers had moored up to the factory-ship and which had cast off. Only once, I remember, when there was some hold-up in the work, I straightened up and looked at the sea. Out there among the green wave-crests, a little boat with an outboard motor was passing – red sides and a white half-cabin – with two young, red-bearded men sitting in the stern and looking at us. Where were they going? God knows where – just out to sea. And I didn't know whether they had enough fuel for their little outboard, or whether they had a sail with them, but they weren't worried about this, and I thought : no doubt they're going where they want to go. The chief thing is to go where you want to go. Maybe I should do the same: push off, go aboard the factory-ship and sail back to port with her, and from there without delay take a train inland and, for a start, go home to Oryol . . . What was stopping me? Surely not this barrel?

At that moment someone reminded me about the barrel by poking me in the back. 'Go on, keep rolling! What have you stopped for?'

And I forgot about that little motorboat.

The sky was darkening a little, and the wind freshening. In those parts the weather changes quickly; within half an hour a calm can change into a heavy swell.

After the next sling, another hold-up developed. The derrickman shouted down to us: 'You can knock off for a bit. I'll give you a shout when we're ready again.'

Shura and Seryozha went back to the cabin and started playing cards, while the rest of us sat down on the steps of the companionway. I took the top step, so as to keep an eye open for the derrickman to appear again.

'We won't finish unloading today,' said Vanya Obod. 'And that means I won't get to see the doctor before evening.'

'So go now,' said Alik.

'Go now! How would I get paid for this work then? The doctor might sign me off as from today.'

'We would have finished the unloading,' said Dima, 'in three hours if the officers had gone on "watch below".'

'Who wants us to unload in three hours?' asked Vanya. 'They want to spend three hours lounging around on the factory ship. If we unloaded straight away, they'd send us off fishing again.'

'But it could be done another way,' said Alik. 'Suppose we *all* pitched in and did the work in one day, then we'd have two free days to spend on board the big ship. That would be fair.'

Vanya laughed so hard he started coughing. 'If you robbed a man and were tried for it, would you say that was unfair?'

Alik was puzzled. 'What sort of logic is that?'

'Don't you understand, greenhorn? Look – you applied to sail on a DWT. Why didn't you go on a factory ship? There are sailors there too. Or why didn't you take a job on shore? Because us galley-slaves are paid four times more, that's why. You came for the money. So what's unfair about it? To earn that money you've got to sweat your guts out. And while you're doing that, the fellows who live in those after-cabins are going to relax, drink vodka and sleep with women. Because they've got diplomas and certificates and you haven't. If you fall down on deck, they won't even offer you a hand to help you up. Or rather, they will give you a hand – just so you can get up and keep slaving away. It's all quite fair!'

Alik said no more, but sniggered to himself.

Vanya asked: 'Have you learned now, you apprentices, how herring are caught?'

'More or less.'

'Well, when you've learned it completely, you won't want to eat another herring again. If everyone knew how herring are caught, the fish would stick in their throats!'

'It's better not to know, then.'

Vanya agreed. 'You're right, young fellow. Because if they did know, no one would buy any fish.'

A voice came from the factory-ship: '*Galloper*, ahoy!'

I looked out. It was Zhora the mate.

'Shalai, call an apprentice.'

'There are two of them here.'

'Either one will do.'

Dima climbed out on deck.

'How's the Third Mate getting on with his exam? Is he burning with a bright blue flame?'

'Only a dark blue flame so far. He threw me this note. He's decided to write his essay on a general topic. This is it: "I am glad that my labour merges into the collective effort of my country."'

'Splendid!' said Dima. 'He can scribble away about "inspiration" and "creativity".'

'That's exactly what he intends to write. But he wants to know how to spell "inspiration". Does it have two i's or two a's?'

'"Inspir . . ." The second syllable has an "i" too.'

'OK, got it.'

Zhora disappeared. A minute later we were hailed again: 'Sling coming!'

The sky had begun to look threatening and dark, and the sea was getting choppy, the wind driving it towards the Faroes.

Vanya stood for a moment in the doghouse and shivered. 'Storm coming up, lads.'

'Well, let it come,' said Alik. 'At least we can have a rest then.'

'You fool, we're not fishing. If there's a storm when we're fishing you can lie in your bunk. Here they make you stand off, but you may be ordered to moor up at any time. As soon as there's a let-up in the weather, you have to come in again and start unloading. You can't work, but you can't sleep either. That can last a week – and you say "let it come"!'

We loaded up another ten slings and then went back to the doghouse. Aboard the factory-ship they hadn't yet managed to stow any of our barrels, and a lot of them had piled up on deck. As a rule that wouldn't matter, but now the weather was making the factory-ship roll too.

Vanya turned gloomy again: 'We won't finish loading tomorrow. Or the day after.'

'Why are you in such a hurry?' I asked. 'You're going back to port anyway, that's for sure.'

'No it's not. This factory-ship only stays here for three days. After that, you have to wait for the next one.'

How had he found that out? I suppose he must have heard it somewhere, since he had made all his plans in advance. Personally, I was still worried about that motorboat. And because I wouldn't see Lilya now.

'Does it really only stay three days?' I asked. 'Yes, we won't finish in that time.'

Vanya sidled up to me. 'Know what? Why don't we both of us sign off together? Haven't you just about had enough of all this?'

I looked at them all sitting on the companion-way steps, leaning against the bulkhead. From the cabin came the sound of someone being slapped on the nose with a wad of cards: '. . . a hundred and forty-eight . . . a hundred and forty-nine . . .' He was right; I'd just about had enough of all this.

'Can anyone sign off?' asked Alik.

'You stay where you are,' said Vanya. 'Anybody can, but not everybody. Otherwise they'll think the whole crew is deserting and they'll declare an emergency. You can sign off on the factory-ship. No one will stop you.'

'I wasn't planning to,'

'Then don't ask, if you're not planning to.' Vanya turned to me. 'Well, what about it?'

I hadn't time to reply before a shout came from the factory-ship: 'Sling coming!'

As I rolled barrels and loaded slings, my mind was busy with other things. I had never yet signed off in the middle of a trip, although it's allowed – no one will stop you. Except that you're supposed to give the skipper a week's notice, so they can send out a replacement from port. But then they can always find a replacement on the factory-ship – there are always people who'd like a change and are willing to spend a week or two as a deckie on a DWT. What's more, thanks to this load I'd already earned a fair bit of money. Yet I still wanted to see *her* first. Then I would probably make up my mind to sail back to port with her, and maybe we'd work things out between us on the way – at sea everything's different from on shore.

Soon, though, we had worked ourselves up into a fury, a mood of angry obsession in which we no longer noticed what was going on around us. All we could see was the barrels and the slings and how they swung away up aloft when they were loaded.

It was then that I had another run-in with the cooper.

Some nut-case shouted down from the factory-ship: 'Hey, lads, you couldn't chuck us a few herring, could you? Two or three would do.'

Were we supposed to feel sorry for him? Asking for fish on a trawler is like asking for snow in winter. Anyway, that misery the cooper picked up a few fish from the scuppers and started throwing them up to him. I thought he'd throw them back in the cooper's face, because those herring had been swilling about in the scuppers since God knows which catch, maybe since last week. But the bloke actually thanked us: 'Thanks, lads! They're fine!'

This really made me see red.

'Throw them away at once!' I shouted to him. 'They're just carrion!'

'Why throw away good fish?'

I seized a hammer, ran over to a barrel, knocked the lid off, grabbed the top three herrings in my mittens and tossed them up to him like hand-grenades. The cooper looked at me and grinned.

'What's he up to?' the other man asked the cooper.

'Playing games.'

The man on the factory-ship shook his head and went away.

'You stingy bastard!' I said to the cooper. 'You couldn't even give the man a few decent fish – and which haven't cost you a kopeck.'

He unhooked the claws from a barrel and looked at me with a kindly, almost pitying frown. His eyebrows were a sort of grey, as if they'd been sprinkled with ash. Gazing at me with this look, he swung the steel chain with its hooks.

'Get down into the hold,' he said to me.

'What for?'

'Because I say so. You can roll out the barrels from below.'

It crossed my mind that he could always fix it so that the hooks came unfastened 'by mistake'. Just over my head.

'I work in the hold every day. When we're at the factory-ship I prefer to be on deck.'

'So you won't go?'

'No, I won't.'

'I'm ordering you to go.'

'And I won't obey. You're not my boss.'

He half closed his eyes and asked: 'Do you want me to thump you one?'

'Keep you hands to yourself.'

He came towards me. I gripped the handle of the big hammer so hard that it hurt. He stopped and said wearily: 'OK, put the lid back on that barrel. You can stay up here.'

And that was the end of it. No one had even dared to run over and stop him.

We unloaded the second layer of barrels and had started on the third when the derrickman shouted down to us: 'Go and eat, lads. We're taking a break.'

In the saloon I found myself sitting opposite the cooper. Without looking at me, he ate his food like a pig, a muscle behind his ear twitching as he did so. At first it disgusted me to watch him, then I somehow began to feel sorry for him. He was older than all the rest of us, older even than Vasya Burov, and I'd been told that on shore no one had ever seen him sober; he was apparently quite capable of flogging everything – his jacket, his shirt, his shoes – to buy drink. He had a son who was nearly eight, but who was so backward he could only say 'papa' and 'mama'. Perhaps this was why the cooper had such a filthy temper. What could he look forward to? Sooner or later he'd ruin himself from drinking too much, and they would refuse to allow him to sign on as a seaman.

I was thinking to myself on these lines when Mitrokhin came in and set us a poser: 'Look, lads,' he said, 'let me go aboard the factory-ship for a spell. My brother's moored up on the other side. Just so as I can meet him for an hour or so – I haven't seen him for six months.'

We pondered his request in silence. Of course it wouldn't just be for 'an hour or so' – that was only a manner of speaking. And Vasya Burov had already gone. When you're a man short on deck, you notice it.

He stood there, waiting for our verdict. We were the only ones who could give him leave to go.

The cooper spoke first: 'I haven't seen my brother for a whole year. He's in the Navy.'

'So does that mean I can't go?' Mitrokhin sighed. 'He's right here, alongside. And maybe I won't see him again for another year. We always come into port at different times.'

'I may not see my brother for another three years,' said the cooper.

Mitrokhin was still waiting. So far only one of us had given his opinion.

Mitrokhin looked a pathetic sight; tears were almost starting to his eyes.

I said: 'Go on, off you go. What's there to discuss? We'll replace you somehow or other.'

Shura, too, agreed to let him go: 'Push off, you skiving bastard. And give my regards to your brother.'

Then Seryozha and the apprentices consented, and finally Vanya Obod – with great reluctance.

'Thanks, lads.'

Mitrokhin beamed all over his face and galloped off to ask for a net to be let down for him. Then all the others went out, leaving me alone with the cooper. He wouldn't look in my direction, but I lit a cigarette and sat there calmly looking at him.

One day I had taken his trick at the wheel for him, because he had cut his finger on a rusty barrel-hoop; it had got infected and his whole hand had started to swell up. He had refused to take his turn at the wheel and every one yelled at him – this was a ship, not a kindergarten, and so on. Gesha, the trawlmaster's mate had demanded that the cooper should untie his bandage and show everyone exactly what was wrong with his hand. This drove me mad. Maybe too, I was curious to see how the cooper would react if I stood up for him. And what d'you think? It made him hate me all the more – if it was possible to hate me more than he did already.

I asked him, calmly and with a smile: 'Felix, why do you hate me, you pig?'

He replied at once: 'Because you're good-natured. And you're a clever dick. That's why. I'd take all you irresponsible goody-goodies and hang you from the masthead. Every Tuesday.'

'By the neck?'

'By the feet. Until you've dried out. And because everything in your head's upside down. You can't see what the world's really like.'

'And what *is* the world really like?'

'What it's really like is that everyone's a bastard. Everyone in a different way – but they're all bastards.'

'I see. And what about that bloke who asked for a few herring? What do you know about him?'

'Exactly the same. He wanted *you* to open one of your barrels because he's too sodding idle to open one of them up on the factory-ship. He'd have thrown those rotten ones away anyway, and then gone and scrounged some more from another trawler.'

'You're probably right. But even so, you don't hate the apprentices as much as me.'

'The apprentices? What do I care about them? After this trip they'll go away and we won't see them again. But you're one of us, you rotten slob. You'll always be around.'

'I won't. But I suppose you and I will get through this trip somehow or other. Enjoy your dinner.'

'Sod off.'

There was still no sling, so we sat down on some barrels for a smoke while we waited. Vanya Obod sat beside me and whispered: 'I've had an idea. I'll ask for *two* sick-notes. I'll say you have more or less the same trouble. He'll sign you off without even looking at you.'

'Who will?'

'That doctor – Volodya the Saint. Have you ever complained about mental trouble?'

'No.'

'Does no harm to complain of it now and again. It can come in useful. Ever had a bash on the head?'

'Not that I can remember.'

'You fool, no one can check up on it. Just say you've had one and since then you can't sleep properly, it's affected your ability to work, and you don't want to be a burden on your shipmates.'

I honestly didn't want to get mixed up in this lead-swinging lark. If ever I signed off, it would be for one reason: 'Mind your own fucking business.' Why should I tell all these fairy-tales if I wasn't going to stay at sea after this anyway? Vanya would be sailing again, I knew; he'd loaf around a bit, then he'd sign on again – there was sod-all else he could turn his hand to. If I signed off, it would be for good and all. For a start I could at least get a job in the railway depot back home. I would have to think about it seriously before making up my mind, and not just because I was pissed off.

'Well, what about it? Shall we push off together?'

'No.'

'But you agreed to!'

'When?'

He looked at me with contempt 'Huh – there's one born every minute. I was giving you a bit of advice because I thought you had some sense, thinking you'd follow my example.'

'Sign off yourself and don't bother your head about other people.'

'I'll sign off all right. Think I haven't got the guts to do it on my own?'

'I don't think anything.'

'That's obvious. If you'd thought about it, you . . .'

He didn't finish what he was saying, but walked away. Was his conscience worrying him because he was leaving us, I wondered?

The derrickman shouted from the factory-ship: 'Ahoy, lads, stand by to take on provisions!'

Vasya the cook chucked us a line, on which were tied a sack and a cow's leg. He was already good and merry, was our cooky. The trawlmaster and Marconi appeared alongside him, both with faces the same colour as his.

The trawlmaster bellowed: 'Stand from under, I'm throwing down some nets.'

He threw us eight green sisal nets and two white ones made of nylon.

'Put those in my cabin.'

Obviously he wasn't going to use them for trawling. He'd keep them stashed away until we got back to port, economizing on nets by mending the old ones over and over again, then he'd give these new ones as presents to his mates to use as landing-nets when they went fishing in rivers inland. There was no point in using them for trawling, anyway – nylon nets take a long time to tear, but on the other hand they cut the fish and make them bleed, which scares off other fish.

Vasya the cook lowered his load and warned us: 'Leave me at least half a sackful of dried fruit. They wouldn't give me any more.'

'We don't need more than that,' said Shura, who had already plunged his hands into the sack up to the elbows. 'You've been drinking for us, so we can eat your share.'

Marconi came aboard with some canisters of film. I helped him carry the canisters to the saloon. Suddenly he stopped and slapped himself on the forehead.

'Senya! I clean forgot. There's a girl up there asking about you. Wait a minute . . . name of Lilya. Yes, that was it, Lilya. Grakov has brought three of them on this trip, young research scientists. Would you like me to fix it so you can meet her?'

I was putting the canisters into a locker and reading the titles. I said nothing.

'Listen,' said Marconi, 'I've got to hand in a duff transmitter for testing. It's on the blink. Well, I'll say it's on the blink. I can't manage it on my own, so you can come and help.'

'And who'll be left on deck?'

'You're not indispensable, are you, Senya?'

'I don't know about that, but the others are going to raise hell. Two of us have shoved off already.'

'What's to be done then? We'll have to think up some dodge.'

While he was thinking, we were hailed from the factory-ship: 'Sling coming!'

We loaded it, then the derrickman let down a net for Marconi. I helped him to climb into it.

'What shall I say to her?'

'Hello. That's all.'

'Is that really all, Senya? No, I'll think up something.'

As he rose up, he held on with one hand and waved to me with the other. The derrickman swore at him and pulled him inboard by his belt.

The ship was rolling noticeably, and the sling was swinging over the whole length of the deck from mast to mast. We were expecting them to stop the unloading operation; the fenders were riding up above our ship's side. Even so, we managed to finish unloading one hold. Half the job. Shura swept the hold clean with a broom and climbed out.

'That's it,' said the derrickman. 'You can knock off for now. They'll soon decide what's to happen. You may have to stand off.'

While they made up their minds we all ran down to the cabin, where we fell into our bunks, some of us still wearing our boots.

I was just dropping off to sleep when I heard someone calling me from the deck.

2

'Senya!' Marconi was shouting from up topside. 'Stand by to receive visitors!'

He was in the net, swinging, along with two others who were not sailors, being too brightly dressed – and the net was heading straight into the hold. One of the two was squealing like a stuck pig and I realized then what sort of visitors were calling on us. I took the net, swung it away from the hold, and they jumped out.

Lilya was wearing a leather coat, blue trousers and a blue fur hat stuck on one side of her head. At first I couldn't see what her girlfriend was wearing – it was something so bright, it dazzled me.

'So this is what you look like!'

Lilya surveyed my working rig, smiled and held out her hand. For some reason I took off my cap, then shook her hand, which was firm and dry. Mine was wet, but she didn't seem to notice it.

'Let me introduce you – this is Galya.'

Marconi also confirmed that this was Galya. Pale-faced, with lots of make-up and curly hair, she was wearing a red woolly hat with a pompom. Gazing around, they looked up at the side of the factory-ship with horror – had they really come down all that way?

'Well, what's life like for you on board?' asked Lilya. As I mumbled something, Galya came to my rescue: 'Oh, how interesting it is here! Will they show us absolutely everything?'

'This way, please!' Marconi crooked his arm for her to take. He knew how to behave, having served on MTBs in the Navy.

The First Mate glanced out of the wheelhouse, looking very thoughtful. Strictly speaking it was against the rules to bring women on board, and he might have told us off for it. But he might also have got a flea in his ear in reply, which he wouldn't have liked in front of ladies, so he preferred to fade back into the shadows.

'But it's nice here!' Lilya's voice was very slightly hoarse and hard to hear in the wind. It annoyed me somehow that she was copying Galya by putting on that voice. 'And what's this – a winch?'

'Yes,' I said, 'it is.'

'And are those the holds?' – from Galya.

'Where is your cabin?' asked Lilya.

That was all we needed – for me to take her down into the crew's quarters, where the men were snoring in their bunks with their boots dangling over the edge. Anyone not asleep would be effing and blinding as he talked to his mate, and they wouldn't stop using four-letter words for the ladies' benefit.

'What's there to see in the cabin? Nothing of interest.'

I could feel through my back that someone was staring out of the doghouse at the wonderous sight. Sure enough, Shura had clambered up for a look and was shouting to the others down below: 'Hey lads, come and see what horses they've brought on board!' And, of course three more were coming up, unable to sleep now.

'Oho!' said Lilya. '*What* a good-looking crew you have! They should all be in the movies.'

'Do you really have horses on board?' asked Galya.

Marconi and I nearly collapsed.

'My dear girl, please don't disgrace me. *We're* the horses. You know how gallant sailors are.'

Galya blushed the colour of her hat. None of all this seemed to upset Lilya, who was calmly looking at the men and smiling – but only with her lips. I knew, though, how embarrassed she really was, only she wasn't showing it.

'Now lads,' Marconi explained, 'these are our guests. From the, er . . . ship's committee of the Komsomol . . . Girls, meet our comrades the seamen.'

'Why are there only two of them?' asked Shura. 'We'd like to meet the whole ship's comittee.'

Someone else sang in a squeaky tenor:

'She has such little, little breasts
And lips as red – as red as poppies . . .'

Marconi explained to the visitors: 'That's our traditional greeting whenever ladies come aboard.'

'We guessed that,' said Lilya.

Quickly we led them towards the saloon. On our way we showed them the engine-room through the skylight. Down there Yurka was sitting, half-naked, at the workbench and singing something; luckily the words were inaudible.

Marconi could now restrain himself no longer: 'Now we'll show you the upper deck, with your permission. Every ship starts with the upper deck.'

We climbed up to the bridge. The First Mate nearly jumped out of his skin and disappeared into the chartroom. He was still young and shy, was our mate from Archangel, and Marconi dragged him out again by the arm: 'Let me introduce you. This is the First Mate, the captain's right-hand man. An expert in fishery and navigation, my best friend and comrade-in-arms.'

The First Mate resisted as if he was being taken to the scaffold, mumbling something about being on watch. When the visitors shook his hand, he at once started to sweat like a pig. Marconi condescendingly dismissed him.

From the wheelhouse the whole deck could be seen, with both holds wide open. The beachers were standing in the doghouse, sniggering to each other, Galya suddenly felt the urge to show off in front of them.

'Is that the wheel? Can I turn it?'

The wheel had been put hard aport and was held in position with a rope's eye.

'No, you can't, you can't,' the First Mate shouted from the chartroom.

'Why not, comrade First Mate?' asked Marconi. The First Mate didn't reply but only rustled some papers, as if he was busy doing calculations.

'You may, girls, you may.'

Marconi removed the eye, Galya stood up to the wheel and he put his arms around her from behind.

'Oh, what big handles!'

'Those aren't handles, they're spokes.'

'Spokes? Oh, how interesting!'

'And you turn them like this, Galya.'

He was swinging her body almost in full view of the beachers. Galya and Marconi were thoroughly enjoying themselves and laughing their heads off.

'Did you get my letter?' Lilya asked me.

'Yes.'

We went aside into the corner of the wheelhouse. Through the glass upper panel of the door we could see the open sea; a steady white-capped swell was running at us like regiments in the assault and the birds were flying in slanting circles.

'Were you cross because I didn't come to see you off?'

'No.'

'This is a funny sort of conversation – "yes" . . . "no" . . .'

How else could it be? There was I in my oilskin, covered in fish-scales and rust from the barrel-hoops. The First Mate could easily have ordered me off the bridge and I'd have had to obey.

'I understand,' she smiled. 'You're not on your own territory here.'

'That's about it.'

'And this is the compass-card,' Marconi explained. To look at the compass-card Galya had to lean over the wheel and he had to press himself to her cheek.

Galya slapped his hands.

'So this is how you live, is it?' Lilya asked me. 'On shore, I somehow imagined it differently . . . I thought I more or less understood you, except for one thing: what made you go back to sea, when you were intending to leave the fishing fleet?'

'It's a long story. Later, maybe, I'll tell you.'

'Yes, but why . . . I think I roughly understand why and how you make your decisions. When you told me about wanting to leave the sea, I somehow thought the outcome would be the exact opposite.' She was talking to me in a slightly condescending tone, which depressed me. 'You're a funny sort of fellow. You're not stupid. And you're a man with a dream, as they say. What makes you prefer this life?'

'I make good money.'

'That's not the reason. I know your attitude to money. You and I went to the Arctic together three times, didn't we? You didn't spend your money the way a man usually does in front of a woman, when he wants to show off his generosity, but as if it was burning a hole in your pocket and you couldn't get rid of it fast enough.'

'Maybe I simply find it interesting. I want to find out something basic about people.'

'You mean to say you don't know everything about people already?'

I shrugged my shoulders: 'I don't even know about myself.'

'Tell me – why don't you transfer to the merchant navy, if you're so fond of being at sea? After all, it's a better life. The trips are short and you go to foreign ports. You'd see the whole world.'

'I did sail with them on one trip, to Reykjavik. Had a row with the bo'sun. They wouldn't take me again after that.'

'What did you quarrel about?'

'I don't remember. We just couldn't get on together. Our views on life didn't match up.'

'But you could have asked to sail on another ship, where the bo'sun was a better sort.'

'He might have been better, but the mate might have been worse. Or some other reason.'

'Couldn't you come to terms with them somehow? Just ignore them, that's all. Anyway, this bo'sun that you had a row with – why should his views matter to you?'

'It didn't bother *me*. He was the one who forced himself on me. "I want you," he said, "to report to me on the mood of the crew." He picked the wrong person to be an informer! Why me?'

'What did he mean by "report"?'

'Well, for instance, to tell him if someone was trying to take gold abroad and bring back foreign currency. Or any kind of prohibited goods. Or books. Or if anyone was planning to jump ship and stay abroad.'

'So that was it! And what was your answer to him?'

'I spat, and just walked away from the shameless bastard.'

'But you might have handled it differently. You might have said: "The mood of the crew is excellent and I haven't noticed anything suspicious."'

'Well . . . that somehow didn't occur to me.'

She smiled and gave me a sidelong glance: 'One has to keep one's feelings in check.'

'I'll learn. But here I can blurt out exactly what I feel. Nobody's going to kick me out of this job.'

Pushing her hair away from her cheek, she asked: 'So you prefer to stay at the very bottom of the social ladder?'

I didn't understand what this ladder was, nor why I was at the very bottom of it. I shrugged my shoulders.

After a moment's thought, she said: 'I suppose it has it's attractions. In effect you live a sterile life, clean and uncomplicated. One might even envy you . . . But I think I understand now who you are. You're Ichthyandros, you know, the hero of Belyaev's novel *The Amphibious Man*. You can only live at sea, and on land you suffocate.'

Again I couldn't understand her.

Galya annouced: 'That's enough. I'm bored with just turning the wheel. Show us something else.'

'We've only been turning it for five minutes, and *he*' – Marconi pointed at me – 'has to keep turning it for two hours at a time when he's on watch – two hours without a break. And he doesn't get bored.'

Galya looked at me with respect.

'He does get bored,' said Lilya, 'only he's so brave and manly that he never complains.'

'Who – Senya? My best friend!'

'And what's in there?' asked Galya, pointing to the door into the radio operator's cabin.

'That's where I work, my home from home.'

'I want to see your home,' Galya demanded.

Marconi hastily made his bed. His sheets were grey, the bedspread not exactly starched either. Galya turned away and prodded the tape-recorder and the transmitter with her finger.

'We could put on some music. Would you like to?'

'The twist? Oh, what fun!'

He hastened to thread the tape through the heads and immediately broke the tape; somehow his fingers wouldn't obey him.

'Don't bother,' said Lilya, 'we only popped in for a moment.'

Marconi was still struggling with the tape and tearing it.

'And what's that?' Galya was pointing to the clock above the transmitter.

'That? An ordinary ship's clock.'

'What are those little stripes?'

'What little stripes?'

'There – those red ones.'

'They're not stripes, they're sectors. Three minutes each. That's when we listen out for any SOS signals. All radio operators at sea listen then.'

'Do they listen to music too?'

'Good God, no! No music allowed. Only distress signals.'

'Now then, my girl,' said Lilya, 'You're disgracing me completely. You have to know the sacred laws of the sea. It's sixteen minutes to the hour now, somebody may be sending out a signal that they're in distress.'

'Really?' said Galya. 'Then why aren't we listening?'

'We're moored up to the factory-ship,' Marconi explained, 'so their radio operator is listening out. In any case, we've unshipped our aerial.'

The girls were fascinated by the clock. Marconi winked to me to go out with him. He locked the door behind us.

'Wouldn't you like to have the key?'

'What key?'

'The key of my cabin. I'm going back to the factory-ship with Galya, she has a separate cabin there. The First Mate won't poke his nose in here, I'll tell him not to.'

'Forget it!'

I opened the door. The two girls were standing there, bored and restless. They couldn't have heard us, of course; the ship was rolling and the fender was banging against our side, but Lilya looked at me and grinned.

'What were you two saying out there?' asked Galya.

'That it's time for us to go, or we'll outstay our welcome,' said Lilya.

As Marconi let them out he waved his hand around his ear – behind their backs.

'The main thing, my girl,' said Lilya,'is not to outstay one's welcome and to leave in good time.'

Someone hailed us from the factory-ship. The First Mate leaped out of the chartroom and lowered a window.

'Number eight-one-five!' came the shout. 'Stand by to cast off!'

We came down from the upper deck. The deckies had gone below. The deck was grey again, washed by spray from the waves coming in astern. The factory-ship was no doubt turning on her anchors in order not to lie beam-on to the swell, and we were turning with her.

'Shalai!' shouted the First Mate. 'Call up a crew to man the mooring-lines. They don't hear the loudspeaker, the idle devils.'

'Summon the slaves, Shalai,' said Lilya.

I went below to call them. It was true – they had fallen asleep, and they took a long time to respond. Then someone mumbled out of the darkness: 'All right, we're coming, no need to shout.'

When I came up on deck again, the net had not yet been lowered and both girls were looking apprehensive in case the net didn't come at all and they would then have to stay on board the trawler. I reassured them – we wouldn't cast off until they'd been lifted back.

'If Senya says it,' said Lilya, 'so it will be. When he says something he means it.'

I said nothing. The net arrived. Marconi caught it and pulled it clear of the hold.

'Oh dear, I'm scared,' said Galya. She was smiling, but rather feebly.

'Now, my girl,' said Lilya, 'coming down was much worse. Just keep looking upwards.'

But her own hand was trembling when she squeezed my elbow. Without saying anything, thank God.

Marconi climbed in with them.

'Where d'you think you're going?' I said, and started to pull him back. He'd gone completely crazy and was showing off in front of the girls, holding on with only one hand.

'Got to get some equipment, Senya. Honestly, there's a radio of mine there. Don't you believe me?'

'Number eight-one-five!' the loud-hailer called, adding a four-letter word. 'What's happening with that net?'

I let Marconi go. To hell with him. No sailor had ever fallen out of the net. If only the girls didn't fall out. The net was swinging hard, and I was afraid it might hit the side of the factory-ship. But all went well, the derrickman held it steady, then wrenched it inboard with one pull. Still looking down, slightly pale, Lilya waved to me before disappearing. The derrickman let them out and chased them away.

A wave broke over our stern and the ship lurched forward, the fenders creaking between the two ships' sides.

'Number eight-one-five!' came a shout from the big ship. 'Cast off at once!'

The First Mate stuck his head out of the wheelhouse.

'Some of our men are still on the factory-ship!'

'Do as you're told – stand off!'

He dashed away from the window. I thought he had gone to switch on the ship's loudspeakers, but suddenly the screw started to thrash, we began to go slowly astern – and hit the factory ship. The side of our flying bridge hit the big ship's upper fender – it was just a tarpaulin cover for the back of a lorry – with a loud clang.

'Where are you going?' they shouted from the factory-ship. 'Why are you going out that way? Have you got eyes in the back of your head?'

The First Mate appeared in the window again. 'Cast off aft!' he almost screamed.

At that moment we struck something astern. The stern rose up and then sank down – at first slowly, then faster and faster until it hit the water with a crash.

I was knocked off my feet. When I got up again, I heard from the factory-ship: '. . . stand off immediately, for fuck's sake! Isn't that enough for you?'

I saw the First Mate running towards me, white, his lips quivering. I couldn't understand when he'd managed to jump down from the wheelhouse, nor why he'd jumped.

'Get an axe!' he shouted to me. 'Cut the stern line!'

I rushed to the trawlmaster's locker then ran with an axe to the stern. The mooring-line was so taut it wasn't just twanging, it was singing. I didn't have to cut it, though, because it suddenly slackened and I was able to cast off several turns. By the time it began to tauten again the stern was already clear. I waited until it slackened once more, cast off the last turns and the line whipped out through the fairlead.

The side of the factory-ship was moving away, the fenders – like thick black sausages – were jerking up and down on their rusty chains. It was then that I saw the bow of the trawler that had been moored astern of us, and which was now standing off too. Her gunwale was crushed, the broken forestay was dangling in the air, and all her bow plating was bent inwards. I hadn't had time to notice it all at first, being too busy with the mooring-line, and only now did I realize what had happened when that clumsy oaf had tried to move away by going astern. Our poop had ridden up on a wave, while the other ship's bow had gone down, then they had both come together in collision . . . A pure example of a 'kiss'. But what was the damage to our arse-end?

I bent to lean over the rail – and there I saw an enormous dent, with a crack in it near the rudder. The rudder itself was not jammed and was still working – I could hear the rudder-chains clanking.

By now the factory-ship could hardly be seen through a veil of rain. I hadn't noticed when it had started to rain. Everything was hidden in a blue-grey shroud. As if through cotton wool, I could just hear them hailing us: 'Number eight-one-five, proceed to Fuglø-fjord!'

I went forward to the main deck. A wave broke over it, hissing, and the holds were wide open, with just one man in oilskins struggling to put back the hatch-planks. I started to help him.

'Where have you been skiving?' A wet face was turned towards me, water dripping from ginger whiskers. The cooper.

'I wasn't skiving. I was casting off the stern line.'

'Bit late with casting off, weren't you?'

'I cast off when I was told to. And you can belt up, pig.'

'They've all buggered off, nobody cares if we sink.'

'We're not sinking yet, so relax.'

We put all the hatch-planks in position and began to cover them with the tarpaulin.

'Cuddling with your Lilya, were you? Pity I didn't catch you two together, I'd have killed you both on the spot.'

'I know you want to kill me, but why her?'

'No bitch should come aboard a trawler. It all started with them.'

We'd spread the tarpaulin, and now we were wedging it down. He was banging away with a mallet and swearing blue murder. When he started up about Lilya again, I blew a fuse. I stood over him with my mallet and said if I heard one more word out of him I'd smash his skull in and throw him overboard, and no one would know. I forgot we were in full view of the wheelhouse; as far as I was concerned, we were alone on deck, alone on the whole sea, lashed by rain, and although we were doing a job together there couldn't have been any worse enemies than the two of us.

He just grinned at all this, but he shut up. I was, after all, the only one who was helping him.

'OK, don't waste your energy, we've still got the other hatch-cover to put on.'

We closed the other hatch in silence, went into the doghouse and took off our oilskins in the heads.

'That's the end of this trip, warpman,' he said to me. 'I can't see us going on. They'll recall us to port.'

'Think so?'

'Have you seen the hole in the plating?'

'From outside.'

'Go and have a look at it from inboard.'

We went below and parted to go to our cabins. In ours it was like the kingdom of the Sleeping Beauty. I couldn't tell whether they'd heard the bump or not, or whether they were so tired they couldn't care less. Some playing-cards were fanned out on the table, along with someone's oilskins, and boots and footcloths lay all over the deck. I went to look at the hole in the stern.

3

In the galley, the cabin-boy was busy at the stove, stuffing in kindling-wood and newspaper.

'Come to have a look? There's plenty to see.'

The hatch-cover leading into the storehold was open. I went over to look in. There was a metre of water in there, and kindling-wood, boxes of macaroni, a cow's leg and tins of jam were floating in it – a miserable sight, I can tell you. But worst of all was the hole itself. I had no idea it was so enormous and horrible; the split ran literally from top to bottom. I could see the sea through it – the grey-green storm waves. Whenever the stern dropped a little the sea came pouring in as if it was a sluice, gurgling and foaming.

'We might try getting the food out,' I said to the cabin-boy.

'What for? The things that are sodden will have to be thrown out anyway. And what harm can the tins come to?'

'That's true.'

'Want some *kasha*?'

'I'll have a little.'

'I didn't want to come on this trip, you know – sort of premonition!'

'Were you here when it happened?' I asked.

'Where else? I was talking to the cooper, and just about to go into the storehold, when it was as if someone put the idea into my head to poke the fire first, to heat up the stove, and *then* go down and fetch the food. Otherwise I'd still be down there swimming, I shouldn't wonder!'

'What do you think?' I asked. 'Will they recall us?'

'Can you doubt it?'

If this had happened on a cruiser, I would have doubted it. But then a cruiser's different. With damage like that, she must not only be able to keep sailing but go into battle. In the Navy, coping with a hole like this would even be made part of the training programme. But fishermen have enough troubles without that. So it was the end of the trip. We'd get a bit of money, that would be that – and back to sea again.

I went out. The Faroes were emerging from the curtain of rain, their cliffs towering above our foc's'le and shutting out half the sky. It almost looked as if we would run into them at any moment, but the cliffs parted, a stretch of calm water gleamed ahead of us, only a narrow strip but of an intense blue that separated it sharply from the open sea. At the mouth of the fjord there were piles of rocks jutting out of the water, covered solid with seagulls and guillemots. As I remember, these rocks at the mouth of Fuglø-fjord had split off from the cliffs about 300 years ago. A wave broke over them with a roar and a rumble, the rock shook noticeably and the birds flew up, circled around and immediately settled on them again when the wave had passed and left the rocks bare to their base.

We passed beneath the cliffs and reduced speed. The channel here twists and turns, the cliffs are like the sides of a wall, and it seems as if you could touch them with your hand or scrape them with the mast. The rain was running down the cliffs in rivulets and on the ledges were countless numbers of birds, making an unbelievable noise with their cries. Sea-birds are used to us; they settle calmly on the shrouds, on the decks, and sometimes a whole flock of migrants will take a rest on board, quite without fear. But land birds are frightened by everything – smoke from the funnels; the hooter; the overloud noise of the propellor in a narrow, landlocked channel; or a man coming on deck to chuck out a bucket of slops. For them, these are major events.

We rounded one bend, then another until there was no more sound of the open sea; the calm waters divided at our stem in two even bow-waves and slapped against the base of the cliffs. Only twice did we meet vessels coming towards us, and their fishermen ran out on deck to have a look at us. You could hear every word that was said, like in a speaking-tube. Pity I didn't know Danish, because I'd have liked to hear what they had to say about the damage to our stern. The Faroese are first-class sailors; here, according to the official sailing directions, a captain is allowed to take on any local person over the age of fourteen as a pilot, girls as well as boys.

All at once the bay opened out: clear, milky-blue. Only if you look upwards and see the clouds scudding over the hills can you sense what is going on out there in the Atlantic. Laid out in straight, even rows are five-storey houses, painted green, red and yellow, all bright against the white snow. Above them rose the hills, covered with grey heather – the snow had been blown off by the wind – and, scattered over them like clusters of flies, the herds of sheep. The little boats stood motionless at the jetties, mast to mast, like sedge by a river bank: yachts, skiffs, seiners and luggers; here almost every family has its own little boat.

We anchored in the middle of the bay. According to the international convention we don't moor up to a quay, but in an emergency a sick man can be taken ashore by launch. From there we could see people walking about, dogs running, cars crawling between the houses and up the slopes of the hills where a little road has been built.

Everyone came on deck to watch as we dropped anchor. Being in calm water, no one wanted to sleep any more.

We crowded on to the foc's'le. Shura ran down from the wheel with a pair of binoculars and we all took it in turns to stare at the shore. A fisherman's wife came out to hang her washing on a line, two friends met for a chat to swap Faroese gossip – but we thought it was wonderful.

'Just look at her legs! We should moor up alongside, then I'd have something to remember all my life.'

'Go on, swim – what's stopping you?'

'Hey, First Mate! Why don't we go alongside the pier?'

The First Mate was also gazing through binoculars from the wheelhouse.

'Aren't you clever!' he said.

'Go on – just for an hour or so, while the skipper's not here. Nobody'll split on you.'

To that he gave no reply, as if he hadn't heard it.

Looking through the binoculars everything was just gorgeous: a little dog, a Faroese dog, was running over the snow, fawning on its Faroese mistress, who was teetering along in little Faroese shoes – fashionable but cold to wear. A Faroese boy was giving his little brother a ride on a Faroese sled, the strings on his earflaps dangling loose . . . Why did we feel such an urge to look at all this? It was nothing out of the ordinary, just people like ourselves who walked upright as we did. We've arranged things pretty stupidly in this world of ours: there's the sea, the same for everybody; there are the hills, the same as ours; here's a bay, a refuge for all sailors – yet we couldn't go alongside, we couldn't throw them a line, we couldn't just go and talk to these Faroe Islanders.

'Just think, beachers,' said Shura, 'we're *abroad*! Even the air seems different.'

'You aren't anywhere of the sort,' Vanya Obod said to him gloomily. 'It's just the same as in Russia. And the air's the same. Don't know why you bother to look at a foreign country through binoculars, you can see it at the cinema back in port – in fact, you can see it even better there.'

There's always someone like Vanya Obod to spoil the mood. The sun had come out, and it was slightly warmer, with the faintest hint of spring to come. When you're ashore on days like this you want to go to sea. And when you're at sea you want to go ashore.

'Take off your oilskins, lads!' said Shura. 'Let's all put on our shore-going rig. We won't be casting or hauling in again before we reach port, and what's left of the fish will be unloaded by the folks ashore.'

We looked at the First Mate. He was still gazing at the shore.

'First Mate, ahoy!' said Shura. 'Is it true we're going back to port?'

'If we get the order, we'll go.'

'What does that mean? We still may not go? Are we going to keep on fishing? Not bloody likely!'

You could never get a straight answer out of the First Mate. He may have been young, but he already had a firm grasp of the first commandment for all officers: if you don't know something, pretend you do – only you must never admit this. He didn't even know, poor Flatnose, whether he would keep his rank of First Mate. He just kept staring through his binoculars, like a general working out the plan of battle.

'For the time being,' he said, 'we'll be doing some repairs.'

'That's for sure,' said Shura. 'With a bloody great hole like that, even sailing to port wouldn't be any fun.'

More than any of us, Shura believed we would be going back to port. He was as restless as a stallion in its stall. Yet when you came to think of it, what were we missing back home except for the January snow, the blizzards, and the Arctic? In any case, even these joys pall after a week, and we hadn't earned enough money to go anywhere on leave. But it's a great word – 'home'!

Anyway, we went and changed out clothes. I put on my jacket, and we came back on deck as if we were out for a walk on the promenade.

'I'm not going to do another stroke,' said Shura. He was wearing a jacket and tie. 'If trawly says: "Chmyrev, go and cut out the headlines," I'll tell him to sodding well cut them out himself, I'm not a seaman any longer, I'm a passenger on this good ship.'

'Would you like a cigar?' asked Seryozha.

'And why not, sir?'

Seryozha pulled out a packet of Belomor, we all lit up, leaned on the rail and spat into the water. We might for all the world have been on a pleasure-launch, somewhere off Yalta.

'Look, First Mate,' said Shura, ' – don't you worry.'

'Why should I be worrying?'

The First Mate had put down his binoculars and was standing framed in the open window, like a portrait. It was not a happy portrait.

'Liar,' said Shura. 'You're worrying all right. But you shouldn't. So what if they demote you to Second, maybe even Third, you'll just go sailing for a year or so and you'll be back at First Mate again. You're a good lad, you have discipline, you respect your seniors.'

'Why should they demote me? It was the Third Mate's watch, not mine.'

'Pull the other one,' said Seryozha. 'He handed over his watch to you.'

The First Mate frowned, wondering how he could wriggle out of this business: 'They'll ask whose watch it was from noon.'

'No-o.' Shura laughed. 'They don't put the question like that, don't count on it. They'll say "Who was on watch from noon?", that's what. Expect the worst, and who knows – it may turn out for the better.'

'You're not allowed to hand over your watch.'

'But you took it over.'

'So what? As an exception . . .'

'And hitting another ship – was that an exception?' But then Shura took pity on him: 'Well, maybe they'll let you off, First Mate. Who knows, it can happen. But even if they demote you to seaman, you shouldn't let it bother you. Just think how much you'll learn! After a spell on the lower deck you won't give us any more shit. First of all, let them sleep longer. Don't get them up at six, but at eight. The fish aren't going to jump out of the nets and men are worth more than fish. Then you can fix it so we have two days off in the week. Who thought up the rule of no days off at sea? You must abolish that rule, First Mate. You be good to the deckies and they'll be good to you. Got the message?'

'OK.'

'Like hell he's got the message!' said Vanya. 'If they leave him on the bridge, he'll go on shouting at you just the same.'

A feeling of gloom came over us. We were simply bored with standing about.

'What are we going to do, lads?' asked Shura. 'First Mate! Got any orders for us? I'd like to hear your voice for the last time.'

'If I have, I'll call you.'

'If you haven't, I'm going back to sleep.'

Shura, though, was even bored with the idea of sleeping. There was such a springlike feeling in the air that it really seemed you could just jump overboard and swim ashore. Suddenly Shura remembered something: 'Listen you lot, we missed seeing any films on the factory-ship, didn't we? Let's have a picture show.'

We came off the foc's'le and yelled down the companion-way: 'Hey, you apprentices! Stop kipping, there's work to be done on deck. We're showing films.'

They didn't come out. They were so tired, they couldn't even wake up in calm water.

Marconi had collected some so-so films. One was about a ballerina, who was being advised by her teacher not to get too remote from ordinary people, otherwise she would ruin her talent. We didn't even bother to run the second reel. We put on another film about a religious sect that was persecuting a young girl, and the local Komsomol organization was doing nothing about it. Then, of course, a new Komsomol secretary arrived, fell in love with the persecuted girl; she naturally loved him in return, although she was terribly afraid of what her fellow-sectarians would say. Then he persuaded her of the joys of love in a lovely clearing in the birch woods and the birch trees circled round and round and the clouds above them danced a waltz. We ran that reel twice. The cabin boy, who was watching from the galley-hatch, even asked us to run it a third time, but by then we were getting hungry. And the hole in the stern interested us more.

First one then another went to see if it had got any bigger. They all came back satisfied and tucked into their food.

'Now if only the rudder pintle had been bent, they'd be sure to recall us for that. You can't straighten in at sea – it has to be replaced in dock.'

'Even better if the screw had been damaged.'

'What's a damaged screw? Divers can replace it. D'you think they haven't got any spare ones on the factory-ship? No, the rudder pintle is your safest bet.'

The apprentices had also come in to eat and were listening to us. Dima burst out laughing: 'You're a keen lot, I must say! What about "the call of the sea"?'

'The sea's calling us all right,' said Shura,' – back to port.'

The First Mate called up on the loudspeaker: 'Deck-crew out. Someone wants to come alongside us.'

Another Soviet DWT had come into the bay and was approaching us to the moor up. A bearded man in oilskins was standing in the bow and uncoiling a mooring line.

'Hey, lads.' he shouted, 'can we make fast to you?'

'You can make fast,' we said, 'only not where we've been kissed on the arse.'

'Nice work, lads! Where did you get that one from?'

'The same place where you got your beard.'

'Have a good trip back to port.'

'Thanks,' we replied, 'we may just about make it.'

Everyone in this other DWT turned out to have beards: the skipper and the Chief were bearded, and the deckies too. Apparently they'd made a promise not to shave until they had doubled their target figure. They were given a double target figure because they'd decided to stay at sea for six months. After sailing for three months in the Arctic Ocean, they were now on their way to the Grand Banks. Sort of Flying Dutchmen in a way.

Standing on their deck were all of our crew who'd been on board the factory-ship, all silent and looking a bit crestfallen, although they weren't to blame for what had happened. I understood their feelings, though; for some reason you always feel guilty when some emergency happens on your ship while you're away from it.

The skipper jumped aboard frowning, and didn't even go to look at the damage, but disappeared straight into his cabin. The Third Mate, his face flushed with drink, went to console the First Mate: 'Accidents will happen. Once when I was on watch we lost all the nets but it turned out all right in the end.'

'Are you saying it didn't happen on your watch?'

'What's the matter with you – soft in the head?' The Third Mate's smile disappeared instantly. 'Who did that bump – you or me? The ship was entrusted to you and you blundered . . .'

The First Mate had been hoping – but what a hope!

The Chief didn't stop to look at the damage either, but the trawlmaster, Mitrokhin and Vasya Burov galloped off to see. When they came back they could only shake their heads and click their tongues.

The beards from the other ship showed interest too: 'Well, is it a good one?'

'You know,' said the trawlmaster, 'I had no idea it was going to be such a good one!'

'Will you get back to port like that?'

'We'll get back to port even if we have to cut off the whole stern.'

Then someone said as an afterthought: 'The Chief's in his cabin making out a report. I looked in through his window.'

I went up to see the Chief. It was true; he was sitting at his little table writing a great long essay.

'Look in that little cupboard,' he said. 'I'll be finished in a minute.'

I took out a bottle of brandy and two mugs. The Chief always brought me something from the factory-ship if I didn't manage to go aboard. I began to lay it on thick about the damage, and how it was good cause to have a drink. The Chief brushed this aside with some annoyance.

'Why are you all panicking about this hole? Give the scatterbrain who caused it a rap over the knuckles, that's all that needs doing. And you talk about going back to port! It would be positively shameful to return to port just because of a little hole like that.

'But you haven't seen it.'

'Yes I have. From outside. It's nothing – no problem.'

'If you look at it from inboard, you can see the sea!'

'We'll weld it, then you won't be able to see the sea.'

I waited till he'd finished writing his essay, meanwhile pouring brandy into the mugs. I actually felt downcast – we'd got too used to the idea of going home.

'Well then,' I said. 'In that case, shall we drink to a good catch?'

'We won't be doing that either.' The Chief picked up his mug. 'It's back to port all the same.'

'But you just said it was no problem.'

'I mean the damage in the stern. But we've also got a patch on the ship's side.'

I couldn't remember a bump on the side as well; maybe I just hadn't felt it, because the collision at the stern had been so violent.'

'Wait a minute,' I said. 'We moored up to the factory-ship on the starboard side and the patch is on the port side.'

'What's the difference? After a shock like that the whole hull is liable to be deformed. When the plating is strong, it doesn't matter, because it just springs back into shape and that's that. But if there's a weak spot . . . Now all the plates on both sides probably need rewelding.'

'The welding-seam hasn't parted so far.'

'Come, come,' said the Chief grinning. 'It's easy enough to say it hasn't parted, but have you been and felt it? Have you looked at it? If it hasn't parted yet, sooner or later it will. One good blow from a big wave . . .'

'Can we weld it all out here?'

'No, in dock. It'll have to be very carefully examined. Well, down the hatch!'

That evening, when I left the Chief's cabin, I went and had a look at the patch all the same. I leaned right over the gunwale, but could see nothing – smooth seams covered in paint, with no sign of a leak or a sucking noise.

Shura Chmyrev came up and leaned over too. 'What are you looking at?'

I told him what I'd been talking about with the Chief.

'Go back to port for *that*?' asked Shura. 'But there's sod-all the matter with it!'

I thought the same.

In the foc's'le Vasya Burov was sitting astride a crate, waving a nail-claw and trying to solve a problem – to open it or not to open it? He had brought three crates from the factory-ship, containing apples, tangerines and chocolates, and the problem was: if we stayed at sea, then of course he should open it – but what if we went back to port? Once opened, we would be charged for them, and we, maybe, hadn't yet earned even the minimum needed to cover the amount of our pay warrants.

Neither Shura nor I were much help in the matter.

'I don't know what to say.' Shura flopped on to his bunk. 'The Chief's off his rocker. He says we need to go into dock – not to mend the hole, but to reweld the plating.'

Vanya Obod sat up in his bunk and looked out over the tops of his boots.

'Is that what he's writing in his report?'

I said yes, it was. Vanya's boot-tops shook with laughter.

'Now,' he said, 'I see it all. I see why I'm a seaman and not a Chief engineer. How could a simple sailor think up such a thing?'

Vasya Burov scratched his bald patch.

'So what's it to be lads? Shall I open them? I'll do whatever you all decide.'

'Don't fret yourself,' Dima advised him. 'Just open them. Let's have a look at those apples of yours.'

'You apprentices speak last of all. You're sailing second-class, you haven't yet earned enough for them.'

'Is that so?'

'That is so. Do you want the whole crate?'

'Not the whole lot. You can put Alik and me down for two kilos.'

'Wouldn't you like fifteen? Either you take the lot or I push it under my bunk and it can stay there till we're back in port.'

'OK, to hell with it,' said Shura. 'I'll take three kilos.'

'Who else?'

'You should take three kilos for each of your kids, Vasya.'

'I won't have any,' said Mitrokhin.

'To hell with your apples,' said Vanya Obod.

Vasya Burov tapped on the crate with his nail-claw to see if there were any more calls for apples, and then started to push it under his bunk.

'Put me down for the whole lot,' I said to him. I was bored by their niggling calculations. 'I'll hand them out all round.'

At once the plywood was ripped open. The whole thirty kilos were shared out in a moment.

We were lying on our bunks, munching apples, when Marconi announced over the loudspeaker: 'Seaman Shalai, collect a radio-telegram.'

I took a dozen apples and went off to the radio cabin. It was dark by now, and we were alone in the bay; the bearded crew of the other trawler had already left for the Grand Banks. The lights of the little town were glowing like in a fog, while red tail-lights and white cones from headlights were flickering along the little road.

Marconi was fully dressed on his bunk, hands clasped behind his head. He sat up and shook his head, as if he had a hangover. The whole of one cheek was scratched.

'Want a drink?' he enquired.

I realized there was no radio-telegram; he'd simply wanted to call me alone to his cabin. He produced a half-litre of Moskovskaya vodka. We each took a slug straight from the bottle and ate apples as blotting-paper.

'What d'you think of this?' He pointed to his cheek. 'All part of the game, eh?'

'So the separate cabin wasn't much help?'

'Precisely. But we did get close. I find, Senya, that I don't need it the first time. You can be more sure of it the second time.'

'So do you think we'll be going back to the factory ship?'

'Not just once and not just twice, Senya. The skipper won't go back to port, that's for sure. He'll drink salt seawater if only he can stay out for the whole trip. What's more, he may stay out for an extra month – until enveryone has forgotten about that little "kiss" on the stern.'

I was about to tell him about rewelding the plating, but somehow I didn't believe in it myself, so I just said: 'In cases like this the whole crew has to decide. The ship has been damaged.'

He gave a crooked grin.

'What does the crew consist of, Senya? It's you and me.'

'Quite right, so let's drink to a successful catch.'

We each took another swig from the bottle.

'By the way,' I said, 'before I forget – Vanya Obod is going to sign off, he wants to go home and catch his wife red-handed. Why don't you send his wife a radio-telegram to say he's coming? Otherwise he really might catch her with another man.'

'I will.'

He shook his head, sighed, and touched his cheek again.

I could see he wanted to talk some more about his Galya.

'Listen,' I said to him, 'what good is this girl going to be to you?'

'I wonder that myself. On the whole, no good at all.'

'You'll only get tangled up in a serious affair again.'

'Huh! Catch me getting involved this time. I've got three kids to stop me getting caught up in anything serious, and my wife is the sort who won't let me out of her clutches this side of the grave. But I can get my own back on her out here, at sea! And I don't care if she does get to hear about it – I'd even be glad. I want to win back at least what's left of my youth from my old woman.' He ruffled his hair. It was very thin. 'See? When the bald patch reaches right down to my temples – then I'll relax and give up.'

I was waiting for him to make some passing remark about Lilya. No doubt he'd talked to her about me. He somehow guessed this, and said: 'Your girl kept asking me what sort of a person you were and what you were really like. I praised you so much, my tongue wore out.'

'Why should she want to know?'

'Why?! Maybe she feels it's time she got married.'

'To me, you mean?'

He laughed.

'You're still young, Senya. Young and untaught. If a woman's in love, there's no worse husband for her than a seaman, but if she's not in love then there's no better. You're at sea, sailing over the waves all the year round: all she gets from you are telegrams and money. It's obvious she's in clover.'

'Well, she's not thinking on those lines.'

'Fancy that – she must be someone *really* special! She may not think it, but the idea will be there, even if she doesn't admit it to herself. Would you marry her?'

'I don't know.'

'When you don't know, Senya, it's dangerous.'

'She's not for me. And I'm not for her.'

'Why not, Senya? She's an educated girl, isn't she? A graduate? From the Institute of Fisheries? So what? Does she know more about fish than you do? Has she read more books?'

'She probably knows which ones to read.'

'No one knows that until they've read them. Ah, Senya – what you and I need is something quite different.'

'What do we need?'

'Well, as a minimum, they should miss us when we're away at sea. And most important of all – they shouldn't stop us from living our own lives when we come home. They shouldn't hang round our necks like millstones. We give our all for them, and then we find ourselves caught in mousetraps. Mark my words, Senya, she won't let you live your life either. Know how she'll keep you tied to her? By making out she did you a favour by marrying you. She'll make you feel under permanent obligation to her. She's that sort of girl, I feel it in my bones.'

After that I could have stopped him from going on. I'd find out for myself what I wanted to know about her.

'I expect she asked you if I had a "difficult" character, didn't she?'

'Yes, she did, Senya.'

'And did she say that I needed to be handled in a special way?'

'She did, Senya.'

'And she said, didn't she, that not every girl would be bothered to cope with me?'

'Yes, Senya, she said that too.'

It was then I suddenly felt sad. No doubt because she hadn't been lying when she had said, 'I'm like all the others.'

'Well, that's enough of that,' I said. 'Are you going to get some sleep now?'

'I'd like to, but they're supposed to be calling up the skipper from the factory-ship. Over there it seems they're coming to some decision about us.'

We waited until two o'clock and finished off the bottle, and still the call hadn't come.

4

Next morning a motor-launch from the factory-ship came alongside us.

It was after morning tea and everyone was loafing around as he pleased, when we saw it – cutting through the mirror-smooth water of the bay and approaching us on the starboard side, although our port side was nearer; obviously we were being honoured by a visit from some high-up.

We pulled the launch alongside with boathooks, fixed a ladder over the side and up it came none other than . . . Grakov himself.

Since I last saw him in the Arctic he had managed to get a bit weather-beaten and he looked healthier, He jumped up on deck like a young man and flashed his gold teeth at us in a fatherly smile.

'Down in the dumps, are you, you poor drowned sailors? Well, I can understand it. It's depressing when something stops you from reaching your target.'

So that was the start of it. The skipper came out to meet him. Grakov had barely greeted him when he turned again to us deckies: 'How can you be depressed with a captain like this? Well, captain, lead the way and show me your wounds.'

Grakov was accompanied by the Group Chief Engineer, a skinny, stooping man in a blue cloak with a hood, and a couple of welders, carrying boxes that contained welding-torches and other tools.

They all crowded into the stern. Grakov was the first to climb down into the storehold. There the bo'sun had already laid down planks, so the bosses shouldn't get their feet wet. Grakov walked along them, the boards bending under his weight, took off one glove and felt the edge of the hole with his finger.

'Mm' yes. You've taken a nasty knock.'

The Group Chief also went down and had a look, but without saying a word. He looked bored, his face wrinkled and tense like a drinker before downing his first glass.

Grakov asked: 'And what does the Chief Engineer think about this?'

Someone had called for the Chief, who was now standing at the hatchway. He cleared his throat and said: 'He thinks it's not serious, a minor matter.'

Grakov started at the sound of the Chief's voice, bent his neck round to look up at him, and his expression darkened very slightly.

'Well, not quite a minor matter. But if the crew is really keen . . .'

'The crew's keen all right. Until it starts to leak.'

'That's a funny sort of attitude to take, Sergei Andreyich. It's not like you at all.'

Grakov started to climb out. The Chief was the closest to the top of the ladder and could have offered his hand to him, but didn't. The Chief's polished boot was right beside his face; Grakov looked at it and frowned, but the Chief did not remove his foot until Grakov had climbed out.

'It's not like you,' Grakov said again. 'You say yourself it's a minor matter, yet your attitude . . . You'll demoralize the crew like that.'

'Come to my cabin and I'll explain. And I'll show you the report I've made out.'

'Already written a report, have you? Well, well. Can the Group Chief come too?'

'Of course,' said the Chief, shaking the Group Chief by the hand. 'He, I hope, will understand me.'

Grakov frowned again, but said nothing.

They spent about fifteen minutes in the Chief's cabin, then they came out and leaned over the gunwale. We stood around in a half-circle at a distance.

'A bit dubious.' Grakov looked at the Group Chief. 'What's your opinion?'

The Group Chief took another look, as if one hadn't been enough.

'It would be a good idea to pay attention to Babilov.'

'And what are we doing, Ivan Kuzmich?' Grakov asked with irritation. 'Haven't we just been paying attention to him? But we've got to make a decision and act on it.'

The Group Chief shrugged his shoulders. He very much didn't want to make the decision. Grakov waited a while, then turned away from him to face the Chief.

'Well, Sergei Andreyich, your arguments carry a lot of weight, of course, the more so as you've already made your report. You've expressed, so to speak, an official viewpoint. By doing so you have, as it were, absolved yourself of responsibiliy . . .'

The Chief seemed not to be listening to him, as he stared at the hills of the Faroe Islands.

'Well, you're naturally bound to consider the safety of the ship. That's why you're a Chief Engineer. Nobody is going to blame you if you find the vessel sufficiently damaged to need to go into dock. In such cases it's better to be safe than sorry, as the saying goes. Nobody will blame you. You're doing the right thing. But the country needs fish – that's the problem. We all know that. The country needs fish.'

The Chief gave him a weary sort of look.

'The country also needs fishermen.'

Grakov laughed, appreciating the joke.

'You're indulging in metaphysics, Sergei Andreyich – separating the men from the job. Well, then – let *them* decide. What about it, fishermen? What is it to be? Shall we return to port or stay on the job and do our duty as workers? The crew must speak first. You don't object, do you, Chief?'

The Chief was going to reply, but turned round and walked away. We made way to let him pass.

'Well, you drowning sailors.' Grakov came over to us. 'It's up to you. No one's going to decide for you. There is a certain danger, of course. Babilov is an engineer who knows his job. But you and I also know a thing or two. We know what it's like to sail in trawlers – I mean the conditions we work in. When it's a case of needs must. You can't put that sort of thing into an official report . . .'

The bunch of us stood there, shifting from foot to foot. Then Shura asked: 'What does it all add up to? Are we going back to port?'

Grakov smiled at him: 'Do you want me to order you to go? On the contrary – I want to hear your opinion.'

'What's the point in listening to me? You should look and see how they kissed us on the arse.'

'Call that a "kiss"? I think it's called something else. That was just a "glance" at your arse. That's more like it, isn't it? Why, Babilov, your own Chief – did you hear? – called it a minor matter, that can be welded in no time at all.'

'He's not talking about that.'

Shura brushed me aside, almost angrily. 'That's enough of you and the Chief talking all that balls. You've gone nuts about that plating.'

Grakov exchanged glances with the Group Chief.

'I told you he was completely demoralizing them.'

The Group Chief did not reply and only shrugged his shoulders. At this point Vanya Obod stepped forward. 'Personally I want to sign off . . . Can I do that or not?'

Grakov gave him a stern look. Vanya cringed.

'What's your name?'

'What's my name got to do with it? Can't I ask a question?'

'Well, all the same you've got a name, haven't you? Or are you ashamed of it? I've got a name – Grakov, everyone knows it. Are you an orphan, or what? Ivan the foundling?'

Vanya hesitated, then said reluctantly: ' 'Course I'm not an orphan. Ivan Obod . . . So what?'

'At last your mother's given birth! So you want to sign off, do you, Ivan Obod, and leave your comrades?'

'I'm already on the sick-list to see the doctor. From last time.'

'Oh, so you're ill? You don't feel well? That's another matter. I'm sorry. So it's not a matter of principle. Of course, we won't hold you back. That's a perfectly acceptable reason.'

The cooper asked: 'Can anybody else sign off? Rebrov's my name.'

'They can, Rebrov. Believe it or not, they can. Anybody who wants to sign off can do so, in accordance with the established procedure. Hand in your notice to the captain, get a reference from the Second Mate, and so on. We're not trying to prevent you. We don't need the chicken-hearted. This is a sound crew and if we get rid of any ballast, it'll be even sounder. Isn't that right, lads?'

He smiled, showing all his gold teeth, and put his hand on the shoulder of the man nearest to him. This happened to be Mitrokhin, our nut-case, who was blinking his ash-blond eyelashes. At this Mitrokhin suddenly jerked into life, flushed and actually shuddered, perhaps with anger, perhaps because he'd seen some vision.

'That's right – why are we standing around chattering? We must work! Repair the damage. Sod all this thinking and talking. Let's get on with the job!'

'Oh!' Grakov was amazed, and patted Mitrokhin on the shoulder. 'Look at this, Ivan Kuzmich. Here we are worrying about metal plating, but there are still some real men sailing in this tin box!'

Our nutter rushed away, no doubt to fling himself into some strenuous piece of work.

'Well now, lads,' said Grakov. 'Let's get down to it. There's more than enough to be done. No time for idle fancies.'

We stood there for a while longer before dispersing. Only then did we notice the welders had already strung cables to the stern and brought a couple of plates of sheet steel from the launch. All this had been done while we'd been chewing the fat with Grakov.

'Look lively there on deck!' It was the First Mate shouting from the wheelhouse. 'Gone to sleep?'

Shura shouted back cheekily: 'You pipe down. Just thank your lucky stars you haven't been demoted.'

'Who are you talking to?'

'Who? You!'

'Open your eyes a bit. I'm not the only one here.'

He was right: behind him stood the skipper – looking grim, his cap pulled down low on his forehead. The remark could have been aimed at him too.

'I was just saying in general – it wouldn't be a bad idea if someone was demoted.'

The skipper moved away out of sight. I pulled Shura away by the sleeve, before he put his foot further in it.

The hatch-covers were opened and we started to shift the barrels up on to the foc's'le. This was in order to lift the stern out of the water. Everyone worked in silence. but they were ready to break out in fury at any moment – which happened very soon.

The skipper got the idea of moving all the nets up to the foc's'le, too. This meant ruining the neat layout of nets ready for the next cast and then putting them all back again. And it wasn't as if shifting the nets would make any difference – each one only weighed about thirty kilograms, so to raise the stern another centimetre out of the water would have meant moving at least fifty nets. We heaved net after net, then we began to wonder: why the hell are we doing this? Or rather, the trawlmaster tripped over something and blew his top: 'They send us jackasses instead of officers to give us orders – stupid sods!'

It was quiet, and of course the skipper heard him. He probably regretted having given the order anyway, but he couldn't bring himself to countermand an order once given.

'Skorodumov – who are you referring to?'

We dropped the nets, sat down on them and lit cigarettes, looking forward to a scene.

'I was talking about the people it concerns.'

'I've had my doubts about you for some time, Skorodumov. I don't like you, Skorodumov.

'I don't got to sea for people to like me, and that's not what I'm paid for, either.'

'Very well, Skorodumov – you and I won't be sailing again either.'

'God forbid! As soon as we're back in port, it'll be goodbye. I suppose we can put up with each other for another week or so.'

'No, it won't be just a week or so, Skorodumov. The decision on whether or not we return to port has already been taken.'

The trawlmaster sat down in amazement: 'When was it taken?'

'I'm sorry we didn't consult you. But you can sign off and go back to port on an individual basis. We'll find a replacement for you.'

The trawlmaster picked up a net and carried it forward. We followed his example. His face had gone the colour of beetroot, and the words were stuck in his throat.

'Enough!' the skipper ordered at last. 'Don't shift any more nets.'

We had only moved about twenty of them.

'Why "enough"? Either we should move them all or we shouldn't have started it in the first place . . .'

But the skipper had already gone, and the First Mate was watching us in his place.

'OK, Skorodumov, you've blown off steam – now shut up. You were told "enough".'

'Does that mean we've got to carry them all back?'

The First Mate throught for a moment. 'Yes' he said, 'Take them back.'

That did it! The trawlmaster gave a roar so loud that all the seagulls in

Fuglø-fjord took off in a flock. He staggered over to the rack suspended between the mast and the doghouse, pulled out a boathook, pointed it like a rifle with fixed bayonet and charged towards the wheelhouse. The First Mate, probably thinking his last hour had come, stood there petrified, like the monument on his own tomb. Five of us grabbed the trawlmaster, turned him around and led him away to the crew's quarters. Twenty minutes or so later he had calmed down and went back on deck with his mate to cut the head-line out of the nets. Whether we stayed fishing or went back to port, he had to cut it out of the old, worn-out nets anyway and hand it in at base – it's a sisal rope and expensive.

We kept on rolling barrels until we were told 'enough'; the stern had risen sufficiently to weld new plates over the hole.

The bo'sun rigged up a cradle – two lines and a plank – and we lowered the two welders on it over the side. One began drilling holes in the plating, while the other flattened the edges of the hole with a sledgehammer.

'Hey, welders!' Shura shouted to them, 'mind you do a good job. If we sink, it'll be on your conscience.'

The bo'sun had given Vasya Burov and me a shovel apiece, with orders to throw the wet coal in the storehold out through the hole. A hell of a lot of it had piled up in there, because the pipe that carries the coal down from the bunker had also been broken; all the water was blackened with coal.

'Hey, welders,' Vasya whispered to them through the hole, 'don't bust a gut on this job – got it? Just listen to us beachers. Weld it any old how. So it splits open again later.'

'Which one of you lads are we supposed to listen to?'

They didn't listen but kept banging away at the plating, while the drill squealed like a stuck pig.

'Come on, Vasya, keep shovelling,' I said to him.

'Relax, warpman. Let's knock off. Nobody's going to see us in here.'

So I shovelled on my own. What's the point of skiving, when you're cooped up in a stinking hole, deafened by banging and squealing? But Vasya's so idle, he'd skive even if you hung him up by his feet. He sat down on a tub full of cabbages and took a permanent smoke-break.

The First Mate came to see how we were getting on. 'How much have you shifted?'

'A hundred and sixty-three shovelfuls.'

'So he does the work and you keep count, is that it?'

'We've got to keep count, haven't we? We take it in turns. If two of you are working, there isn't enough room to turn round, so it lowers the productivity.'

He's a good, trained skiver. He even asked eagerly: 'How much should we shovel? A thousand or three thousand?'

'Until the coal starts coming dry.'

'OK, that should be about a thousand seven hundred.'

The First Mate had had enough, and went.

'Go ahead and smoke,' Vasya said to me. 'You heard what he said – "until the coal starts coming dry".'

'In that case there's enough work for us here for three days.'

'What are you talking about? If you want to know, there's no need to do any of this shovelling at all. Think it won't burn when it's wet? Why, they wet it specially – ask the cook.'

I threw down my shovel. 'Then why the hell are we doing this?'

'I'm not doing it! I told you – go ahead and smoke. All right, just keep going gently, otherwise they'll make us go and work on deck.'

I picked up the shovel again.

'Don't strain yourself,' said Vasya. 'We can always say the coal's coming dry.'

'But they'll see if it isn't.'

'We can always sprinkle on some dry coal. We'll bring it down from the bunker and stuff it up the pipe. You're still young, Senya, so just do as an old storeman tells you. I've lived all my life with fools, and believe me, you learn more from them than you ever will from clever people.'

But this pleasant interlude didn't last long. Grakov appeared – I could see his suede-topped shoes. He stood watching us so long that Vasya had to start working too.

Suddenly Grakov asked us: 'Who told you to do that?'

I kept on shovelling.

'Who ordered you to throw the coal into the sea?'

'Plenty of clever people on board,' I said.

'Haven't you got a head of your own on your shoulders?'

I stood up, leaning on my shovel, and looked upwards: 'Keep your voice down, I'm not used to being shouted at.'

'You're a rude seaman,' he said to me. 'You're doing something that's doubly wrong and on top of that you're being rude to your superior. The coal should be dried, not thrown into the water. And secondly, you're polluting the bottom of the bay. Under the international convention we don't have the right to throw so much as a cigarette-end overboard here.'

What he said was absolutely right, but I still felt the urge to needle him.

'I'm just a nobody. Tell the First Mate to cancel his order.'

'Very well – I'm ordering you to stop it.'

'You? And who are you aboard this ship, if you'll pardon the question? I simply don't know you.'

He remained standing there while I shovelled away with enthusiasm.

'Well,' he said, 'I suppose you're right, lad.'

'And by the way,' I said, 'less of the "lad", if you don't mind.'

He made no reply and went away. Soon the First Mate came running up, looking hot and bothered.

'That's enough!' he said. 'How much more have you shovelled out?'

'Only four shovelfuls,' answered Vasya. 'We'd only just begun.'

But they wouldn't let us out of the storehold. The Group Chief climbed down through the hatch to look and see how they were getting on with flattening the edges of the hole.

'OK, you can attach the new plating.'

The welders lifted up a sheet of metal, and as they laid it against the plating the storehold grew dark. We pushed the steel hawsers of a block and tackle to them through the holes they'd drilled, made the block fast to a pillar and then all three of us hauled on the tackle. The sheet moved into place with a terrible grinding and squeaking. As they started welding it from outside, laying down a blood-red seam with their welding-torches, there came a reak of hot metal and acetylene gas. We nearly suffocated as we hung to that hellish block and tackle. Then the Group Chief picked up another welding-torch and began to weld it from inside. We were immediately dazzled.

Vasya let out an obscenity: '. . . Let me out of here, or I'll singe my beard!'

He let us go, and we coughed the gas out of our lungs.

Up on deck, Shura and Seryozha were mixing cement, and the bo'sun was planing boards to make shuttering. Although the patch was being welded, it still had to be backed with a concrete slab. They were all working with such enthusiasm, it was incredible to think that only that morning they'd been shouting: 'Back to port, back to port!' Shura was positively dripping with sweat from so much effort. Then he ran over to the welders, took a welding-torch from them and himself welded the upper seam. He enjoyed this so much, he stuck his tongue out as he was doing it. In fact, the seam he welded was a first-class job – smooth and even, and later when we'd cleaned it up, red-leaded it and painted it over with black enamel paint, you couldn't see it at all.

Shura spat on it and walked away proudly, hands in pockets. I reminded him he'd sworn he wouldn't have anything to do with the repairs.

'Well, it's not fishermen's work. I just did it for fun.'

'The fishermen's work starts tomorrow. We'll be unloading the rest of the barrels and casting the nets.'

'Oh, sod casting the nets!' Then he thought for a moment and pulled a wry face. 'Yes, of course we'll cast the nets, and all the rest of the caper, too. Just don't remind me of it, that's all, otherwise I'll fetch you one round the ear!'

I knew how he felt; I no longer had any rosy illusions about going back to port either.

By evening the repair was finished and the inboard side of the patch had been filled in with cement. An hour later the cement block started to leak; this happened when we took all the barrels off the foc's'le, replaced them amidships and so put the ship back on an even keel. What were we supposed to do then – lift the stern up again?

'Where are our two storemen?' asked the bo'sun (by this he meant Vasya Burov and myself). 'Get bailing, lads.'

Vasya bailed down below, while I hauled up the bucket and emptied it over the side. But the water kept on coming.

Vasya stopped bailing: 'Come on, warpman, let's go for a kip. We'll say we bailed it all out and it must have filled up again afterwards.'

'Then they'll make us do it again.'

'The main thing is to push off now, before the First Mate comes back on watch.'

But the First Mate came running up before he was due to go on watch.

'There's water in there,' he said.

'There will be,' said Vasya. 'You'll never bail it all out.'

'Bail out half of it.'

We went on bailing, but it kept coming. It reminded me of when I was a kid and didn't want to eat. My father would take my spoon and draw it across my plateful of soup. 'Eat up this half,' he would say, 'and leave that half.'

The First Mate scratched the back of his neck and took a decision: 'Well, close the hatch and to hell with it. We won't use the storehold.'

In that case, why did we patch the hole at all? I wanted to ask. They welded it and cemented it . . . But who was there to ask?

We left the bay soon after dawn, when the lights were still burning in the little town. The Faroese were not going fishing that day, and no doubt they were staring at us with amazement – were we really such idiots as to leave the fjord when there was God knows what weather brewing up in the Atlantic? By now, though, we didn't give a damn about the Atlantic. We just crawled out on deck to take a last farewell look at Fuglø, then flopped back into our bunks and only woke up when the ship started to roll.

'It's at least Force 6, lads,' said Mitrokhin. 'They probably won't let us moor up to the factory-ship.'

'Yes, they will,' replied Shura. 'We'll have first priority.'

We all knew by now that we'd be fishing till April, and then no one – not even Grakov – could keep us at work any longer.

There was a clicking and crackling in the loudspeaker. We sat up, thinking they were about to call us out on deck, but it was only Marconi calling the factory-ship. He just hadn't switched off the shipboard intercom, either because he'd forgotten to or because he'd left it on purposely to give us a bit of fun in the crew's quarters.

'Grakov speaking.' The familiar voice cut through the air. Everyone looked up. Seryozha stretched out from his bunk to turn up the volume.

'. . . the damage is serious, but they've welded on a patch and cemented it. They've decided to stay at sea and reach their target figure. The crew themselves took this decision, and almost unanimously. There were, of course, some individual objections, but on the whole they're a tough lot of lads, a sound collective, in other words – seamen.'

'Roger,' replied the factory-ship. 'Understood. Greetings to the crew. Come alongside on my port side.'

We lay in our bunks for another minute, then the cheerful bass voice of Zhora, the Second Mate, ordered us up on deck.

5

The four of us found ourselves in the stern-sheets again – Vanya Obod, the apprentices and myself. The stern came alongside, started to bump against the fenders, and they passed us a mooring-line from the factory-ship.

'Watchkeeper!' shouted Vanya. 'Are you the same one as before?'

The watchkeeper peered down at us for a long time. It was hard to recognize Vanya under his earflaps.

'Well, did they patch you up?'

'Yes, they did.' Vanya spat. 'Only I don't have much faith in it. Did you put me on the sick list to see the doctor?'

'Aah . . .'

'I'll give you "aah"! Obod's the name.'

'Oh yes, I put you on the list. He'll see you.'

They were already lowering a sling from up above. We had left our barrels on deck when we sailed out of Fuglø-fjord, and we transhipped them by working four hours non-stop. There was even one barrel short in the last sling, and in place of it Shura tied on a broom.

'And that's that,' said Vanya Obod. 'I've done my seaman's duty and helped unload the catch. So I'm seeing the last of you, my beauties.'

The derrickman lowered a net for Vanya, and he went up in it without even looking back at us.

'Open the hatch-covers, lads,' said the derrickman, 'I'm going to lower your empty barrels.'

We opened up both holds and ran for cover. Twenty-five empty barrels in a sling is a terrible thing. It sways from mast to mast until the derrickman chooses the moment, then he drops the load over the hold and the barrels go rolling all over the deck. There's barely time to shove them into place in the holds, because another sling is swinging overhead and you must keep well clear of it.

We took eight slings, then sat down for a smoke, because they were having a break on board the big ship.

'Your captain's wanted!' shouted the derrickman.

Zhora the mate stuck his head out.

'The captain's in his cabin, writing a report. Who wants him?'

'One of your seamen wants to sign off.'

'Which seaman?'

Vanya Obod appeared alongside the derrickman, looking very glum and embarrassed.

'Is it you, Obod?'

'Yes,'

'Signing off, you skiver? On what grounds?'

'I've been put on the sick-list.'

'What's the matter with you?'

'I hardly like to say . . .'

'Caught a dose of the clap, have you?'

'Worse.'

'What's worse than that?'

Vanya tapped his head with his mitten.

'Something wrong up here.'

'Oh well, off you go and give your brain a rest. We don't want any nutters on board, we're all pretty crazy ourselves.'

'I need a reference. And my gear's down in the cabin.'

I went below, found Vanya's suitcase and threw his crumpled shirts and socks into it. Zhora wrote him out a reference at top speed and handed it down to me. Vanya paid out a line, I stuffed the reference inside the suitcase and tied it to the line.

'Sorry lads,' said Vanya. 'I just can't go on.'

'Shove off,' said Shura, 'and drop dead, you son of a bitch.'

We were bad-tempered because we envied Vanya, and no one had a good word to say to him in farewell. Why did we envy him? Was it because we lacked the brass neck to do our own thing and see it through to the bitter end, as he was doing?

'Stand by to take a sling!' said the derrickman.

Shura and I dropped into the hold, and the others passed the barrels down to us. Compared with barrels full of fish, empty barrels are as light as a feather, and they simply flew through our hands.

Marconi looked in on us.

'Hey, Senya – want to go over to the factory-ship with me? Got to fetch some equipment.'

I looked at Shura.

'Off you go, pal.' Shura gave me permission. 'I'll manage on my own. Buy me an electric razor while you're there.'

Marconi and I flew up in the net. When you're standing down below, you can't imagine what it's like. The net is slow to go up and it takes your breath away when you swing between the masts, while underneath you is the tiny deck and the fenders bumping between the two ships' sides; that's what is terrifying – the chance of falling down between them. Then when you fly over the side of the factory-ship the wind catches you and threatens to pull you out of the net, while all around is just empty sea.

The derrickman caught the net, guided it down to the deck and we jumped out.

'Take a look around for a while,' said Marconi. 'I'm going to find Galya.'

'Do we fetch the equipment after that?'

'They may not have fixed it yet. If I see your girl, shall I tell her you're here?'

'Don't bother.'

'OK, but I can if you want me to. Come here in about twenty minutes' time, in case they have fixed the radio set. But I could always manage it myself, the thing's no trouble to carry.'

I went off to look for the shop and at the same time to inspect the factory-ship, as I'd never been on this one before.

The fish-hold was open, and down there, on various decks, stevedores were stowing the barrels full of our fish. So that was where it went. We always say there's nothing harder or more dangerous than working on a DWT, but this place was no sanatorium either. The sling goes down and swings around in the hold until someone from one of the decks pulls it over with a boathook. The hold is deep enough to take a seven-storey building, and if you lack the strength to haul the sling on to your deck, or if a wave makes it swing, then you can be pulled over the edge – and you'll be smashed to pieces.

Here, above a hatchway, a conveyor belt was rumbling away as it carried boxes of salted herring – top quality, packed in tins – while women were scooping saline solution out of a tub and filling the tins with it. At first sight you couldn't tell they were women; wearing boots and oilskins, with caps on their heads, they were swearing no worse than men.

I asked one of them how to find the shop.

'Go below to No. 4 deck, then ask the way there.'

'Thanks.'

'You're welcome. Give us a smoke.'

I took out a Belomor. She shoved her mittens under her armpits, sniffed her hands and frowned.

'Hell, you hold it while I smoke. You get soaked in fish, you breathe fish, so why should you smoke fish too?'

I lit it and gave it to her to smoke.

'Thanks, pal. Without this I'd go round the bend.'

I couldn't tell whether she was twenty or forty.

As I walked around the decks I didn't meet anyone I knew – though I was hoping to – and was just about to go on down below when I suddenly froze, as if I'd been stuck to the deck. Who should I see but . . . Klavka Perevoshchikova!

This was someone I *wasn't* expecting to meet. She was standing sideways-on to me – on the open deck, beyond the coaming of a watertight door – just as I'd seen her in the restaurant: in a grey dress with short sleeves, a white apron and a little lace cap on her head. Facing her was an officer with two gold rings on his cuff, who seemed to be trying to pick her up. I walked back and forth past the doorway to make sure it really was Klavka. In a moment I would stop and talk to her, say a few kind words, just to make sure I wasn't mistaken.

Meanwhile he was saying to her:'Well, what about it, Klavka?'

And he went into his routine. He wasn't bad at shooting a line. It went something like this: 'If our little romance has any chance of going any further, it must develop either along a hyperbolic curve or along a parabola. If it's to be hyperbolic, then the inclined plane rises headlong upwards. But if we choose the parabolic variant . . .'

'Just tell me this,' was her reply. 'Aren't you afraid of your wife? I'm only concerned for you.'

Standing opposite the doorway, I was waiting until he'd finished making a play for her. If only she didn't walk off with him. Anyway, what if she did? I'd just catch her up and tap her on the shoulder.

What would I talk about to her? About the money? No, that was already dead and buried. And there was no point in demanding it now, when I'd missed my chance at the police station. But then she might find it interesting – just like that, for no particular reason – to talk to someone she'd harmed. It would, after all, be interesting to know what her victim had thought about it at the time, wouldn't it? Take Vova and Askold, for instance – I'd fed them and bought them drinks, and no doubt a good deal of my money had passed into their hands even before the fight. So why did they also have to beat me up, and with such hatred too? Why had they shown such spite? Or take Klavka – what harm had I ever done her? Why did she treat me as she did? It wasn't by chance they took me to her place. Obviously they couldn't have managed it without her: she was behind it all. She'd sent them to fetch me from the Seamen's Hostel when I left the Arctic and told them to drive me to her flat, and there she'd seduced me to the point where I completely lost my head. Say what you like, it was a well-organized job. But what was she *thinking* all the time? Was she just wondering how to wheedle all the money out of me? Even so, you don't leave a man with just forty kopecks when you're grabbing big money like that. There was real malice in it too! So the question was – why the malice?

'I appreciate your concern, Klavka,' he was saying as he went on chatting her up. 'But she's far away, my wife, in the dim distance. I don't even know whether she exists or not.'

'But there are so many eyes watching us!' she said. 'Doesn't it embarrass you?'

At that moment they both turned towards me.

And what d'you think – was she startled? Embarrassed, perhaps?

Her whole face lit up in a smile, as if she'd met her lover.

'Excuse me,' she said. 'My brother's come to see me. I haven't seen my little brother for so-o-o long.'

I, it seems, was the little brother. The officer gave me a very expressive look: Will you kindly bugger off out of here, brother? 'No,' I said, paying him back in kind. 'I've things to discuss that are more important than your sweet nothings.'

He saluted and went.

'Hello, sister dear!' I said. 'Weren't you expecting me? We've lots to talk about. You should have put a coat on, it's cold on deck.'

'What d'you mean? How can I be cold if I've found you?' She held out her hand to me. 'Not expecting you? I've been on the lookout for you for the last three days.'

I didn't take her hand, but kept mine in the pockets of my jacket. Klavka clasped herself round her bare shoulders and shivered. All right, I thought, if you don't want to talk in a place where there are witnesses, then you can wait a bit. We moved further away from the open deck.

'How did you turn up here? Did you decide to have a spell at sea?'

'Only for three trips, as a replacement. One of the girls is on maternity leave – Annechka Feoktistova. Do you know her?'

'I don't know anybody here.'

Klavka smiled – a crooked, malicious smile.

'Nobody at all? What about that girl I saw you with? The one who sneaked on to your ship.'

'Ah . . . And how did you like her?'

Klavka frowned. 'Why does she wear trousers? Tell her to take them off, otherwise everyone will think she has bandy legs.'

'Her legs are straight.'

'Have you seen them?'

'I've seen as much as necessary.'

'You don't know anything about her legs.'

'OK, Does it worry you?'

'No, not at all. My legs aren't bandy. I just felt sorry for her.'

'Really?! So you can feel sorry, can you?'

She was slightly embarrassed but didn't take the hint.

'I'm serious. Surely you don't rate yourself so low? Don't you think you're worth something better?'

It was windy on deck, my cheekbones were caked with salt, there was a blue haze in front of my eyes from looking at the sea and I felt unsure of myself here, even though I was wearing my jacket – and I could feel the anger gradually rising in me; I just couldn't get through her tough skin, with her look of a drowsy pussycat. She was more cunning than I was; for instance the reason why she hadn't put on a coat was for me to get an eyeful of her bust, right down her deep cleavage.

A crane driver shouted to her from up above: 'Klavka, stop showing off your tits like that! Cover them up, or I might cripple somebody!'

She purposely turned to face him and pulled her dress open wider.

'Impossible,' she said. 'No one's ever been crippled because of me. Only because of their own stupidity.'

So there. And I, so she implied, was suffering for *my* own stupidity. I took her by the elbow and turned her round towards me. 'Maybe we can talk all the same, can we?'

'Yes, my dear!' She came very close to me, and her eyes were in love. 'Yes! Why else d'you think I followed you to sea? At least tell me how you've been feeling on this trip. Have you thought about me, or did you forget me completely?'

'I've done nothing but think about you,' I said. 'I think about you in the daytime and I dream about you at night.'

'Do you really?' She simply beamed all over.

'Klavka,' I said. 'Let's leave the jokes aside.'

Again she gave me that crooked smile.

'When you wouldn't shake my hand, I thought it was because your hand was all fishy. But it's quite dry. Ah, my Ginger . . .'

'I'm not your "Ginger" and I'm not your "dear". If you must pick up a gang of admirers, don't include me among them.'

'Why should I? To me, you're separate. You're not jealous of that man I was talking to just now, are you? Why? Typical lady-killer, boring to talk to, and hands like frogs – brrr! Anyway, I'm not interested in anyone else since I saw you.'

'Really. Not counting your Askold, of course.'

'*Ask*old?!'

'Yes, the one you stayed with that night.'

'He's not mine! The idea! For one thing he didn't stay with me. And for another, it's not so easy to stay with me. I have to be knocked off my feet first, I'll have you know.'

Standing there in front of me she looked tough, with legs so strong she could have stood upright on them in a storm without holding on to anything, with shoulders braced back like a soldier on parade, all poised, as if she might pounce then and there. The wind hadn't affected her, except that her face had hardened very slightly and taken on a healthy flush, and her arms and chest showed no signs of gooseflesh. How could I ever penetrate her armour? I felt our talk was running into the sand. It was no use being clever or beating about the bush with her, she could handle that like an expert; I had to ask her straight out. So I asked her straight out: 'Klavka, why *did* you go to sea? Or wasn't my money enough for you? You could have lived for quite a while on that.'

Now at last she was embarrassed. She blushed all over, down to her cleavage.

'My dear, I'll tell you all about the money. Of course, I must. I'll give it all back to you. No doubt I should have started off with that . . . Look, I'm sorry. I was just so thrilled to see you. But . . . you haven't been thinking of me just because of the money, have you?'

'How much will you give me back?'

Again she shivered and clutched her elbows.

'All there was. Three hundred and something.'

So that was it. They'd decided to divide me up between them. To share out my property. They were scared in case I might raise a stink. After all, I'd gone straight from them to the police station: what if I'd made a statement there, what if the police had started investigations and were only waiting for my return, when I might name some witnesses? . . . The merchant navy man, for instance; the cloakroom attendant at the Arctic; the taxi-driver who drove us – there are only about twenty taxi-drivers in the whole town. So better to forestall me, give me back some portion of the money, and we'd be quits. They'd say I must have left the rest with Nina at Cape Abram; let the police look there. Was *this* why she had followed me to sea? My God, fancy going to all that trouble! They should have known I'd written the whole thing off.

'Well, have we finished talking about the money?' she asked.

'Yes, we have.'

She was silent for a while, then said: 'Perhaps there was more than that three hundred?'

'No, there wasn't.'

'Well, thank God for that . . . Aren't we going to talk about something else? Didn't you prepare anything, is that it?'

She said it just like that: 'Didn't you prepare anything?'

'Oh, thanks – I'm also meant to prepare my speeches, am I?'

'Why not? D'you suppose I haven't been thinking about what I'd say when I met you? But it simply didn't work . . . because of the business of the money. I can't get through to you at all. So much for not being able to live without me . . . Did you resent being beaten up by them?'

'Well, I expect I'll settle that little score separately.'

'It served you right, if you really want to know. Just remember how you behaved. Or don't you remember anything at all?'

'OK,' I said. 'That's an end to the whole story. We'll say no more about it. What am I to you? And what are you to me? Get it?'

She nodded in silence.

'You give me back the three hundred-odd, and as for the rest you walloped out of me . . . you can use it, I won't report you.'

'D'you mean there was more?'

'Didn't you know there was?'

'How much?'   ·

'A thousand. Or nearly.'

'Oh dear, that's a lot!' she sighed, with a faint hint of regret. 'How did you manage to lose so much? Maybe it was when you went to Cape Abram? . . .'

'Klavka,' I said, 'why bother to put on an act? I can see right through you!'

'My God, I really don't know what became of your money. They probably spent it all on drink . . .'

'They spent it on drink?!'

Why was I so surprised they'd blued it on drink? Obviously they didn't use my cash to build palaces with crystal halls. But I couldn't help imagining to myself how I'd been sweating away with those barrels today, for instance . . . and there were they, on shore, in some dive, maybe even at this moment . . . Had they had a good booze-up? Had they remembered me kindly? Perhaps they'd each downed a glass to my precious health. So that was it. They'd drunk it all. I'd kill them. Yes, I'd kill them, no other punishment would do. I'd be put on trial. The courtroom would be full of sailors like me, or their wives; they of all people know how I earned that cash – and how those idle layabouts had shown up, those monsters, those gutter-bred pigs, who had steered me towards this girl and robbed me. It wouldn't have been so bad if they'd used that money for something sensible. But no, they'd blued it. Spent it all on drink . . .

'Go away,' I said to Klavka. 'Go away, before I belt you one right here. And don't let me see you again.'

She clutched her shoulders as if suddenly feeling the cold, and she finally covered the open top of her dress.

'Why are you shouting at me?' she asked, her voice close to tears – though I hadn't been shouting but had spoken to her quietly, through clenched teeth. 'Do you think I'm frightened of you, you miserable beacher? What could you do to me? How can you threaten me? I've been shouted at enough in my time. I've been beaten up by men, cursed by my parents, threatened by officials. Nothing frightens me now. Your trouble is, Ginger, you don't understand people. People are nice to you, but all you can do is go for them.'

'I haven't gone for you yet. I haven't finished what I've got to say to you.'

'What else have you been saving up to tell me? . . . I've heard you, and I can give as good as I get.'

She walked away from me, her heels clicking on the deck. From halfway she turned round and said: 'I hear you ship is going to stay out and go on fishing.'

'What's that to you?'

'For the moment, nothing. I wish you luck with that hole in the stern. Let's hope you don't sink. See you in April, then?'

'That's right.'

'Well, in April you'll get your money back. You might at least thank me for taking that much off them, when they picked it up in the corridor.'

'Wait a moment . . .'

'No, I've told you everything that was bothering you. I can't hang around here any longer. I'm not a passenger on this ship, either, you know.'

She went out on to the open deck and closed the watertight door behind her with its securing clips.

My face was burning as if I'd been scalded. So that was what she thought, was it? I didn't understand people? I lit a cigarette and looked down at the trawlers that were riding alongside and bumping against the fenders. Perhaps I *didn't* understand . . . It had all ended so nastily, even though I hadn't meant to make a scene. But why should I believe her, when I'd burnt my fingers so badly? And on top of it I was supposed to thank her! And when I went to get my money in April, I might even end up without a stitch – her place was nothing by a clip-joint. I'd have to take a pal with me, so he could be a witness and help me in case of need. The main thing was not to trust that pussycat, not to trust anybody where cash was involved; it's a stinking business and it turns everyone into a brute . . .

OK, the subject being closed for the time being, I set off to find the shop. I went below to No. 4 deck and immediately found myself in a different existence: carpets all down the corridor, glass doors, the bulkheads lined with plastic made to look like malachite, lads in string vests playing ping-pong.

They can't have been keen to allow us galley-slaves on to this deck: one look at it, and we'd all desert our trawlers. All they want from us is output, while other people live. Admittedly they don't make as good money as we do, though it'd be a good thing if we could manage to hang on to some of that money, which we don't seem able to do.

I still couldn't get Klavka, that enigmatic girl, out of my head. For some reason I suddenly felt sorry for her. To get a foothold in this luxurious life, she no doubt had to grease somebody's palm for a job on board – in fact it may well have been *my* hard-earned cash that came in handy for that. And what a price she had to pay for that lousy money: all that playing up to a 'miserable beacher', the fear of getting caught, and then to have to act as if she loved me. All in all, I decided I wouldn't go and get my money in April, unless she herself wanted to come and find me. When I don't understand something, I do better to keep away from it.

Looking like an elephant in my sea-boots, I blundered into the shop and shouted from the doorway: 'Got any electric razors?'

In there it was as quiet as a church, a fan humming gently, and two lads in string vests were chatting politely to the salesman, choosing a length of material for a suit. All three looked askance at me and shook their heads, as if they'd seen some idiot from the frozen waters.

True – why had I bothered to ask? Stacked up all around was everything the heart could desire: suits of every possible kind, tweed and gabardine; five different sorts of razors; Blue Matador razor blades; transistors and stereo tape-recorders. And you didn't have to pay. Payment was simply unnecessary, that's all. All you had to do was show them your seaman's paybook, so they could enter your name in their ledger, and point at something: 'Wrap me up that one.' And there's that magic word 'later', that makes you feel like Rockefeller: you grab whatever you fancy and only later, when your account is totted up, do you discover you have only about a month's earnings left to live on. You can even end up in debt, because wherever you may be sailing your earnings are also drained away by pay-warrant to your wife, kids or parents. If I could have burned that shop down, how many seamen's problems would have been solved! Including my own, by the way: I've sailed at least two extra trips all because of that 'pay later' system.

I didn't buy anything for myself, but only chose an electric razor on Shura's paybook – the most expensive one, of course. Shura would never forgive me if I bought him a cheap one. As the salesman was droning on about how it could be switched to either 127 or 220 volts, how to change the blades and so on, I thought how lucky it was for Shura that *he* hadn't come to this shop in person; he wouldn't have just bought the razor but he'd have grabbed a couple of suits as well, which then would have hung, unworn, in a cupboard until his wife finally flogged them to a second-hand shop for half their price. When does he ever get to wear a suit? It's amazing – we break our backs and get calloused hands to earn that money, and then we try and get rid of it again as fast as we can! But just because it does cost us so much effort, such callouses, such hard labour, perhaps it's not money at all. Perhaps it ought to be called something else. Am I really giving my life away for *money*? I can't accept that. But for Klavka, now – it really is money. Unlike me, she doesn't squander it but puts it all to good use. So why did I lose my temper with her? Go on, let her use the money; it's quite fair. And all at once I felt better.

There was nothing more for me to do on the factory-ship. Even if any mates of mine were sailing in her, I'd never find them in this ant-heap.

At the foot of the main companion-way I bumped into our trawlmaster, who was talking to some friend of his. The trawlmaster was wearing a quilted jerkin and cap pulled down over his eyes, but his friend had neatly brushed hair and creases in his trousers, and he was wearing a short-sleeved lumberjack shirt. Both, though, were equally merry, glistening with alcoholic good humour.

'Hang on here, Senya, I'm going to fetch the nets in a moment and you can give me a hand.'

The conversation with his friend was a serious one: 'The devil himself put me on this ship!' said the trawlmaster.

'Yes, you've been unlucky,' his friend replied.

'I'm going to transfer to another, I swear to God.'

'Of course. A man must have some self-respect.'

'I may switch to the *Mermaid*.'

'Sure, she's a decent ship.'

'Or the *Chaliapin*.'

'She's a decent ship too.'

'But this *Galloper* – to hell with her, that's no ship to sail on.'

They might have kept on like this for a long time, because there are plenty of ships, but at that moment the clicking of a pair of heels and the swish of a skirt were heard, so their attention was distracted.

Klavka walked past us and started to go up the companion-way, but then stopped. She glanced at me as if trying but failing to remember some chance acquaintance.

'Go on, up you go, Klavka,' the friend said to her. 'We won't look up your skirt.'

'Even if you do, my underwear's clean.'

The trawlmaster snorted with amusement.

'Oh, Klavka,' said the friend. 'Why do we all love you so much?'

He tried to make a grab for her, but she was standing out of reach.

'If only you all did! But that villain in the posh jacket is scowling at me. He wants to kill me.'

'Who, Senya?' roared the trawlmaster. 'He's no villain. Why he's the life and soul of the ship. He's a tower of strength to the whole crew whenever life gets difficult.'

'In that case, you must be working him too hard. He may have had a soul once, but you've taken it all out of him.'

'Senya!' The trawlmaster looked hard at me. 'Yes, it's true, you somehow don't look your usual self. Relax, Senya! You're looking at a queen!'

'He's right,' said Klavka. 'What have you got against me?'

You're not a pussycat, I thought, but a snake. You still want to force me, in front of these people, to say I haven't got anything against you. No, when I made up my mind about you, it was my own decision. So don't expect me to say anything.

'Of course he hasn't got anything against you,' said the trawlmaster. 'Have you, Senya?'

'Why doesn't he say anything? Why don't you say something, Ginger?'

'The silence of assent,' said the friend. 'In that case let's go and get the ladies a bit drunk. Want a drink before you sail?'

'Can I come too?' said the trawlmaster.

'You're merry enough already. But he's sad, and I hate sad people. They spoil everything for other people . . .'

I still said nothing. Klavka suddenly laughed, dismissed us with a wave of her hand and went.

'What's the matter with you?' the trawlmaster asked me. 'That woman was giving you the come-on.'

'It means nothing,' said the friend. 'He was doing the right thing. You did the right thing, mate. You're not the only one she's flirted with. Some of them almost get on the job with her, but then she wriggles out of it at the last moment.'

For some reason the trawlmaster sighed. Then they took up their conversation again: 'And what about the *Boatswain Andreyev*? Isn't she another good ship?'

'I should say so!'

I dragged the trawlmaster away from his friend and we set off for the net-hold. On the way I asked him: 'Will we be coming back to this factory-ship?'

'No Senya. She has a full load and she's going back to port now. So you've missed your chance. Run after her if you really want to – I'll collect the nets myself.'

'No, I won't.'

In the net-hold we lay a while on the nets, smoking surreptitiously – the trawlmaster had found another friend there – and by the time we emerged from the lift on to the upper deck, it was starting to get dark. The wind had freshened, the factory-ship was rolling hard and we would have to leave very soon.

We threw the nets down on to the deck of our ship. She was pitching fiercely, and one net fell into the water. Swearing horribly, Seryozha fished it out with a boathook. It was then that I saw Lilya, wearing a tarpaulin raincoat with a hood. She was looking over the rail at our ship. She'd probably heard me swearing as I gave Seryozha instructions.

She came up and held out her hand. Her handshake was the same as ever – warm, dry and firm. And her smile was the same, sweet and a little embarrassed. But something had changed between us. I didn't know what it was; I thought there wasn't anything *to* change.

'I can tell which DWT is yours now. She has a little aeroplane with a propellor at the masthead.'

'It isn't only our ship that has it – lots of them do.'

'What for?'

'It's just a toy. When the propellor spins, it cheers us all up.'

'But I did recognize *your* ship all the same!'

Noticing that I was being delayed, the trawlmaster decided to dash off somewhere for his own purposes: 'Wait for me, Senya, and we'll go down together.'

Lilya asked: 'Is that hole in your stern serious?'

'With luck we won't sink.'

'Why "with luck"?'

'Anything can happen at sea.'

'Just like that, for no particular reason? They told me the damage was serious.'

'It's nothing. That's not the problem.'

'What is, then?'

I was going to tell her about the Chief's misgivings, but changed my mind. It would have taken too long to explain and wouldn't have meant anything to her.

'It's nothing serious either.'

'I heard one of your crew has signed off. I thought it was you.'

'No, it wasn't me.'

'I know that. I just thought how splendid it would be if it had been you. We'd have sailed home together. The ship's going back soon, did you know? We're only waiting for Grakov. He's on your ship, with the captain.'

I still had the chance to play my hand again from scratch. I could call up Zhora the mate and spin him some yarn; he hadn't asked to see Vanya Obod's sick-note. Somebody would pass me up my gear, and I could lower Shura's razor to him on a line – not forgetting to tell them to release Tommy the seagull. And she and I would sail away on this magnificent liner. Together, the two of us. Ah – a white ship on a blue sea!

'Can't you make up your mind? You know, everyone here was amazed when your crew decided to stay out and carry on fishing – I asked lots of people about it. You're just like children. Such incredible thoughtlessness: "With luck it'll be all right." Don't you realize how stupid that is? Is it being brave just to bash on without thinking?'

For the first time she was showing she minded about what might happen to me. For the first time she was asking me to do something, making a suggestion. This was worth knowing!

'Should I run away like a rat when the others are staying?'

'So that's what bothers you! I suppose it's better if you all drown together, is it?'

'Well, we won't necessarily drown . . .'

'You said yourself – anything can happen at sea. Are you afraid of not being like all the others?'

She was right; I was afraid of just that. But then the Chief wasn't afraid of 'not being like the others', and he was staying with the ship.

'Are you afraid of being laughed at? Is that the worst thing in the world?'

I had once dreamed of a moment like this, when she would be worried about me. Now she was not just worrying, she was afraid for me. But it gave me no joy. If I did sign off, something might happen to the Chief without me, and for that I would never forgive myself for the rest of my life.

'Well, make up your mind.'

The *Galloper* was lifted up by a wave and banged her side against a fender. Lilya gave a start.

'If I was to be hung, drawn and quartered, I could never agree to go on your ship.'

She said this in such a frightened voice that I suddenly pulled her to me and kissed her on the lips. They were cold and slightly chapped. I surprised myself by doing this – she hadn't expected it either and took a step back. Doing so made her even more embarrassed.

'Heavens . . . how romantic.'

A voice came from the loundspeakers:

'Number eight-one-five, stand by to cast off at once!'

Down below Zhora looked out of the wheelhouse: 'OK, OK, we're nearly ready . . .'

The derrickman brought up a net. I went over and took hold of it. Marconi and the trawlmaster came running.

'So what's the answer?'

'The same. It'll be all right.'

She said with a faintly sarcastic smile: 'I think I understand all about you.'

'And what am I?'

'What I thought you were. But it's always worthwhile to make sure.'

'Will you write to me at sea?'

'Do you think that's a good idea? You're not going to change your mind for my sake. There was a moment, you know, when I suddenly wanted to . . . get together with you as they say. But since you don't need that, then I'm sorry, but letters . . .'

I had the feeling she said this not just sadly but also with a certain relief.

Marconi and the trawlmaster ran up and took their places in the net.

'Well, good hunting!' Lilya waved to all of us. 'Hope you break a leg! A hundred feet of water under your keel!'

'Good for her!' the trawlmaster roared triumphantly. 'There's a woman for you!'

The net flew over Lilya's head, over the side, and started to go down. Suddenly it came to a sharp stop – we were heading straight for the mast, and the derrickman had spotted it in time. I raised my head: Lilya was looking down at us, shading her eyes with her hand against the beam of our searchlight.

'You don't seem too cheerful,' said Marconi. 'I was wrong to take you on board the factory-ship.'

'I told you not to bother.'

He was about to wave to her, but the net plunged sharply down towards the holds, and Seryozha caught it. The others at once went their sparate ways, but I stayed where I was. The empty net was swinging between the masts and it was tempting me greatly.

'Number eight-one-five!' came the order from the big ship. 'Cast off mooring-lines!'

A wave lifted us up and dropped us with a crash against the factory-ship's side. There was no one in the wheelhouse; no doubt Zhora had gone to the captain's cabin. An official report is a serious matter; it has to be signed by all the ship's officers – and the occasion always calls for a drink.

Then this is what happened.

I was alone on deck, looking at Lilya. I didn't know whether she could see me or not; she had screwed up her eyes against the searchlight beam and this gave her a sort of scornful look.

Suddenly she had gone. There was just the straight line of the ship's rail with no head showing above it.

I went to put on my oilskins, so as not to dirty my jacket; I was obviously going to have to cast off the lines, because all the others were already asleep. When I came back on deck, someone yelled at me from above: 'Watchkeeper!' It was the derrickman. 'Are all your people back on board?'

'Yes, all of them.'

'And what about our people – have they all been hauled up?'

'Yes.'

A moment after I'd said this, I remembered about Grakov. He was still sitting in the captain's cabin, signing the report, or drinking, or doing God knows what else, and all the time he was expected on the big ship and the waves were knocking our trawler against her side.

'Then I'll take the net away.'

'Go ahead.'

It'd be better this way, I thought. Grakov could stay on board our ship, so whatever happened to us would happen to him too.

The derrickman waved his mitt at me and asked: 'Where's your crew?'

'In their bunks.'

He snorted with laughter. 'Already? Well, so long, watchkeeper!'

I was going to reply that I wasn't the watchkeeper, but then I changed my mind – let him think I was; he'd never recognize me again, dressed as I was all in green oilskins.

A call came over the factory-ship's loudspeaker: '*Galloper*, ahoy – cast off mooring-lines!'

Zhora wasn't in the wheelhouse. With my heart thumping like mad, I went to the stern and cast off all the turns of the stern line. It dropped out of the fairlead and trailed in the water, and the current immediately began to push the stern away from the other ship. It's the truth when I tell you nothing terrible could have happened. It only meant we couldn't haul in on the stern line, and to moor up again we'd have had to turn round and come alongside again, that's all.

When Zhora came back into the wheelhouse, I was standing inside the doghouse, in the dark. He saw at once that the stern line had been cast off.

'Who cast off? I'll have their guts for garters!' Then he switched on the intercom: 'Crew to cast off for'ard!'

I waited a bit before coming out, as though I'd heard the order down below in the cabin. Zhora shone the searchlight on me.

'Who's that? Shalai? Cast off for'ard!'

The watchkeeper on the factory-ship took the line from me and wished us luck. I came aft and stood beneath the wheelhouse.

'Shalai!' shouted Zhora.

'All clear for'ard.'

'OK. Don't go away, we'll have to moor up again straight away.'

The engine started up and we began to move away. Grakov and the skipper came running into the wheelhouse.

'Who gave the order to stand off?'

'I did,' said Zhora.

He was a real ship's officer, was Zhora. He just couldn't have said: 'I don't know, the line cast itself off, I suppose.' He said: 'I gave the order. Emergency situation, risk of damage.'

'What's to happen to me now?' asked Grakov.

I didn't hear Zhora's reply. He switched on the loud-hailer and Grakov himself shouted into the microphone: 'Factory-ship, ahoy! Number eight-one-five calling! Give me the officer of the watch!'

The big ship was moving further away, her lights growing hazier.

'Officer of the watch here . . .'

'Request permission to moor up. A man from the factory-ship has been left on board . . .'

'Permission to moor up not granted.'

'This is Grakov speaking. I demand to speak to the captain.'

'You don't demand to speak to the captain, you request. I'll give you the captain.'

Another voice came over the loudspeaker: 'Captain here.'

'Grakov speaking. Request permission to moor up. I must come back on board your ship.'

'There's a Force 7 gale blowing. No question of mooring in this weather. Remain on board number eight-one-five.'

'I request the captain not to direct my whereabouts. Number eight-one-five is going out fishing.'

'I wish number eight-one-five a good catch,' said the captain of the factory-ship. I thought I could hear him laughing. 'Tomorrow number eight-zero-six is going back to port, you can go back in her. Dmitry Rodionovich, you are in the hands of a sound collective of our glorious seamen. I'm sure you won't mind spending twenty-four hours in their company.'

'But I have to hand over an official report.'

'I believe you. But why must you hand it over to me?'

'I hear you,' said Grakov. 'I regard it as my duty to report this incident to the commodore of the fishing fleet.'

'Good fishing. Roger and out.'

There was silence as the skipper and Grakov left the wheelhouse. I stood up to window and said to Zhora: 'Zhora, I cast off the sternline.'

He leaned out right to his waist so as to get a look at me.

'You did? You son of a bitch! Did you realize what you were doing?'

'Yes, I did.'

'And that there might have been an accident?'

'No chance, Zhora.'

He thought for a moment. 'Tell the bo'sun to send you to swab out the heads.'

'Both.'

'What d'you mean – "both"?'

'Both sets of heads.'

'Go and get some sleep. Send the next man on the list to do his trick at the wheel.'

'Aye, aye!'

'You son of a bitch!'

By now the factory-ship could barely be seen. Even with the most powerful binoculars, I couldn't have seen anyone on her deck. Anyway, Lilya wasn't there any longer, unless she happened to be looking out of some porthole.

The weather was getting worse, and the waves were lashing the whole vessel with spray. Then came a flurry of snow, and as I made my way to the foc's'le my whole face was stung with needles, making it impossible to open my eyes. I had to grope my way by feel, like a blind man.

It had all happened like the words of the song: 'We parted, you and I, just like two ships at sea . . .'

Part 4

The Chief

1

None of us thought we'd be casting that night. Even if a good shoal registers on the echo-sounder, they let it go, to give the deck-crew a full night's sleep after the factory-ship. It's a sacred law, and every skipper observes it, even if all the fish in the Atlantic are passing under his keel. After the departure we all bunked down, except for Seryozha, whose turn it was to take the wheel. This, too, was only right and proper: when the ship is under way in such dirty weather, the mate could never manage on his own – although I've known mates who let the whole crew lie in after a spell at a factory-ship, who take the wheel themselves and sound the hooter if there's fog or a snowfall.

Suddenly, when we were all asleep, the helmsman came clattering down the companion-way, burst into the cabin and yelled: 'Get up, you lot – we're going to cast!'

Not a single curtain moved, so he went round all the bunks pulling off blankets and tugging at people's feet.

'Seryozha – are you round the bend?'

'Get up, lads, this is for real. They won't let you go on sleeping, anyway. The First Mate'll be down in a minute.'

Shura said: 'Maybe they'll change their minds.'

'No, they've been thinking it over too long to change their minds. The skipper, he didn't want to: let the men rest, he said. It was Flatnose who called him through the speaking-tube: "There's an enormous shoal, the sounder's never registered such a big one, and what's more we've lost two days' fishing time." Grakov backed him up: "That's right," he said. "Why are you so soft on them? You only handed in half a load and you're full of empty barrels . . ."'

Vasya Burov said: 'It's obvious. Staying out's not enough for them. They want to earn themselves promotion as well.'

'Well, what's it to be?' asked Seryozha.

'Go and tell 'em we're getting up.'

Outside, we could hear him talking to the First Mate.

'Why are they taking so long to wake up?'

'We'd better go, First Mate. Otherwise, who knows, you might get hit by a boot . . .'

We went up the companion-way like we were climbing the scaffold. Out there it was howling and whistling. As we went to our stations, we couldn't see each other through the snow.

The skipper shouted out of the white murk: 'Skorodumov, what depth of nets have you prepared?'

'I haven't prepared any.'

'Good! Put the nets at zero depth!'

'Zero depth' means attaching the nets without any headlines. The nets are made fast directly to the floats, and they trawl at only half a metre below the surface. It isn't often done, but it means we've struck a really good shoal and it's not deep.

'Let's go!'

In the darkness and spray we couldn't see where the nets were going as they went overboard. This time I didn't shout: 'Mark! . . . Splice! . . .' but simply squatted alongside the trawlmaster and spoke almost into his ear. Besides, he wasn't tying the floats at the marks, but in any old place. Once I thought I even saw him tying the knots with his eyes shut. And he was, too – now and again his eyelids stuck together and I held my knife ready in case he suddenly got his fingers caught in a knot. Even so, I doubt if I'd have been able to cut him free in time.

We went below, threw our wet things on the deck – there's not room for everyone's gear on the radiator – and flopped out. Now just let 'em try waking us at six!

And they didn't. We woke up by ourselves and realized why we hadn't been called: it was blowing a storm.

Grey waves tinged with a sort of rust colour were rolling at us like mountains, hanging over us, threatening to break on us at mast height, then breaking on the foc's'le and flooding along the deck as far as the wheelhouse, hissing and foaming like new beer. We would gradually climb up a wave and roll down from the crest into the trough, where it seemed we'd never get out again. Yet by some miracle we got out every time.

The sea was like an endless ploughed field, furrowed with wave-troughs, and no sooner had we climbed out of one than we'd plunge back into the next, and so on for ever. It made your heart freeze to look at the water – heavy as mercury and shining with an icy gleam. You'd try and look at the wheelhouse, wait until the bow rode up and the wheelhouse was below you and then run for it, like running downhill. Anyone who didn't make it in time or who stumbled would at once be thrown back and the deck would rise up in front of him like a mountainside.

In the saloon we crammed ourselves in six to a bench, so as not to keep falling against each other. Through the porthole you saw first the sky, then the sea, now whitish, now a dark grey-blue like a seagull's wing. Nobody even felt like watching films, so we went for'ard again to get some more sleep.

Vasya Burov said cheerfully: 'Good old wind, give us a blow, so we can stay on "watch below".'

Shura and Seryozha played a hand or two and slapped each other on the nose, but their hearts weren't in it and they soon bunked down. Seems they'd played over a hundred games on this trip; or maybe they'd started again from scratch after the 'kiss' on the stern.

I lay there with my curtain drawn, my feet rising higher than my head as the ship pitched, trying not to think about anything. In a storm, you simply can't think. However long that 'watch below' may last – a week, a fortnight – the time doesn't count in your life. And you can't call it rest, either.

Mitrokhin came back from the wheel and flopped – his boots were squelching, the water was pouring off his jerkin. He started telling us how a wave had caught him. Of course it had caught him just by the doghouse – where else?! The only good thing about a storm is hearing how someone else was caught by a wave, especially when you yourself are warm and dry. The reason is because it's so nice to sympathize, because you know exactly what it's like: you've walked the length of the deck, you've dodged all the spray, you've successfully taken cover from ten waves – and the eleventh one is specially waiting for you, just before you reach the doghouse and safety. Say what you like, the sea is a living thing and spiteful with it – it's not just a mindless force of nature.

Before going to sleep, Mitrokhin said: 'Looks like we're going to have to haul in today, lads, too.'

The engine was running at dead slow ahead, to straighten out the trawl. In the next-door cabin, Mitrokhin's relief – was it the cooper? . . . yes, it was – could be heard pulling on his wet boots. The door banged and he squelched up the companion-way, cursing the Atlantic for all he was worth; no doubt it made him feel warmer. Then everything quietened down again – except the storm, that is.

Unable to restrain himself, Shura pulled back the curtain and asked Mitrokhin: 'What did you say?'

Mitrokhin, as usual, was sleeping with his eyes open. You could never tell if he was asleep or daydreaming.

'Did he say we'd have to haul in today? Or was I imagining it?'

'Lie down,' I said. 'Nobody heard anything.'

'Which one of us is crazy?'

'You, of course. Who ever heard of hauling in when it's Force 9?'

Shura lay still for a while, listening.

'The weather's slackening.'

'It's your brain that's slackening,' said Vasya. 'Go to sleep, it's the best cure.'

'*You* wake up the loony, then! Get him to talk sense, otherwise I won't be able to sleep.'

'If you go on making that noise,' Vasya said threateningly, 'they probably *will* call us out.'

We lay there for another half-hour, until suddenly the intercom crackled and sure enough the order came to haul in.

The spray was slashing my face so hard, it took an effort to wait until that hellish warp came out of the sea. I opened the hatch-cover and dived into the warp-hold, where at least I was better off than those poor buggers on deck.

Tommy was delighted to see me and huddled up close. And you should have seen the way his beak gaped. He could probably sense how much fish was out there in the nets. He was such an efficient echo-sounder, he ought to have been paid a salary – at least as much as the mates.

I could hear the frequent heavy thumping of the nets as they were hauled in, the sound of boots slithering about in roe, the creaking of the net-winch and the squeal of its drum under heavy strain. I was just going to take a look out, but at that moment about three gallons of water came sloshing over my head. I knew by now what it meant when a wave came right into my warp-hold – at least Force 9, and further hauling was impossible.

Somebody shouted, and then the trawlmaster came squelching over to me: 'Senya, come on out of there!'

'What's up? Are we breaking off?'

But he was already off and away, swearing blue murder.

I climbed out. The whole deck was covered in fish. The lads were wading about in it up to their knees, bumping against the gunwale, smothered in roe and in pink, blood-stained snow. The net was coming in over the side, crammed with a twitching, silver mass. I saw all this in a moment, then came a snow-flurry and all I could see was a glimpse of someone's sou'wester, an elbow or a back.

I pushed my way through to the trawlmaster – he was standing by the winch, looking at the sea. I don't know what he saw there, apart from snow and black water. His whole face was stuck together with snow, icicles were hanging from his sou'wester. He stood there whispering to himself: '. . . fucking stupid oafs, drive us up the wall, don't know what the hell they're doing, sod the fucking bastards . . .'

'What's the matter, trawly?'

He turned round towards me, his eyes closed, and barked: 'Haul in from the warp-hold. Haul in as far as a splice and we'll break off! They can do what they like.'

I hauled in half a coil, made it fast, and he cut the line at the splice.

'Shut the hatch-cover, somebody might fall in . . .'

I groped my way to it, threw in the cut length and closed the hatch-cover. Then I went over to the net, to relieve someone at shaking. And I shook the net, seeing nothing, losing all feeling in my hands, shoulders and legs, battered by the weight of about a ton of fish. I couldn't pull my legs out of the fish, except perhaps by shaking off my boots, until finally the others moved me away to help with the second, final shaking of the almost empty nets.

After a time there was nowhere left on deck to shake the fish. The order came from the wheelhouse: 'Don't open the hold. Leave the fish on the deck.'

We fenced it in with the fish-gutting table and with barrels of salt, and we left it there, hoping it wouldn't be washed overboard. We threw off our boots and oilskins on the companion-way and crowded into the cabin, where we chucked our jerkins into a heap on the deck.

'That's it, lads,' said Shura. 'This is my last day in this job . . .'

We could hear the trawlmaster going to his own cabin and saying to someone, maybe himself: 'I'm going to sign off at the next factory-ship. I don't care if they put me to swabbing out the heads. There aren't any more fools left who'll carry on like this!'

Vasya Burov just lay on his bunk and laughed.

'What's up with you?'

'There still are some fools left. Us. If they call us out again, d'you suppose we won't do as we're told and go out?'

'They'll call us out all right.'

'Have you seen the floats?'

'What about the floats?' Shura leaned out over the side of his bunk. 'I don't understand you. Why don't you tell us one of your stories?'

'What, don't you understand? The floats are half-submerged in the water. There's so much fish in those nets that you young puppies have never seen the like of it. At least four hundred kilos per net. I can only remember seeing anything like it once before.'

'OK, so there's four hundred kilos. How are we going to haul it in, when we can't open the hatches?'

Vasya sighed: 'It's like I say – we're the fools. D'you think the officers up on the after-deck are bothered about the *fish*? They were stupid enough to cast in this weather, now they're worried about losing the whole trawl. That's all the skipper needs now – to lose his nets: if he does that, they won't just demote him to Third Mate, but to bo'sun. A trawl costs money. But our sweat costs nothing.'

Somebody came squelching down from the deck. We all huddled into our bunks, trying to look as if we weren't there, or were dead. But the man who came in was Vasya the cook.

'Dinnertime, lads.'

Were we pleased to see him!

'Vasya, why did you have to come along the deck to see us? Couldn't you have announced it over the intercom?'

'There's no microphone in my galley. Well, what about it, lads? The skipper's ordered me to feed the crew properly.'

It's a bad sign, I can tell you, when they give the order to feed the crew 'properly'.

'I don't envy you, lads. You won't get this lot sorted out before nightfall.'

So that was why the cook had struggled along the deck to come in person. He wanted to show us his sympathy.

We sat there in the saloon, a picture of misery, each man's face and hands looking as if they'd been scrubbed raw with a brick. Zhora the Second Mate gave us a sarcastic look: 'Why so miserable? We've got a record catch!'

'How can we stow it aboard?' asked Vasya Burov. 'All we can do is run it through our fingers and throw it back.'

Zhora shrugged his shoulders. It wasn't time for his watch, so he had no cause for headaches yet.

'Are you going to make us haul in?' asked Shura.

'Think I'll let you off?' Zhora suddenly looked at me. '*He's* the one you've got to thank for this.'

Everyone stared at me. Zhora got up and went out. I, of course, understood what he meant: how I'd cast off the stern line and so forced Grakov to stay on our ship. If he hadn't been on board, the skipper probably wouldn't have made us get up. Oh well, I'd have to tell them; they'd find out sooner or later. But just then Grakov himself came into the saloon and sat down at the end of the table by the door, in the place where the skipper always sat.

The cook served him the same food as us, only not in a bowl but in a plate, just as he always served the skipper, the mates and the Chief. Grakov noticed this and handed the plate back to him.

'Why these privileges? Don't you count me as an equal member of the crew?'

Vasya went to get him a bowl, which was simply extra trouble for him. Grakov leaned back, looking at us with a smile, twiddling his spoon in his hands as if he was winding up a reel of twine.

'Down in the dumps, I see. But this weather's mild for real seamen!'

Without raising his head, Shura said: 'It's mild when you're sitting in a cabin.'

'I take the hint. Just try going out on deck – is that what you meant? Well, when you and I have finished our dinner, I'll come out on deck with you. How's that?'

Shura was amazed.

'Fine. If you come out, we all will.'

The Chief arrived. We moved up to make room, and he also sat down at the end, opposite Grakov.

'What do you say, Sergei Andreyich?' asked Grakov. 'Shall we give the deck crew a hand? All of us together? We'll give our bellies a good shake-up. I'm even thinking of trying to persuade the captain to join us. Otherwise these youngsters will lose heart at the sight of a catch like this.'

The Chief took his plate in silence and started to eat.

'You don't have to come, of course. I expect you've got enough trouble with the engines to look after, haven't you?'

The Chief appeared not to hear him. We even began to feel awkward; the Chief might at least have frowned, or something. Grakov kept smiling at him, but with a bit of an effort. Then he turned to us, his face took on a kindly look and he gave a beaming smile: 'He's a bit unsociable today, is your Chief. Well, he and I will be taking a back seat soon. You don't notice time passing, then when you look at all these young faces, all these cheeky young lads – it makes you sad, I can tell you . . . Yes. But you'll never be like your Chief. Ah, what a lad he was! You started with a shovel in your hand, as a stoker, didn't you, Sergei Andreyich? Yes, as a stoker, I remember. Anyway, one day the furnace-bars had got fouled up with cinders and although the firebox was still hot he crawled inside, just imagine, to poke out the clinker with a flat-bladed shovel. He just wrapped himself in wet sacking. And nobody ordered him to – he did it off his own bat. They say the soles curled off your boots, isn't that so, Sergei Andreyich? . . . You'll say it was stupid, why climb into the furnace, couldn't he have waited an hour or so until it cooled? But he couldn't. The whole country was going through such terrible times, it seemed every minute lost would cost us dear. I don't suppose you lot will understand that. Even we ourselves sometimes can't believe things were really that bad . . . But they were! So there you are, you youngsters. As soon as the ship starts to roll a little, you say: "It's a storm! . . . Better wait a bit, better sit it out and smoke a cigarette" . . .'

The Chief looked at him only once – quickly, from under his eyebrows, with lacklustre eyes – but even so those eyes did seem to give out a little flash of warmth. It was as if in their youth some tie had existed between the two of them, something we would never know about.

Yurka the greaser burst into the saloon, stripped to the waist, wearing slippers and an oily rag round his neck. Grakov turned to look at him with a kindly, thoughtful expression, spread his hands and laughed: Yurka was such a cocky lad, with the smug look of a sly tomcat.

'Just try talking to this young, er . . . enthusiast. About rebellious youth. Would he understand anything? Since he thinks it permissible to come into the saloon in such a state. Oh dear, you've let standards slip, Sergei Andreyich.'

'So what? I've come straight off watch,' said Yurka, blushing all over and starting to blink.

The Chief said to him in a gloomy voice: 'Don't put in any more oil. I dipped it before we started the engine, and there's this much – ' he indicated the width of his palm – 'excess oil in the sump.'

Yurka straightened up and said eagerly: 'I'll go and let it out right away.'

'Never take oil out of a moving engine. The oil is at work all round the system. I expect we'll be drifting today, so we can stop the engine then.'

'But maybe we won't be drifting?' Grakov wasn't speaking to the Chief any longer, but was asking us. 'We'll haul in and then search for more fish, shan't we?'

The Chief pushed aside his plate, ate his stewed fruit in one gulp and went. Grakov watched them go, with a mixture of sadness and pity.

'How Babilov has aged. No doubt his hearing's bad. And it's hard to make him change his mind once he's made it up.' He turned back to us again with a smile. 'Well, you seamen? Are we going out on deck, or are we going to take a smoke-break?'

'I'll do as I'm told,' said Shura.

'You keep saying "I'll do as I'm told!" But what do you *think*?'

We got up one by one and sidled out – over his knees. It never occurred to him to stand up and make way for us.

'So you can expect me on deck,' he said to Shura. 'You'll see me there, sailor.'

And we did see him on deck. He came out with Marconi, the engineers, and the First Mate. He was given a new, unused set of oilskins and offered the choice of a rake or a scoop-net: bosses don't shake the big nets. This seemed a stupid choice; you can at least use the rake to lean on against the rolling of the ship, but with a scoop-net you have to slog away without stopping, heaving up thirty pounds at every scoop, and you can conk out in no time. But Grakov hadn't come on deck to conk out; he swung his net with such a will that our eyes popped out of our heads, and he even managed to shout, though in a hoarse voice: 'Come on, lads, put your backs into it! You're not going to let us old fogeys beat you at your own game, are you? Ah, you young people . . .'

By now fish-scales were stuck all over his eyebrows and he was caked in snow. The others who had come with him were flagging, making little more than token strokes with their rakes, but Grakov was scooping away as hard as ever, as broad-shouldered as if he was tossing hay with a pitchfork and giving no sign of being short of breath. Honestly, we too were infected by his example, though we'd been on deck since that morning. Even Vasya Burov said with admiration: 'God, can he move his muscles! First time I've ever seen such a nut-case!'

Then came a snow-flurry as thick as a wall, so that Grakov couldn't be seen or his wheezing heard any more.

Zhora the mate gave the order: 'Break off!'

That wasn't the end of it, though. We came out on deck a couple more times and tried to haul in the rest of the nets. Regular as clockwork, Grakov came out with us, to show us he thought this weather was mild and his generation could do twice the work of ours. We shook the nets for all we were worth, bogged down in fish, wet, frozen to the marrow, and all in vain – the fish kept being washed into the scuppers, they never managed to scoop it out from under our feet, and the head-line was continually getting caught up in the drum of the winch and tearing the nets one after another.

'We're just producing scrap, lads,' the trawlmaster said to us. He was holding a net in his hands: it was a mass of holes, quite past mending. He pulled it out of the trawl and draped it round his shoulders like a priest's cassock. 'I'm going straight to the captain, to show him what we're doing to the nets.'

When he came back he looked terrible, and could only speak in a hoarse bark: 'That's it, lads – I've had enough.'

'What did the skipper say?'

'Break off! Lash down everything on deck for a storm. The forecast is more than Force 10.'

We lashed down in the dark, lit by searchlights. Our fingers wouldn't bend from the cold, and you have to tie knots with your bare hands – you can't do it in mittens, when even they are frozen rock-hard. In any case those canvas mittens don't warm your hands; the best method is to keep your fingers in your mouth. On top of it all, I had to drag out the lead-hawser and splice it to the warp. When we got into our bunks we still couldn't get warm, although we threw everything we had on top of us.

Vasya the cook and his cabin-boy appeared, lugging a two-gallon tea-kettle, from which they served us tea in two mugs as we lay in our bunks. Gradually we began to come back to life. There's probably nothing better in this world than when hot liquid flows into you after being out in snow, wind and freezing cold, and you gradually thaw out: first your arms and legs revive, then your whole body comes back to you from a great distance, soon you can talk and smile, and before long you're thinking – what about getting up and going somewhere? The saloon, maybe, and run some films . . .

Shura was the first to think of it: 'What sort of flick did Marconi bring us back from the factory-ship?'

'Go to sleep,' said Mitrokhin. 'Who wants films now? I'd rather have a nice dream.'

Vasya Burov promised him: 'And I'll tell you a story. Only don't fidget.'

'What's the story about?'

'About a king. In days of old. Who had two faithful sailors.'

'Is it about how they wooed the princess?' Shura climbed out of his bunk. 'You've told us that one already.'

'No, it's not that one at all. It's about how they caught a whale and brought it back alive to the palace.'

'Impossible. My brother in the Indian Ocean catches two of them every day. As soon as you pull a whale out of water it dies from its own weight. Come on, let's go and watch the film.'

Shura was already winding on his foot-cloths. Are we supermen, or what? Only just now we were at death's door!

And believe it or not, the people in the next-door cabin were on the move too. The weather on deck was so awful that you hardly dared to look out, yet they ran aft all the same, plunging into the snow and wind . . .

I stayed behind because I remembered I ought to leave Tommy some food for the night. I don't know whether seagulls feed at night, but he was in a dark hold, after all, where it's night-time all round the clock. All the fish had been swept overboard, but I found him a couple of herring in the scuppers. Then I unfastened the hatch-cover and rolled it back. The hold was so dark, I couldn't see the seagull.

'Tommy! Want some fish?'

I was going to throw it to him, but then I was afraid I might hit his injured wing, so I decided I'd better go down there myself.

I sat on the hatch-coaming, put the fish under my arm and held them there with my elbow while I swung my legs into the hold. A wave and then another hit me in the back, and I still couldn't find the rung with my foot. Then I decided to jump. It was a long way down, but I remembered the warp was coiled down and there was no chance of injuring a leg provided I didn't hit a rung on the way down. I lay prone on the deck, crawled downwards until my elbows were through the hatch, then pushed off and jumped down.

I didn't hit anything or hurt my legs – because I fell into water.

2

I flinched and gave a shout of fright, but I soon realized the water was only up to my waist. Well, maybe a bit higher, but from the waist up I was wearing my jacket. My heart nearly jumped out of my mouth, though. I forgot I should have first closed the hatch-cover behind me, and instead began straight away searching for the leak.

There was one bulkhead between the warp-hold and the cargo-hold, made of thin planking, and the water was seeping in from there. I climbed up the rungs of the Jacob's ladder, grabbed the topmost plank and pulled myself up, but I couldn't get over the top, so I had to wrench a couple of planks out of their grooves.

Beyond that were the barrels. They were rattling about, and I had to crawl right over the top of them on my belly. It was pitch-black, the barrels were shifting underneath me and my worst fear was that I might get an arm or a leg crushed between them. In fact I should have been afraid of something else: if there was a lot of water in the hold, those empty barrels might be floating and might squeeze me so hard that I couldn't breathe. Somehow I didn't think of this, otherwise I wouldn't have crawled in there.

Finally, I somehow reached the ship's side – meaning I simply banged my head against it. Knowing roughly where the leaking seam might be, I'd crawled about half the length of the hold. I pushed two barrels apart, lay between them and groped further down – and my hand was burned by a stream of freezing-cold water. So that was it – the welding seam had parted. I couldn't tell whether it was above or below the waterline, but it really didn't matter a damn where the waterline was, when the ship was rolling from side to side and when half a dozen gallons of water were pouring into the hold at every roll.

I gradually pushed back the barrels on either side of me and slithered further downwards. The water was flowing in with hissing and sucking noises, and I felt a sickening stab of fear: I'd managed to crawl in all right, but how was I going to get out? My two barrels had closed up together again and were sliding towards me. I suppose I should have foreseen this, but then I always act first and think afterwards.

Why had I crawled in there at all? OK, so I'd found the hole – but how could I block it up? If only I'd brought some pillows from the cabin. I lowered myself still further and pressed my back against the leak, found a pillar with my foot and pressed hard against it. The sucking noise seemed to have stopped, but I began to feel the bitter cold through my jacket – to say nothing of my sodden trousers. Even so, I'd got myself into quite a good position; I could survive like this and the leakage was reduced to a gallon or so at a time.

Just as I was thinking this, a barrel hit me with a hefty thump on the forehead. Luckily it struck me with its bottom and not one of its hoops, but it still made a loud boom when it hit me. That's all I need, I thought. You can get a case of meningitis like this, and then I'd be a loony for the rest of my days.

I stuck my elbows out in front of me, so if it happened again the barrel would hit them instead of my head; at least the sleeves of my jacket were lined with fur. The barrels were just lying in wait, though; a couple of them might squeeze my arms, and while they held those, other barrels might bang me on the head. All in all, I was in a right mess. And what if I had to sit there to the end of the film that the others were watching in the saloon? I'd have to wait until they realized I was missing. At least on shipboard they notice it quite soon, and if a man goes missing for half an hour in a storm they start looking for him. They call for him on the intercom and bang on the doors of the heads. But they might think I'd been washed overboard, and start searching the sea with searchlights. This might last an hour, and then, of course, they'd start mourning my untimely end. Who'd ever guess I was sitting below decks, fighting off barrels?

Suddenly I heard someone running over the tarpaulin cover of the hold. The noise was like someone hitting me on the head. He ran past the hatch-cover – didn't notice it was open, the idiot! – and clattered down to the cabin. He was followed by another, then the first one came back and said to him – standing right over the hatch: 'He's not in the cabin, not in the heads.'

'Where else can he be? Overboard?'

What did I tell you? First they'd look in the heads, then overboard.

They called out to me despondently: 'Senya, where are you hiding? For fuck's sake, Senya, answer!'

I was just going to answer when a sodding barrel clouted me on the forehead again. The two went away. I couldn't hear them any longer; there was only the singing of the wind and the sound of a wave pouring into the warp-hold.

But then there came some more footsteps overhead – slow and ponderous – and suddenly a noise as the man tripped over something.

'Who left this hatch-cover open?'

It was the Chief's voice.

'Which one?'

'This one, on the warp-hold . . . Prison's too good for you!'

'But it was closed.'

'Who opened it, then? Me?'

They started to heave the hatch-cover into place. Perfect, I thought –
now they'll bottle me up in here.

I yelled with all my might: 'Hey, on deck! I'm down here, alive!'

The Chief bent over the hatch: 'In the hold! Who's there?'

'Me!'

'Who's "me"?'

'It's *me*, Chief!'

'What are you doing down there? Come on out.'

'I can't, I'm pinned down by barrels.'

'How the hell did you get there?'

The Chief began to climb down into the hold, his boots clattering on the
rungs.

'Chief, don't come any further!'

But he'd already dropped into the water. He swore, then came crawling
towards me, pushing the barrels aside.

'Is it leaking badly, Senya?'

'Not so much now. I'm holding it off with my back.'

'I see,' said the Chief. 'Pretending to be a plug, are you? Well, hang on a
while, old fellow. Take care, though – that seam can breathe, and it might
squeeze you.'

'Aha, thanks.'

The Chief crawled out and closed the hatch-cover. Again I felt a surge of
fear. But the sound of running feet had started up on deck. The alarm
signal for 'making water' was sounded – long blasts on the hooter and a bell
ringing. By now I was frozen stiff; it had soaked right through my jacket to
my shoulders, and my elbows were black and blue.

Someone opened the hatch-cover again: 'You alive, Senya?'

It was Shura Chmyrev.

'I'm alive. But only just.'

'So you're in a bad way, are you? Want a smoke?'

He really put his finger on it. I hadn't even noticed why I was feeling so
awful.

'You'll have a cigarette in a moment. Someone's coming to relieve you.'

Shura jumped into the water and gasped. Someone else jumped after
him. They dragged several barrels away from the bulkhead and flung them
into the water. One of them began to push his way towards me.

'Senya, don't you worry too much, OK? We'll fix it and put everything
right . . .' It was Seryozha Firstov.

'Hey, listen – don't stop talking, Senya. We need to be able to hear your
voice.'

'OK, keep on coming.'

My tongue was already frozen to my teeth, but as he crawled he kept on asking me questions: 'How did you get here in the first place? I'm amazed you managed to find it.'

It took him a hundred years to reach me, but then he wasn't having an easy time of it either. As he talked he was having to push barrels out of his way and pass them back to Shura.

He finally reached me, and hit me in the teeth with his head.

'Sorry, Senya. What d'you think – can I stick it for half an hour?'

'I've been sitting here for an hour and I'm not dead yet.'

'What d'you mean – an hour? We've only had time to see half a reel of the film.'

He spent another fifty years moving barrels aside, then he decided to light up, took a couple of drags and stuck the cigarette in my mouth.

'You can come out now.'

The ship's side rose up, the water subsided and I moved away from the hole. Seryozha sat down with his back against it. Then the ship rolled over again.

'Ow!' he said. 'It's cold.'

'What did you think it would be?'

'I can feel it through my oilskins. You must be crazy, Senya! What an idea – stopping a leak with your backside. We haven't got enough backsides for the job – we'll have to order some from abroad. You might try and find something for me to sit on . . .'

'What can I put there for you?'

'What were you wearing?' He reached out and felt my jacket. 'Look, you could put your jacket under me . . .'

That made me stop and think a bit.

I didn't mind about the jacket itself; anything might happen to it. But the letters from Lilya were still inside it – her last one, and the others she'd sent me on my last few trips. She loved writing letters, which is a rare thing these days, and they were long ones, full of detail. I'd read each of them until I'd worn them through at the folds. To this day I can remember them, even though there's nothing left of them now. There was one bit like this, for instance: 'You assume there's more to me than there really is. I'm an ordinary, common girl, hard as they come, with one ambition – somehow to make a tolerable marriage, have babies and subside into domesticity. The reason why you think I'm an enigma is easily explained! We're all the children of anxiety, something in us is perpetually tossing uneasily about, groaning, shifting. More than anything else we want to be reassured, to fix ourselves on something permanent, and we don't know what it is. But as soon as we reach it, as soon as we land on terra firma we won't be ourselves any more; instead we'll have turned into pretty hard-boiled, complacent old squares. *You* are quite different . . .' And so on like that – about what she saw in me, how I surprised her at our first meeting. Maybe there wasn't any of that in me at all, at any rate I'd never noticed it, but it was interesting to read about it. No one, before her, had ever talked to me like that. And maybe no one would ever write to me like that again. Even when we realized that we were, in fact, parting for good – back there on the *Fyodor* – I still decided to keep these letters. How was I to know I'd have to grope my way through a waterlogged hold clutching them in my fist? And what if I didn't take them out, but left them in my jacket? I wasn't worried that Seryozha might feel them there . . . it was simply a superstitious feeling, d'you see? If something happened to them, it would have broken my heart.

'What's the matter?' asked Seryozha. 'Bothered about your jacket? Don't worry about it. We may not even get out of this alive.'

'Shut up. Don't panic.'

'I just feel it.'

I took off my jacket and folded it with the lining inside. Seryozha moved aside, and we shoved it into the hole.

'That's fine now. Go and get warm. Send Shura here in half an hour.'

As I was crawling out I remembered Tommy. I couldn't leave the bird in the waterlogged hold – God knows what might happen to him.

Tommy was sitting quietly in his little nest, quite dry, but he came to me as soon as I called him: 'Tommy, Tommy.' As I climbed up the Jacob's ladder, he lay sprawled out on my hand, his injured wing hanging down. I was going to take him to our cabin, but suddenly he jumped down, ran away from me and hopped up on to the ship's rail. He sat with his feathers ruffled up, his wing stuck out to one side.

'All right, Tommy,' I said to him. 'Go and see if you can ride out the storm.'

A wave broke over us, lashing the rail, and when the water had flowed away Tommy wasn't there any longer. Worried, I made my way over to the gunwale. Tommy was afloat on a steep-sided wave, wings folded, beak and breast into the wind like a real sailor. He preferred the stormy sea to the hold, even though he was warm and well fed in there. That must mean things look bad for us, I thought. Then a snow-flurry came down and I could see Tommy no more.

Someone was unlashing a pump from under the float-caboose, others were fetching hoses. In the heads I grabbed somebody else's oilskins and ran out to help. Shura, Vasya Burov and Alik were there.

'Where are the others?'

'Where they're needed. We've sprung a leak in the engineers' cabin. The water's knee-deep, their gear's floating in it. That's what comes of watching films. Let's hope to God it doesn't seep through into the engine-room.'

'God forbid,' I said.

'What's so special about the engine-room? It could easily be leaking there, too.'

'We may go under, but we won't give in,' said Alik.

Vasya Burov yelled at him: 'Spit three times, greenhorn! Spit at once, I tell you!'

Alik spat.

'If you can't say the right thing, shut up.'

We dragged the pump to the warp-hold. Loose planks and the fish-gutting table were sliding about our feet, and there was an empty barrel rolling around the deck. We stumbled and fell, picked ourselves up and went on heaving the pump. Then we lowered the hose into the hold and started pumping out straight on to the deck, two on one handle, two on the other.

Pumping away, Vasya asked: 'Hey, beachers – have those barrels got their bungs in?'

'Why do you ask?' said Shura.

'Because if their bung-holes are stopped up, they won't let the water in.'

We stopped pumping.

'You'll have to ask the cooper,' said Shura. 'Where is the cooper? Maybe he's pumping out the engineers' cabin. God knows. I suppose some have got the bungs in and some haven't.'

'Anyway, they haven't been soaked,' said Alik.

He was right; even if its bung is in, a barrel that hasn't been soaked to make the wood swell will let the water in.

'If they haven't been soaked before, they're getting soaked now all right,' said Vasya. 'We're wasting our time pumping.'

Shura thought for a moment, then suddenly bawled at him: 'Sod you, you skiver! Personally I'm not planning to drown.' And he started pumping like a maniac.

Just then came a shout from the wheelhouse: 'Pump to the engine-room!'

Somehow we didn't take this in straight away.

'But what about the holds?'

'Do as you're told – to the engine-room!'

'That's all we need,' said Vasya. 'This is it. And all you can do, greenhorn, is croak: "We're going under" . . .'

Shura was already dragging the pump away from the hatch. As I pulled out the hose I shouted down into the pitch-black hold: 'Seryozha, are you still alive?'

No answer. I was dead scared – had he suffocated down there? Or been crushed by barrels?

'Seryozha, you rotten sod!'

'Ahoy!' came the reply, as if from the tomb. 'Are you coming soon?'

What a relief that was!

'Soon?' I said to him cheerfully. 'The game's only just beginning.'

'Have I got to stay here?'

'No, come out.'

'Aren't you going to put a patch on this?'

'Come on out, there's water in the engine-room.'

He started banging the barrels as he made his way out.

'Then why were you and I sitting here, Senya?'

'Can you get out by yourself?'

'Yes, I can . . . But why were we sitting on that hold, I'd like to know.'

'Don't bother yourself . . . Will you close the hatch-cover?'

'Yes, I will. But mind, Senya, you haven't answered my question.'

I ran off to help with the pump. We dragged it through the narrow gap between the gunwale and the wheelhouse, then opened the door into the passage leading to the engine-room. The coaming there is almost knee-high, and while we were heaving the stupid thing over it, we all nearly wrenched our arms off – but we immediately forgot about them . . .

Steam was billowing out of the engine-room, and through the steam we could see water: black, with oil-slicks. Duckboards were floating here and there, riding up and down on the waves. Yes, on the waves: a whole storm in miniature was raging in the engine-room, surging up against the bulkhead, rolling over the engine-bed. Steam was spurting out from under the engine – in fact it was amazing the engine was still working, still thumping away.

We laid the outlet-hose over the doorway on to the deck, and lowered the inlet down into the engine-room. It was too short to reach the water.

Yurka the greaser emerged from the steam – up to his knees in water, but, as usual, half-naked.

'You idiots, didn't you think of coupling the hose to another one?'

'What could we couple it to?' asked Shura. 'There aren't any spare lengths.'

'Well, if there aren't any, why the hell did you bring the pump here? We're driving a pump off the main engine.'

'Why aren't you pumping, then?'

'Not pumping? We started as soon as it began to leak!'

'Where were you, you idle bugger?' I wanted to ask him. 'Where were you when it began to leak? Bet you were sitting at the work-bench making a cigarette lighter until your feet started getting wet. And when you realized what was happening, you didn't have the sense to call the Chief, you decided to pump it out yourself but you didn't know how to couple the main drive to the bilge pump.'

'So what do we do with the pump now?' asked Vasya. 'Hump it back again?'

'Who told you to bring it here?'

'Look, lads,' said Vasya, 'I'm going back to my bunk for a kip.'

The Chief came out from behind the engine. He too was wreathed in steam, but wearing his tunic and a tie.

'Why are you sending the pump away?' he said to Yurka. 'You and I have bungled it, so at least let them help out with a hand-pump.'

He said 'you and I' because when the greaser is on watch the Chief is supposed to be on too – not for the whole watch, but he should come and take a look-see every now and again. But the Chief had first been watching the film, then he had gone to look for me. But of course it was Yurka who had bungled the job of starting up the bilge-pumps.

'The hose doesn't reach far enough, Sergei Andreyich.'

'Then they can bail out with buckets.'

'So much for your technology,' said Yurka.

Once again we heaved the bloody pump over the coaming. We didn't take it back to its usual place, though, but simply pushed it into a corner, just far enough not to obstruct the gangway. Then we formed a bucket-chain and started bailing – one below, scooping the water, two on the companion-way to hand up the buckets, and the fourth to run and empty the buckets on deck.

Then Shura was called to take the wheel. In his place came Seryozha, who for some reason had taken off his oilskins. His jerkin was covered in snow.

'You should at least have put on my jacket,' I said to him.

'Doesn't matter, Senya, I'm OK like this.' He emptied three buckets, then said: 'By the way, your jacket's gone.'

'What d'you mean – gone?'

'It was sucked through the hole into the sea.'

I was stunned.

'Why didn't you look after it?'

'I couldn't, Senya. It's dark there in the hold. I noticed a stinging cold feeling on my backside, felt for the jacket – and it wasn't there. Remember when I asked you why we had to sit there?'

'You fucking stupid idiot!'

'That's enough bickering, you two,' said Vasya. 'We've got to save the ship. You can moan about that jacket afterwards. Think I don't feel sorry about your jacket too?'

'Honestly, I could have wept,' said Seryozha. 'I'm sorry, Senya, forgive me.'

I could have really lost my temper then, but I hadn't the energy. We'd already shifted thirty buckets. Or forty; I wasn't counting. Vasya Burov, who was counting, said it was sixty-eight. The water hadn't gone down one inch, the engine-room was still blanketed in steam and all you could see was the odd head or arm, while the buckets seemed to be coming up of their own accord – half-spilled, of course . . .

We were relieved by the cook, his cabin-boy and the cooper.

'Go and eat, lads,' the cook said to us. 'We'll give you an hour. I've made some *borshch*.'

He was a real chef, was our cooky, always on top of things in his galley. But right now, the last thing we wanted to do was eat.

'Take my advice,' said Vasya Burov, 'better spend that hour kipping.'

I walked for'ard along the gunwale, wanting to look into the water just in case my jacket might be floating alongside, but you couldn't see anything because the snowstorm was so fierce.

Back in the cabin we flopped on to our bunks, and Vasya immediately started snoring. Seryozha tossed and turned and groaned for a while, then he too quietened down. Suddenly I didn't feel like sleep any more; the thought of those letters was still nagging at me. And the jacket, too, of course. You'll remember what it cost me. But the chief thing that bothered me was this: the wind could change, my jacket was bound to float into the Gulf Stream, which is thick with ships – and somebody might pick up my jacket and read those letters before they were completely soaked. Then how could I ever look Lilya in the face again? It would get all round the fishing fleet – what had surprised her about me at our first meeting, and so on – it would all grow into a legend, no one would remember how the letters were found, and it would look as if I'd let other people read them. And what for? To give a bad name to a girl who hadn't returned my feelings for her. I got cold shivers as I imagined the look on her face: 'Well, I suppose I should have expected that from him.' It'd be better if that damned jacket sank to the bottom. It wouldn't sink at once, though; clothes float on the sea for a long time, until all the air goes out of them . . .

All at once I noticed the engine slowing down, and immediately the water began hitting the ship's side: that meant we weren't breasting the waves any more, but had turned beam-on.

I couldn't lie there any longer, so I went out of the cabin. I met Shura coming from the wheelhouse.

'What's going on?'

'Total chaos. The skipper's having a row with the Chief.'

'What's it about?'

'Go and hear for yourself. I'm flopping.'

In the passage near the engine-room I saw the skipper, tunic unbuttoned, cap on the back of his head, with Zhora the Second Mate alongside him. The Chief was standing on the companion-way, splashed all over with oil, his arms bared to the elbows and black with oil too.

'Do you realize what you're doing?' shouted the skipper. 'Why have you reduced speed?'

'Because there's a crack in the crank-case and oil is spurting out.'

'What caused the crack? Why wasn't it there before?'

The Chief explained patiently: 'It was, but it didn't show up at first. Then the water washed over it, and because it was red-hot it split open.'

'Well, let it spurt, and you keep topping it up. Caulk it with anything you can – cotton waste, rags . . .'

'Nikolayich,' said the Chief. 'Don't be a fool, you make me ashamed to hear you talk like that.'

Zhora stepped in front of the captain.

'Who d'you think you're talking to?' he yelled at the Chief. 'You're talking to the captain. "Don't be a fool", indeed!'

'You're right, Nozhov,' said the Chief. 'I am talking to the captain. Not to you. So shut up, young man, and keep your place. The captain, though, must understand that if all the oil leaks out of the crank-case the engine will jam, and worse still – the pistons will seize up, and then it can't be repaired.'

'Don't tell me you're planning to try and repair it!' the skipper literally screamed.

'I don't know yet. But it's got to be stopped. We'll use the Schönebeck* for pumping.'

'Are you in your right mind?' said the skipper. 'We're being carried on to the Faroes!'

At once I felt my legs go weak and a cold stab in the pit of my stomach. He was right; an east wind had been forecast, and that meant we were being blown towards the Faroes and their cliffs. How far was it, I wondered, to those cliffs?

'It's the nets that are pulling you,' said the Chief. 'OK, so you cast before the storm got up, but you should at least have cast them deeper. As it was, you put them at zero depth. So now you must stop and think whether you shouldn't cut the nets away.'

'I don't want to know! Increase speed!'

The Chief frowned as if he'd suddenly got toothache, took one step up the companion-way and closed the door. Zhora pushed it, but the Chief had managed to turn the clip to lock it.

There's one other way into the engine-room, along the passage and around the corner, opposite the Chief's cabin; they ran round there. The Second Engineer emerged from the door as they reached it and spread his hands apologetically, implying: 'I'd be glad to obey you, but Babilov has kicked me out.' Zhora pushed him aside, but at that moment Yurka's little beret appeared in the doorway, followed by Yurka's well-rounded shoulder and Yurka's mighty chest. By the time he'd climbed out, the Chief had had time to nip up the companion-way behind him and slam the bolts shut.

'Don't worry,' said Yurka. 'He'll manage on his own.'

The skipper hammered on the door with his fists, and for good measure Zhora kicked it with his shoe. But that was just stupid; you could never break that door open even if you put the whole crew on to it. They ran up on to the boat-deck, where there's a skylight with glazed shutters, like a greenhouse, giving on to the engine-room. Steam was pouring out of the open shutters, mixed with snow and spray. Down below, the Chief could

---

* An auxiliary engine, used for pumping out the bilge, charging accumulators, etc. At one time these engines were imported from a German firm called 'Schönebeck', hence the name. (Author's note.)

just be seen standing by the engine.

'Babilov!' shouted the skipper. 'I'll have you in court for this!'

The Chief raised his head: 'You'd do better to be thinking about those nets. I'm stopping the main engine.'

'Don't you dare, Babilov!'

The engine turned a few more revolutions and was silent. Now only the auxiliary was left, working the bilge-pumps.

The skipper straightened up. Somewhere he'd managed to lose his fur hat with ear-flaps; the snow was falling on his bald head, the wind was making his open tunic flap, but he noticed none of this.

'We're being carried on to the Faroes,' he said miserably. 'Now what? Do we shoot at him?'

We had the means to shoot at him – three army rifles in a sealed locker; a ship can't be sent to sea completely unarmed. I was wondering what I ought to do: start a fight with them then and there, on the boat-deck? Or call the lads to come and help?

'But that won't do any good,' said the skipper. 'Well, we shall have to send out an SOS . . .'

'There's nothing else for it,' said Zhora.

They went into the wheelhouse. Down below in the engine-room the steam was gradually dispersing and I could see the Chief bent over the engine, pouring oil into a huge funnel, where it was spurting back and foaming, splashing his bare arms and face.

'Chief, want any help?'

He looked up and frowned: 'Is that you, Senya?'

'Can I help you?'

'Don't worry. I'll try and manage on my own. I don't want to open the doors.'

'Will it take long, Chief?'

'If only it had happened sooner! We could have welded it and been saved all this trouble.'

'I'll send you down a first-rate welder, Shura Chmyrev. He'll weld the crack for you – so well you won't be able to find it afterwards.'

'All right, go ahead. Tell him to knock three times.'

'Why? I'll lower him down to you on a line through here.'

The Chief said cheerily: 'Good idea!'

It took me a long time to drag Shura out of his bunk. He moaned and kicked, couldn't remember what had happened to us. I reminded him. Then we got Seryozha up. We grabbed a head-line from the rack and cautiously made our way aft to the boat-deck. Shura was still dozy when we sat him in a French bowline and pushed him through the open shutters.

'Where are you sending me, beachers? To hell? I'll never forgive you.'

'To paradise,' said Seryozha. 'Where it's warm and the bugs don't bite.'

We braced ourselves against the coaming and lowered away, while Shura, it seemed, even managed to fall asleep again. The Chief caught him by the legs and pulled him clear of the engine.

'We'll chuck the line away,' said Seryozha, 'just to be on the safe side.'

We threw it into the sea and were leaving the boat-deck when Seryozha suddenly stopped and grabbed me by the sleeve. A figure was standing on the flying bridge, capless, his tunic flapping.

'The skipper,' said Seryozha.

We hid behind the funnel. The skipper raised his arm and fired the rocket-pistol. For a split second we saw a red flash just above the barrel, then it seemed to be instantly cut off. He reloaded and fired again. Again there was just a flash and a hiss.

'That's our lot, Senya. I tell you – we won't come out of this.'

When we reached the main deck, the skipper was still firing. From there only the shot could be heard, the flash was no longer to be seen.

3

Just as we were going into the doghouse, the bo'sun came crashing up from below and bumped into us.

'You and you – come with me. We're dropping the anchors.'

Clinging on to each other, the three of us made our way to the capstan and started to pull off its tarpaulin cover. It got caught on something and wouldn't come off. Seryozha yanked at it by one corner, groaning with the effort, and the bo'sun yelled at him to get it untangled first.

A wave broke over the gunwale, pouring over us and the capstan, and suddenly the tarpaulin came free of its own accord, like a living thing. It was snatched up and swept away. To hell with the tarpaulin – where was the bo'sun? He seemed to have vanished. Had he been washed overboard? If so, there was only one hope – that the next wave might wash him back on board again. Such strokes of luck do happen. But no, he came crawling back to us on all fours.

'I'm alive, but I've nearly smashed my arm. Wanted to try and catch that tarpaulin.'

Seryozha went for him: 'You're always so bloody stingy – you'd do better to try saving your life!'

'Bo'sun!' came a shout from the wheelhouse. 'Look lively with those anchors.'

We waited while another wave broke, then released the pawl on the capstan. As the chain rattled in the hawse-hole, the anchor ran out and splashed into the water. We waited for it to 'catch' on the bottom. You can always feel that by the jerk it gives; sometimes it knocks you off your feet, but this time there was no jerk.

'No bottom,' said Seryozha. 'Must be too deep.'

'How come?' asked the bo'sun. 'The echo-sounder is showing forty metres.'

'Let's try the other one.'

Again we waited for the jerk, and it didn't come.

'They're dragging,' said the bo'sun glumly. 'The ground won't hold. Nothing but shingle here. And flat rock.'

'Plenty of sailors' bones, though!' said Seryozha.

'Any amount of bones, only you can't get a grip on them. Come on, no point in hanging around here.'

A hefty great wave caught us in the back. It was like being hit with a sack of wet sand and I was flung forwards against the doghouse, where I collapsed, doubled up, blacked out with pain. Somebody pulled me up by the collar. Seryozha shouted something to me, but I couldn't hear what it was. He gripped me under the armpits and pulled me up: 'Stand like that, sideways on! Hang on to the handrail.'

Aha, there was the handrail. I'd forgotten it was welded to the bulkhead. Seryozha pulled me away from it, dragged me after him and pushed me through the door.

We stood in the doghouse, huddled together, teeth chattering. I still hadn't got my breath back after the blow.

The bo'sun said: 'The anchors aren't working.'

'Don't speak too soon,' said Seryozha. 'I think I felt a jerk.'

'That's just the chain clanking. It's not taut.'

How could he have heard it? All we could hear was the wind, and the waves slapping against the side.

Zhora the mate shouted from the wheelhouse: 'Strashnoi, what's happening with your anchors?'

The bo'sun cupped his hands to his mouth: 'We've let go anchors!'

'But we're still drifting!'

'They haven't caught. They're dragging.'

'They're just scrap, your anchors!'

'They're all we've got.'

Zhora didn't answer, but closed the wheelhouse window.

I remembered how those cliffs had towered above us, as smooth as if they'd been polished, covered in frozen snow. Of course, we'd all land up in the water, there was no avoiding it; in any case we were already soaked to the skin. It would be at least a ten-mile walk to the nearest village; we'd never make it, because we'd freeze to death in the wind. Not that we'd even be able to start walking – we'd have to climb up those cliffs first, and no one had ever done it before. Yet we all wanted to live.

'Scrap!' the bo'sun suddenly said. 'That reminds me – I *have* got another small anchor. But it really *is* a piece of scrap.'

'Bullshit,' said Seryozha. 'Where is it?'

'A killick. About a hundred kilograms. Where is it? In the bo'sun's locker. I hid it there. Last time in port I was inspected for scrap metal, and they asked about that very anchor. I said it'd been lost at sea, 'cos I thought – who knows when it may come in handy?'

'You can tell you're from Vologda!' said Seryozha. 'Calculating bugger.'

The bo'sun was the first to step out of the doghouse, followed by

Seryozha and myself.

We walked bent double, holding on to the lead-hawser of the trawl. As a rule you shouldn't hold on to it, and in a storm you're not even supposed to go near it – but what else was there to hold on to?

Vasya Burov and Mitrokhin came towards us along the hawser, and we turned them round.

'We can use a couple more,' said the bo'sun.

'Where are the apprentices?' Seryozha asked.

'They're pumping out the engineers' cabin. We don't need them. We'll get the cook and the cabin-boy.'

We reached the stern-sheets and went into the galley through the after door. The stove was burning, a saucepan sliding and puffing on top of it; the cook was asleep on a stool, his head resting on the zinc-topped table.

As we shook him awake, he grabbed a ladle and rushed over to look at his saucepan.

'Later,' said the bo'sun. 'Right now we need your help with an anchor. Where's the cabin-boy?'

'He's asleep in the saloon.' The cook removed his apron and pulled on a jerkin that had been steaming as it hung to dry over the stove. 'Can we do without the cabin-boy? He's even more whacked than I am.'

'Can we manage with six of us?'

'If we can't, we'll wake him up.'

The six of us went up on to the after-bridge and opened the door of the bo'sun's locker. The place smelled of linseed oil, mould and some other horrible smell; the bo'sun really was a great one for collecting junk. We pushed aside an assortment of cans, scrap lengths of hawser, chain-links, sacks and planks, while the bo'sun shone a torch and cautioned us: 'Careful, lads, there's enough stuff here for three ships.'

'Look,' said Vasya Burov, 'maybe that anchor of yours isn't here at all. Perhaps you just imagined it.'

The bo'sun was offended.

'If you want to know, there's everything in this locker that a fool like you could imagine, so it must be here.'

We took a long time digging through all the junk, until Vasya suddenly yelled: 'Got it! I'm holding it by one of the flukes.'

'Hang on to it!' the bo'sun yelled back. 'Give it a good pull.'

It wasn't so easy, though, to get it out. The other fluke was so badly stuck, all five of us couldn't pull it free.

'Let's hope it holds on to the sea bottom like this,' said Seryozha.

The bo'sun was delighted: 'Is it stuck hard? Well, who knows, it may stick on the bottom, too. If it only takes hold, though!'

Finally we pulled it out on to the after-bridge. I don't know how much it weighed – maybe a hundred, maybe even three hundred. We heaved it along with our combined force of five hundred kilos. Two pulled it by the flukes, three by the shank and the bo'sun made up the sixth, holding it by the shackle.

We lowered it down the companion-way . . . How it didn't crush us to death, I'll never know. Two of us put their shoulders against it from below while the others lowered this lethal weight towards them – each only using one hand, the other gripping the rail. We dragged it through the narrow gangway under the wheelhouse, then along the open deck, where it first caught on a taut rope, then on the backstay, and finally contrived to get fouled up around a bollard.

'Not bad for a piece of scrap!' The bo'sun was still very pleased with himself. 'Hang on, lads, we'll secure it in a moment. It's our only hope now!'

Our 'hope' lay on the foc's'le – the most ordinary admiralty-type anchor, light enough for a yacht, as we could now see. We lay down prone under the gunwale; the waves couldn't hit us there, except when some water splashed on us from above, and we waited while the bo'sun secured a hawser to the shackle and led the hawser through the fairlead. He wouldn't let anyone help him, but did it all on his own.

'All right, lads – let's spit on it.'

We all spat heartily on it, our 'only hope'.

'God help us. Now let's drop her overboard. Steady does it.'

For some reason we didn't hear the splash; one of us leaned over the gunwale to see what had become of it.

'Stand clear of the hawser!' roared the bo'sun.

He turned the beam of his torch on to it, and we watched as the hawser flew through the fairlead and the coil unwound itself like a mad thing. Then it suddenly stopped and we all caught our breath. The hawser jerked, twanged, and began chafing the fairlead.

'It's taken hold, has our bit of scrap,' the bo'sun said, almost in a whisper, patting the hawser with his mitten.

We stood a while in the doghouse, huddled together again, listening. No, the hawser hadn't snapped. And the wind was blowing on our other cheek, which meant the bow was swinging round on the hawser.

'If we'd known it'd hold,' said the bo'sun, 'we should have secured it to a chain.'

'And have you got a scrap chain?' asked Seryozha.

'I've got everything.'

A window was lowered in the wheelhouse, and Zhora shouted cheerfully: 'Strashnoi, those anchors are holding!'

'For the time being.'

'Then why don't you report it?'

'I'm reporting it now.' He was still listening hard. 'It's rubbing,' he said gloomily. 'Can you hear? The hawser's rubbing against the fairlead. It's chafing.'

'It won't chafe through,' said Vasya Burov. 'Perhaps we should pad it with some sacking?'

'I'll go and have a look at it.'

He came back all white with icicles, which clinked on his oilskins like chain-mail.

'It'll snap,' he said hopelessly. 'It'll hold for a bit, of course. But then it's bound to snap.'

'What can we do?' asked Seryozha. 'We've done all we can.'

'We ought to cut the nets away. Only up there in the wheelhouse they refuse to do it.'

'Maybe we should tell them? They don't know we've put out the scrap anchor. They don't know what we've been up to.'

'They know all right,' said Vasya Burov. 'When we were dragging it down from the after-bridge, someone was looking out of the wheelhouse. I saw them.'

'Even so . . .' said Seryozha. 'What's the matter with them – don't they want to live?'

He was the first to go, and we followed him. They saw us from the wheelhouse and lowered a window. We could see Zhora, and behind him the skipper.

'What's the matter, Strashnoi?' asked Zhora.

The bo'sun clambered up on to the hold and steadied himself on the derrick-boom, while we held on to his oilskins.

'We ought to cut the nets away, Nikolayich.'

The skipper stuck his head out – fur cap pulled down to his eyebrows – and asked: 'Do you realize what you're saying?'

'The hawser won't hold. One good wave and it'll snap.'

'And the nets?' asked Zhora. 'What's worrying you about the nets?'

'I'm not talking to you, Nozhov. I don't suppose you've ever seen a ship founder because of the nets. But the way things are, they'll be the death of us all.'

'We know what we're doing,' said the skipper. 'There are people up here with brains in their heads too, you know.'

The bo'sun was about to say something else, and went right up to the wheelhouse, but Zhora closed the window.

'They don't know what they're doing,' said the bo'sun, shaking his head.

We turned and went for'ard to the doghouse.

'They're worried sick about the gear, but they don't seem to care about their own lives! What are they hoping for? Oh well, let them do as they like. I'm going to get some sleep.'

He went down the companion-way, still shaking his head. Someone switched on the light for him; the bulb was glowing at half-strength, and in the dim light our bo'sun looked like a hunchback.

'Well, I'm going too,' said Vasya the cook. 'Doesn't anybody want some of my *borshch*?'

We stumbled our way aft again.

4

The cabin-boy was asleep on a bench in the saloon, wearing a singlet and white cook's trousers, and barefoot. His head hanging over the end, he was sliding up and down the bench, his singlet rucked up over his stomach, but he didn't wake up.

The cook ladled us out some *borshch* and sat down on the end of the bench, his face wrinkled into a painful frown. The bowls were beastly hot, so Vasya Burov took off his cap and put his bowl into it, holding it tight against his chest. We all did the same. The cook kept topping up our bowls until we said 'enough'.

Then we asked him for a smoke, as ours were all soaking wet, and we lit up. The light in the deckhead shone dimly and we sat there swaying in the smoke like ghosts; there were green patches on our cheeks, and everyone's eyes were sunken.

'Know what I'm going to do,' said Vasya Burov, 'when all this caper's over? I'm going south, to the Crimea.'

'On leave?' asked Mitrokhin. 'It's early yet, you should go in May.'

'No, for good. I'm fed up with this cold. I ask you – is the human race meant to put up with cold? We'll never get used to it. I'll chuck the kids, chuck the old woman. At first I'll just sunbathe. I won't even bother about food.'

'They have a winter there too,' said Mitrokhin.

'Winter? Even our summer isn't like their winter. Some people are just lucky. Then when I've warmed up a bit, I'll build myself a shack. Right on the beach. Well, somewhere by the sea. In Gurzuf.'

Seryozha said: 'There's Alushta, too. It's better than your Gurzuf.'

'I don't know. I've never been to Alushta, but Gurzuf's a good place. I once spent two months there. Only thing that spoiled it was the old woman and the kids were there too. Rented a cottage, did our own cooking. But if I'm alone, I don't need anything. I'll just lie on my back all day in the sun. And I'd be Vasya Burov from Gurzuf.'

'So we'll write to you like that,' said Seryozha '– "To Vasya Burov in Gurzuf".'

'Don't bother to write. Just come and visit me. There'll be room for all of you, it's a big beach. I'll let you know secretly how to find me there. Only don't tell my old woman, or she'll make me go back to the Atlantic again. But in Gurzuf I'll hide myself away like a mouse, so she'll never find me. We'll live there with no women and no families. And the only fishing we'll do will be with rod and line. You should see the grey mullet I've caught there on a line, with bread-balls for bait. And the *barabulka*! Smoked, eh? Whatever we catch, we'll eat. Right there, by a camp fire.'

'You've just made up your best fairy story,' said Mitrokhin.

Vasya was astonished: 'Why's that a fairy story? Think there aren't people who live like that?'

'But it must be a fairy tale,' said Seryozha, 'if you're not going to have any women. You can't do without them.'

'Women would ruin it. No, lads – somehow or other, if it's going to be paradise, it's men only.'

'No,' said Seryozha. 'Say what you like, it's impossible without women. A woman's the biggest trap of all, you'll never escape her. We all know that. And still we can't get away from them.'

'So you can't do without them, can you?'

'Me? Maybe for a year. But it's *they* who can't do without *us*. So they'll find out where you are, don't worry. And they'll ruin your little paradise.'

Vasya sighed. 'You're right. So that's why our little plan won't work, beachers. Well, we might hold out for ten days, but it's not worth going for that long, so we might as well take the old woman and the kids with us from the start.'

We sat in silence and smoked another cigarette.

'Someone's coming,' said Seryozha.

It was the First Mate. His evening watch had just ended. Or maybe the skipper and Zhora had let him go early, because they could manage on their own in the wheelhouse. But he arrived looking as if he'd just finished some job of great responsbility and could now take a well-earned rest; he'd put on his fur-lined jerkin, wet his hair and brushed it down over one side. The cook went into the galley for some more *borshch*. The First Mate sat down, tapped the table with his spoon and gave us all a sarcastic look – why, God knows.

'Phew, you've been sitting here long enough, smoking like chimneys!'

'What's it to you?' asked Vasya. 'We've done our job. Now if you don't bother us, we won't touch you.'

'If you don't want to bunk down, you could at least sing songs.'

Again this was said with a sort of contempt, as if we'd just ruined the ship and he'd just saved her.

'What's happening up on the bridge?' asked Mitrokhin. 'What's the buzz?'

'Do you want to know it all?'

'I don't,' said Vasya. 'I know it all already. We've sent out an SOS, now we must just wait and see what comes of it.'

'Yes, you haven't got much to worry about.'

'And have you got bigger troubles?'

The First Mate smirked and started eating his *borshch*, but even that he did with the same mysterious, self-important look on his face.

'Is someone coming our way?' asked Seryozha. 'Even one ship? Just don't play games with us, now – we're asking you seriously, as a human being.'

The First Mate blushed to the roots of his hair. Seryozha looked at him calmly, almost with a touch of pity.

'What sort of a ship would you like?'

'You're dodging the question again.'

'The factory-ship has altered course. Satisfied? Only how far d'you think she has to go to reach us?'

'Isn't there anyone nearer?'

'Well, there is one. From the Riga flotilla. But just imagine what it's like – nearer or further, it makes little difference if she has to sail beam-on to the weather.'

'I see. I wouldn't go in this weather, either, if it meant taking it on the beam. Unlucky we may be, but there are always reasons for it.'

'You don't suppose we're the only unlucky ones, do you? There's a foreigner in trouble out there, too, a Scotsman. He's got it even worse than we have, because he's drifting right under the lee of the Faroes.'

'God help him,' said Vasya. 'Why was he out fishing, the fool, instead of taking shelter in the fjord?'

'Well, he just didn't take shelter.'

'Anyway, how far does she have to go to reach us?' asked Mitrokhin. 'The factory-ship, I mean.'

'How far, how far! Seven versts – and through the forest all the way.'

'You're at it again,' said Seryozha. 'You're such a dummy, for God's sake. The man's asking you because his life depends on it. He could ask you any stupid question and you're supposed to give him an answer, got it?'

The First Mate threw down his spoon: 'Why must you nag like this? Can't even eat my dinner in peace. Go and ask the captain all about it.'

'Won't he tell *you*?'

The First Mate, already in the doorway, turned to snap back at him, when he stopped still, his mouth open. The jerk was barely noticeable. Only the bowls rattled slightly and the cabin-boy, asleep on the bench, shuddered and woke up: 'Wha'? Where must I go?'

'Nowhere,' said Vasya. 'It's all over now. That was the hawser snapping . . .'

The First Mate slammed the door behind him and ran.

'It was unreliable anyway,' said Seryozha. 'The hawser, I mean.'

Stamping of feet and shouting came from the upper deck, and just as we were finishing our cigarettes the alarm signal was sounded. This time it wasn't for damage to the hull but it was 'abandon ship' – one long blast and six short ones.

Half-awake, the cabin-boy rushed for the door as he was, in singlet and beret, then suddenly came to his senses and began to put on his light linen cook's jacket.

'Pull yourself together,' said Seryozha. 'You can't get into the lifeboat like that. Find your oilskins and a quilted jacket.'

'Will I have time? Don't hurry, lads, I'll be ready in a moment.'

'Why should we hurry?' said Vasya Burov. 'We ought to sit in silence for a minute before the journey.'

We all wanted to stay a little longer in the last warm place, to soak up a bit more of it, and now we had an excuse – to give the cabin-boy time to get dressed and the cook time to collect a sackful of emergency rations: ship's biscuits, canned food, dried fruit. He also had the idea of taking a thermos flask full of *borshch*, but we advised him not to: how could we eat it in the lifeboat – out of our hands?

The cabin-boy's quilted jacket was drying over the stove, and now it wouldn't meet over his chest. Half the buttons were missing from his oilskins, but instead he had the sense to fasten them by tying a dishcloth round his waist. Like that, belted with a white-tasselled sash, he followed us up on to the boat-deck.

Five or six men were already at work on the lifeboat, pulling off its tarpaulin cover. The First Mate, wearing oilskins, was running round them and yelling: 'Not that one! The other one! You can't lower the boat on the windward side! Use the one on the leeward side! . . .'

A figure emerged from behind the lifeboat, and from his voice I recognized the trawlmaster: 'Can you tell which side is to windward at the moment? The ship's yawing.'

'Look at the windsock!'

'Windsock yourself. Go away, it's sickening enough without you.'

'I'll find a way to get my own back on you, Skorodumov.'

'OK, you can be thinking about it. Meanwhile I'll give the orders.'

The snow-flurries had stopped, the moon was shining through ragged blue-grey clouds and the sea could be seen all the way to the horizon – big black waves with leaden crests, which the wind was blowing into spume. As the ship plunged down the icy slope of one wave, the next one would rear up above mast-height. God forbid anyone should ever see weather like it. It was better not to look, but to keep yourself busy with some job as long as your soul was still alive and there was a spark of warmth left in it.

It was this boat, after all, that had to be launched first. The trick was to judge it precisely, and to lower it at exactly the right moment when the wind was blowing from the other side. She was pitching terribly, was our poor old ship. The nets had swung her round again, so she was stern-on to the weather, which isn't the same as being head-on – the waves hit you much, much harder.

We leaned our weight against the davits. The trawlmaster took a run and put his shoulder to one of them, shouting hoarsely: 'Move it, lads, move it!'

The davits creaked but would not give way, until they moved of their own accord when the ship heeled over. The lifeboat fell outboard and started to swing. A wave-crest passed under it and licked its bottom.

'Stop!' shouted the trawlmaster. 'Three men get in. Pay out the painter.'

'Where is the painter?'

Three of them had already climbed into the lifeboat and were sorting out the oars, but they still couldn't find the painter. Suddenly I saw Dima, standing calmly to one side, holding the painter in his hands.

'You've got it, greenhorn!'

'Oh, is this the painter?'

'But it's too short!' said Seryozha, peering at it in the darkness.

At that moment I was holding the falls, and both my hands were full.

'Splice it!' I said to Dima. 'You've been taught how to do it.'

'What with?'

'Get a cod-line from the bo'sun's locker. Know where it is?'

As soon as he dashed off, I regretted sending him, but he came back right away with a coiled line.

'Tie a sheet-bend.'

'Sheet-bend. Is that a double hitch?'

'Yes. Only don't hurry.'

'Quickly!' shouted the trawlmaster.

Dima didn't listen to him, and he did right, because you can't splice a painter in a hurry; if you do, it can mean the loss of a lifeboat. I liked the way his hands weren't shaking and the fact that he wasn't in haste to get into the lifeboat.

'Enough!' I said to him. 'I'll pay it out. You get in.'

'Why?'

'To get a place in the boat, that's why.'

'What, as I am, without any of my gear?' He looked around. 'Alik, where are you?'

'Go on, get in, I expect Alik's already in.'

Four of us were left on the boat-deck, two on each of the falls. I knew we wouldn't get into this boat once it was lowered. By the time we came to get in, it would be full. We would then have to lower the other boat for the officers. And a good thing, I thought, because that meant I'd be with the Chief. If anything happened to our lifeboat, at least he and I would be together.

The trawlmaster shouted from below: 'Lower away – slow and steady!'

There was a delay at that moment, because the falls jammed for some reason, and then when the boat did start to go down, it was the wrong moment – instead of lowering we should have held it fast. Just then the ship righted herself and started to heel over the other way, and the lifeboat, swinging wide, hit the ship's side. The men in it fell to the bottom of the boat, but nobody seemed to have been injured, because no one cried out.

'All's well!' yelled the trawlmaster. 'Keep lowering away! She's not made of straw!'

I suddenly felt the falls slacken. A wave was lifting the boat up. It was too late to get into her now – in fact this was the moment to shove her off with a boathook or an oar, but someone was still trying to clamber over the ship's rail and couldn't manage it . . . The lifeboat was lifted up and flung against the gunwale with a splintering crash.

We flung ourselves on to the falls to haul the boat back, and we felt her weight as she rose up.

'Get out!' yelled the trawlmaster. 'I'll hold her!'

Sure enough, he held her at the rail until they had all clambered out, then he jumped across himself and pushed the boat clear of the rail: 'Haul away!'

As we hauled her up, she hit the ship another couple of times. The whole of one side of the lifeboat was stove in from stem to stern and water was pouring out of the cracks. The water hadn't come in from above, and it was then I noticed she'd been leaking through the bottom.

We put her back on the chocks and made fast the ends of the falls, but we might just as well have thrown the lifeboat overboard.

We started to go below. The First Mate met us on the way: 'Where d'you think you're going? Why have you left the lifeboat?'

I was in front and said to him: 'The lifeboat's smashed. You can give it to the cook for kindling-wood.'

'Call yourselves seamen, you idle sods! Well, back you go and lower the other one! And repair this one!'

I went on past him.

'I'm talking to you! Go back!'

Somebody said to him: 'Repair it yourself. You can call us when you've fixed it.'

We had already reached the doghouse, but the hooter was still roaring, calling us to the boat-deck.

Down in the cabin Shura was packing his suitcase. I had a sudden feeling their efforts to repair the engine had failed. And Shura realized, too, that we'd made a mess of launching the lifeboat.

'Did you weld it?' asked Seryozha.

Shura closed the suitcase and threw it on to his bunk.

'I welded the crack all right, but three of the pistons have burnt out. The Chief felt them through the fuel-injection ports. And you can't mend that by welding.'

'How many pistons are left? Nine?' said Seryozha. 'You can run on them.'

'But how far?'

The hooter was booming through the cabin loudspeaker.

'Switch it off,' said Shura. 'It only disturbs us.'

I went over and pulled out the wire.

'That's better.' Shura scratched the back of his neck, pulled his suitcase towards him and got out his pack of cards.

Seryozha sat down opposite him at the table.

'What's the score?' asked Shura. 'And who's winning? I seem to have forgotten.'

'Deal!'

Dima arrived and sat down in the doorway on the coaming. As he watched them playing, he smoothed down his wet forelock and his cheekbones darkened with tension. Suddenly he said: 'No offence meant, but you lot really are the dregs. I thought you would at least keep going to the end. There are still things that could be done, but you've just given up and sat down on your bottoms.'

Looking at his cards, Seryozha said: 'There's a raft on the rack. With oars. Do you want us to get it down for you and Alik? If you're so keen, maybe you can tow us home.'

'Think I'm talking about myself? It's you I'm ashamed of. I don't know . . . if you were at least panicking, or something . . .'

'What for?' asked Shura. He looked at Vasya Burov. 'Weren't you and I sailing together when No. 105 went down?'

'Yes, we were.'

'Well, things were better for her. She hadn't shipped so much water, and the engine hadn't completely given out. Even so, we didn't manage to save her. So what have we got to worry about?'

'Nothing, so play – it's your turn,' said Seryozha.

'Hoping to play your way out of a tight corner, are you?' Shura asked him, gloating. 'You won't pull it off.'

'It's simply disgusting to listen to you!' said Dima.

'So don't listen,' Shura retorted.

Vasya Burov sighed – a long, mournful sigh – stood up in the middle of the cabin without holding on to anything, and pulled off his wet sweater and his vest. True, he'd once been a strong man, but now his shoulders were drooping, and his muscles looked like ropes that have been torn and spliced again many times. Pleasurably, Vasya towelled himself dry, as if he'd just come out of a river on a July day, then took a shirt out of his suitcase – a dry, ironed shirt – and held it up against himself.

Dima looked at him, frowning and baring his teeth in a mirthless grin: 'Pardon me, but is there some sort of ritual of putting on white shirts? I didn't expect that!'

'Oh,' said Vasya, 'white, grey . . . it doesn't matter, so long as it's dry. Haven't you got one of your own? If you haven't, I can give you one.'

'Oh, no thanks.'

Vasya put on the shirt, which came down almost to his knees, turned back a blanket, lay down and stretched out blissfully. Dima got up from the coaming and looked at him, holding on to the doorpost.

Vasya folded his arms on his chest and linked his fingers: 'Who's going to give me a smoke?'

Shura threw him a packet.

'Ah, this is the life!' Vasya inhaled the smoke and slowly blew it out at the deckhead. 'I think we'll go under bow first. It's much better that way. No need to run anywhere, no need to go on deck.'

Dima spat, left the cabin and slammed the door.

I looked at Vasya's face, so calm, at Shura and Seryozha, and at the four bulkheads – the place where it would all happen to us. That one over there, the for'ard bulkhead, would give way at once, and the water would come pouring in through the crack. You might still jump out of the door, but only if you were sitting near the door – you'd never make it from your bunk. No, we wouldn't have to suffer for long. Maybe we wouldn't even have time to think of anything. When you're near a shore, the waves fling you all the harder, the cliffs smash the ship's plating like an eggshell . . .

So, I thought to myself, what is all this for, why is it happening? What are we guilty of?

I even laughed – with fury. Shura and Seryozha glanced at me and turned back to their cards.

Was it all for nothing, I wondered? Could it really be for nothing at all? Maybe we deserved it, after all. Because we *were* the dregs; that apprentice was telling the truth. We were so much junk, riff-raff, scum, trash blown in the wind. And now we had it coming to us – for everything we really were guilty of. Not for having done things to others, but for what we'd done to ourselves. For having behaved like wild beasts to each other; no, worse than wild beasts – if they live in packs, at least they never go for each other's throats. For having worked at a job we didn't like, but which we didn't give up. For not having lived with the women we really wanted to live with. For having listened to fools, when we could see from a mile off what fools they were.

It had got darker in the cabin; no doubt the accumulators were running low, but Shura and Seryozha kept on playing, even though it was hard to make out the suits on the cards.

'Don't worry,' said Shura. 'In a moment your nose will be glowing like a candle, and it'll be so bright we can even turn out the deckhead light.' He threw down a card and asked: 'Vasya, who do you feel sorry for? Apart from your mother, of course.'

Vasya replied with closed eyes: 'I haven't got a mother. I feel sorry for the kids.'

'Not for your old woman?'

'Not so much. She's not my flesh and blood. She had a rough old time with me, so it'll be easier for her now. But the kids are mine and love me.

What's to become of them? . . . But don't ask me. I'm going to lie in silence for a bit.'

'I feel sorry for my wife,' said Shura. 'What has she seen of me? We'd only just got married and we were bickering already. We even had a row just before I sailed.'

Seryozha played a card and said: 'Well, that was all right, that was just jealousy.'

'But there was plenty of it that wasn't all right, too . . . Who do you feel sorry for?'

'Lots,' Seryozha replied grimly. 'Too many to remember them all.'

'And what about you, Senya?'

Who did I feel sorry for? Not counting my mother and sister. Well, I hadn't made any special pals . . . Nina, no doubt, would cry when she heard the news, even though it was all over between Nina and me, and maybe she'd had more luck with Cheekbones, but even so she'd cry, she was good at that. And Lilya would be sad too, but she would soon console herself: I had, after all, done nothing to her – nothing good and nothing bad. If only those letters in the jacket didn't come to the surface; though she'd forgive me, in the circumstances, and in any case there was nothing special in those letters, nothing to get upset about. As for Klavka, I'd done more to her – I'd behaved like a lout . . . For some reason I suddenly remembered Klavka's room: a wardrobe with a mirror in it that took up half of one wall, so tall it almost reached the ceiling, and then there was a picture cut out of a magazine – right above the divan where she'd made up a bed for that Lidka. What was in that picture? Some woman on a horse. She was dressed all in black, the horse was black too – it was rolling its eye wildly, rearing up a little on its hind legs – and you could tell it was whinnying. Stretching out her arms to the woman was a little girl, standing on a balcony or the steps of a porch, at any rate stretching them through a stone balustrade; she was a lovely girl, all in white and her hair was black like her mother's. Yes, they were most probably mother and daughter, because they looked very much alike. That was all I could remember; most of all, my mind had been on Klavka herself. She was so cuddly and sweet in her dressing-gown, though everything had started to go crazy as soon as we burst into her flat. Another woman would have thrown us out, but she immediately rolled up Lidka's bed-clothes, fixed us something to eat and drink and even personally brought me a glass of vodka when I was sitting on the floor by the radiator . . . My God, that little room, where we made so much noise, was her *home*, so no wonder she hissed at us: 'Quiet, you lunatics, you'll wake the neighbours!' – and everything I saw in that room she had acquired by her own efforts. Think of it, what a looter, what a robber she must have been! Yet, it hadn't worked out too well with Klavka. I suddenly felt a sense of shame, burning shame, when I remembered her standing in front of me in the cold with her bare elbows and chest. Supposing she really hadn't been guilty of anything? And even if she had been, no money was worth the things I'd said to her. How would she remember me?

'There's one girl I feel sorry for,' I said. 'I hurt her for no reason at all.'

'Did you hurt her badly?' asked Shura.

'As badly as can be.'

'Will she forgive you?'

'I don't know. Maybe she will. But she won't forget me.'

'Is she a good girl?'

'I don't know that either . . .' I got up and went out of the cabin. The door of the next cabin was half-open. There, too, they were lying on their bunks under the blankets, dressed in clean clothes and smoking. No one turned his head to look at me.

5

Up above, in the doghouse, Alik was pouring water out of his boot while Dima held him steady by one elbow. As I climbed up towards them, Dima looked at me and grinned: 'Dynamic, aren't they? What a bunch of comedians!'

'Don't,' Alik begged him. 'Stop it.'

'What's the matter? Don't say *your* knees are knocking too?'

'Well, so what if they are?'

'Nothing,' said Dima. 'Just nothing, Alik my friend. It's all quite natural. If you have personality, death *should* be terrifying, because you have something to lose. I don't suppose the Chinese get terrified. You can slaughter them by the dozen without hearing a word of complaint.'

'Shut up, I said.'

'No, but where are those famous old sea-dogs we hear about? I thought they'd be clinging to the last bits of wreckage.'

'Wait a while,' I said to him, 'we haven't got to the last bits of wreckage yet.'

'Oh, so we still have to wait for that, do we?'

What could I say to him? I was thinking the same as he was.

'Has it ever happened to you before?' Alik asked me.

'Not once.'

'That's why you're calm. You don't believe it can happen, do you?'

'Makes no difference if I believe it or not. What will be, will be.'

'Even so, I can't believe in it until the very end.'

'Lucky you. It's easier that way.'

He was shaken by what looked like a convulsion. I regretted having said that to him. He was still such a kid, he couldn't believe in death. I believed in it, though. Once when I was in the Navy I got into a fight at Severomorsk naval base; someone whacked me on the head with a belt-buckle – and I woke up in hospital. I realized then – this was how it could happen. I might have simply not woken up. Death isn't when you go to sleep; death is when you don't wake up. Since then I've believed in it.

'Go below to the cabin, lads,' I said to them. 'Until they call us all on deck, my advice to you is – flake out.'

'We've heard that brand of philosophy too,' said Dima. 'Don't stand if you can sit, don't sit if you can lie down. So will everything just work out on its own without us?'

'Of course,' I said. 'All on its own.'

Alik smiled: 'Chief, your words inspire us with confidence.'

'Why else d'you think I try so hard?'

They went. How easy it was, I thought, to reassure people. If you start trying to prove to them that for this or that reason we can't possibly drown, they'll pester you with doubts and questions – how, what and why. But just tell them: 'With luck it'll be all right', then the thought of that puts their minds at rest.

Suddenly a light shone into the doghouse. I realized it meant that someone from the wheelhouse was coming to see us and they were lighting his way with the searchlight. Sure enough, it was someone in an officer's raincoat. He saw me and threw back his hood. It was Zhora the Second Mate.

'Are you going to come out on deck?'

'Already been. They smashed one lifeboat. What's the point now?'

But he was in a determined mood. He wasn't wet through yet, and someone who's dry never can understand a person who's soaked to the skin.

'Come below with me.'

Shura and Seryozha were so caught up in their game, they didn't even look at Zhora. The apprentices had only just started taking off their boots, while Vasya was still lying there, eyes closed and fingers clasped on his chest, though he wasn't asleep but muttering something to himself.

Zhora went up to him first: 'Get up.'

Vasya looked at him with indifference, as if he was looking right through him and staring at the bulkhead.

'Who d'you think we've been sounding the alarm for?'

'I don't know. Not for me. Nothing alarms me.'

At that moment Zhora noticed the wire I'd torn out.

'Idle slobs! Can't even be bothered to save your own skins! Better in a tin coffin than on deck, is that it?'

His eyes were already as red as a rabbit's, and now they turned bloodshot with fury.

'You should have a machine-gun,' said Seryozha. 'Then you could mow us down with a few bursts, couldn't you?'

Zhora strode towards him and took a swing. Seryozha turned a bit pale, but he didn't flinch. Zhora turned away from him and went for Vasya Burov again.

'Are you going to get up or not?'

He picked him up by the collar with both hands and sat him up in his bunk. Or rather he held him suspended. He's strong, is Zhora. He could have smashed him against the deckhead with his left hand alone. Vasya began to wheeze, as his collar was choking him.

Dima and Alik froze into silence. Suddenly Dima's face went blank and he said through clenched teeth: 'If anyone did that to me . . .'

Zhora looked at him and threw Vasya back on to his bunk.

'You can have it too, if you like.'

Dima shook his head, hunched his head down and stood up in a boxer's stance – left fist forward, the right guarding his jaw. But I guessed how it would end. Zhora had never learned to box, but he had learned how to keep his feet on a rolling deck with nothing to hold on to. He didn't stagger when the cabin heeled over, but Dima fell backwards against the bulkhead, and his boxer's stance was gone.

Alik leaped forward and held his arm out.

'What are you doing? Come to your senses! . . .'

I could see he was ready to hit both of them. He would hit out furiously, till he drew blood and teeth flew. All of us together couldn't have held down that young bull. I stepped in front of Zhora and hit him in the stomach with both hands. He doubled up and sat down on a bunk. I bent over and picked up the heaviest thing I could find – a boot.

'You won't get anywhere by beating people up,' I said to Zhora.

He sat there on the bunk with his knees almost up to his chin. Before he could have got up, I'd have had time to smash his face in with the boot, and I could have pushed him back again with no more than one finger.

'OK,' said Zhora. 'Let me get up.'

I dropped the boot. He clambered out and went to the door.

'If you don't come out to man the lifeboats in five minutes – everyone that's here – I'll dock your pay by thirty per cent.'

'Why so little?' said Shura. 'Go ahead and make it a hundred.'

Suddenly Vasya gave a sob. His eyes were full of tears. Shura turned to him: 'What's the matter, Vasya? Don't.'

Vasya wiped away his tears with his fist, but that only made them flow harder. It's unbearable to watch a bearded man sobbing his heart out. Even Zhora was embarrassed: 'Don't whine like that, I haven't done a damn' thing to you.'

'Go away! I wish you were dead, you brute!'

'Shut up,' said Zhora. 'Stop it, or . . .'

'Hit me, then, you pig. Hit a man lying down.'

'Get up,' Zhora grinned, 'and you'll be standing.'

'I'm not getting up. I don't care if I die here, but I'm not getting up. Why should I live, when there are brutes like you alive? . . .'

Vasya was completely choked by his tears.

'Go away,' said Seryozha. 'Seriously, Zhora – go away.'

Zhora looked round at us all and stopped grinning. No doubt it had got through to him that we were finished, and no amount of force would get us moving.

He punched the door open with his fist and went out. When he was halfway up the companion-way he shouted: 'Shalai! Come on out.'

I went up to him.

'You realize you're in deep trouble, don't you? You won't sail again after this, your career's finished after you've raised your hand against an officer. Well, not your hand – a boot.'

'I musn't do it to an officer,' I said. 'But you can do it to a seaman.'

'You fool, I'm not going to lodge a complaint. I'll cripple you for life in my own way. We'll settle our score in port – agreed?'

'Always provided we get back to port.'

'Balls! You've all turned into so many snivelling infants!'

He turned to go, but stopped again.

'Has it occurred to you, Shalai, that this whole cock-up started with you? Don't you feel guilty? Incidentally, I haven't told anybody you cast off the stern line. So you should be showing a bit of gratitude, you fool. Instead of which you prevent me from getting the men up in response to an alarm. You know what happens to people who do that sort of thing? They throw the book at you – and hard.'

'But, Zhora, what *are* we doing?! We're sending out distress calls, we're getting into the lifeboats, we're abandoning ship – but we won't cut the nets away!'

'Shut up! The nets are no business of yours.' He suddenly leaned towards me, right up to my face: 'But if you want to sacrifice yourself, so to speak, then go ahead – cut the trawl-warp.'

I said nothing.

'But I don't advise it,' said Zhora.

He shot up and out, ran aft along the deck, and the light in the doghouse faded. I sat down on the step. Yes, it did look as if I'd been the cause of it all – if you didn't count Grakov's talk to the crew on deck in Fuglø-fjord, when we all voted to stay at sea and carry on fishing. That was the whole point: we had *all* decided; you couldn't point the finger at any one person. Well, OK, maybe you could point it at me. In that case, what was I doing just sitting there? The axe, after all, was in a locker just for'ard of the doghouse. Four good whacks at the trawl-warp – that was all the sacrifice involved. I had to do something for my shipmates if I really had, as it seemed, got them into this trouble.

Suddenly I noticed Dima down below, lit by the faint light from the cabin. I'd no idea how long he'd been standing there; perhaps he'd heard the conversation between Zhora and myself.

Dima carefully shut the door, climbed up and sat down beside me: 'We must do something, chief.'

'That's what I'm thinking, too. The trouble is, it's a bit late.'

'Chief . . . Is it true there's a raft on the rack?'

'Haven't you seen it? Well, it's always piled up with head-lines, so you mightn't notice it. It's painted red and white.'

'Is it inflatable?'

'The raft? No, it's metal. Made of hollow tanks.'

'Can two people get into it?'

'Well . . . it's really an ace.'

'What's an "ace"?'

'A single-seater. Two people can get into it, but it's dangerous.'

'Would it sink?'

'It'd be a squeeze with two. Hard to row. Still, if you're determined to survive . . . Have you and Alik decided to take the raft?'

He shifted closer to me.

'Chief, listen. It's not so crazy as it sounds . . . If we can hold out for two days, we'll be picked up. This is a fishing ground here, and a shipping lane. It's idiotic, don't you see, to stay in this floating coffin. They've all given up already, lying with their paws in the air. Except for us two. I realized this just now . . . You and I are not going to die, chief. I'm telling you – people don't die because of a storm, they don't die of hunger. They only die of fear. It's been proved, chief. Books have been written about it. But we're only delaying a bit – to salve our consciences.'

He was talking exactly like a preacher. Even his eyes were shining. And I thought: of course, we could do it. We could also launch the second lifeboat. We could make a raft by lashing some floats together, or some barrels.

'If only they were all like you,' I said.

'Come on, chief – let's go!'

He stood up, tugging at my sleeve.

'Where to?'

'Let's go and get into the raft, before it's too late.'

'But there's only room for two people.'

'Chief. They've all died of fear already. And a man's alive so long as he wants to live. You want to, don't you? If we don't take the risk now . . .'

'You see, I want to get the chief out of this too. I won't leave the chief. Or Shura . . . or Seryozha . . . or Marconi . . .'

'Will it be any easier for them if you and they all go together?'

'Well, how can I explain it? Anyway, what is there to explain? You wouldn't abandon Alik, would you?'

He looked away from me.

'I asked Alik. He won't risk it. chief, in a case like this, the rule is simple: anyone who wants to get into the raft, gets into the raft. If it's two of us – OK, so it's two. Otherwise nobody will be saved.'

He said this so sadly and hopelessly, I actually felt sorry for him, the poor devil . . .

'Now listen.' I sat him down beside me. 'All right, so I get the raft down from the rack for you. I grab you a lifeboat box – it contains ship's biscuits, fresh water, bandages and so on. Try by yourself. It's easier for one in an ace, anyway. Put on two sweaters under your oilskins: people die of cold, too, not just of fear. Maybe you'll save yourself. And who can blame you for wanting to live?'

'No.' He shook his head. 'One person on his own will die. I know that for sure. What cretins you all are! What a cretin I am!'

'Don't go on like that, for God's sake. If you really wanted to, you'd push off by yourself.'

'And what about you?'

'I would too, if there was nothing holding me back.'

He sighed: 'No, it won't work.'

Alik came out of the cabin – with only his socks on his feet – and climbed up towards us.

'Well?' he said in a carefree voice. 'Can't you make up your minds, you vikings?'

'You keep yourself warm,' I advised him. 'Don't walk around without boots, the cold always starts with your feet.'

'Go and get some sleep, Alik,' said Dima. 'We'll come and flop too. With our paws in the air.'

Alik watched him go and said to me: 'Chief, if you're holding back because of me – I pass. I'm no good at this sort of thing. It's true, it really is. Dima and I agreed on it.'

'I don't understand you. I just don't, that's all. How can you agree on something like that?'

'Simple calculation, chief. Simple and sober.'

'Off you go to God up in heaven, then! Go away. I don't want to know either of you.'

'Why get angry, chief? Who are you angry with?'

'With myself, that's all.'

'But what about us?'

'You're both such good kids – I can't bear it'

I gripped the handrail, stood up and started to climb the companion-way. Suddenly I lost my grip and fell backwards, but by some miracle I managed not to get knocked out, by twisting myself round with a kind of instinctive jerk. My heart nearly jumped out of my mouth.

I found the trawlmaster's locker easily enough, but while I was looking for the axe among all the junk, my face was stung all over by driving snow. I clutched the axe to my chest and wiped my face, but still couldn't make up my mind to go on up to the foc's'le. I couldn't even see the foc's'le through the murk and the roaring blizzard. But it was me who had to cut it – my warp. Or rather, not the warp itself – cutting a hemp rope is no problem – but the hawser, plaited out of steel strands, which could kill me. Well, OK, I thought, it's my job as warpman after all, no one else would do it for me. And no one was likely to help me.

I noticed Alik looking out of the doghouse, huddled up against the cold.

'Go over to the winch,' I said. 'You're wet through anyway. You know how to release the pawl. I'm going to chop off the hawser where it passes over the rail.'

'Who told you to do it?'

'Ah, who indeed!'

I groped my way like a blind man, found the hawser and then felt my way along it, moving sideways. It was as taut as a steel bar, and when I reached the canvas 'scotchman', lashed around the rail to keep the hawser from chafing, I hit the hawser hard. The axe bounced back as if it was made of rubber. I felt the hawser – there wasn't a trace of my blow.

'Let me help you.'

I looked round. Alik was standing behind my back, his oilskins iced up, his face covered in snow.

'Keep away!'

'Why lose your temper? Let's do it together. How can I help you?'

'Get into the doghouse. When the end whips free, it could kill you.'

'What about you?'

'Will you get out of the way?'

A wave drenched us both, but though I'd managed to crouch down under the gunwale, Alik was knocked over, and all I could see was a glimpse of his socks. Believe it or not, he started struggling back towards me again. I couldn't be bothered to warn him again.

Two or three strands parted after each blow. The hawser was twanging like a mandolin and throwing the axe back into the air like a live thing. Many times I hit the ship's rail or the scotchman. But I was in a frenzy by now, hacking away like an automaton. It was getting thinner and thinner, ready to snap at any moment, and I looked behind me to see if there was anyone on deck. Alik was standing hunched up by the doghouse.

'Stand clear of the hawser!'

With one hand I pulled my padded jacket over my head, while I hacked away with the other.

The foc's'le rode up and the hawser began to creak on the scotchman – I was wary of hitting it again – but just then it snapped by itself. I didn't see it whip through the air, but it hit the doghouse with a blow that might have come from a riveting hammer and bounced back off the doghouse to whack me on the shoulder. I fell over and slid towards the hold, where I managed to get to my feet. There seemed to be no sign of the axe.

Alik was standing in the same place, holding on to the handrail. God knows how it hadn't hit him. He was a lucky lad, that apprentice!

'And that's all there is to it!' I said to him, almost cheerfully.

He looked at me in silence.

'Let's go.'

I pulled him after me into the doghouse. He kept on looking at me, but I was peering towards the wheelhouse, trying to see through the windows.

'They won't have heard anything in there,' said Alik. 'No one looked out. What'll happen to you for this?'

'What'll happen? Deliberate damage to shipboard equipment. About ten years, probably. How much would you give me?'

'Nobody saw you, though.'

'What about you?'

'I didn't see you either.'

What a good lad! How I liked him!

'What else do you want?' I asked. 'To have the captain demoted for losing the nets? Or for the whole crew to be made to pay for them?'

'How much do they cost?'

'A hundred thousand. Have you ever seen so much money in your life?'

'New roubles?'

'Real ones. In gold.'

'But the warp could have parted on its own.'

'Could have done. But it didn't. And there are axe-marks on the rail.'

'What do we do now?'

'Sleep. Or save our lives. Only I think it's too late for that.'

Down in the cabin everyone looked at me; but nobody said a word. I took off my quilted jacket and noticed that one shoulder was all torn, the cotton padding sticking out of it. I threw it on the deck, sat down on it and leaned against the radiator. My shoulder was just starting to look inflamed, although the first pain had gone.

'Chill, Senya?' Shura got up and covered my back with his jacket, which was as sodden as mine. 'Wait a moment, I'll tidy up a bit for you.'

He threw everything off the heating pipes so I could lean against them, but they were hardly warm at all. But perhaps it would be better to press myself against something cold? I closed my eyes and started willing my shoulder to stop hurting. Sometimes it works. Shura went back to his game of cards with Seryozha.

I didn't know whether what I'd done was good or bad. But I'd done it.

Suddenly Mitrokhin, who was sitting beside me on the deck, asked in a frightened voice: 'What's that, lads?'

I opened my eyes. The light was starting to fade. The filament in the bulb was barely pink.

'Look, lads,' said Mitrokhin, 'this is the end!'

'Don't talk crap,' said Shura. 'The Chief has switched all the power on to the pumps. Or he's saving it for the starter motor.'

'No.' Mitrokhin shook his head. 'I didn't want to believe it was the end either. But no – this is it, lads, we're finished!'

He started to thrash about as if he was having a fit. Maybe it even was a fit: he always had been a bit barmy. Shura and Seryozha threw themselves on him and grabbed his arms, but he was struggling so violently that the two of them couldn't restrain him.

'It's all my fault, lads! I was the ruin of you all when Grakov spoke to us. It's because of me we didn't go back to port. Forgive me, lads. Can you forgive me?'

He fell against my injured shoulder and I almost howled, but kicked him instead.

'Then you should be keeping quiet about it now, pig . . .'

He began thrashing about even more violently, shouting something through his tears, but it was impossible to make it out.

'Tie him up, lads,' Vasya begged. 'I'm going out of my mind.'

Shura gagged Mitrokhin's mouth and he calmed down at once, except for a low moaning noise. They lifted him up and carried him over to his bunk.

'Close his eyes,' said Vasya. 'He never sleeps.'

'Yes, he does,' said Seryozha. 'He sleeps with his eyes open.'

The light went out completely; all that could be heard was the sound of the waves and the pitiful groaning of the ship's hull.

I leaned back against the radiator again and closed my eyes.

6

A torch was shining in my face. I screwed up my eyes and pushed it away
with my hand. Maybe I was seeing him in a dream – a little man in a
raincoat with a pointed hood.

'It's quiet time, I see! And who's going to stand watch?'

From his voice I recognized the Third Mate.

'Where is Burov sleeping?'

'Why do you want him?'

'"Why, why." Nothing but questions. He's due to take the wheel.'

I rubbed my eyes with my fist.

'Why should anyone take the wheel? We're not under way.'

'What's the matter with you? Still asleep? Something wrong with your
ears?'

I listened – and something really had changed. The open door was
banging slightly, and someone's boot was creeping over the deck from
vibration.

'Has the Chief fixed the engine?'

'It's coughing. But it still won't get us out of this. Where's Burov, the
storeman?'

'Why waken him, if I'm not asleep?'

'What's wrong with him – sick?'

'Does it matter to you which of us goes?' I stood up.

'There's a rota, got it? Must be discipline, then everything gets done
properly and there's none of this chaos. All right, if you want to – you can
come.'

On the companion-way it was more audible: the engine was thumping,
but unevenly, as if it might stop at any moment. Chuff, chuff, chshsh . . .
Chuff, chuff, chshsh . . .

'And they say that engine's working!' said the Third Mate. 'What a
joke!' He plunged ahead into the dark, then came back. 'Hey, you haven't
gone to sleep again, have you? I don't want to have to come and get you a

second time.'

'I'm coming.'

'Are you going like that? In your jerkin? What about your posh jacket?'

'It's gone.'

'You are a fool. I told you we should swap. If I'd had it, it wouldn't have gone.'

Half-asleep, I followed him, guided by the hood of his raincoat. We reached the float-caboose and clambered up the netting to the flying bridge. The door hit me in the back, and sent me flying halfway across the wheelhouse, throwing me right against the wheel. Then I looked around – the skipper was there, Zhora the Second Mate, and Grakov. Marconi was sitting in the radio cabin, wearing earphones and talking into the microphone: 'Hello Base, Number eight-one-five calling . . . How do you read me? . . .'

I gripped the spokes, pressed my chest against the wheel and spread my legs wider. Then I reported in the proper form: 'Seaman Shalai. Permission to take the wheel.'

'You've already taken it,' said the skipper. 'Why isn't it Burov? Is he sick, or what?'

Zhora the mate answered for me: 'I know what he's sick with. And I also know how it's cured. Well, stand fast, since you've come.'

The skipper was standing by the engine-room telegraph and moving the handle.

'Starboard your helm,' he said to me. 'Hard astarboard. Don't let her lie beam-on.'

'Starboard.' I pushed the wheel over as far as it would go. With no way on, it moved quite easily. 'Wheel's hard astarboard!'

The skipper grinned. 'I see you haven't forgotten how to do it.'

'It's amazing,' said Grakov, 'how your crew hasn't forgotten how to go on watch.'

The skipper didn't reply, but took the whistle out of the speaking-tube to the engine-room and blew into it. The whistle sounded below, but nobody came to the tube.

'Are they all dead down there, or what?'

The door swung open, someone stumbled in and stood by the farthest window, legs apart. I squinted sideways – the Chief was wiping his hands on some cotton waste and looking out of the window, that was spattered with snow and spray.

'What's the word?' asked the skipper.

Without turning his head, the Chief replied:'The word's up to you now.'

'Are we under way?'

'Certainly.'

The Chief blew down the speaking-tube, to be answered from below 'Second Engineer here.'

The Chief went back to the window.

'Hullo!' came the call from below. 'I'm listening.'

'You don't say!' The skipper went over to the tube. 'Put on a few more revolutions, please. Can we at least have half speed?'

Again without turning round, the Chief said: 'I've forbidden him to run at half speed. He can give you slow.'

'What did you repair it for, I'd like to know? If you hadn't stopped it back there, we'd have met up with the factory-ship by now. I suppose you'll say I'm talking rubbish again, will you?'

'Yes, you are.'

The skipper sighed.

'You might at least not make me look a fool in front of a seaman.' He said into the speaking-tube: 'Slow astern.'

The spokes pressed against my hands, and the rolling changed character as the ship turned stern-on to the waves.

'Thanks, Sergei Andreyich, for at least giving us slow speed,' said Grakov. 'Now we can launch the lifeboat on the leeward side.'

'Is there only one lifeboat now?' asked the Chief.

The skipper replied, though not very confidently: 'The other one can be repaired. We'll secure a tarpaulin under its bottom.'

'Well, we'll count that one *when* it's been repaired. Meanwhile, only one is seaworthy. So . . . who will get into it? Grakov, who will you put in the lifeboat?'

'I don't understand the question. There are regulations that lay down who goes first.'

'Passengers are supposed to be the first.'

Grinning, Grakov said: 'Well, I suppose I'm the only pasenger. I can give up my priority.'

'Give up your priority, or give up your place in the lifeboat altogether?'

'Sergei Andreyich, as I see it the rule is as clear as can be: older people first. The younger ones can use whatever other means of flotation are available. What objection can there be to that?'

'None,' said the Chief. 'Except that young people want to live too.'

Grakov spread his hands. Or rather one hand; with the other one he was holding on to the strap used for lowering the window.

'Well, let's not give way to premature despondency. Experience tells us otherwise. Men have hung on like this for several days, not just for hours. And in what conditions! By the way, Sergei Andreyich, your own experience during the war is also instructive.'

'But it was easier for me,' said the Chief. 'After all, I was helped by the Germans, as you know.'

'Stop it,' The skipper intervened. 'This is no time to be settling old scores.'

'What old scores, Pyotr Nikolayich? It's just that Sergei Andreyich has seen fit to suspect me of personal cowardice.'

'I don't suspect you,' said the Chief. 'I'm simply making a visual observation.'

Grakov was silent for a while, then said sadly: 'Look, Nikolayich, you're the boss in this wheelhouse, if you don't mind me saying so. Kindly intervene, and perhaps ask someone to leave. In this instance, you can disregard my senior position. One of us two – the choice is yours.'

'Oh, stop it . . . I've got enough headaches without you as well.'

'No, Nikolayich, you must decide.'

Breathing hard through his nose, the skipper paced the wheelhouse from door to door.

'Well?' asked Grakov.

'Oh, to hell with you . . .' The skipper clutched his head. 'Look, Sergei Andreyich,' he said to the Chief, 'will you kindly keep your tongue in check, for God's sake?'

'I see,' said Grakov. 'One of us is asked to keep his tongue in check. Consequently, it is the other who must leave. Myself, in other words. Thank you, Nikolayich, that's fair enough.'

He left the wheelhouse, but without slamming the door as I expected him to do. On the contrary, he closed the door behind him most politely.

The Chief turned away from the window: 'Nikolayich, is it really possible to lose one's head the way you lost yours? Why on earth did you signal "Abandon ship" when the vessel was still afloat, when she had to be saved and there were the means of saving her?'

'What do you mean? Am I going to let my men be destroyed?'

'You're destroying yourself first of all. And your crew, too. It didn't occur to you that you and they could founder in weather like this. And you thought it better to lose the whole ship along with the nets instead of just the nets. If you'd have cut the nets, you wouldn't have been taken to court – because you would have saved the crew. As it is, you'll probably be prosecuted for casting the nets when you knew a storm was blowing up. I don't know if that was your idea or whether someone advised you to do it . . . I appreciate the position you were in. But if you're forced to choose between two evils, then at least make up your mind which is the worse! Then you only have to fear that one.'

Pacing the wheelhouse in silence, the skipper stopped behind my back.

'Are you going to keep the wheel hard astarboard all the time? Midships.'

I let go of the wheel and it swung over by itself. I couldn't stop it with my elbow, so I had to lean my weight against it and could hardly steady it by the spokes.

'Take care, helmsman,' said the Chief. 'When the ship's going astern it can break your arms . . . It'd be better to be going ahead, of course, the way people normally go, but it's a shame to abandon the nets.'

'As for the nets,' said the skipper, 'we're having no debates on that subject.'

Again he paced from door to door, like a tiger in a cage; he was really getting on my nerves. Then a whistle came from the speaking-tube to the captain's cabin. The skipper took out the whistle and put his ear to the tube, which delivered a rumbling, crackling message.

'All right.' The skipper plugged the tube again. 'He's reminding me to check the depth of water. As if I need him to remind me. OK, let's take a sounding.'

The Third Mate went into the chart-room and the echo-sounder squealed.

'Thirty-five. Maybe less.'

'The lead-hawser of the trawl will soon begin catching on the bottom,' said the skipper. 'Perhaps it'll hold?'

'It's never been known to happen anywhere in the world before,' said the Chief. 'So who knows – we may even chalk up a first!'

We stared in silence through the black windows. A shower of snow would tinkle against them like needles, to be swept away be spray.

Suddenly the radio began crackling and Marconi answered briskly: 'Hello Base, Hello Base . . . Number eight-one-five here, I am receiving you . . .

'How are things, eight-one-five?' asked the factory-ship.

The skipper ran into the radio cabin and grabbed the microphone.

'We're relying on you. What's become of you?'

'We've been talking to the tugs. Two salvage tugs are proceeding towards you from the North Sea. The *Desperate* and the *Komsomol*. They may even reach you before we do.'

'Out of the question,' said the skipper. 'I know those two old tubs. We're still relying on you.'

'We're sailing at full speed. You could get a bit of a move on, too. How do you read me?'

'We're reading you well. We just can't move.'

'What about your engine? Didn't manage to repair it?'

'Yes, we did. But we're not making enough way to move under our own power.'

'I don't understand.'

'All we can do is to slow down the drift a little. That should be easy enough to understand.'

'Use maximum revolutions. How do you read me?'

'We can't run at maximum revolutions. We're at "slow".'

'I see,' said the factory-ship.

'And then there are the nets,' said the skipper. 'The nets are pulling us.'

There was a moment's silence at the other end.

'What have the nets got to do with it? Are your nets outboard?'

'That's the whole point. And the head-lines are at zero depth.'

'Why did you cast? Didn't you get a storm warning?'

The skipper sighed. 'We heard the warning. But they're not always accurate. Well, so we took a risk. We were greedy. What am I to do now?'

'Proceed on reciprocal course to mine. How do you read me?'

'But what about the nets?'

'Proceed on reciprocal course to mine. Make your own decision about the nets.'

Heavy interference started up, and it became impossible to make out what was being said. The skipper waited a while, and came back into the wheelhouse – but the factory-ship got though to us again:

'. . . -one-five . . . much water under your keel? Report sounding.'

Marconi gave them the answer.

'Understood,' said the factory-ship. 'Yes, you must make your own decision about the nets.' And went off the air.

'Make your own decision, he says,' said the skipper, 'but he doesn't give us any advice.'

The Chief turned to him from the window: 'That's not what you've got to decide. And the people at Base aren't thinking about your nets. Just now you had thirty-five metres under your keel. Soon it'll be twenty. And the factory-ship can't go there.'

'She'll sail in twenty metres.'

'I'm not so sure. You have to take the rough weather into account, too,'

The skipper stopped behind my back: 'You're letting her yaw. Keep a better course.'

'Aye, aye.'

He walked away. Marconi's radio started howling and crackling. The voice came through: '. . . -one-five . . . read me? . . .' and then it went dead. Before the skipper had time to reach the radio cabin, it changed to a crackle of morse.

'What's that?'

'It's that Scots ship in distress,' said Marconi.

'Again? What a time to choose.'

'Why? It's the proper time.'

I turned my head and looked at the clock above Marconi's instrument panel. It was a quarter to three; the minute hand had just entered the red sector.

The first minute's silence had begun.

7

'Well, listen if you want to,' said the skipper. 'Tell us anything you hear.'

The morse was barely audible.

'They couldn't start their engine,' said Marconi. 'They're drifting.'

The skipper turned to me. Thinking he was going to give me another telling-off, I started turning the wheel.

'Do you remember her? The *Girl Peggy*?'

I was amazed – he hadn't forgotten I'd been at the wheel that time. I thought he couldn't tell our faces apart.

'Yes, I remember.'

I remembered her overhauling us to starboard, all blue and snow-white, as neat as if she'd just come down the slipway. She'd passed us as if we were standing still, and the cook had come out of the galley and emptied a bucket of slops right ahead of our bow.

'Rude fellow,' said the skipper. 'Oh well . . . now his ship's in trouble too. What's her position?'

Marconi told him. The Third Mate went into the chart-room and started rustling a chart.

'Oho! She really *is* in a bad way. Her keel's probably touching bottom.'

'I expect he can see the cliffs already,' said the skipper.

'Not yet. But he soon will.' As the Third Mate came back into the wheelhouse, he said to Marconi: 'Ask him if he can see the Faroes.'

'Don't you dare,' said the skipper. 'Don't get in touch with him.'

'I couldn't anyway,' Marconi replied. 'You have to know English really well for that. I can only talk a bit of slang.'

'Don't even try in slang. Some radio operator we've got, who doesn't know English!'

'You tell me what to say.'

'OK,' the skipper sighed. 'Come off that frequency, 600 metres. Try and pick up the factory-ship. We can't help that Scotsman anyway.'

'Soon . . . Another two minutes.'

I looked at the clock again – the minute hand was still in the red sector. The second minute's silence had passed.

'What's the point?' asked the skipper.

Marconi didn't answer; he was tapping away on his morse key.

'Why are you transmitting to him? I told you not to contact him.'

'I'm not calling him, I'm calling the shore station. They may not have heard him. We have a more powerful transmitter.'

'OK, go ahead. We'll help as far as we can.'

'Quiet, please,' Marconi begged.

Someone was talking on the air – a truly astonishing voice, velvety and fruity.

'Can you understand any of it?' asked the skipper.

'Well . . . a bit, here and there. In a moment they'll repeat it in Russian.'

It was not a man but a woman, who spoke in Russian. She had a slight accent, and her 'R's were very throaty, but you could hear her as if she was standing in the wheelhouse with us:'Attention all shipping. This is the Jutland Peninsula shore station calling all those at sea: all vessels sailing in the North Atlantic or anchored in the ports of northern continental Europe and islands, all coast-guard helicopters, all rescue craft on patrol. Two vessels are requesting assistance – one Russian and one Scottish. Wind and tide are carrying them on to the cliffs of the Faroe Islands. Their positions are as follows . . .'

Suddenly the Third Mate said: 'She knows her stuff, that woman. Probably an emigré.'

'All you can think about is women,' said Zhora. 'A fine time to choose.'

'I was just thinking aloud.'

'Well, keep it to yourself.'

The woman stopped. I looked at the clock again. The third minute of silence had passed.

'Why isn't anyone responding?' asked the skipper.

'Why should they?' said Zhora. 'They've all got charts.'

'Yes,' said the skipper. 'And those Scotsmen have landed up where there's no other shipping. Except us, and we're wallowing too.'

The hand of the clock had passed out of the red sector.

'Switch over,' said the skipper, 'and try to contact the factory-ship.'

As Marconi searched for the factory-ship, we heard: 'Number eight-one-five, how are things? . . .' but is was immediately blotted out by morse, twittering and cascading like a nightingale's trill.

'Hey,' said Marconi, 'that joker is horning in on our frequency too.'

'Who is?'

'The Scotsman on the *Girl Peggy*.'

The skipper was amazed: 'How on earth did he find this frequency? Say what you like, he's a bright boy.'

'He wants to live,' said Zhora.

It was impossible to make out the speech transmission behind the morse.

Then the factory-ship began to answer the Scotsman – also in morse.

'What are they saying to him?' asked the skipper.

'Same as they said to us. Asking him to proceed towards them.'

The speaking-tube from the captain's cabin gave a whistle. The skipper put his ear to it.

'No contact yet,' he said into the tube. 'That Scotsman who's so fond of sea-bathing has stuck his oar in. He's managed to contact the factory-ship. Well, let him talk . . .' He plugged the tube with the whistle.

Suddenly the Chief turned towards him: 'Well, how about it, Niko-layich? Now's the time to cut the nets.'

'Why do you keep harping on that? Maybe we can still save the nets. I somehow feel more hopeful now.'

'Why? Just because some others are worse off than we are?' All at once the Chief lost his temper. 'I don't understand you! He's been sending you an SOS signal for hours, and the only thing that's bothering you is the nets!'

The skipper stopped in the middle of the wheelhouse: 'Which of us is out of his mind? Tell me, Babilov?'

The Chief didn't answer, but simply looked at him.

'The captain of this vessel,' said the skipper solemnly, 'has always helped another ship when necessary. But when she had way on her! And the hull wasn't full of holes! In these conditions no one can blame me.'

'Nikolayich,' said the Chief. 'You'll never live it down, if you save your nets but abandon a shipload of fellow human beings. You'll be disgraced for the rest of your life. Why bring that on yourself?'

The skipper suddenly roared at him: 'But what if the ship isn't under way? Why haven't you given me any power?'

'You are under way. You only have to turn and get the weather astern, and the wind will carry you to the Scots ship.'

'And what then? That same wind will fling us on to the cliffs! We'd never get through into the fjords now.'

'Nokolayich, you can think about all that *later*. First you save them.'

'"You'll never live it down"!' the skipper yelled. He pulled off his cap and stood in front of the Chief, a head shorter than him. 'See how bald my head is? Well, it's earned the right not to be lectured or preached at by anybody!'

'Why are you shouting? My eyesight's bad, but I'm not deaf yet.'

'I'm not shouting!'

'Yes, you are. You can't hear yourself. And in the wheelhouse you don't shout. You give orders.'

The skipper asked quietly: 'What orders should I give, in your opinion? What am I to say to the crew? That we're going to look for some people to keep us company when we drown?'

The Chief looked at him in silence.

The skipper tapped his bald head and put his cap on again.

'But why not?' the Third Mate suddenly asked. Let's hoist the sail and go like a bomb! We must act fast! Are we seamen or aren't we?'

'You shut up,' said the skipper. 'When it comes to the crunch, that "kiss" on the stern happened during *your* watch . . . and don't forget it.'

'What d'you mean – during *my* watch?'

'Shut up,' said Zhora.

The Third Mate buried his nose in the collar of his fur-lined jerkin and subsided.

'There are seven of them on that Scots trawler,' said Marconi.

'Unlucky number, so they say. It's hardly more than a little motor-boat with a car engine.'

The skipper went over to the radio cabin.

'Why are you talking to *him* in morse and not trying to contact the factory-ship?'

'He's transmitting on our frequency.'

'I can hear you're transmitting to him, too.'

'Not yet.'

'I suppose you told him our call-sign, did you?'

'I had to, didn't I?' said Marconi. 'Otherwise he couldn't have given me his position.'

'So now he'll write in his log: Number eight-one-five received my SOS. And didn't come. Why the hell did you answer him? You might easily not have heard him.'

Marconi swung round on his chair to face the skipper: 'But we *did* hear him.'

The skipper didn't answer, and walked away. Once again the speaking tube whistled.

'No, no contact,' the skipper said into the tube. 'Anyway, what's the point in nagging them? They're doing what they can . . . No, I'm not being irritable. Some people here . . . want us to go and help the Scotsman . . . I tell you – they've taken leave of their senses.'

The Chief suddenly strode over, pushed the skipper aside and gripped the speaking-tube with both hands: 'Listen, Rodionych. This is Babilov speaking . . . Don't badger the man. I didn't intend to talk to you, because we haven't anything to say to each other, but I must. Stop badgering him. He's lost his head – ever since *you* came on board. Why make him act like a shit? I beg you, we all beg you . . .'

The tube didn't let him finish, and gave a squeak. The Chief frowned, took the whistle from the skipper and closed the tube. The whistle blew again immediately. The Chief removed the whistle, and in its place he plugged the tube with the cotton waste he'd been using to wipe his hands.

'You're rude,' said the skipper. 'Don't you respect *anybody*?'

I remembered the compass – the lubber's line on the compass-card had veered a long way to starboard – and turned the wheel.

'Are you a seaman or aren't you?' the skipper asked me. 'Don't port your helm. If you do, the trawl-warp will break before long.'

'Aye, aye.'

Marconi was calling the factory-ship again: 'Number eight-one-five calling, do you read me?' and when they answered we all froze in silence and the skipper dashed into the radio cabin. Suddenly the Scotsman came up on the same wavelength and began tapping and twittering in morse. Three dots – three dashes – three dots. Save our souls! Three dots – three dashes – three dots. I am in distress, I am drifting on to the cliffs, depth of water . . . position . . . I am calling you and you're not answering!

No doubt they had passed under those cliffs a thousand times before and knew what to expect. No doubt, too, they had lost all hope by now. There was nothing they could do. No angel would appear, not even a seagull would fly over them. There was simply their Marconi's hand mechanically tapping out – three dots, three dashes, three dots.

Then there was silence; not because the Scotsman had stopped transmitting but because our Marconi had switched to 600 metres. It was a quarter to four, and the minute hand was already in the red sector.

The Scotsman began twittering again. We listened to him for a whole minute, then the shore station came on the air once more: 'Following signal received from the Scottish trawler: To all who have tried to save us. You have done all you could. We understand. We wish you all good luck. Send greetings to our families.'

And no one answered the call. It was true – they all had their charts.

The skipper stood looking out of the window, hands clasped behind his back. The pane was lashed first by spray, then snow, then spray again.

I said: 'The nets aren't there any longer.'

I could feel my hands trembling on the spokes. Everyone in the wheelhouse stared at me.

The skipper asked: 'What makes you think so?'

'He's the warpman,' said Zhora. 'He ought to know.'

The skipper looked at me: 'What, did you cut the hawser?'

'Yes.'

'What with?' asked Zhora. 'Not with an axe?'

I said: 'Yes.'

'Yes, I thought I heard something,' said Zhora. 'There was a bang on the rail.'

The skipper took off his cap and wiped his forehead with it. In that one moment he'd broken out in a sweat.

'Why didn't you say so before?'

The Chief answered for me: 'He's as frightened as the rest of us, Nikolayich.'

'Do you realize,' asked the skipper, 'that you'll be prosecuted for this?'

'I know.'

'And that I'll be prosecuted with you?'

'When I cut the hawser, you didn't know.'

The Chief said: 'He's right.'

'Oh well, we'll both be sitting side by side in the dock. Perhaps it'll be more fun with the two of us, what d'you think?' The skipper put his cap on again. 'Turn the ship around to go ahead on the same course. Let's proceed like human beings. Port your helm.'

I put the helm over. The Chief switched the telegraph to 'ahead'. The wheelhouse heeled over almost vertically – this was as we turned beam-on – then righted itself.

'Steady as you go,' said the skipper. 'Right. Thank you, helmsman. And now get to hell out of the wheelhouse. And don't let me ever see you in it again.'

'Off you go,' said the Chief.

Zhora took the wheel from me.

'Go and wake up Firstov.'

As I was going out, the skipper said to the Chief: 'You're still hinting about those Scotsmen. But it looks as if we won't make it, even without the nets . . .'

I walked straight ahead, without dodging the waves. I even thought I wouldn't mind if they washed me overboard and to hell. Precisely – to hell.

I'd never been dismissed from my watch before.

The deckhead light in the cabin was hardly burning. Cards were scattered all over the deck. I didn't know how Shura's and Seryozha's game had finished, who had won.

I shook Seryozha, who said: 'OK, just coming' – and went to sleep again.

I pulled him down from his upper bunk on to the table. Swaying, he asked me with closed eyes: 'Are we going somewhere?'

'To the factory-ship.'

I stuck a cigarette between his teeth and lit it. He took a drag on it, came to his senses and started getting dressed. I saw him out and crawled into my own bunk.

'Senya,' Mitrokhin suddenly asked, 'what do they say up on the bridge; are we going to sink?'

This made me a bit wild: 'D'you suppose the people on the bridge know any more than you do? Your brain box not working?'

He wasn't offended, but said sadly: 'You see, I found a letter in my jacket. One I'd written home. I meant to post it on the factory-ship and I forgot.'

'Well, at least you met your brother.'

'Yes. I said goodbye to him. But my old woman won't get my letter now.'

'Go to sleep. Do you want me to switch off the light?'

'Don't bother.'

'You won't go to sleep with the light on.'

'I won't sleep anyway. And I feel a bit better if the light's on.'

I lay down and stretched out. I was more tired than I'd ever been in my life.

'Listen,' I suddenly asked, to my own surprise. 'Why do you sleep with your eyes open? Do you know why?'

'Yes, I do. I've done it for a long time. I was sunk once. And the light went out, just like this one. Afterwards I went into a mental hospital for a while.'

'Well, at least you were saved that time. Maybe this time, too . . .'

'How many turns can you give to a rope, Senya?'

He began telling me something about some premonitions he'd had, but I wasn't listening and dozed off. And being tossed about in my bunk didn't bother me a bit.

How long did I sleep? It seemed like a minute to me. And that's probably how long it was.

I heard someone come running and bursting into the doghouse, heard his wet sea-boots clattering down the companion-way – twenty steps, twenty blows in my ear – and heard him shout: 'Beachers! Get up, there's work to do on deck!' It was Seryozha yelling, like he was trying to waken the dead in a cemetery. 'The Scots ship is sinking! We're going to rescue the Scotsmen!'

Part 5

Klavka

Wretched he may be, the poorest rustic churl,
In distant hamlet, far from your warm hearth;
Yet if there grieves for him one true and loving girl,
Then there's some reason for our life upon this earth.

Japanese tanka

1

As I climbed up the companion-way I saw both searchlights were switched on, though they were only shining, as they say, like two glow-worms in a fog: a snowstorm was blowing, the like of which I've never seen. On the deck the snow was at least being swept away by the waves, but the masts and shrouds were growing beards of frozen snow like pine trees in Siberia.

Some time had passed since Seryozha had run back to take the wheel again, and still no one was stirring in the foc's'le. Like a fool, I was the only one who'd come out on deck. Suddenly a huge figure loomed up out of the snow, the face invisible under a hood. As the figure came towards me, I recognized the Chief.

'Is that you, Senya?' He led the way down below. 'Why aren't they coming? There's work to do on deck.'

A man was sitting on the coaming. The Chief tripped over him, swore and shone his torch. It was Mitrokhin, his eyes wide open and staring.

'Not bad. One more who's woken up.'

But I knew Mitrokhin was asleep, even though he'd managed to get dressed and move here from his bunk. I picked him up under the armpits and heaved him aside.

'Show a leg there!'

No one moved.

'Well,' said the Chief, 'this won't do.'

He strode into the middle of the cabin, kicking aside boots, oilskins and jackets, and began pulling back the curtains in front on each man's bunk.

'Ah, the welder!' The Chief recognized Shura and shook him. 'You asleep, welder? Come on, up you get . . .'

Shura groaned, but didn't open his eyes. The Chief dragged him out and sat him on the table. Shura's face lolled back, quite lifeless.

'You hold him up,' said the Chief. 'We need him in our team. I'll deal with the other one.'

The other one was Vasya Burov. He was lying there so calm, arms

folded on his chest, his little beard pointing up to the deckhead – all he
needed was to have two coppers put on his eyes. The Chief sat on his bunk,
gripped him by the shoulders and sat him up.

'Get up, storeman! You're not asleep.'

'All right, so I'm not asleep,' said Vasya, his eyes still closed.

'We've got to go and help some other people, that's the situation. And I
thought our storeman, the senior seaman, would be first on deck, setting
an example to the others. But you're lying here, all in a nice clean white
shirt . . . Planning to die, were you?'

'What's that to you?'

'Why anticipate? It comes to all of us when it's our turn. And there are
people out there who are going to drown if you don't get up.'

'Damn those Scotsmen! I'm not going anywhere.'

'Oh yes, you are. And I'm not joking.'

'Chief,' I said, 'whatever you do, don't hit him.'

'Why should I? He'll get up by himself.'

Shura's head flopped over on to my shoulder. Groaning, he began to
come to his senses. The Chief shook Vasya, who opened his eyes. His face
had puckered up, and at any moment he might burst into tears.

'We're goners ourselves.'

'But at least we have some hope. They have none. Come on, storeman.
At any rate tell me what you're thinking about . . .'

'All sorts of things . . . Why pick on me? There are younger ones. I'm
old.'

'How old are you?'

'Forty-two.'

'You don't say! What about me, then? Senile, I suppose? No, this is a
pointless conversation.'

The Chief hauled him out of his bunk. Vasya stood up and gave a sob.

'Where's his cap? Hey, welder!'

Without a word Shura bent down and picked up Vasya's cap.

'There you are!' said the Chief. 'Cover up your bald patch, and you're a
young man again.'

With the cap crammed on his head, Vasya shut his eyes and sobbed. 'I
don't care, I'm going to lie down again.'

'Lie down then, damn you!' The Chief lost his temper. 'What a sight –
you scarecrow!'

Vasya leaned down to pick up his quilted jacket. The Chief went over to
the apprentices. 'Well, how are our romantics? Do you need help to get
up?'

'We're already up.' Puffy-eyed, Dima was swaying on the edge of his
bunk, dangling his legs over the side. 'Alik, you're not asleep, are you?'

Alik silently crawled out of his bunk. The Chief went to the next cabin.
There the door was on the hook. He rattled it, then charged it with his
shoulder and burst into the dark cabin.

'Why are you still in your bunks, when the storeman's already up?'

'You go to . . .' the cooper replied, and told him where he could go – to somewhere more horrible and distant than you'd ever imagine.

The Chief didn't let him finish. There was the sound of a juicy punch, a roar, a kind of savage growl and the crash of a falling body. A brawl started, boots crashed and a stream of hoarse swearing poured out of the cabin. At once I saw red and ran to help the Chief – I was terrified in case someone, half-awake, hit him on the head and knocked him out. But I met the Chief coming out of the cabin.

'Go up on deck, I want you to be the first man ready.'

As I went, I looked back – the Chief was bursting his way into the bo'sun's cabin. The light in it was suddenly switched on and the trawlmaster came flying out, barefoot and wearing only his underwear, followed by his boots and jacket. Then the bo'sun's gear flew out and after it the bo'sun himself.

'We're getting up, why all the fuss?'

The bo'sun clutched his cheekbone and spat. The Chief came out, pushed him back into the cabin and came up the companion-way towards me. His face was white and terrible, big drops of sweat had broken out on his forehead. Breathing hoarsely, he suddenly closed his eyes and collapsed on to me, heavy and limp. I was going to sit him down on the steps, but he had already recovered.

'Don't worry,' he said. 'They'll get up now . . . they must. That Scots ship was a stroke of luck for us.'

'How are you? Can you stand? Do you feel bad?'

'I can stand . . . I must go and make sure they all come up on deck.'

He went down again. There was a steady bustle in the cabin, though someone was still swearing to relieve his feelings, and soon they came out as if they'd been ordered to cast the nets.

His face still puffy, the trawlmaster emerged from the doghouse. He stood and shivered, warming his hands under his armpits, mittens gripped between his knees.

'It's all gone, trawly,' I said to him. 'You sisal's gone to the bottom.'

In a flat voice he asked: 'Cut the nets loose, did you? Fool. There was a lot of fish in them. I suppose you didn't attach a flashing buoy to them, did you?'

'Would it have held them?'

'We could have picked them up . . . If we're still alive, that is . . .'

'Where? On the cliffs?'

The cooper came up into the doghouse, and the trawlmaster said to him: 'Hear that? Our Senya the warpman has distinguished himself by sinking the trawl. No brandy for the crew now.'

The cooper squinted at me angrily. He still hadn't cooled off after the brawl.

'Cooked your own goose this time, have you, idiot? Thought you knew what was best for all of us? Well, just don't expect me to bring you any food parcels in prison, that's all.' Then he noticed my injured shoulder and said, looking away: 'Rub that shoulder of yours, otherwise the arm will go numb. Then you won't be any help to the rest of us.'

The bo'sun climbed up, swaying from foot to foot: 'Lousy devils,' he said. 'What a time to choose to go and sink! Well, what are we standing around for? Since we're up, we might as well work.'

'The Chief's going to give us special orders any minute now,' said the trawlmaster.

'Why do we need the Chief? We can give orders ourselves.' The bo'sun cupped his hands to his mouth. 'Bridge, ahoy! Power to the capstan!'

The answer came from the wheelhouse: 'Giving you power . . .'

Immediately the searchlights dimmed. So much for the power.

The capstan would barely work; it couldn't haul up both anchors at once, and only just managed them one at a time.

'It's got the droops,' said the trawlmaster. 'Like this, it'll only just haul a cat up. I'm fed up with this ship!' He took a boathook from the racks and used it to hook on to the anchor-chain and heave it up link by link, as if that would help the capstan.

'Bo'sun,' the Chief called out, 'that sail – do you remember where you stowed it?'

The bo'sun growled: 'In the forepeak. Where else would it be?'

Looking like a snow-covered rock, the Chief made his way for'ard to us on the foc's'le, felt for the hatch-cover of the forepeak with his boot and began rattling the clip.

'Wait a minute!' The bo'sun couldn't bear this. 'Don't you go messing around with *my* gear. If we ship water in the forepeak it'll leak into our cabin.'

He opened the hatch-cover himself, while we either crouched round it on our haunches or lay down on the deck to protect the forepeak a little from the waves coming over the bow. For a long time the bo'sun fumbled around in the dark, banging and clanking.

'Now where is she, my beauty? Where did I put her? Come on, shine a light in here, you idle devils!'

The Chief put his hand into the hatch, holding a torch. The bo'sun was sitting on some canisters, with the sail on his knees.

'But you've got it there!'

''Course I have! Think I was looking for the sail? I'm trying to find the head. I folded the sail specially, with the head-board on top, and now I can't find it. No, that's the clew . . .'

The trawlmaster yelled: 'Bring it out! We'll sort it out up here.'

'No you won't. Ah – found it!' He pushed the folded sail up through the hatch. 'Mind your hand. I'm holding it by the head.'

Without letting go of it, he somehow contrived to close the hatch-cover with one hand, then as he ran behind us along the deck he tripped, but still managed to hang on to the sail. It unfolded in our hands, the corners dragged in the water and swelled, making it heavy. The trawlmaster got tangled up in it and fell over. A few others ran to help us, picked it up and dragged it to the mast. And the bo'sun was still clinging on to his corner.

'Got it, lads, got it! The main thing is not to lose the head.'

The sail was spread out on the tarpaulin-covered hold. It was almost completely unwrapped, lying splayed out in heavy folds and covered in snow, until the head was made fast to the main halyard.

A shout came from the wheelhouse: 'Bo'sun! What's happening to the sail? Is it hoisted?'

'Any minute now!'

He jumped up and grasped the halyard, two others hung on to it with him and the sail – a sodden, heavy mass of cloth – jerked and started to crawl up the mast, while down below it flopped into grey folds that would scarcely bend. Wasting no time, we pulled the foot of the sail along the derrick-jib, which had now become the boom, and belayed the main sheet to a cleat on the gunwale. As the three of them hauled on the halyard, the luff of the sail climbed up the mast. Gradually the folds straightened out as they began to catch the wind, and the boom started to jerk. At that moment the canvas came to life: there was a bang like a sledgehammer hitting a log, the sail snapped flat and then immediately bellied out in a curving arc. The battens creaked, sending down a shower of icicles. The cold blasted our faces, burning foreheads and lips, but we kept standing there, heads thrown back, and at that moment something inside us changed: it was no longer just a heap of canvas but a sail, a sail – a white wing above the black abyss of destruction. It was just as it was three hundred years ago, when men had sailed the world like heroes, knowing nothing of those stinking engines that always break down at the wrong moment. Having achieved this miracle, we even felt maybe all wasn't lost, we might yet come out of this alive and see dry land again.

The Chief licked his finger – though why did he have to lick it? – raised it, and said: 'A broad reach on the port tack!'

I saw his face under the hood – for all its wrinkles, it was a young face.

'Bo'sun! Thanks for the sail!'

'We can always dream up something,' the bo'sun answered. 'We're not completely wooden-arsed.'

'Well done! Now let me have four men on the pumps.'

2

The pump was where we'd left it, in the narrow space between the
superstructure and the gunwale, only now it was powdered with snow and
wrapped in a tarpaulin – the one from the capstan. So *that* was where the
wind had blown it.

Four of us – Shura, Alik, Vasya Burov and I – hauled the clumsy thing
over the coaming again. Only when we lowered the intake hose did we
remember it was too short.

'It won't reach, sod it!' said Shura. 'Now let's think up a way to make it
reach. We'll lower the bugger down.' He was already standing on the
engine-room companion-way and pulling the pump towards him.

'That's not logical,' said Alik. 'That way, the outlet hose won't reach far
enough up. Nose to tail or tail to nose, it's still the same crocodile.'

'Heave, you crocodile!'

'But what d'you want to do?' I asked.

'Questions, questions! We'll put it on the work-bench – that's still a bit
higher. And don't you come down, greenhorn. Your job's to hold the
outlet-hose.'

We heaved it on to the work-bench. I took one handle, Shura the other,
and Vasya, standing below us in the water, pulled alternately on my handle
and on Shura's. The hose jerked, the pump slowly began to work.

'We're pumping, lads!' said Shura, delighted. 'How are things up there,
greenhorn? Does it reach?'

'Perfectly!' Alik replied from above. 'Only it doesn't need holding – I
can jam it in position with the door. I'll do a bit of bailing with a bucket.'
He lowered a bucket on a cod-line, filled it and hauled it up.

This pleased us a lot, even though about half a bucketful was spilled each
time. Alik laughed: 'Low-level technology!'

'He's growing up, is our greenhorn,' said Shura. 'He's as clever as a
dolphin.'

'Dolphins are the intellectuals of the sea. We're a long way behind them!'

'Keep pumping! If we don't pump her out, we're in trouble.'

'Tell me, Shura, why didn't we think of this before?'

'Think of what?'

'Putting the pump on the work-bench.'

'One thing at a time. You keep bailing!'

'But still, Shura – why?'

'Use your loaf, greenhorn – people out there are drowning and you want to talk. Bail!'

But the apprentice wouldn't give up.

'You poor idiots,' he said, 'now I really like you.'

'Oh?' said Vasya. 'Why?'

'I like you a lot.'

Shura asked him: 'You haven't gone off your rocker by any chance, have you? If so, tell us, and they'll send someone to relieve you.'

'It's not impossible. We're all a bit crazy. But I'll always remember this moment. And you must remember it too, please. It's the moment of truth!'

'What's that?' Shura actually stopped pumping.

Alik was beaming gloriously, but there was also a look about him as if he might just have gone a bit barmy.

'How can I explain about "the moment of truth"? Well, it's . . . it's when a matador kills a bull really well. Beautifully, by all the rules of the game.'

'What's good about killing an animal?' asked Vasya.

Alik was thoughtful for a moment. 'No, I haven't got it quite right . . . But I stick to my opinion.'

'Don't worry, greenhorn.' Shura began pumping again. 'We like you all the same. But still keep on bailing.'

'By the way,' Alik asked, 'how long do I go on being an apprentice?'

Again we stopped pumping.

'Yes, by God,' said Shura. 'Shall we make him into a seaman? Of course, we could have lowered you into the water on a line here and now, but you're wet through already. So just take it as read – next time you step ashore you'll become a fully-fledged beacher of the fishing fleet.'

'I'll do it symbolically, so instead of myself I'll dip this bucket in the water.'

'Right!' said Shura. 'That's the best thing to do. Bail away, non-apprentice, bail away!'

We pumped like absolute lunatics. Then we began to flag. Vasya took over from me on the work-bench, and I stood in the water. In every job there has to be a bit of a let-up, and for us it was standing in the water.

Vasya spat on his hands and said: 'I'll do seventy strokes and then I'll die.'

He started to count the strokes, but soon lost count. Then Shura stood in the water and I climbed back on to the work-bench. We pumped for an age, wrapped in steam, while the noise of the engine battered away at our eardrums and the air in the engine-room made it harder and harder to breathe. I started to have a funny feeling, as if it wasn't me who was banging away at that stupid pump – up, down, up, down – and trying hard not to fall off the work-bench when it swayed and rocked underfoot; it all seemed to be happening to someone else while I watched from alongside, wondering when that someone would bust a gut. It came very close to that . . .

'Senya,' the Chief called me from up above. 'Come up here.'

Our relief-shift was coming down the companion-way – the trawlmaster, the cooper and Mitrokhin.

As the Chief pulled me up by the hand, he leaned down into the engine-room and called out: 'Shepilov! Are you hiding down there?'

Yurka the greaser emerged from the steam as if he was appearing from a cloud.

'Give her a few more revolutions.'

'But Sergei Andreyich, we'll overheat the engine again.'

'Can't be helped,' said the Chief. 'We must go for broke now.'

The Chief went up on to the flying bridge and I followed him.

'Why did you call for me, Chief?'

'We're getting near the Scotsman. We'll have to come alongside.'

'How will we do it?'

'You and I must think up a way.'

All the time – when we were hoisting the sail, when we were hauling the pump into position, and when we were pumping – I'd been wondering how on earth we would come alongside. Closing on another ship in a sea like that could be death. And what else might we be running into? Really, we had all gone barmy.

We went out on to the flying bridge. A light was on in the radio cabin. I put my face against it and peered in: Marconi was sitting at the desk, leaning on his elbows, hands gripping a pair of earphones to his head. His lips were moving, like someone having a fit. The skipper was pacing up and down outside the door, his hands clasped behind his back. He came into the cabin and said something to Marconi. He'd aged, had our skipper; he was bent like a hunchback. He took off his cap and wiped his bald head with a handkerchief.

'What are you doing there?' asked the Chief.

He climbed up to the boat-deck. There the wind was enough to blow you over and you couldn't see your hand in front of your face. The Chief shone his torch, but the beam lit up no more than a couple of feet ahead of him.

'What did you say to him?' I asked the Chief.

'Who to?'

'The skipper. Why did he suddenly change course?'

'Oh, nothing special. I told him no one would ever sit at his table in the Arctic again.'

It gave me a funny feeling just to think what you can say to a man to scare him so badly he'll forget all his other fears.

'Don't you laugh at him,' said the Chief. 'He's still going to have to answer for your exploits. It'll be easier to get you out of trouble . . . Where does he keep it?'

'What?'

'The line-shooting pistol.'

Standing over the bo'sun's locker, the Chief was shining his torch into it and rummaging about among the lines, hooks, bottle-screws and shackles.

'Here it is.' He pulled out the line-shooter from the very bottom. 'Look – and a full set of cartridges. There's a bo'sun for you!'

'Are we going to set up a line connection?'

'We'll try. But it seems like these cartridges are as damp as hell.'

'Was the lid open?'

'Yes, it was. Ah, if I could lay my hands on the man who did it . . . OK, we've all done stupid things, including me. Well, now – shall we fire one, just for fun?'

The Chief loaded the cartridge, pointed the line-shooter astern and pressed the trigger. The only sound was the click of the hammer.

'We're going to disgrace ourselves,' said the Chief. 'We'll disgrace ourselves in front of these foreigners.'

'Maybe we can dry them out?'

'It'll take too long. They're not just slightly wet. Five minutes was probably enough to soak them.'

'Longer. Know how long the locker's been open? Since we tried to launch the lifeboat.'

I now knew precisely who had failed to close the locker. It was Dima – who else? When he was splicing the painter.

'We'll have to do it by hand,' said the Chief.

'Can we heave it that far?'

'I can't. You'll do it. You're young and you've got good eyesight.'

We pulled out a manila hawser, coiled it into two loose 'running' coils, and in the middle I used a double sheet bend to make fast a block and a heaving-line – also manila, but much thinner and with a weight on the end.

'Take a rest,' said the Chief.

I sat down on the deck, my back to the locker, holding the weight in my hand. It was then I remembered my shoulder. I'd overworked it on the pump as well, and now how could I throw a heaving line? It was my right shoulder, after all. Maybe I should tell the Chief; it was nothing to be ashamed of. And suddenly I heard the Scots ship. We had been calling her with our hooter, and now she was answering with a faint little toot.

The Chief pushed back his hood and cupped his hand to his ear. So he had heard it too; it wasn't my imagination.

'Well, this is it,' said the Chief. 'We've arrived.'

The hoot came from somewhere abeam. We had almost sailed past them.

'The sail!' shouted the Chief. 'Have they reefed the sail?'

Someone answered from the main deck: 'We've already lowered it. We're not deaf either.'

The Chief ran to the speaking-tube on the flying bridge: 'Vessel on the starboard bow. Power to the searchlights!'

He grasped one of the searchlights, aimed it – and through the spray and snow-flurries I saw a dancing shadow on the waves.

'Do you see her, Nikolayich?' the Chief asked the skipper.

The whole ship shuddered as the engine went astern. Slowly, slowly we edged towards the Scotsman. By now we could see clearly – she was lying stern-on to us. Lying! If only she had been! Instead, she would first ride up on a crest, even higher than us, then slither downwards to hell into the trough of a wave.

'Can't you come any closer?' shouted the Chief. 'OK, Nikolayich, this will do – we'll manage somehow.'

Men could be seen in her stern-sheets, wearing black oilskins trimmed with white. I was still resting, one shoulder leaning against the locker, the weight in my hand. Our people were already coming out on deck, clustered along the starboard side.

'*Peggy*, ahoy!' The bo'sun's voice cut through the dark. 'Where's your line? Am I supposed to provide the lines? Greenhorns! Landlubbers! Idiots! . . .'

The Chief leaned over the rail: 'Quiet, Strashnoi! The line's here. We're going to pass it to them.'

'Why do *we* have to do it?'

'Because they're the vessel in distress.'

'Aren't we in distress too? I'll say no more. But why is it always poor old Ivan the Russian who carries the can?'

'You want to know a lot, Strashnoi!' the Chief yelled back cheerfully. 'Too much, in fact!'

The Scotsman's stern had drawn a little nearer.

'Heave your line, Senya!'

Holding my weighted line, I went over to the rail. The Chief lifted the two running coils and put them at my feet, where I felt for them with my boot just to make sure. The Chief shone one searchlight on me, so the Scotsmen would see me with the heaving line, then he trained the other searchlight on to their stern.

'Don't delay – heave your line!'

There were three of them standing there, the one in the middle slightly taller than the others. Which of them would catch the line? Almost the whole length of the heaving line was in my left hand, coiled in small loops, while the two coils of the hawser were under my boot; I felt for them once again. I leaned my stomach against the rail and threw.

Snake-like, the weighted heaving line flashed in the beam of the searchlight and hit their rail. They all grabbed for it with their clumsy, mittened hands and got in each other's way – either that, or they hadn't spotted exactly where it fell. I felt it go slack in my hand.

I hauled it back, coiled it again in my left hand and gripped the weight end with my right. At least I now knew the exact length needed.

Someone yelled from the wheelhouse: 'What's happening with that line?'

'Don't listen to them,' said the Chief. 'And don't hurry.'

Maybe my arm simply failed me, thanks to that damn' shoulder, because this time the line fell short of their stern, where you couldn't have picked it up even with a boathook.

'You're in too much of a hurry!' said the Chief.

I coiled it again, clenching my teeth to force myself not to hurry. And I threw it well, taking a slow swing and throwing with a jerk and a slight twist, so that the weight spiralled its way through the air.

I saw it quite clearly as it hit the tall man on the shoulder. He slapped his chest with his mittens as if swatting mosquitos, then he dropped out of the searchlight beam. Their stern rode up, we plunged down, and my heart sank as I felt the line once again slacken in my hand.

'Clumsy bastard!' I shouted to the tall one. I could have wept when he dropped that line. 'Killing's too good for you!'

'What's the matter you?' the Chief yelled at me. 'You're as hysterical as a pregnant girl. Heave your line!'

'How many times do I have to throw before they catch it?'

'You'll go on throwing until they do catch it!'

I hauled it back, took enough in my right hand, judging by its weight, and waited until the two ships were level again.

The weight flew right at his face. I did this quite deliberately. He saw the weight coming straight for him. He jumped aside, and the weight fell over the rail. I didn't see them catch it, because their stern rode up again and moved out of the searchlight beam, but the line flew through my hand, burning my palm.

'They've got it!' I yelled at the Chief. 'It's worked!'

Both coils began to unwind.

The Chief ran over, picked up one coil in an armful, walked to the rail and flung it to the deck below.

'Hold it, Strashnoi! That's your running-line.' Then he threw the second coil: 'And that's your standing-line. Is the raft ready?'

'Raft? Ready in a moment!'

'Idle fucker! *We're* the landlubbers when it comes to doing a job . . .'

I was watching to make sure the heaving line passed over all the rails without fouling.

'You can go now,' said the Chief. 'Or has your arm gone numb?'

'A bit.'

'Even so, go below and don't stand in the wind. We're aiming to come out of this alive!'

I followed him down to the main deck. Someone was busy at the stowage-rack, throwing out the head-lines that were piled up in the raft, while the bo'sun moaned at him not to fling the tackle around but stow it neatly in the doghouse. At last they pulled the raft down, made the running-line fast to one end, and dropped it overboard. The raft vanished from sight, and the lads gently hauled the standing line taut. 'Gently' is only a manner of speaking, of course, because with each wave the line was jerked out of their hands and soon it was hung with mittens frozen to it.

I did nothing, but simply sat down on the cover of the hold, hanging on to a shackle, and watched. No one yelled at me for sitting down and doing nothing – not even the cooper. I'd done my bit, so now it was my turn to sit and watch the others. The lines wrenched themselves out of their hands, pulled them over the deck and flung them, belly first, against the gunwale.

'Vasya!' yelled the trawlmaster. 'Burov, where are you? Skiving as usual? Your stomach's fatter than mine – come over here and be the anchorman!'

Vasya, of course, was skiving somewhere at the back, but he stepped forward with a self-sacrificing look.

'What'll be left of my dear old gut now?'

'You'll survive. Stand there and anchor this line.'

The trawlmaster and the Chief towered above them all, making it look as if they were the only ones holding the hawsers and all the rest were only 'anchoring'.

Suddenly Vasya shouted: 'Stop! Stop, lads, they're jerking the line! It's the signal to pull the raft back. Haul in on the running line!'

They hauled. Someone asked: 'Is the raft empty?'

'Doesn't seem to be. It feels heavier.'

'There's someone sitting in it!'

The bo'sun leaped out of the crowd, cupping his hands to his mouth: 'Bridge, ahoy! Train the searchlight on the raft!'

A door banged in the wheelhouse, and there was a clumping of boots as someone ran to the upper bridge. The beam swung around over the furious, seething wavetops, over the black troughs – and amid the lashing spray it picked out the raft. Like a hand it gripped the tiny little red-and-white raft . . . and the man in the raft.

3

He was all in black, except for the trimming of white fur round his face and his cuffs. We could already see he was wearing no mittens. He was clinging to the rope hand-holds and screwing up his eyes against the searchlight beam.

'Careful, lads!' said the Chief. 'Don't smash the man as he comes alongside. Take up on both lines.'

The raft had come right under the ship's side and then drifted away. They were waiting for the next wave, while the wretched Scotsman bobbed up and down, dropping out of the beam and then being picked up by it again.

'Trawly,' the Chief called. 'Let you and me do it, while they hold the lines taut.'

The two of them stood side by side at the gunwale and leaned over. The others moved back, planting their feet firmly against the deck so as to keep the lines under tension. The Chief gave the orders: 'Haul in on the left . . . Now a bit on the right.'

'Got him!' roared the trawlmaster.

'Hang on and don't let go! Right, now I've got him too . . .'

They heaved together, and the Scotsman literally flew over the gunwale.

'Slippery oilskins they've got!' said the trawlmaster. 'Feels like they're coated with grease.'

The Chief grasped the Scot under the armpits, pulled him towards himself and collapsed with him on to the deck. Some of our men ran to pick them up.

'Get back!' roared the Chief. 'Hold those lines. We can stand up by ourselves.'

The Chief got up all right, but the Scotsman stayed sitting under the gunwale, tucking his legs under him so they wouldn't get trodden on.

'Senya,' the Chief called to me. 'Show this man to the saloon. Look, he can't move his limbs.'

The Scotsman gave me a sort of guilty, agonized smile. His face was like chalk. He raised his hand – it was covered in blood, flayed skin was hanging from it in strips. He said something to me, but knowing no English I couldn't understand him.

'Khello! Pliz in saloon.'

He shook his head: he wasn't going anywhere. A wave washed over him up to the waist, he rinsed his hand in the water and held it up to me, meaning – this is the best treatment. What could you do with him?

'Let him sit there,' said the trawlmaster.

The second man came aboard fairly easily, but we had a bit of trouble with the third one. Twice he tried to jump on board and missed, until the trawlmaster caught him by the elbow. Gripping the man like that, by the elbow, he flung him face down on to the deck. Alik and I brought him round, dragged him to the gunwale and sat him down beside the first one. Slowly he came to his senses, then got up and began helping our lads.

The last to come was their skipper. He was as small and agile as a monkey. And as bold. While the raft was being pulled alongside, he crouched, waited for a wave and jumped. His jump was accurate as a sniper's bullet – he landed with arms and stomach across the rail. He would certainly have climbed over the gunwale by himself if Vasya Burov hadn't tried to give him some misplaced help – by grabbing the seat of his trousers and tipping him inboard head first. They didn't seem to realize he was the skipper.

Afterwards, Vasya would reminisce about it: 'My career in the fishing fleet didn't come to much. My head's bald, and I never made it to bo'sun. But there were some achievements, beachers: I once held a skipper by his stern end! Sure, not one of ours, but a Scotsman . . .'

The skipper recovered his dignity and made a sign that meant: that's all, no one else is left on board. The trawlmaster drew his knife to cut the lines.

The Scots skipper said something to his own men. They stood up, holding on to each other, and looked at their *Girl Peggy*. She was already drifting away from us. Now and again our searchlight caught her and then lost her again. The skipper unfastened his hood and pushed it back. His head was as bald as a billiard-ball – like our own skipper's. All of them pushed back their hoods, and standing in silence they crossed themselves.

'*Girl Peggy* – good ship?' the trawlmaster asked sympathetically.

The Scots skipper nodded and crossed himself again.

Then, without anyone showing him the way, he went into the saloon. He obviously knew the layout of our DWTs. The other Scotsmen followed him, two of them supporting the one who had come aboard first and who could hardly stand on his feet.

I looked – the *Girl Peggy* had vanished from sight. Only her hooter could still be heard booming spasmodically. They had purposely left it switched on so no other vessel would collide with her in the dark. It was like a live animal complaining at being left to die.

All our lads crowded into the saloon, of course – standing in the doorway, squeezing up along the bulkheads. The Scotsmen were sitting in a row along one of the benches: they had red faces, like us, only their eyes were different. And there was a look they all had in common, even though some were younger and some older, and their skipper was well into middle age – a bit over fifty, probably. I can't even begin to tell you what it was, that look in their eyes. It was like it is with young sucking calves, before the blue film has fallen away from their pupils, as if there was something they didn't know and never wanted to know. There was no sense of life's experience reflected in their looks. As our First Mate from Volokolamsk used to say – though admittedly about Norwegians: 'Their faces have not been ennobled by suffering.'

The cook and the cabin-boy served them with bowls of *borshch*. They smiled and nodded, but were in no hurry to eat – they pointed to their wounded shipmate. Someone had already run off to fetch the Third Mate, who brought with him a pillow-slip from his cabin.

'You blockhead,' said Vasya Burov. 'Why bring a whole pillow-slip?' And what are you going to treat him with – green liniment? You should bring it to him in a bottle with a label on it, that's the proper way to do it.'

The wounded Scot took the bottle, inspected the label and nodded. The Third Mate began to cauterize his hand with cotton-wool, and everyone watched intently. The injured man grimaced and yelped, but he seemed to be doing it on purpose: 'Oh! Ow! Ow!' – and he smiled.

The Third Mate bandaged him up somehow or other, and the Scot, of course, displayed it for everyone to see how good and how thick it was – '. . . thank you very much.'

Then they started to eat. They clasped their bowls to their chests, just as we did. The injured man's mate fed him out of his own bowl, because he couldn't manage it by himself – and he fooled around, grabbing the whole spoon with his mouth, winking at us and clicking his tongue: Ah, how delicious, only he wasn't getting enough of it, his mate was too greedy and was filling the spoon fuller for himself.

Dima said something to their skipper, who listened to him with his head bent forward, then answered with a long, long reply. Well before he'd finished, Dima spread his hands hopelessly – he couldn't understand a word of it.

'First time I've ever heard English like that.'

Shura had a bright idea: 'We must get Marconi. I expect he and their Marconi can understand each other somehow.'

Somebody ran to fetch Marconi. Meanwhile we looked at them and smiled. What else could we do?

Marconi arrived, red in the face with embarrassment before he'd even begun, and when we pushed him towards the Scotsmen he began sweating like a pig.

'Which is their radio operator?' he asked. 'Khoo eez Marconi?'

The radio operator turned out to be the little man with the injured hand. 'Ah!' said Marconi. 'So are you the villain who sent me that signal: "Ivan, call a Komsomol meeting"?!'

The little fellow nodded delightedly and even tried to tap it out in morse on the table-top. And that started them off jabbering at each other – speaking a kind of English that made Dima simply shrug his shoulders. Their Marconi had a Scottish accent, ours had no accent at all but simply spoke the words as they're written: 'o-u-r', 't-i-m-e', 's-a-v-e'.

The Scots skipper put a question to his Marconi, who 'translated' it to ours.

'What's he saying?' asked Shura.

'They're asking what's up with us. He understood we were in distress too.'

'Rubbish,' said Shura. 'You tell him we wouldn't let that happen.'

'But then who sent out the SOS?'

'Someone else did, someone not even in our flotilla. We're just practising for emergencies and rescue operations.'

'Think they're fools?' asked Marconi. 'They've seen the water in the engine-room.'

'Of course,' said Shura. 'We let in the water through the sea-cocks. Now we're pumping it out. How else could we do our training?'

'Do they have to be told everything?' Vasya asked. 'They've suffered enough shocks already.'

The Scotsmen were listening, and had even stopped eating. Marconi translated what we'd said. They exchanged glances with each other and the skipper, smiling, asked another question. He talked for a long time, while their Marconi translated it to ours.

'He's asking us why we didn't take them in tow, if everything's all right with us. That's about the gist of it, I think. Well then, he says, we could have practised towing in storm conditions. I tell you it's no good lying to them, they understand it all, the devils.'

'Tell him,' said Shura, 'that pumping and lifeline practice are on our current training programme. Towing is the next exercise.'

Marconi told them. Their skipper listened, nodded, then stood up, leaned across the table and offered his hand.

'How do I say it? You are *seamen*.'

Marconi sweated all over with embarrassment.

'Oh, to hell with them. I've got to get back to the radio cabin.'

The other Scotsmen jumped to their feet and stretched over towards us. My hand was shaken by the tall one, the fellow I'd thrown the line to. He turned out to be a very young lad with fluff on his upper lip – I don't suppose he'd ever shaved in his life. He remembered me, though, having had a good look at me in the searchlight beam, and now he acted out again how it had all happened.

The First Mate appeared, with an invitation to their skipper from ours to make use of his cabin. He was sorry he couldn't come and join him, but he was busy on the bridge. The Scotsman thanked him and declined the invitation.

'I greatly respect your captain,' he said, 'and thank him for rescuing us, but I know he hasn't much room in his cabin. Apart from that, I'm very interested in talking to the crew.'

Just then the intercom was switched on. The effect on everyone was like an electric shock. We all somehow flinched and went silent, including the Scotsmen. Well, of course, nothing was a secret to them by now.

Zhora the mate's bass voice boomed out of the loudspeaker: 'Marconi to the wheelhouse. Marconi to the wheelhouse.'

Marconi apologized to the Scotsmen, putting his hand on his heart and saying: 'Ai em sorry – job!'

Again the Scots leaped up, shook him by the hand and smiled – they understood: he had a job to do.

I went out after him and asked: 'Are you going to talk to the factory-ship?'

'No, probably going to get a fix on our position by the radio beacons on shore. Come on, Senya – how can the factory-ship help us now? We're probably no more than a mile off the Faroes.'

'So where do we go from here?'

He went on climbing the companion-way.

'Oh, Senya, ask me something easier. The only thing left for us to do is to jump out on to those cliffs.' And he ran off.

The bo'sun and Alik tumbled in through the outer door, carrying life-jackets for the Scotsmen. I realized they must have got them from the lifeboat.

The intercom was switched on again, and Zhora said: 'Crew – stand by! Take your stations!'

What was there to stand by for? And where were our stations now? Nobody asked any questions, but we all trooped out of the saloon – all except the Scotsmen and the cook.

4

And once for all, let me tell thee and assure thee, young man, it's better
to sail with a moody good captain than a laughing bad one.

from Moby Dick *by Hermann Melville*

Dawn hadn't yet broken – although it can't have been far away – and both
searchlights were switched on, pointing forward. All around was blackness, from which snow was blowing, and spray glittered in the beams.

A voice from the loudspeaker boomed out over the deck: 'All hands
clear of the for'ard quarters! Bo'sun – check the cabins!'

We were all on deck, though, and nobody was left in the crew's cabins –
but our gear was there, and all at once everyone rushed to get theirs; each
man wanted to save something. I didn't feel like getting any of my things,
now that my jacket was gone. There was no point in fetching my suitcase,
with nothing in it but a couple of shirts and some socks, so I decided to save
myself the trouble. I just took my life-jacket, put it on at once and tied the
tapes.

Shura picked up his cards and shoved them under his oilskins. Vasya
Burov pulled out a crate of tangerines from under his bunk, but Shura
persuaded him against it: 'It'll get smashed on deck, and here it may keep
whole, provided we don't go under . . .'

We went on deck and stood on top of the hold, everyone holding on to
whatever he could – and each other.

A shout came from the wheelhouse: 'Anyone left in the for'ard cabins?'

'No one!' Shura answered. 'They're all out.'

Literally at that very second Seryozha came bounding towards us – from
the wheel. 'I'm not out yet!'

He ran into the doghouse. A minute passed, then another, and he still
hadn't come back. Shura and I ran after him.

And what was he doing there in the cabin? He, the rascal, was taking
down his collection of pin-ups from the bulkhead – all his Valyas, Nadyas

and Zinas – and he wasn't just ripping them down but carefully unpinning them and putting them into a neat little package. So far he'd only managed to remove half of them.

'Seryozha, have you gone crazy?'

Shura crammed a life-jacket over his head, we grabbed him by the sleeves, and as we dragged him away he dropped the whole packet on to the deck.

Who else had we forgotten?

'Has the helmsman got a life-jacket?' Shura asked Seryozha. 'Who relieved you at the wheel?'

'The skipper.'

'The skipper himself?'

We looked at the wheelhouse: in the feeble glow from the binnacle, the skipper's face could just be seen above the wheel – black pits under his eyes, his chin catching the light. Zhora and the Third Mate were standing beside him.

'What about the Chief?' I asked.

'In the engine-room, standing by the reversing gear.'

'Has he got a life-jacket?'

'You fool,' said Vasya Burov. 'We're all issued with life-jackets!'

I ran down to the cabin, and before they could catch up with me I grabbed a spare one – from Vanya Obod's bunk – and dashed back on deck again.

. . . The Chief was standing beside the reversing gear, up to his knees in black, oily water, holding the lever in his hand, his gaze fixed on the engine-room telegraph. The half-naked Yurka and a Scotsman in black oilskins were flogging away at the pump on the work-bench. All of them were wreathed in steam billowing up from below.

'Chief!' I shouted down into the engine-room. 'Take this life-jacket!'

He probably couldn't hear me. The engine was thumping away – very unevenly – and no doubt his ears were straining to listen to it.

'Chief!'

He answered without turning round: 'Go back on deck, Senya! I've done enough swimming for one lifetime.'

I wanted him at least to give me one last look, but he just kept staring at the telegraph dial and holding his hand on the reversing-lever. I called him again, but he didn't turn round.

Who could I give this life-jacket to? Maybe Yurka would take it. I showed it to him, meaning – should I throw it to him? Yurka winked at me and said: 'Want a chat, Senya?'

Have you ever seen such an idiot?

'OK, let's have a chat.'

'What about? Women or politics?'

'It was women last time. So politics it is.'

'What shall we do about Cuba?'

'My view is unshakeable: *Cuba – sí, yanqui – no!*'

Suddenly the Scotsman turned towards me and whinnied with laughter, his teeth flashing. What lunatics!

At that moment I saw someone in the half-dark corridor, pushing at the door leading out on to the deck and rattling the clip.

'Where d'you think you're going?' I yelled at him. 'Don't try and open that door! We can ship it green through that door when she heels over on that side. Isn't there enough water in the engine-room already?'

He grunted something and pushed at the door. I wondered if it was someone who'd gone off his head . . .

'You'll be washed overboard!' I went up to him and pulled him by the shoulder.

It was Grakov, his tunic unbuttoned, his hair all over the place . . . He breathed hard in my face and I suddenly realized: he was dead drunk. I went wild – surely he couldn't have been getting drunk? At a moment like this?! When we'd all been knocked off our feet but had got up again, to save our lives – and his precious life, too . . .

'Go into the cabin!' I said to him. 'If necessary someone will come and get you, they won't leave you behind.'

'Are things bad, sailor?' His eyes were bleary, his face purple.

'They could hardly be worse.'

'Will we go down? Tell me honestly.'

I offered him the life-jacket.

'With luck we may be able to swim for it.'

'Who ordered this?'

'What?'

'Life-jacket . . . for me . . .'

'The captain.'

'You're lying, sailor . . .'

'Would I lie to you?'

I put the life-jacket over his head and tied the tapes.

'No point in all this, sailor . . .'

I thought – you're right, there's no point in it. You'll be able to swim, you great fool, but no one will save the Chief, except maybe Yurka. And by the time he's pulled even a sweater over his biceps, the whole engine-room will be flooded. I should have stayed there, but my station was on deck, and I might be needed. But I'd try all the same. I'd run to the engine-room and drag the Chief out.

I led Grakov back to his cabin and pushed him through the doorway.

'You will come for me, won't you, sailor? You promised . . .'

I ran out on deck and stood on the covered hold alongside Seryozha and Shura. The engine was making the deck vibrate, my teeth were chattering and the life-jacket was bumping up and down against my stomach. My face was being lashed by snow and spray, but I couldn't shut my eyes – I dared not, because I'd seen the rocks. We'd all seen them.

The searchlights were groping for the rocks in the darkness. A wave broke on them, sending up fountains of spume, and we could see the black, slippery rocks shuddering under the impact. Suddenly they dipped down and vanished from sight as our foc's'le heaved upwards and seemed to head straight on to the cliffs. The engine roared as if it had been given full revolutions and the screw spun in the air, then hit the water again. No doubt the Chief had put her in reverse, because when we saw the rocks again they were further away. I looked round – the wheelhouse window had been lowered, the skipper was standing at the wheel bareheaded, his jacket open. The spokes began to spin, he leaned his chest against the wheel but couldn't hold it. Zhora and the Third Mate dashed up to help him.

Again the bow was pointing at the rocks. Standing just abaft the mast, I could see it was aimed at a point midway between the piles of rock, and then, dead ahead of us, I made out the black gap that was the mouth of the fjord. The waves were rolling towards it at an oblique angle and curling around the wall of rock: this flow caught us up, turned us round, and the mast overshot the mouth of the fjord. Again the engine raced, the whole deck shook and we moved away to seaward. The searchlights shone all over the place – now up in the sky, now picking out the rocks. The sea at the foot of the rocks was churned up by whirlpools, sending the shingle flying and drumming against our sides.

Slowly, slowly we turned around again until once more we were opposite the black mouth, no further away, no further forward. Suddenly we were caught, picked up – higher and higher – and carried forward on the crest of a wave. The rocks flashed past on both sides, and then the wave broke over them with a roar. I just had time to think 'We're through', when I saw the cliff, pitch-black, beetling above us in the sky. Water was pouring down it in streams, and it was right beside us, on the very deck. The men standing at the gunwale jumped back amidships. The bow began to yaw again and the cliff was heading straight for the mast, at us, at our heads . . .

I screwed up my eyes and fell to my knees. I sensed all the others were kneeling or squatting. My lips began moving of their own accord. What was I whispering? Was I really praying? If Thou indeed art God, save us! Save us, don't fling us at those cliffs! We'll never climb up them, no one has ever done it. Save us and I will believe in Thee for ever, I will live as Thou commandest me, as Thou teachest me to live . . . Save the Chief. Save Shura. Save Marconi and Seryozha. Save the cooper, too, even though he's my enemy. Save the Scotsmen – why should they die a second time today? But Thy will be done. Thou art God, I believe that, I will always believe it. But don't let us hit those cliffs . . .!

Something cracked over my head, fell down from above and slid along my arm, some piece of wire – oh God, it's the aerial, Marconi's aerial! – and some heavy metal object hit the canvas hatch-cover alongside us. It might have been the top of the mast. But that's not the end, it's not death!

And I opened my eyes.

The roar of the sea was already behind us and the engine could be heard rumbling and coughing as its sound echoed across the narrow channel between the cliffs. Our searchlights groped around the overhanging walls, looking for the bend in the channel. The sea was still grumbling astern of us, then we rounded the bend and all we could hear was the splashing of waves at the base of the cliffs. Those waves were coming from our ship – from the bow and from the propellor – and for us the storm was over.

I stood up. My knees were trembling and the life-jacket was pulling downward like a ton weight. I untied the tapes and pulled it off. Shura took his off, too. And Seryozha. And everyone.

Then the bay opened out – still water, without a ripple. Two or three lights were burning in the little village and the silence was so deep, it made your ears ring.

We reached the middle of the bay and the engine stopped. The searchlights immediately went dim, and it was clear that dawn was not far off; the hills, the little village houses and the boats at the short jetty were already turning grey. The broken-off masthead was lying on top of the hold, wires looped around it in rings. Someone threw it aside.

Then the bo'sun went over to the capstan – silent, without calling for anyone to go with him. We heard a splash and the rattle of the anchor-chain. All the windows in the wheelhouse were open, someone stuck his head out and looked at the village.

The ship was still rocking, from inertia. When we'd been at anchor for a day she would settle down.

It was then I suddenly felt seasick. It had never happened to me before, from my first day at sea. I only just had time to reach the gunwale and hang over the side. With steam still coming off him, the Chief came up to me and held me by the shoulder. Then he gave me his handkerchief to wipe my mouth, and threw it into the water.

'Don't worry,' said the Chief. 'It's quite normal, Senya. A real sailor's only sick in calm water.'

God, did I feel terrible. And so ashamed, although no one seemed to be looking at me.

A door slammed. The Scotsmen came out on deck, wearing their black one-piece oilskins, in twos and threes, embracing like brothers.

Just people, like any others. I went below.

5

For some reason nobody woke me up. Through my sleep I heard someone being called to man the pump, someone coming back, slamming the door, kicking off his boots. Then I remember a shout: '*Molodoi* coming alongside . . . stand by to secure lines . . .', and I couldn't understand who this 'young man' might be, because the tug's name, *Molodoi*, means young . . . And I remember the thumping of an engine but not ours, and a sucking sound from the ship's side, but then it all went quiet again and I fell back into blackness.

When I woke up, it was quite light in the cabin. Well, it never gets completely light in there – the porthole in the deckhead is tiny – but even so I could see everything clearly. The lads, nearly all still wearing their quilted jackets, were lying on top of the blankets. In Vanya Obod's bunk there was a Scotsman asleep in his oilskins, face down, without having even pushed his hood back.

Why had I woken up? From cold, probably. Or because there was a gasping, sucking noise coming from somewhere, and I thought we must have sprung another leak.

I came on deck – and there was the bay, milky-blue, bathed in sunshine. A few sparse clouds were floating across the blue sky. The village had already woken up, little human figures showed black against the snow, the houses were no longer grey but bright-red, green and yellow, and small boats were leaving the jetty.

So that was the cause of the sucking noise: the salvage tug *Molodoi* was moored up alongside us. Her very name cheered me up – one look at that old tub, with her tall funnel, was enough. Our holds were open, the barrels that had been taken out were lying around all over the deck and several thick hoses were laid from the *Molodoi* over our side – one into each hold and one through the door into the engine-room.

Down in the hold, two men were rewelding the burst seam. One was hanging in a cradle, the other walking up and down on duckboards. The water there was still up to their ankles.

I sat down on the hatch-coaming and lit a cigarette.

315

'Look,' said the man in the cradle, 'one of them has come to life.'

'I'm alive all right,' I said, 'but no thanks to you. What the hell were you doing in the North Sea, where no one was sinking?'

'How were we to know you lads would go off course? We came as fast as we could, but there was no sign of you in the square where you were supposed to be. And no radio contact. We thought you'd gone to the bottom.'

'You came as fast as you could?! To our funeral.'

The other one, on the duckboards, said gloomily: 'Yes, that's the sort of salvage tug we are – as long as nobody's sinking, we do a great job.'

'Don't worry,' said the fellow in the cradle. 'When you're saved at sea, it means you're going to live long.'

'Yes,' I said, 'at least there's that to be said for it.'

I went on smoking and watched them at work. They had already finished welding the new plating, and were now slapping on wet cement.

'Why don't you call us out to help you?' I asked.

'Good God!' said the man in the cradle. 'We won't allow you to lift a finger. You heroes need your sleep.'

Wasn't there something else I wanted to ask them? Oh, yes: 'I lost a jacket down there. You haven't found it, have you?'

'What sort of jacket?'

I sighed: 'Oh, it's not worth telling you if you haven't found it. It was a good one, kept me nice and warm.'

'Well, if we'd found it we wouldn't have pinched it, whatever it was like.' Then a thought came to him and his face took on a dreamy look. 'Listen, I saw one of those Scotsmen take off his oilskins. He was wearing a sweater under them – the sort I dream about. Tell him how nice it is, and he might give it to you.'

'But he'd give it to *me*, not to you.'

'It's still a nice thought. And then perhaps I could swap it with you for something.'

'No good, I'm not going to ask him.'

'Pity. You'll miss your chance.'

Then the glum one, down below, asked me: 'How did you come to lose it? I suppose you used it to plug the seam, did you?'

'Yes, something like that.'

He shook his head: 'You'd have needed a lot of jackets to do *that*. You were leaking in three places. In the holds, in the engine-room and through the afterpeak.'

'So it was leaking from the stern into the engineers' cabin?'

'Sure was.'

'You don't say! And we didn't know.'

The man in the cradle asked: 'And what about that Grakov – how did he behave? Lost his temper, I suppose, when he should have been getting worried?'

'Not too much. When we were sinking, he was pretty harmless.'

'Harmless!' said the glum one. 'Wolves in flood-water are harmless and they don't touch the rabbits. But when they get back on dry land, they suddenly remember they've got teeth.'

'Maybe they do,' I said. 'Even so, he was taught a lesson.'

'Lessons have no effect on people like him.'

I didn't argue. If there was anyone I *didn't* want to think about, it was Grakov. And for some reason I still couldn't get warm, even though I was sitting in the sun. Well, not that it's much of a sun in those parts! The man in the cradle noticed my teeth were chattering.

'You look to me, lad, as if you've got a fever. Not surprising, after what you've been through. Go to the galley, the stove's burning there.'

'Is the cook up?'

'Yes, he is.'

I was just about to go, when a motor-launch from the factory-ship came alongside. I took her mooring-lines.

'Watchkeeper!' came a shout from the launch. 'Call Grakov.'

So I'd been made watchkeeper again . . . But I didn't have to call for him: Grakov himself came out of the officers' quarters – shaved, tunic buttoned up, his face only slightly puffy from a hangover. He was followed by the skipper, also in his tunic, then by Zhora and the Third Mate. The First Mate, wearing his fur-lined jerkin, came to the gangway to see them off.

Then came the bo'sun – glowering, with a greenish blotch on one cheekbone – and Mitrokhin, our nut-case, both wearing caps and greatcoats. I couldn't understand why those two were going in the launch too.

'What's happening about our guests?' the First Mate asked Grakov. 'The Scotsmen, I mean?'

'Don't wake them up as long as they're asleep. And let our men sleep as long as they need to. You'll bring the Scotsmen with you when you come to the factory-ship this evening. Just make sure, somehow or other, that they're kept separate, know what I mean? We don't want too much of this unsupervised fraternization.'

The Third Mate waved to the First from the launch: 'Just try not to have another collision when you're under tow.'

'Justify the confidence placed in you,' shouted Zhora.

The skipper said nothing, but spat in the water.

The launch cast off. Grakov hadn't noticed me.

The First Mate turned to me, beaming all over: 'Hear that, warpman? I may come out of all this without getting into trouble.' And he skipped off back to his quarters.

And why not? I thought to myself. Of course he'd get out of it, we have a soft spot for fools. If you're a first mate, then I'm Shostakovich. You've learned how to give political lectures, about what the imperialists and their hirelings are planning to do to us and all that stuff, but put you on the bridge – and you'll set a course across dry land, you'll put the ship astern without looking where you're going, and you can't even tell which lifeboat should be launched first. Any minute now you'll be promoted to captain. God forbid I should ever sail under a skipper like that. And others, who are more competent, will be under you – Zhora, for instance, or even our Third Mate. I never could understand the way these things are done.'

I was still beastly cold – not so much from the air, because the temperature that day was above freezing, but I somehow felt cold inside me. I went to the galley.

The cook, as it turned out, was baking a cake. He had put the mixture in the oven and was now whipping up the filling, made with butter and sugar.

'Is that for our guests?' I asked.

'Why just for them? It's for you. Well, for the guests too. You're all the same to me.'

Gradually the crew trickled into the saloon. Then came the Scotsmen. To the cook's delight, we all ate the cake together, with our tea. It was only a pity there was nothing stronger to drink, then we could have really got friendly with them. The cook said regretfully: 'If I'd known sooner, I'd have made a fruit cordial out of jam. I've got the recipe, and there's plenty of jam, but there wasn't enough time for it to ferment.'

But we fraternized anyway. Each one of us took a Scotsman – and we managed to communicate, in God knows what sort of language. Vasya Burov jabbed a finger at 'his' Scotsman's chest and said: 'Me – yes? – Vasya Burov. That my *Vorname*. My job on this ship – senior seaman, in Russian: *artelny*. Now say – who you? What your name and *Vorname*? What your job on ship?'

In fact, he managed to find out more about those Scotsmen than the rest of us.

'Listen,' he said, 'their crew is like one family. Their skipper is father of them all. That tall one, the one Senya the warpman threw the line to, he's the youngest son. Those two ginger-heads there – Archie and Phil – are the oldest and the middle one. And those two are sons-in-law – the skipper also has two married daughters. Only one of them isn't a member of the family – their Marconi. They pay him a wage, and they keep the earnings of the catch for themselves. But their ship's not their own, they pay the owner fifty per cent of the catch as rental.'

'How much will they have to pay back to him now?' asked Shura. He felt very sorry for the family.

'Not a bean. It's all covered by insurance. They'll even get compensation for the loss of the *Pegushka*.' He called the *Girl Peggy* – *Pegushka*. 'And they'll also get some compensation from the firm that supplied them with a defective engine.'

We felt a little better, knowing the Scotsmen were not completely ruined.

'And how much salvage money do you think we'd have been paid, beachers, if we'd saved their ship? Five thousand pounds, no less.'

'OK, OK,' said Seryozha. 'What a question to ask!'

'Think I asked them? They told me themselves.'

The First Mate kept prowling around us, like a tiger on his soft paws, his ears practically out on stalks – but we appreared to be keeping off politics and sticking to economic matters.

'Now tell me this,' said Vasya Burov. 'How come they pay money for a ship or some other kind of property, but they don't pay out a bean for the people?'

'Would you take it if they did?' asked the cook.

'Me? Not likely. I wouldn't take it for a ship, either. But as for taking it for *people* – that's just a sin. Others might, though. If you didn't promise them money in advance, they wouldn't lift a finger to get anyone out of trouble.'

'So are those others worse than you?' again the cook asked.

'I don't know if they're worse or not, but even so there ought to be some payment for saving people too. Surely a living soul isn't worth less than a piece of property?'

'There is a payment, but it doesn't go to us,' said Seryozha. 'Their minister just owes something to our minister, but you'll never find out how much it is.'

Shura said: 'There's no such payment. Just the moral satisfaction. It's like doing voluntary social work on a Saturday.'

'Well, you know what happens on those unpaid Saturday jobs – people just go to fool around and skive. What's more, it's not voluntary: they tell you to go, and just you try and get out of it! No-o-o,' Vasya Burov still couldn't agree. 'Material incentives are a powerful force. Isn't that so, First Mate?'

The First Mate could find nothing to object to in this force.

'So I say – a human being is worth something after all. He must be!'

'He isn't worth anything,' said Seryozha gloomily. 'Would anyone give half a litre of vodka for you? So dry up.'

'Blockhead! Can't talk about anything seriously with you . . .'

'Well, now, you see . . .' Shura said thoughtfully. 'It depends on what sort of a human being it is.'

'Ah! So according to you he *is* worth something. The only question is how much?'

Alik the apprentice had been listening to all this with his head on one side. He smiled, then blushed as he said: 'No doubt you have to calculate it like this . . . how much value do other people place on a man? That's what I think.'

Vasya thought for a moment and disagreed: 'That slob – you heard him, didn't you – wouldn't give half a litre of vodka for me, but you ask my kids – to them, ten million wouldn't be enough for their dear old dad.'

'But to them you're not just anybody,' said Shura, 'you're their parent. So what's the argument about? How much a person earns – that's what he's worth.'

'Hey!' said Vasya. 'In that case our First Mate is worth more than four apprentices.'

We looked at our First Mate, then at Alik the apprentice. No, we decided silently, that was no way to calculate it either. By now, we felt we valued the apprentice more highly.

'And then again,' Vasya went on, 'we'll only be paid the guaranteed minimum for today, because we haven't brought the country any fish, even thought we've been doing seamen's work. But the day before yesterday we *did* deliver a load of fish. So what, then – were we worth more the day before yesterday? If so, when you come to work it out, fish have a value but people don't.'

The First Mate decided the time had come to stick his oar in and proposed we should make a clear distinction between what kinds of people we had in mind: Soviet people or foreigners. At this we all rounded on him in chorus. We asked him at least to mind his tongue in front of our guests – they might understand. What's more, Seryozha hinted to him, if a person was a foreigner you couldn't calculate his value in our roubles – you'd have to price him in foreign currency, and that might come more expensive. The First Mate withdrew his proposal.

Vasya laughed: 'Well, I never expected this . . . Grown-up, bearded men, fathers of children, and we don't know how much a human being is worth!'

'Maybe we don't need to know,' said the cook. 'The Lord knows – and that's all that matters.'

'Oh, is that the one who doesn't exist?' the First Mate asked with a giggle.

'It hasn't been proved yet,' Alik remarked.

'What d'you mean – "hasn't been proved"?'

'What I say. Great minds have argued about it, but they've never been able to agree on the answer.'

'Who are those "great minds", I'd like to know?!'

'Well, whoever they were,' said the cook, putting an end to the argument, 'since they couldn't agree on the answer, nor can we. Who wants some more tea?'

So we all agreed – that we couldn't say how much a human being was worth.* The Scotsmen had simply been watching us with wide-open eyes; we tried to explain to them what we'd been talking about, but they didn't understand and shrugged their shoulders. They did say, though, there

---

* International maritime law doesn't know the value of a human life either; it is regarded as priceless, and for that reason no reward has ever been stipulated for saving life at sea. (Author's note.)

ought to be more contact between us. They invited us to come and visit them at their homes in Scotland. They produced ballpoint pens from under their oilskins and wrote down their addresses, then gave us the pens. We took the addresses, just in case. We invited them – someone to Mtsensk, someone to Vologda, someone to the village of Makarievo in the province of Penza.

Meanwhile the work on deck was all being done for us. The fitters from the *Molodoi* really weren't allowing us to lift a finger. On their own they stowed the sail in the forepeak, cleared away the barrels, and welded the broken section of the mast back in place – it turned out to be a yard, and the mast itself had been very slightly bent. They even re-rigged Marconi's aerial.

The Chief came out to have a look, waved his hand and said: 'We'll stagger home somehow.'

Then we slept again, us and the Scotsmen, and only woke up towards evening as the *Molodoi* was towing us through the fjord. Out in the Atlantic the gale had slackened, which I could see from the birds – they were sitting all over the cliffs and shrieking as we sailed past them. When there's a storm, they hide themselves away somewhere.

As we came out into the open sea, the sun's rays were coming through clouds at a slant, the ocean was dark and threatening, low wavetops a-glitter. But the cliffs were now powdered with snow, once again they were white with lilac-coloured shadows and orange-red tops; I couldn't believe we'd seen them pitch-black not so long ago. About a mile out of the fjord some fragments of wreckage were floating in the surf – no doubt from the *Girl Peggy*, or from someone else. Our Scotsmen looked glum and crossed themselves again.

The factory-ship was waiting for us on the horizon – lit up all over. There were lights on the masts and the rigging, and ten rows of lighted portholes. A whole town was there in the middle of the sea, all reflected in the water. As we came closer, the water all around her hull seemed to be shining with a blue light, as if it was lit from under the water. The whole ship's side was dotted with people, heads were sticking up all along the rail, on the upper decks and the superstructure. A flag signal in the international signal code was strung between the masts and lit from below by searchlights: 'Greetings to the brave Scottish seamen saved from the sea.' I'd been a signalman in the Navy, so I was able to read it out to the other beachers. As the *Molodoi* towed us smartly to the factory-ship's side, sailors from the tug's crew jumped over to us and secured the mooring-lines. They also took the net when it was let down from the big ship by the derrickman. We didn't have to do a thing about it – just like passengers.

The Scotsmen were standing ready. We came on deck to say goodbye to them.

'Five at a time in the net, and hold tight!' shouted the derrickman. 'Show them how, lads!'

Someone from the factory-ship shouted something in English through a megaphone. No doubt the same instructions.

'Couldn't you have let down a Jacob's ladder?' the trawlmaster asked. 'Illiterates!'

The derrickman clasped his head with his mittened hands: Blundered again!

Two of the Scotsmen seated the little one with the injured hand in the net, and helped him to put his legs through the mesh. He hung on with one hand and waved goodbye to us with the other, bandaged hand. Suddenly they said something to each other, one jumped down and pointed to us and to the net. They were inviting us to go with them.

'What's there for us to do there?' asked Vasya Burov.

'Who cares?' said Shura. 'Let's just go!'

He was first to grab the net and pulled me after him: 'Come on, Senya, since they're inviting us.'

Vasya made up the fifth. The net started to rise – no going back now! The derrickman ran over to us: 'Where are you going? Guests first . . .'

'Ai luv yoo, meester derrickman!' was Shura's reply.

The little Scotsman added something too, no doubt very much to the point; the man with the megaphone didn't try to stop us either.

The second net brought up three of ours – Seryozha, the trawlmaster and Marconi. Then came the apprentices and Gesha, the trawlmaster's mate, and in the last net, along with their skipper – just imagine – Yurka the greaser. So the whole gang of us came aboard and passed down a living corridor: everyone, of course, had come to have a look at the Scotsmen – officers, seamen, herring-canners, laundresses, doctors. And we got a hero's welcome too.

We took the main companion-way down three decks, and there the officer of the watch – two gold rings on his tunic – flung open the double glass doors for us and showed us where to go: down a long, long corridor carpeted in red, straight into the officers' wardroom. There the doors were already open and the table set for a banquet – I'm not telling a lie, it was for a hundred and twenty people – in a glittering array of bottles, decanters, cakes and God knows what else to eat, and decorated with Soviet and Scottish flags.

It was then we started to feel shy and awkward. The Scotsmen, in their glistening black oilskins, went on into the wardroom, and we stood aside to let them pass. The officer of the watch eyed us up and down: 'Look here, lads, you can't go in there in *that* state! You might at least have cleaned yourselves and smartened up a bit . . .'

The trawlmaster mumbled something in reply, but very unconvincingly. On deck he had a voice like a foghorn, but now he just turned as red as a rose in May and lost all his bluster. Only Yurka the greaser was able to get past, but then he was wearing a jacket and shoes; not such a good jacket as mine, but still respectable. The rest of us were all wearing our quilted jackets, some still wearing wet sea-boots that squelched as they walked, and the cotton-wool padding was sticking out of the shoulder of my jacket. We'd had no idea this banquet was being held, and everyone had just come in what he was wearing at the time.

We stood in a tight little bunch by the bulkhead, gaping at the crowd of people, and I can't tell you how awkward we were feeling. We couldn't even get out, either; how could we push our way through that mob when all our clothes were still soaking wet?

'Look,' said Marconi, 'as I see the situation, it's like this: if no girls come to escort us, we'll just have to make ourselves scarce.'

He'd put his finger on it. The officer of the watch was a sailor, after all, and very gallant with it; almost every one of them on board here had his bit of skirt – maybe some nurse or a woman doctor, or perhaps a fish-packer.

Vasya Burov was the first to spot one.

'Over there,' he said, ' – that's Irochka.'

Irochka wasn't so much walking as flying along on stiletto heels, her black skirt flaring out like a bell, wearing a white lace-trimmed blouse and little red clips in her ears. As soon as you looked at her hands and neck, though, it was obvious she worked on deck, in the wind; maybe she was one of the girls who filled the cans of herring with saline.

We liked the look of Irochka.

'Is she reliable?' we asked Vasya.

'She's my next-door neighbour at home! Irochka – don't you recognize me?'

Irochka fluttered her mascaraed eyelashes. 'Vasya! What an unexpected meeting! . . .'

But just then she caught sight of Shura, and Vasya's hopes slumped badly. No one could help being struck by Shura's looks. She immediately fastened her eyes on him as if the rest of the world didn't exist.

'Oh, Vasya – I would so like to be introduced to your shipmates.'

Shura looked at Vasya, Vasya looked at Shura. They understood each other.

'Come on, let's go.' Shura took Irochka by the elbow. 'We can introduce ourselves over there.'

The officer of the watch frowned but let them pass . . .

From then on it was a dead loss, because only couples came in. Finally, one bird floated in on her own, wearing a chiffon scarf, and so dolled up we were almost dazzled. She had such a huge beehive hairdo, it was a wonder her neck didn't break under the strain.

The trawlmaster fixed his eye on her.

'That's Julia, the hairdresser. She cut my curls off, on the last trip.'

That 'last trip' sounded a bit dubious to us.

'How's life, Julia?' he asked her, in his best on-deck voice.

Julia actually jumped, then looked at him coldly with her blue, blue eyes.

'Are you talking to me?'

'Yes, Julia. Who else?'

'What d'you mean – Julia? I'm not Julia, I'm Verochka.'

'Ah, Verochka . . .'

'That's better. Call your Julia, if it's her you want.'

And Verochka passed on. The trawlmaster slapped himself on the forehead and subsided completely.

'Well, beachers,' said Vasya, 'do we give up? We don't seem to be having much luck in this direction.'

'It all depends,' said Marconi. 'Personally, I'm still hopeful.'

He had just spied two more girls coming out of a cabin not far from where we were standing.

'Torpedo tubes – stand by to fire! If these ones don't scoop up at least two of us . . .'

The others edged forward a little, but I had already spotted who the girls were and stood aside, behind their backs. One was Lilya, my unsung song, and the other was Galya.

I recognized Lilya by her walk. And by the colour she was wearing, her invariable green. Her walk was fascinating – never in a straight line but slightly wavy, with a kind of uncertainty about it. How it had thrilled me once, when she was walking towards me, as though she somehow didn't want to but was drawn onwards despite herself. And still she *was* pretty, I had to admit it. Well, not like Klavka, who has the sort of looks that make a taxi-driver turn his head and drive slap into a lamp-post. Lilya had something special about her, though, that not everyone noticed – not that I had wanted everyone to notice it.

Suddenly she smiled, her face lighting up all at once, and came towards us with outstretched hand.

'Boys!' She'd recognized the two apprentices. 'Well . . . I hope you've got enough to fill up your biographies now?'

'Details later,' said Dima. 'Right now, old lady, we're relying on you. Will you escort us to the party for auld lang syne?'

'In there? Why not? But will the officer of the watch let us?'

'What a question, old lady. A woman's will is God's will. And the watchkeeper's, naturally.'

'Oh, I'm so glad to see you . . .'

As she looked at us again, her glance flickered over my face – and I couldn't have been mistaken – she didn't recognize me. Well, she always was a bit short-sighted, and she was also a bit shy in front of so many men.

Alik turned round to me. I shook my head. We, too, understood each other perfectly.

The officer of the watch was extremely reluctant to let them pass – two men with one lady. She had to smile at him – such a sweet, embarrassed smile – and, of course, she slew him.

And Galya escorted Marconi.

'Galya,' he said to her, 'the memory of you is graven on my heart.'

'It's graven even more on your cheek,' said Galya. 'Come on, big-mouth.'

Marconi turned round to us and spread his hands: 'Best of luck, lads.'

'Off you go,' said the trawlmaster, and to us he said: 'OK, let's go, no point in standing here huddled up against this bulkhead.'

He was right, there was no point. The crowd had thinned out a bit, we could easily move away now – and I wanted to do that more than anything else. I was desperately cold. The most enticing thought at that moment was to climb into my bunk and pile on all the blankets I had.

Klavka came towards us from the middle of the wardroom, threw a cheerful glance at the officer of the watch, who gave her a slight bow and reddened a little. I was glad to be standing behind the others' backs, because I didn't want her to see me just then. Yet at the same time it was lovely to see her – so alive and flushed, so beautifully turned out in a blue dress with a lacy something on her chest, a sort of standaway collar – I'm not much good about these things – and little gold earrings dangling from her ears. Something had changed, though, in her expression – it had become somehow brighter, perhaps because she had brushed her hair back into a bun and her forehead was completely open.

Klavka saw us and came over: 'Aren't you from the *Galloper?*'

'My queen!' said the trawlmaster, in his on-deck voice again. 'Sure we're from that very ship!'

'Where's that gingery one who was sailing with you, the one who's so angry? I don't seem to see him. He wasn't drowned, was he?'

'We've got lots who are angry but no gingery ones. May I take his place?'

Klavka smiled at him.

'Well, no – there's too much of you for me . . . I just call him "Ginger", but he's really fair-haired. He used to wear a beautiful jacket.'

'Oh, you mean Senya?'

'That's it, Senya.'

The trawlmaster waved his great paw and said gloomily: 'His jacket's floating in the waves now.'

Klavka gave him a horrified look, and I felt a stab to the heart to see how she turned instantly pale and clasped her hands to her chest.

'But nobody reported it . . . I wish you'd bitten your tongue off!'

The trawlmaster already regretted having said it.

'Wait, don't squeeze your tits like that, none of us was drowned. Senya, where are you? Come on out. Come out when a lady's asking for you.'

The others pushed me forward.

Klavka looked at me and said nothing. Her clear, bright face had turned pink again, but for some reason she suddenly hunched her shoulders and clasped her elbows – just as she'd done before, when we met on one of the lower decks.

'Why are you all standing here?' she asked. 'Watchkeeper, why do you keep them hanging about here? They're the lads from the *Galloper*.'

'Now, Klavka,' the officer was slightly flustered. 'How could I tell? It's not written on them . . . of course, there must be representatives from the crew. But not in the state they're in.'

'What state d'you expect them to be in? They're heroes of the sea. Go on, let them through, I'll find a place for them in a corner.'

'Well, Klavka . . . it's your responsibility.'

'Of course it is . . . Go on, lads,' she pushed them by the shoulders – 'in you go.'

They tumbled into the wardroom, but the officer of the watch still held me back.

'Does he *have* to be walking around with his stuffing coming out?' He pulled out a wad of it and showed it to her. 'Couldn't you sew it up for him? Then he'd look like a hero, too.'

'You're right, it won't do.' Klavka put her hand to her collar, feeling for a needle, but couldn't find one and pulled me away by my sleeve. 'Come on, I'll sew you up.'

A party of officers was coming towards us, some with four rings on their cuffs. Then Grakov passed – again he didn't recognize me – followed by our skipper and the mates. The Third Mate devoured Klavka with his eyes and shook his head at me. Our Second Engineer went by, then the bo'sun and Mitrokhin – all of them wearing suits. So these were our 'representatives' . . .

We went down several more decks, then walked along the same corridor, only this time it had a green carpet. Klavka let go of my sleeve and took my hand.

'You hand's cold.' She suddenly stopped. 'Listen – how would you like a shower? I'll take you there. You can be getting warm while I sew up your jacket. You do seem very cold.'

'Good idea.'

'Couldn't be better!'

A snorting sound was coming from the shower-room. Klavka banged on the door with her shoe, but there was no answer – just snorting.

'Oh, well,' said Klavka. 'Some oafs are steaming themselves. It'll take too long. I'd better put you in the women's shower-room, there's no one there at the moment.

'Yes, but . . . in the women's shower?!'

'Come on!' She pulled me after her. 'Hold on to Klavka and you won't come to any harm.'

On the way she stumbled, and bent down to straighten her stocking. I supported her by the elbow.

'When you hold me like that,' she smiled, 'it's nice, believe it or not.'

She was right – there was no one in the women's shower-room. Again using her shoe, Klavka pushed open the door and shoved me inside.

'Have a good wash in here and don't worry, no one will come in. You'll still be finished in time for the most interesting part.'

'How will I find you then?'

'I'll find you myself. Take off your jacket.'

She unbuttoned it for me, frowning, then pulled it off my shoulders.

'Aren't you fed up with walking around in something that's stiff with salt?'

'Pretty fed up . . .'

'There, you see – what a good thing I thought of this. Now I'll fix it in two ticks.'

Klavka went out with my quilted jacket, and then I undressed and threw all my gear into the corner by the door. It was just the right place for it. The shower cabinet was spacious, not like ours on a DWT, and it had a little mirror. I saw myself in it – hair matted with salt water, sunken cheeks, eyes somehow wild and staring. It was enough to give you the shivers; not surprising they wouldn't let a scarecrow like this into a respectable wardroom. I stood under the shower, but it would only run tepid, and however hard I turned the tap I couldn't get warm, probably because the cold in me was so deep-seated – in my very bones, no doubt. Or in the place where one's soul is. My teeth wouldn't stop chattering, and I was shivering as if I was out in the frost.

Someone knocked on the door. Before I had time to remember whether I'd shot the bolt or not, the door opened and Klavka said: 'I won't look. There – I've sewn it up. And there's a towel for you.'

'Thanks.'

I was standing with my back to her. Klavka asked: 'What's happened to your shoulder?'

'Nothing.'

'"Nothing" indeed! It's all black and blue. God, what happened to you?'

'Oh, it doesn't hurt any more. This water's hardly warm.'

Klavka came over, pushed back her sleeve and tried the water, then turned the tap and punched the mixer-valve with her fist. Steam began to bubble and hiss. No doubt she'd unblocked an obstruction caused by rust.

'You see, everything here needs a special knack. Is that better?'

'Couldn't you make it hotter still?'

'Good God! I couldn't even stand *this* for a moment. You really must have been cold!' She said nothing for a while, then suddenly leaned her head against my bad shoulder, where the shoulder-blade was hurting. I felt her hair and a slight prick from her earring. 'So beautiful, and your shoulder's all blue. Why do we lead such stupid lives?'

'You'll get wet,' I said.

'If I get wet, I can always dry myself. Here, let me rub you dry.'

She didn't towel me, but only rubbed my shoulder with her wet hand, and it was probably just what I needed, because the pain went away a bit. And the cold, too.

She said: 'Wait here for me, OK?'

'Where are you going?'

'Just something I must do. Sit down a while, rest yourself . . . Only lock the door, otherwise someone else besides me may see you.'

Again she trotted off somewhere. I sat on the bench, until I started to feel cold again. I actually burst into tears – from weakness, I suppose. I got under the shower again, and decided to stay there until she came back. She was away for an age, and then I suddenly realized I couldn't leave the place without her anyway – she'd taken all my gear with her. Finally she came back.

'That's enough, my dear, you're crimson all over. It's bad for your heart.'

'Where have you taken my things to?' I asked.

'To the laundry. I threw them into one of the washing-machines. I asked them, and they'll wash and dry them for you in no time. Don't hurry, they'll be making speeches there for a long time yet. Put on my dressing-gown for the time being.'

'The same one? With tulips on it?'

'The very same. What difference does it make? . . . You're not a virgin, are you?'

I said: 'Turn round, all the same.'

'I've already turned round. In that dressing-gown you don't turn me on at all. Not like when you're wearing your jacket. Is it true your jacket went to the bottom?'

'Yes.'

'Well, come on then. My cabin's the fourth door on the left, on this side.'

The corridor was deserted, and I reached the fourth door in safety. In the cabin, a lamp was lit on the night-table and a faint light was coming in from the corridor through a frosted-glass panel above the door. The porthole was constantly splashed by the waves, which also gave off a bluish light. Klavka was standing by a little table with her back to me.

'Who do you share with?' I saw two bunks.

'Sit on this one. The other one is Valya's, she's a laundress. It's she who's washing your clothes right now. As they say – semi-detached with separate entrance.'

'Two of you – that's hardly separate.'

'That's what watches are for on shipboard. I'm joking, of course. Are you at least a bit warmer?'

'More or less.'

'Would you like to eat now? I want to feed you up?'

Klavka turned round to face me. There was a tray on the little table, covered with a napkin.

'Thanks, but I just don't feel like it right now.'

'All right, later. Your nerves are just overstrained. What would you like? How about a drink? Would that put you back on your feet?'

'Now that's an idea.'

'Vodka? Or rosé?'

'Have you got both?'

'What else am I here for?'

I laughed, already drunk in advance.

'Let's have some rosé.'

Klavka swiftly inserted a corkscrew, gripped the bottle with her knees, twisted herself round a little and pulled out the cork. I watched her pour the wine into two wineglasses.

'A full glass for you, too.'

'Yes, of course. To keep you company. Now let me kiss you.' Klavka bent down to me, put her bare arm around my neck and kissed me hard and long. She gasped for breath. 'Now here's to you. I hope you'll outlive me.'

She looked at me, biting her lip. I felt young and strong again, as if life had come back to me. Soon I was really drunk – with the wine, with the warmth and with Klavka.

'Klavka, do you have to go?'

'Of course, I must. But you will wait for me, won't you?'

'Yes, I will.'

'Please don't die. You won't die, will you?'

She went over to the door – in her stockinged feet – and turned the lock.

'Klavka, they'll notice you're missing up there.'

'So what if they do? Does it matter?'

'What does matter, Klavka?'

She didn't answer. But what did matter was the way that woman turned her head. Nothing in the world mattered more: the way she turned her head, took off her earrings and put them on the table; the way when she put her hands behind her head all her hairpins scattered but she didn't look for them, and her hair untied itself from the bun and fell all over her shoulders; the way she looked at the porthole and smiled – no doubt she saw something out there besides blue water; the way she put one hand behind her back and tilted the shade of the night-light with the other; the way she quickly dropped all her clothes on to the deck and stepped over them . . .

6

'Was I good for you? Tell me . . .'

She pressed herself against me, stretched out and put her head on my shoulder.

'You know you were.'

'But I want to hear you say it! Was I very good for you?'

'Yes.'

'Well, there you are.' She sighed. 'You've had a drink and you've had Klavka too, so you're all right now. I know. People forgive me everything for that.'

Everything was perfect, except that my shoulder was trembling. I really had overstrained myself for those damn' Scotsmen, blast them.

'Does it still hurt? What a fool I am for lying on this side. I should have been on the other side. Did I arrange it badly?'

'Don't worry, it's better like this . . . Klavka, why did they curse you?'

'Who?'

'Your parents. You told me once.'

'Oh . . . Why did you have to bring that up now?'

'Tell me.'

She said nothing for a while.

'I was such a little tramp, it's awful to think of it now . . . Anyway, I was reconciled with them. Did you ask because I said "People forgive me everything"? What else do you want to ask me?'

'I want to ask you about myself. When did you first fancy me?'

Astonished, she answered: 'Right from the start! Didn't you realize I fancied you from the very first? As soon as I saw you. You were sitting in a corner with those two beachers and some man from the Merchant Navy. I walked across the whole room towards you, and you were the only person I was looking at. You looked so good, sitting there in your jacket! Generous, not a care in the world, and your face – it just shone!'

'Not true – I was absolutely furious.'

'Well, you looked good because you were sitting with the dregs. Nobody thinks of Vova and that Askold as men. All they ever do is come running to me: it's either – "Klavka, give us something to eat on tick", or – "Klavka, give us a drink, we're going to sea tomorrow and we'll square up when we get our advance of pay". God knows what they think about me, but I just feel sorry for them. You can't be angry with *them*! . . . But it was bad of you not to notice me. I wiped the clean tablecloth in front of you, I did this and I did that . . . You should have said to me then: "Come away with me, Klavka", and I'd have gone then and there, wherever you liked. I'd have only stopped to take off my apron.'

She looked out of the porthole, smiled, and her eyes glistened moistly. I asked: 'And what happened then?'

'Then? Must I?'

'Right now you must tell me everything.'

'Well, then – you disgraced me in front of those two layabouts. You invited me, and kissed me behind the ear . . . So I changed, put on all my make-up, got into my No. 1 rig. And you, it turned out, were waiting for your scientist girlfriend – the fish expert, or was it meat? – forgive me for being crude. Then you went off to Cape Abram. I saw her too – both of them in fact – surely they're not better than me? Never! . . . And then when neither of them wanted to see you, you turn up on my doorstep and it's "Klavka, I can't live without you!"'

'I was drunk, though.'

'And how. Filthy drunk. Anyhow, I realized it wasn't the real you. Somehow I didn't even feel sorry for you when they beat you up. They won't kill him, I thought, they can't kill his sort . . . It was only afterwards that I got a shock, when they told me you'd had to go to sea – because of the money. I'd been thinking that when you'd slept it off you'd come looking for those two, and then you and I could have had a sensible talk. After all, we'd never had a chance to talk properly. So I cursed myself . . .'

'You cursed yourself – for *what*?'

'Well . . . you were probably in love with that girl scientist of yours. It wasn't all so simple. I've been saying nasty things about her, too. Did you love her?'

'I don't know now.'

'Don't say that. One day you'll be saying about me: "I don't remember if I liked being with Klavka or not."'

I began to make love to her.

'No, you won't say that,' she laughed. 'You most certainly won't say that!'

I embraced her even harder.

'Wait a moment. No, wait, I'm not going anywhere. And you're tired.'

She made love to me so hard, she forgot about my shoulder – in fact she was completely oblivious to everything else, as if she was sharing her very life with me.

331

'We're good,' she said. 'We're good for each other.'

And later: 'Well, I suppose it's no miracle, neither of us are sixteen any more. No, it *is* a miracle.'

Again she lay with her head on my shoulder, eyes closed, her mouth half open. And the waves rocked us so beautifully when they splashed against the porthole.

There was a gentle knock on the door. It might have come from another planet.

'Oh . . .' Klavka shook her head and swore through her teeth. 'Can't be helped, I'll have to open it.'

'But why?'

'It's Valya. She's brought your laundry . . . Oh, what a little boy you still are! D'you think Valya doesn't have a love-life? No-o-o, our Valya's no virgin!'

She opened the door a little. Valya asked: 'Everything OK?' and laughed.

Klavka answered in a slightly hoarse voice: 'Couldn't be better. Thanks, Valya.'

'But if you haven't been to the banquet . . .'

'Oh, to hell with the banquet. We're having our own banquet in here. Thanks very much.'

Klavka didn't come back to me, but picked up all her things from the deck and started to get dressed. I asked her: 'Did she miss the banquet because of me?'

'Of course not. Not everything is because of you. Two of her boyfriends happen to be here at the same time – an old one and the current one. At any moment they may start fighting each other there, at the banquet. So she decided it was better to keep out of harm's way.'

'She won't split on us, will she?'

'Who, Valya?' Klavka burst out laughing and ruffled my hair. 'Relax, my love. The whole ship knows you and I are in here together. From keel to truck, as they say. So what does it matter to us what Valya says!'

I laughed too: 'So it seems you and I are married now?'

'Seems like it . . .'

After a pause I said: 'I didn't just ask that for fun, Klavka.'

'What for, then?'

'What's going to happen when we leave here? What will I be tomorrow without you?'

'Oh dear, that's just what you *shouldn't* be asking. I beg you, Senya. You'll be exactly the same as ever.'

'No, I can't face it.'

I suppose I had no right to say that to her. I still had to face prosecution when we got back, and no one knew how that trial would end; I did, after all, have some excuse on my side. At least we could live together for those weeks before sentence was pronounced, and then it would be up to her to decide whether it was worth waiting for me. No, in fact she'd better decide here and now – I would surely come clean with her if only she'd say 'yes'!

Klavka sat down on the bunk beside me: 'Why did that idea come into your head? Now you've gone and spoiled everything. Why, I wonder? Just think – nothing has started between us yet, and before this, things couldn't have been worse. Poor us! What sort of a future can we look forward to? I'd be a sailor's wife. You'll go away for three and a half months at a time. I'll see you off at the gangway and snivel into my handkerchief. Then I'll have to be faithful to you – just that: sit at home and be faithful. I'll ask for songs to be played for you on radio request programmes: "Are you listening, Senya? They're now going to play 'A Sailor's Dancing with a Sailor'." I'll phone the personnel office – how's my husband, has he fallen overboard "at his own request"? . . . Then I'll join the crowd at the pier to meet you, and by now there's a little baby in the basket, a little ball-and-chain so that you aren't tempted to have a bit on the side and don't blue your advance of pay on drink. So I'll give you a drink and take you home, to the couch, and at last we'll lie down together. Was all that really worth it for that little scrap of happiness? What harm have I done you, for you to wish that sort of life on me?'

I said: 'But I don't want that sort of life either. I'd be ready to pull up stakes any day you like and look for something else.'

'That's possible . . . Of course, it's equally possible to describe a sailor's life quite differently, so that anyone listening to you, far from being put off, would come running to sign on. Plenty of them do, don't they? You're not from my part of the country, are you?'

'What made you think that?'

'I don't know. I just had the impression you might be.'

'I'm from Oyrol.'

'Well, I grew up not far from you – in Kursk. And I used to dream, too, of going away to some magic place where you can breathe freely and the people are somehow special. I saw an advertisement and signed on at a building-site in the north. God, how keen I was! I was looking for somewhere as tough as possible, fool that I was. And what did I find? Bricklaying? Heaving planks? Mixing cement? Or dying of boredom in an office? I wasn't afraid of any work, as long as I didn't cripple myself or stop being a woman . . . And what for? The people around me were exactly the same as anywhere else: they suffered and made others suffer, and how would all my heroism improve anything in their lives? So I fixed myself up with a sort of life that was easier for me, and where at least they'd pass in and out of my life quicker and without hanging around – it was somehow a bit more fun, because when something lasts a long time it can get sickening to watch them. I expect you've probably arranged your life like that too – so you don't have to work too hard at living with people, or so you don't have to depend on someone – haven't you?'

'You've more or less guessed it.'

'It's bad, I've no doubt – but that's how it is! But all the same I am a woman, I'm supposed to attach myself to one man – and then put up with everything for his sake and, what's more, be glad of it. And you say to me: "Let's go away and look for something else." No, if something's not in you already you won't find it anywhere else. And you'll never give it to me. You can't change into a different person, my dear!'

'What sort of person am I, Klavka?'

'Shall I tell you? You won't be offended?'

'No, I won't.'

'You're not the kind that women marry. They can fall in love with you, even lose their heads over you. It would be easy enough to drown in your little green eyes . . . But marry you? Better to lie down across the railway tracks. Or jump out of that porthole fully dressed. Do you know what you are? You're a solitary soul! All alone in the middle of the field. You've got lovely hands.' She took my hand and pressed it to my cheek. 'But your soul is a lump of ice. And I could never make it melt. It was awful when you shouted at me.'

'I didn't shout.'

'It'd have been better if you had shouted – better, even, if you'd hit me. But you . . . sort of hissed at me, in a whisper, like a snake. You may have been thinking all sorts of things about me. But didn't you *see* the way I was looking at you? I was standing on deck, in the wind! I wasn't faking or putting it on then.'

I could see that now, from the look on her face. And I remembered Alik shouting down to us from above: 'I like you – this is the moment of truth!' No doubt there are some feelings you can't fake – the only problem is in telling which they are! . . . And then I remembered how I'd yelled at that Scotsman when he'd probably just been asleep in the stern, worn out by fear and exhaustion . . . My hands had done what was necessary, but my soul had been a block of ice.

I said: 'Maybe it's because all my life has been . . . always on the move, like a wheel turning.'

'Think mine's been any different? Yet surely we live for something else besides turning round and round. Sometimes when you stop and look . . .'

'There's a star twinkling?'

'Well, call it what you like. But whatever it is, it must be somewhere. I mean, not just anywhere but inside me. Perhaps it's God, or something, I don't know . . . There, I've told you now. Have I offended you?'

'Klavka,' I said. 'I know one thing: I can't live without you now.'

'You musn't say that. I wish you all the good in the world, but I'm going to run away from you as fast as I can go. This is the second time I've seen that look on your face . . . the first time – do you remember? – was when I asked you; "What have you got against me?" But I'll see it again – I will! No matter what else, I'll see it. People may say horrible things about me – and I'll see it. So I've got to run a long way away from you! If you're fond of someone, you've got to run further from them than if you aren't.'

'Tell me, then, why did all this happen?'

'Why did *what* happen? Nothing's happened.' Now that she'd put on her dress, the lace on the front of it made her different, distant. And anyway, the best thing of all had passed – the moment when she'd first leaned her head against my shoulder. 'What are you asking? Why did we make love? Well, because . . . because my life's been empty lately. And you came along, uninvited, into that emptiness. And you've just escaped death by the skin of your teeth. Forgive me. I probably shouldn't have said that . . .'

No, I thought, it was all necessary, if only so that you'd have told me everything. From now on I'd never think one could pass by someone and touch them – with hand or word – and not leave some trace on them. But why did you come to me just to go away again? You yourself asked: 'Why do we lead such stupid lives?' Yet we all live like that. We go away just to return. We return to go away again. And I was just thinking: at last I'd reached a safe haven, and the mooring was, as they say, 'promised'. Somewhere I once heard the expression 'the promised land'. I don't know what it is, but no doubt it's a good place. Only now it, too, was going away from me.

I was going to tell her this, but I didn't have time, because there was a loudspeaker in the cabin, and an announcement came over the intercom: 'Our Scottish guests are invited to go to the upper deck. A Norwegian warship has come alongside to take them home.'

'They'll still take a long time seeing them off,' said Klavka. 'Rest a little longer, I still have to feed you. They won't be bothering you for a while.'

'It won't be long now.'

And it wasn't: 'The following comrades are requested to return to their ship, to stand watch while the vessel is prepared for towing . . .' – and they listed practically all our names except the engine-room crew.

'Have they called you too?'

'Didn't you hear?'

Klavka walked over to the table, put her hands behind her head and shook out her great sheaf of hair so that it all fell down her back again, then began to wind it into a bun.

'I don't even know your surname. I only know you as Senya.'

I told her.

'I'll know now. Must you go?'

'It is an order to go on watch, even though it's only for preparing the tow.'

'A pity. I was thinking you and I might at least sail back to port together. I'd have fixed you up with a job on this ship.'

'I'd have fixed myself up. Only there's no point.'

I now had to get up and go; but getting up was like setting off to my own execution – and where was I supposed to go when I left her? I had no idea.

Still, I got dressed. And I put my foot in it yet again. I asked her: 'Are we never going to meet again?'

'I don't know. I'm confused. I really should go away somewhere, but where? . . . Please go. Go, and don't torment me. I don't even know how I'm going to walk out of this cabin. And I've got another little problem to cope with.'

'What problem, Klavka?'

She smiled with an effort: 'Aren't you grown up yet? Don't you know how babies get made? . . . Oh, I shouldn't have done it today!'

I never did know what to say at such moments. I went towards her, but she begged me: 'Don't, don't kiss me. Or I'll fall apart completely.'

'Goodbye, then . . .'

As I was going out she turned away towards the table and started putting on her earrings.

I reached the main companion-way and stopped. Perhaps it was here that she'd asked me: 'What have you got against me?' I stood in the shadow behind a fire-extinguisher. I wanted to look at her one more time.

Klavka walked away down the corridor – slowly, as if she was drunk. Not like drunks who stagger, but like people who are very drunk yet can still walk straight. She was dragging her heels along the carpet. She stopped, straightened her hair and smiled to herself, but her smile, too, was a drunken smile and somehow pathetic.

With other women, after making love with them, I had wanted more than anything else to be on my own and relax, because I always felt completely empty. But with her it was as if the parting had been violent and painful. I couldn't even call out to her as she passed by without noticing me. It'd have been better if I hadn't stayed to look at her.

When I reached the upper deck, it was noisy and bright and the whole of the port side, where the Norwegian warship was moored alongside, was crammed with people. They were still saying goodbye to the Scotsmen – they couldn't seem to let them go. People embraced them and had their pictures taken with them under the searchlights.

I didn't join in. I wanted to go back to our ship in the first available net, so as not to see Lilya when she came to see the apprentices off. They were delayed somewhere, thank God, and the first two to show up were Shura and Marconi. The derrickman produced a net for us and we flew up over the side and down. Marconi was seen off by Galya, who waved her handkerchief to him, roaring with laughter. Shura was accompanied by Irochka, but she didn't seem to be in the mood for laughter.

As we swung through the air, Marconi shouted to me: 'Well, Senya, did you score? Can we congratulate you?'

'How did *you* make out?'

'Same as before, Senya. But she says it could be third time lucky.'

The Chief was waiting for us on deck. He was wearing someone's quilted jacket thrown over his shoulders and slippers on his bare feet. He sniffed at us and pulled a face.

'I can see you've been at the port wine, you villains. Aren't you ashamed of yourselves?'

I felt embarrassed: 'Chief, I forgot to bring you anything.'

'*You* forgot him, but I didn't.' Shura produced a half-litre bottle of Stolichnaya from his jacket. 'Well, it wasn't really me – someone asked me to give it to you.'

'Who was it? Interesting to know.'

'They asked me not to say.'

'Mysterious,' said the Chief. 'Two other anonymous people each lowered a bottle of Armenian brandy to me on a cod-line. And by the way, they haven't been broached yet.'

Seryozha and Vasya Burov came next. On his way down, Vasya was talking about a bottle of Italian vermouth, which had been standing on the table unopened, and he hadn't dared to reach out and grab it.

'Couldn't you just have asked them to give it to you?' asked the Chief.

'I felt shy. Anyway, the officer of the watch wouldn't let us through.'

'And I should think not!' said the Chief. 'Why should he let in such scarecrows? And you can't even behave yourselves. Why did you go, Marconi? Both you and I were on the list to go, we both refused – but you upped and went.'

Marconi scratched behind his ear.

'I'm amazed at myself. Well, I suppose I went because everyone else went.'

'When will you learn a little dignity? Well now – did you take note of what I said about those two bottles of Armenian brandy? So I invite you all to my cabin. Got that? I invite you. But mind – I won't let you in looking scruffy.'

The Chief shuffled away to his cabin. The beachers immediately ran off, but I hung back for a while to take a look at the side of the factory-ship – just in case Klavka might have come out to look at me. But no, she hadn't.

Suddenly I noticed a lonely figure standing in the shadow by the doghouse, with his cap over his eyes so you couldn't see his face.

'Is that you, Obod?'

'Yes.'

He came towards me sort of reluctantly, looking awkward, in an overcoat that came down below his knees.

'Why aren't you on the factory-ship?'

'What's good about it? I'm coming back to port with you. As a passenger. Will you take me?'

'You can sail with us. We're all passengers now.'

Marconi shouted to me from the wheelhouse: 'Senya, you haven't forgotten we're invited to the Chief's, have you? Got a tie? If not, I can lend you one of mine, it's Japanese.'

Shura also lent me a pullover, so that I looked respectable. Vasya Burov dug out his suit; God knows who it had been made for – it was tight across the shoulders, while you could have pulled Vasya through the trousers with room to spare. Seryozha advised him not to wear a tie, otherwise with his little beard he'd look a complete scarecrow.

For some reason we were all a little excited, although there was nothing special about the Chief's little cabin. We went to see him as if we were going for a medical. The Chief apologized for not wearing a jacket, but his suit had been splashed with oil, and his uniform tunic would make it somehow too formal. We all squashed in on the couch and on the Chief's bunk. Vanya Obod sidled in behind us, quiet as a shadow. He asked timidly: 'May I come too? I haven't come empty-handed.' He pulled a half-litre bottle of vodka out of his pocket.

'Come in, you wretched deserter,' said the Chief. 'What do you say? Shall we accept him?'

We accepted the deserter, only suggesting he should take off his overcoat and cap. The Chief pointed to the table: 'Help yourselves, lads.'

For snacks there was a plate of ham and some bread sliced up on a sheet of newspaper.

Shura jumped up: 'I'll just go and squeeze a bit more out of the cook.'

He came back with a fair amount of booty – in one hand half a bucketful of stewed fruit, two chunks of sausage under one elbow, mugs on his fingers and a loaf of white bread under each armpit.

'The galley's pretty well bare. Our foreign friends have eaten what there was, and the cook hasn't got the dinner ready yet because he's found a mate of his on the *Molodoi*.'

Vasya Burov said: 'Fancy that. The first time our cook's skipped his watch, and it's a tragedy. But we'll forgive him, beachers.'

We forgave the cook. The Chief sniffed at the bucket and asked: 'What was that bucket last used for?'

'It had coal in it,' said Shura, 'but I washed it out.'

'You scavenger-fish!' The Chief laughed. 'I don't know how the sea tolerates you!'

Marconi poured brandy into the mugs and offered the first one to Vanya Obod. Vanya took it cautiously: 'Why do I get it first?'

'Because the first toast is to those who've returned,' said the Chief. 'So far you're the only one who's returned, deserter. We haven't – yet.'

'I'm not a deserter, lads. I wanted to untie the family knot.'

'With an axe?' Marconi winked at us.

'Yes, if I'd caught her in the act.' Vanya sighed again. 'I got this idea into my head . . . Then I thought – who've I got besides her? If I'd have broken it up, I'd have been left all alone.'

'Well, you won't be,' said Marconi. 'A message has already been sent to your Klara that you're on your way home. By the way, you owe me fifty kopecks for the radio telegram.'

Vanya was thoroughly embarrassed. He stared into his mug and muttered: 'Forgive me, lads. It's like you're all heroes . . . but what am I?'

'Don't feel bad about it,' said Seryozha. 'We're just the same as you.'
The Chief raised his mug: 'Down the hatch, lads!'

We sent our drinks down the hatch and surfaced again to eat some sausage and chase it with stewed fruit drunk out of the same mugs.

Marconi began to tell us what had happened at the banquet, about the speech Grakov had made and how he'd mentioned the signal the Scotsmen had sent, in which they thanked everyone who'd tried to save them and asked for greetings to be sent to their families. He'd read all that in our ship's log and remembered it word for word. When people began to protest at his quoting that signal, he'd even gone on to ask the Scotsmen: 'Did you think you couldn't rely on Soviet seamen? We have a saying: "I may go to my grave, but a comrade . . ." – and a foreign comrade, too, of course – "I must save."' In reply the Scots captain had said he thanked the Russian seamen and hoped he would never again have to send signals like that to Mr Grakov.

I looked at the Chief; he was frowning, as if he had toothache. He and I were talking once, and he'd made a strange remark to me: 'I pity that wretched man.' I'd asked: 'Haven't you come to tolerate him over the years?' – 'Well, he and I are the same age, though he's very slightly older than me . . . Yet he can't do anything. All his life he's done nothing but say stupid things. If they sacked him tomorrow, he'd die in some gutter. Except, of course, that he has his pension . . .' Ah, Chief, I was thinking now, we still don't yet know which of you two has more clout! . . .

'Pity,' said the Chief. 'I thought he might at least have had some spark of human feeling in him.'

'Well, I must say, there was no sign of it,' said Marconi. 'And his voice – he just went droning on and on like a tape-recording. Our bo'sun, Strashnoi, sensed this, and that must have been why he let fly at Grakov.'

'Come on, tell us about it,' said the Chief, perking up. 'Don't tell me the bo'sun dared to speak out?'

'Not straight away. He needed three slugs of vodka to get his courage up. He'd moved over to sit with us, while only the mates and Mitrokhin stayed with Grakov. Mitrokhin, incidentally, made a speech too – he spoke about the "efficient co-ordination between the captain and the crew". The bo'sun was sitting there getting hotter and hotter under the collar. "No," he said, "*I'm* not an arse-licker, I'm going to tell the whole truth." – "You'd die rather than do that," I said to him. "I may die," he said, "but I'll have my say first. Now's the moment – I can feel he's afraid of me." And he got up to speak. "Well now," he said, "all that's true – I may go to my grave but a comrade I must save. We weren't sure we'd be sitting down at this table, though. We had no such certainty. But someone – I won't say who or how much – began celebrating well before this banquet started by hitting the brandy bottle in his cabin."'

'Good old Strashnoi!' the Chief grinned. 'By tradition we must now drink to our bo'sun, with a wish that he at least stays a bo'sun.'

'Well, yes . . . *if* he'd stopped there. But then he went on to prod a few more sore spots. "My misfortune in life has always been this: somehow the person I want to drink with is never at the table. It's always the wrong people who seem to be giving the orders and making the speeches. Right now, the man I'd really like to clink glasses with is Babilov, our Chief Engineer. But where is he? I don't see him at your banquet . . ."'

'No, he shouldn't have said that,' said the Chief. 'I chose not to go.'

Again I glanced at the Chief and thought how cunning people could be when they bore a grudge. Who was that list of 'ship's representatives' at the banquet compiled for? For you, Chief, and no one else. Grakov made it up just so you'd take one look at it and refuse to go. He knows you better than you know him.

We tossed another one down the hatch – to the bo'sun – and surfaced again. As we did so, it was nice to know there was plenty more where that came from and it'd be a long time before the party broke up.

It was then we heard orders being given to cast off. The *Molodoi* was towing us away from the factory-ship. No one noticed it amid all the talk, but I was sitting by the window facing the big ship's side, and I saw her moving away, saw how there was first one row of portholes, then two, then four. But when I noticed the waves splashing against the bottom row of portholes, I almost groaned aloud.

I looked up – the Chief was talking about me: 'Our Senya seems a bit sad.'

Marconi winked at me: 'Senya's totting up his score. Trawly told me Senya's found something worth mooring up to.'

'Maybe it's more serious than that?' the Chief enquired. 'In that case we'll drop the subject.'

I waved my hand: 'Talk about whatever you like.'

Shura quickly filled all the mugs again: 'To our warpman! To my dear and good neighbour. May he live long and be lucky in love.'

It's really something, I can tell you, when a golden boy like Shura wishes you that.

'Down the hatch, lads!'

Again we took a bit more on board as we drained our mugs, and Vanya Obod told us what it had been like on the factory-ship when we were sinking, and how uncomfortable he'd felt – it's a sign of bad luck when someone signs off, and it looked then as if he really had brought us bad luck. Everyone had kept running to the engine-room and begging them to put on more revolutions, even though the engines were already at full speed. Apparently, too, the skipper of the factory-ship had said to the mate on watch in the wheelhouse that if all ended well, he would see that Grakov was made to answer for it, even if he had to hand in his Party card.

'That's a legend,' said the Chief. 'But it's nice to hear a legend like that one.'

There was a knock at the window: it was the trawlmaster flattening his nose against the glass and pulling funny faces at us. We waved to him to come in, but he wasn't alone – with him were the bo'sun, the apprentices and God knows who else. There wasn't room for them all in the cabin, so they stood in the doorway and the mugs were passed from hand to hand. And of course everything started all over again – the talk and the toasts . . .

I sat with them drinking and laughing. And I felt good again. Yes, I really think I did.

7

The good old Gulf Stream!

It's two thousand miles from the fishing-grounds to port, but the Gulf Stream helps us along, the wind's astern too – by whose kindness I have no idea – and we bowl along like this right as far as Kildin Island; the main problem is not to miss the mouth of the Murmansk Sound. And we arrive a day early.

Now, though, the *Molodoi* was towing us. All we had to do was spit on the towing-hawser so it wouldn't break. For the first few days we could see the factory-ship ahead of us: her smoke by day, her lights by night. Then she passed over the horizon.

We just slept and watched films – the same old ones, of course. Then on the third morning our dear Bo'sun Strashnoi came on deck, looked at the sun, at the blue water, at the snow-topped cliffs of the Lofoten Islands – and spake thus: 'I've got work for you beachers. You've been stuffing your faces so hard, you're as round and fat as floats. But who's going to clean up the ship for you?'

'You go back to sleep, bo'sun,' Seryozha advised him. 'The ship's going into dry dock as soon as we arrive, anyway.'

'But before it goes into dry dock, we've got to go into port. And in what? It's not a ship, it's a disgrace.'

Well, we all grumbled and blew off steam, and then, of course, we got hold of paint-scrapers, wire-brushes and paintbrushes and began to clean up the ship. We scraped the rust off the sides and the bulkheads, then we red-leaded them and painted them. Somebody washed out the crew's quarters with soda, someone scrubbed out the wheelhouse and someone else swabbed out the heads. For some reason the apprentices asked to go up to the masthead, where they painted the crow's nest with whitewash and black paint, bellowing to each other in raucous voices: 'Alik, hold the bucket, I'm going up to the truck, it has to be painted red.'

'OK, Dima, I've got it. We'll paint everything, from keel to truck!'

The trawlmaster and his mate painted their net-winch in a horrible acid green that hurt you to look at it. The Third Mate glared at them from the wheelhouse and spat: 'You bumpkins! All machinery is meant to be painted red. For a seaman, you've got a horrible taste in colours.'

Just to please him even more, the trawlmaster then painted the capstan green.

Shura Chmyrev and I were told to clean up the outside of the galley. Nice job. The sternsheets are a good place to be; you can't hear the wind, the bulkhead gets warm from the sun and screens you from the officers. Later, Vasya Burov joined us – a sure sign we'd got the cushiest job of all.

'Mind if I join you for some honest skiving?' he said.

'Skive away,' said Shura. 'Only hold a paintbrush in your hand. And watch out for anyone coming.'

'Don't worry, I can smell someone coming a mile off.'

Vasya, in fact, didn't pick up a paintbrush the whole way. He just sat down in blissful idleness.

The cook and the cabin-boy, who were cleaning the galley on the inside, often came out and joined us to sit on a bollard and discuss life.

'As for me, I'm going back to work in a factory,' said Shura. 'I'm a trained welder – and that's not something to throw away lightly. As for roaming all over the sea – sod that for a lark! The apprentices can climb up to the masthead if they want to, they haven't had a bellyful of the "romance of the sea" yet. Do you agree, cooky?'

Vasya the cook not only agreed, he developed the theme further: 'But I'm telling you, Shura: the sea has given us something, you know. Take me, for instance: ship's cooks have to pass an exam. If you're not a real professor at your job, you'll never stick it out on board ship – no sir! The skipper won't take you on another trip – he wants to eat well too. So I have a good chance to fix myself up in the Gorka restaurant. You need pull, too, of course. But in principle it can be done.'

Shura wasn't sure they'd take our cook at the Gorka, but he nodded and agreed. Fine weather and sunshine has a marvellous effect on people. What's more, we were heading for port.

'Hey, cooky!' said Vasya Burov. 'I've made up a story about you. And about God.'

'Let's have it then!'

And Vasya span him a long and tangled yarn, but if you listened carefully and unravelled the story, it was a good one.

It went more or less like this: One day we shall reach the end of our tortuous paths on this earth and we shall come to the Lord (who doesn't exist). Cosmonauts, marshals, writers, great scientists and famous actors will be sitting there already – they have an atuomatic ticket to heaven. But there'll come a day when Vasya our ship's cook arrives there, and the angels and archangels will lead him to God's Judgement Seat. And the Lord (who doesn't exist) will ask him with iron in his voice: 'Who are you and what do you hope for? Answer this minute!' – 'I'm a chef, or rather a ship's cook. I hope for your mercy, O Lord. What else is there to hope for?' – 'Tell what you did when you lived on land and on sea.' – 'What was special about my life, O Lord? I did what everyone does. And I sinned, of course. I deceived my wife with her sister, who came from the country to stay with us; my wife found out – and she yelled her head off . . .' – 'That is a great sin, cook. It will be counted against you. But most important of all – what did you do?' – 'I cooked *borshch* with Bulgarian peppers.' – 'What's so clever about that? A woman can do that, and you did wear trousers, after all.' – 'But it was blowing a gale, O Lord. Force 11. You sent it to us!' – 'Force 11, you say? Then it wasn't me – that was Satan's doing. I only send up to Force 6, anything more comes from him.' – 'That's true, O Lord. In a Force 6 life's still possible – you can moor up to the factory-ship and you can still cope in the galley. But just you try it in a Force 11. If your stove's in gimbals it's OK, but if not, you're liable to get half a saucepanful all over your stomach.' – 'And did the beachers appreciate your skill?' – 'They didn't complain, judging by the noise they made eating. I should think they did appreciate my work – other cooks give up and serve dry rations in a Force 7, they're allowed to by regulations, but I only served hot meals and what's more I baked fresh bread every day. But to be honest with you, O Lord, they didn't care what I did by then. They were about to drown, they were blowing bubbles already.' – 'Stop!' the Lord (who doesn't exist) will say: 'So they were expecting to die, were they? Therefore they should have been thinking about their immortal souls, preparing for My Judgement – and you make them *borshch*! What does that mean, cook? Were you against me?' – 'O Lord, how could I ever be against you? You wouldn't want to cope with a crew of starving beachers, would You? Then they wouldn't be thinking about their immortal souls but simply about how to get something to eat. I'm a little man, but I know my job. Whether we were going to drown then or survive, whether we were going to stand before Your throne or wait a while to see if You're going to send us to the golden palace for lead-swingers in paradise or make us lick red-hot frying pans – I'm not going to send any beachers to You hungry. I must feed them first, and what's more with hot food. No matter what the wind and waves are doing. And then You may judge me as You think fit. But I did my duty as a ship's cook.' The Lord (who doesn't exist) thought for a while. 'I think you're right, cook. But I have one more question for you: were *you* expecting to die?' – 'Who could have doubted it, O Lord? The wind was blowing us on to the cliffs, the engine had conked out and the anchors wouldn't hold. What else could I have been thinking when I watched the beachers pumping?' – 'And still you cooked *borshch* for them?' – 'Truly, O Lord. Good *borshch*, with peppers. That was my job, and I did it conscientiously.' And the Lord (who doesn't exist) will say: 'I have no more questions. Come to me, my son, Vasya the ship's cook. Look into my auburn eyes. You're a sinner, of course. But damn it, let's not quibble over trifles. Basically you're on our side. And I hereby assign you to the most heavenly paradise of all, to the golden palace for lead-swingers!' And He will say to His angels and archangels: 'Carry this beacher away in your pure white arms. And write in the Book of Regulations: There is no such thing as heroism on earth, but there is duty done . . .'

To be serious, though, I agreed with Shura – and with the cook, and with the cabin-boy, who was aiming to go and raise geese on a collective farm – that bumming around the oceans was no sort of life. They asked me: 'And where will you head for, warpman?'

'I don't know – I haven't made up my mind yet. For the time being I'll go to Oryol, to see my mother. Then I'll look around. I did train to be a milling-machine operator once.'

Shura was delighted. 'That's it, neighbour! We'll push off to Oryol together, it's our home territory. We'll drop anchor in the same factory, get jobs – and work like hell! The apprentices can stay at sea if they want to.'

So each of us had found an ally and was glad of it. And it had somehow slipped my mind that only the previous day I'd been in Marconi's cabin and seen all the radio-telegrams they had been sending – to the fleet administration, asking to extend their engagements for another year. And why had I gone to see Marconi? To send the same radio-telegram, because on the day before that we'd been called individually to see Zhora the mate, who was compiling lists of personnel for the next trip. He sent for me, too, and, avoiding my eye, he asked me: 'They're mustering a crew for a new trawler of the "Ocean" class, to fish for cod in the Barents Sea. For twenty days. What about you? Will you sign on?'

'Zhora,' I reminded him, 'I'm going to be prosecuted when we reach port.'

'Are you crazy? Those nets will be written off. Mean to say you've been worrying about it all this time? You should have asked me . . . They're only looking for the right section of the regulations that will allow them to write the nets off. In the cause of international good will, or something. The Soviet government is kind – it'll write off anything you like.'

'Was Grakov trying to help me?'

'Well, yes, amongst others . . .'

'Give him my thanks. He's a good man.'

'You're not so bad yourself,' said Zhora. 'But I just can't imagine how you're still walking around a free man. You're a prime candidate for jail – the prison people must be missing you badly! So just watch your step.'

'I'll try.'

'Like hell you'll try!'

I didn't bear a grudge against Zhora for having advised me to cut the trawl-warp. Of course, he advised me *against* it, if you remember; the hint had to be put into effect. And I could understand Zhora's position, too: the skipper could have been demoted and prosecuted for those nets, while all they could do to me was prosecute me – you can't demote a mere seaman. In any case, it had come out all right in the end.

I asked Zhora: 'Are you going to sign on?'

'I haven't decided yet. I feel like taking a bit of a rest, after all the excitement.'

In fact, though, he put his own name second on the list; the first was Marconi, because Marconi would have put his own name at the top of the list anyway when he radioed it to port.

Marconi himself said to me: 'I'm swotting up a textbook to learn to be a driver. Mind you, it's hard to remember all the rules, they're enough to make you cross-eyed. But I've got a mate in the Traffic Police, I'll give him a bottle and he'll fix me up with a licence. What do you think of the idea?'

And I thought: what are we, for heaven's sake? Just children . . . that's all.

8

We reached port in the early morning.

The *Molodoi* took a long time towing us in – past the lighted channel-buoys; past the floating docks giving off sounds of hammering, drilling, and the hiss of welding-torches; past the hills where not a single light was burning yet; past the Arctic, its windows still blank and empty – until in the middle of the harbour she made fast alongside us and pushed us into a berth.

By then we were all standing on deck, the cook's last meal inside us, dressed in our shoregoing rig – although I'd had to beg a quilted jacket off the bo'sun.

I could tell you what usually happens: how the trawler eases herself into the berth and bumps the quayside with her bow, while the Second Mate is standing ready with a little suitcase and, while the ship's still moving, leaps on to the pier and belts off to the office for all he's worth – to fetch the cash for our advance of pay. Meanwhile the ship is manoeuvring and we moor up properly, making fast all mooring lines – head and stern ropes, bow and stern lines, springs – and just as we're finishing that job the Second Mate comes dashing back at full steam and shouting: 'Got it!' We all crowd into the saloon, breathing down each other's necks while he unseals the bundles of money on the table, ticks off the amounts in the ledger, and its – 'Sign here' for the sum each of us has requested: two hundred, three hundred. Then the stevedores will unload our fish, and when the amount due to us for the whole trip has been calculated, the office will pay out the balance in full. The women are already waiting for us on the pier to hustle us off home – that's it, we've had our fill of sailing!

This time, though, it was all different. Since the whole trip had gone wrong, the trouble lasted right until the final mooring-up. We looked – and couldn't recognize the familiar quayside. It was empty; there wasn't even anyone to take our mooring-lines. Then a man appeared – a little runt in a fur hat with dangling ear-flaps like a spaniel – and said gloomily: 'Why've you moored up on your port side? The harbourmaster told you to moor up to starboard – didn't you hear him on your radio?' And he threw us the eye of a warp from a bollard.

'Dear man,' the skipper said to him, 'we have no power, so it would take a day for a tug to turn us round in this berth.'

'I only do what I'm told. The order was – starboard. If you want to get a suntan out in the roads, I can arrange it for you.'

The bo'sun picked up the eye of the warp and threw it over the man's shoulders. He went on mumbling something, but we weren't listening – we were jumping across from the ship to the pier.

We walked along the quay at a leisurely pace, stretching our legs. The snow creaked loudly underfoot, much louder than on the deck of a ship. Suddenly we saw the women – running at us for all they were worth, weeping and calling out:

'Vasya . . . Seryozha . . . Kesha . . . and they told us Quay No. 8, so like fools we were standing and waiting there. That harbourmaster – I'll . . .' And they told us what they'd do to the harbourmaster. Sailors' wives have a pretty good vocabulary too.

Vasya Burov's wife had brought their two little daughters – all wrapped up in scarves, only their sleepy little eyes visible. She'd had no qualms about getting them up when it was still dark – either that, or they themselves had begged to come: it wasn't every day daddy came home from a trip, and not on every trip was he nearly drowned. Vasya even shed a few tears when he saw his kids. He kissed them on the tips of their noses and felt their foreheads.

'They're a bit hot.'

'Nonsense!' His wife tried to take them back from him. 'Hot? You must be crazy. Who else has such lovely, healthy little kids?'

Vasya tucked each of them under one arm and carried them off like that. Then he sat them on his shoulders.

'Let them down, you old fool!' his wife shouted at him. 'They're big girls now, I expect they can walk home by themselves.'

'No, I won't! I'm going to carry them home like this. They're not that big, let them ride on their dad for a bit longer, the darlings.'

She smiled, wiping her tears with a handkerchief. She turned towards us with a sort of guilty look on her sharp little face, as though making excuses for Vasya: 'You see what it's like with him!'

Vanya Obod's wife, on the other hand, turned out to be almost a head taller than him; smartly dressed, too – in little boots, a fur coat of grey Persian lamb and a fur hat with a scarlet top. Under that was a slanting gypsy eye, a fringe of tight curls and bright red cheeks. You'd *need* an axe to keep a treasure like that.

'Ah, my old scarecrow!' She slapped Vanya on the shoulder. 'Playing tricks, are you? I met the factory-ship, but you gave me a surprise.'

She squeezed and fondled him, shrieking with laughter as if she was the one being tickled.

Vanya was very embarrassed: 'Klara, we're not alone, you should at least meet my shipmates first.'

'And why not!' She thrust her hand, with its blood-red fingernails, at all of us. 'My name's Klara Obod, pleased to meet you.'

When she shook my hand, I almost winced; she even tackled the skipper: 'Klara Obod, pleased to meet you. I hear you had a bit of trouble on this trip – don't worry, everything will be fine!'

The skipper's wife gave her a frightened look. Klara reassured her: 'We silly women, we worry ourselves to death and then they come sailing home, as fit as fleas and nothing's happened to them at all. You brave boys, how glad I am to see you. Your money's already been worked out, you can go and pick it up at half past two.'

We walked on with the women, turned off the quays to the central causeway and gradually spread out, breaking up into couples.

Walking alongside me was Marconi's wife – not exactly God's gift, I'd say. Waddling like a duck, she had legs like bottles and a face – well, the sort they say looks as if she's always just about to start a row; arrogant, dry lips pressed together, eyes half-covered by their lids and somehow bare, without any eyelashes, white with fury. Even here she couldn't restrain herself, but nagged away at him in a whisper so loud we could all hear it: 'I don't see what you have in common with all these grey little men! They can all go to hell. But you're a specialist, a qualified radio-operator. And you treat them as equals!'

'Oh, Raisa, do stop it,' he said to her in a pained voice, frowning. 'Come on, pussycat. We are back safely, after all . . .'

'Oh yes? And how am I supposed to get over the shock to my nervous system? I'm absolutely shattered. By all your carryings-on.'

'You can tell me all this at home.'

'I've got more than this to tell you. The things you get up to out there! No doubt with vulgar tarts like that one, I suppose.' She stabbed Klara in the back with a glance; it was a wonder her fur coat didn't start smoking. 'But of course you couldn't remember what yesterday's date was, could you?'

'What was it?' Marconi asked in horror. 'Oh my God, I clean forgot!'

'Ah, so you forgot! And what *were* you thinking about, may I ask? What prevented you from sending a few words by radio for my mother's birthday?! Who, by the way, has done so much for you. Everyone keeps saying to me: "Your Andrei is such a pig, he never thinks of anyone but himself!"'

It made me feel sick. If he did 'get up to things', it was only to snatch himself a little piece of life. I walked on ahead, before they started fighting.

Three women turned up to meet Seryozha – all so similar it was amazing. They were like little round-faced 'Matryoshka' dolls – all wearing smart white felt boots and little short overcoats, all with red hair and extravagant hair-dos under polka-dotted headscarves, looking like steeply-pitched roofs. It was amazing he could tell them apart.

'Well, how are you, Zinochka?' he drawled. 'How are you Allochka, Kirochka?' Although they could only whinny and giggle, they didn't quarrel among themselves, even contriving to take it in turns to hang on his arms.

A little figure emerged from a shadow by the wall of a warehouse. She stood there timidly, then took a step towards us, not daring to come right up to us but just standing, tugging at the collar of her overcoat.

'That's mine waiting for me,' said Shura. 'Come on over, I won't eat you.'

She took another pace towards him and burst into tears.

'Shura . . .'

'Well, what is it? We were out of luck this trip, that's all.'

'What d'you mean "out of luck"? You might have died, Shura.'

'All sorts of things might have happened. But I didn't die.'

'If you had, do you imagine I could have stayed alive? I'd have committed . . .'

Shura took her by the shoulders and said to us: 'Go on, lads, I'll calm her down.'

And so it was that Shura was the first one we said goodbye to. We waved to Shura and his wife: 'See you in the Arctic!'

'It's the law. We'll be there at eight.'

We went on, over the dirty snow, between the fish-curing sheds and the warehouses. A locomotive crossed our path, pulling empty goods wagons with frost-encrusted sides. We stopped to let it pass and bunched up into a crowd again. Suddenly the engine stopped in front of us, making the couplings clink all the way down the train. The engine-driver looked out of the cab – a white-haired man with a squint, his cap stuck on the back of his head. His name was Kolya; we knew him, and he knew most of us.

'That's funny,' said Kolya. 'I see Seryozha from the *Galloper*. It's less than a month since I saw you go to sea. Has something happened?'

'Don't you know?'

'Haven't heard anything. Must have missed the story. What was it all about?'

'Oh, you know – had a bit of bad luck.'

'I see,' said Kolya. 'Are you all alive?'

'Yes, all of us.'

'Will you at least get paid for one load?'

'Yes.'

'So what's the problem? Don't worry, lads.'

We said to Kolya: 'Keep going. People are waiting for us at home.'

Kolya thought for a moment, took off his cap and put it on again.'

'I can't go forward as long as you're standing there. I'm pulling empty wagons. I'd better put her in reverse.'

So he did, and we stepped across the track.

A nasty moment was awaiting our Third Mate: his lady had come to meet him, the one that was 'big enough for one and a half blokes', wearing a hat and an overcoat with a fur collar. His keen sailor's eyesight did not let him down, however; he spotted his 'dear Alexandra' from a distance, as she was walking under a street lamp, slapping her handbag against her knees. He hung back a bit, hiding behind us: 'I won't say goodbye. Don't forget – I wasn't here with you, OK? And he vanished round a corner.

She peered at us short-sightedly and asked in a low voice: 'Excuse me, is this the crew of No. 815? Was Third Mate Cherpakov sailing with you?'

'Yes, he was. We saw him only just now. Oh, no, he's been held up on board.'

'But he's alive and well, at least?'

'Nothing wrong with him.'

She nodded: 'Thank you. That's all I need to know.' And she set off again with a broad stride.

At the fleet management office the skipper, his wife and Zhora the mate broke off from us. They had to go in to fill out forms: the official notification of our arrival and the claim for the nets. Zhora said to us: 'See you all on board at half past two. Adios!'

We reminded him:

'And we'll see *you* at eight in the Arctic . . . Will you be there too, comrade Captain?'

Frowning, but with solemnity, the skipper replied: 'The captain of your ship also respects the law.'

A little later, at the port café, Vasya Burov went his own way, while the cook and Mitrokhin turned off to go to the ferry terminal, as they had to cross the Sound.

After another hundred paces our little cohort thinned out a bit more: Marconi and the bo'sun had to turn off along the southern causeway, as they were going to Nagornoye, and with them went Vanya Obod and Seryozha.

'Shall we be seeing you in the Arctic?'

Marconi's wife said: 'We can't promise. It depends on circumstances.'

Klara shut her up by saying: 'Are you a sailor's wife or a witch? You're in such a hurry to get your husband back under your thumb, you might at least give him an evening off.'

Marconi's wife said nothing, but clamped her lips into a thin little line and her face went pale with fury. 'Marconi' spread his hands, smiling guiltily: 'I'll make every effort.'

Then the apprentices left us; they were hoping to fix themselves up in the Polar Institute hostel. I went over to them and asked: 'Well, will you be coming to the Barents Sea with us; or are you fed up with it?'

'We're going to think about it,' said Dima. 'So it's goodbye for now, chief.'

I asked Alik to step aside so I could have a few words with him; Dima turned away and waited for us.

'It's most likely we *won't* go, chief,' said Alik. 'We've got to get back to our own work.'

'Of course. Fishing's not your job anyway.' But I wanted to ask him something quite different. 'Tell me, why did you hang back and not get into the raft?'

'How can I explain it to you?' Confused, he looked down at his feet. 'You probably won't understand. Well . . . I wanted to share it all with you. Whatever happened. I actually felt curious to know what it would be like. And somewhere inside me I couldn't really believe the worst would happen. Perhaps I did, though, for a moment – when the light went out.'

'What's hard to understand about that? It's quite right and proper.'

'Don't blame Dima, either.' He looked me firmly in the eyes, although he blushed a little. 'How could I have let him go? What if he'd decided to go and a wave had washed him off the raft? We'd have both been to blame, chief. I still don't know who should forgive whom.'

I laughed. 'Forget it, lads. Where's the blame? We all did stupid things, and yours wasn't the worst.'

'Good, if that's what you think.'

'Going to sea with us at all was enough . . .'

'Yes, it meant a lot to us. You can't imagine . . .'

I interrupted him: 'Are you coming to the Arctic? You can tell me everything there. They'll all be listening then, not just me . . . Oh yes!' – I remembered – 'Will you be seeing Lilya today?'

'Shall I tell her to come too?'

'I'm not bothered.' I was surprised at how easily I said that. 'If she wants to, let her come. But give her my regards, of course. And say "thank you" for me. She'll know why.' I shook his hand, and simply waved to Dima. 'See you in the Arctic!'

We were quite a small group by the time we crossed the central causeway and walked up to the station. There, on the square, the last of us parted to go to Rosta – the cabin-boy, the trawlmaster and the cooper. They shook a sleepy taxi-driver and explained where they had to go.

'No hard feelings,' I said to the cooper. 'I know you're not going to the Barents Sea, so shall we say goodbye?'

He didn't take my hand.

'Who has any feelings about you? You're not worth it.'

He tapped the taxi-driver. 'Let's go, pal.'

From there on I walked with the Chief. He lived quite near our hostel. That was how he and I had originally met: the others had all gone their separate ways, and he and I had slogged our way onward through a snowstorm together; suddenly we'd got talking and he'd invited me home for lunch – yet for the whole trip we hadn't spoken a word to each other.

As I walked beside the Chief, he said to me: 'I'm worried about your future, Senya. In spite of everything, you shouldn't leave the fishing-fleet – there's no point in breaking your life in two. Maybe we've already lived through the toughest part, and now, you'll see, they're introducing a mass of technical improvements in vessels like the "Ocean" class and the "Tropic" class and conditions are getting much better. As for me, I'm through with the game, that's for sure. This trip was my last. Thirty years I've spent with engines, but when I looked at that sail, I suddenly realized – I've finished with it all.'

'Oh come on, Chief! You and I will sail again. You promised to teach me your trade.'

Instead of replying he just grinned, and I remembered how he'd said: 'But it's nice to hear a legend like that.'

When we reached his corner, he stopped and asked hesitantly: 'Maybe you'd like to come up to my place? We can feed and give you a drink and you can sleep wherever you can find a space. You don't want to go straight from the ship to the hostel, do you?'

I remembered their one little room and the little divan where they had made up a bed for me . . .

'But I'm not going to the hostel,' I said to him cheerfully. 'I've got somewhere else to flop.'

'Ah!' He smiled at me. 'Well, then – see you in the Arctic?'

We shook hands and the Chief trudged on – his heavy body in its short fur-lined coat, his shaggy fur hat and his boots. He turned round to me once more, knowing I was waiting for him to do that, and waved goodbye. Then I went on my way alone, turning first one cheek then the other to the wind.

Two weird creatures were coming towards me. One was booming away and waving his long arms, the other was moving at a slow jog as he hid his nose in his upturned coat-collar. I stared at them: I knew those silhouettes – it was Vova and Askold. I went over to a street lamp and waved to them.

'Ahoy there, mates! Off to sea, are you?'

They stopped, rooted to the spot, trying not to look as if they had been walking together. Then Askold smiled and opened his thick lips: 'Senya! What brings you here? Where've you sprung from?'

'From the usual place – the sea, where you've never been.'

'We were expecting you back in April. How come you're here?'

I didn't feel like telling them.

'You're a bit late today, beachers. All the others have gone home. We had a spot of bad luck, so you won't be able to milk us for much this time.'

Vova sighed: 'We could at least have sympathized.'

It all seemed so funny. I didn't feel any resentment towards them, but I felt no pity either.

'You're still just the same, mates,' I said. 'Still in the same filthy old caps with earflaps and quilted jackets. You didn't put my money to good use.'

Askold looked surprised: 'What money, Senya?'

'Come on, own up. It's all in the past, anyway . . . How much did you pinch off me? Except for the cash Klavka took.'

Vova, my friend, my faithful pal, racked his brains and confessed: 'Well, Senya, we did pinch some . . . In the taxi. You probably don't remember how you were chucking your money around then. It was enough to tempt anybody.'

'I see . . . And what you pinched – did you really spend it all on drink? Oh, you fools!'

'Senya,' said Vova, 'you know as well as I do – no money's ever enough for the damn' booze.'

'You're a couple of fools.'

Askold decided to try needling me: 'But look, Senya, you're wearing an old quilted jacket too. Where's your own jacket, our present to you?'

'When it comes from you,' I said, 'even a present doesn't last long.'

I walked away from them. Vova called out: 'Maybe we can have a quick one to say goodbye to your jacket?'

'That's an idea!'

'So are you inviting us?'

'I would, mates. But you weren't with us when it happened. I'm sorry, but you weren't with us.'

They hung around under the lamp-post for a long time.

Snowdrifts were building up all over the town, and as I walked my footsteps were immediately covered with snow blown by the ground-wind. On Militia Street the wind was blasting like it was being funnelled through a tube and it went right through my quilted jacket. Even so, I stopped for a while in front of the wing of the Polar Institute, and was even slightly amazed when I felt: No, Lilya means nothing to me any more. Just 'thank you', that's all. Do we really get over these things so quickly?

The snow had blown into a drift in front of the entrance to the hostel too, and I had to push it aside with my shoes before the old janitress could open the door. She was the same one who'd seen me off when I left.

'Recognize me, dear?'

'You've come back, have you?'

I could see she didn't recognize me.

'I've come back and I've come to pay my debt. Thirty kopecks. Remember?'

Now she recognized me. 'Why are you back so soon? Has something happened?'

'Oh, nothing to speak of . . . we were just unlucky, that's all.'

'They should all be so unlucky – at least you're all in one piece. And your debt's been written off. They started a new ledger.'

'I see,' said I. 'Well, life doesn't stand still, does it? Give me a bed, there's a dear. Near a window if possible.'

'You can take any bed you like. One whole room is empty at the moment. Just give us time to clean it up and you can move in.'

'Are you expecting any ships in today?'

'There's a ship coming in at five o'clock this evening.'

I worked it out – they wouldn't be here before seven, and at eight I'd be going to the Arctic, so I had the whole day with the room to myself. I could lock myself in, lie down, smoke.

'Thanks, dear. I'll leave my suitcase with you for the time being.'

'Leave it, it won't come to any harm.'

'There's nothing in it to get lost, anyway. I'll go out for a walk. I've missed this town badly – our northern gateway to the sea, our bastion of peace and honest toil.'

She looked at me over her glasses: 'Something must have happened to you out there . . .'

'I told you: we were unlucky.'

The station buffet opens at six; I occasionally used to go there before going on morning watch. The barmaid came out looking sleepy, her hair tied up in a grey scarf, and squeezed two glasses of coffee out of the urn. The coffee was hardly warm – or so it seemed to me, having come in from the freezing cold – and I drank it without bread or anything else, simply in order to chase away the sleep and have a bit of a think. Because in the evening we'd be meeting at the Arctic and there, of course, we'd have plenty to drink and everything would again take its usual course. In the meantime, thought, it would be a good idea to try and understand what we live for and why we go to sea. And about those Scotsmen – why did we go and save them, when we seemed unable to save ourselves? And about what might happen to me in the future, as the Chief had said: perhaps I might go to him for instruction or pluck up my courage, apply for the Nautical Academy and become 'a hard man' – in an officer's mackintosh and a white scarf! – or would I really break my life in two and look for something completely different?

Was it so important, though, how I organized my future? Because Klavka wouldn't be with me, and I didn't want any other woman in my life – ever. And anyway, one thought wouldn't give me any peace: why were we all such strangers to each other, why were we always each other's enemies? No doubt this is to someone's advantage; sad to say, we are all simply blind and we can't see where it's taking us. What disasters we need to bring us to our senses, for us to recognize our fellow-men as our brothers! But we are good people, that's what we have to understand – I couldn't bear to think we were worthless – yet we put up with pigs; like sheep, we obey people who are stupider than we are, and we torment each other for no reason . . . And so it will be – until we learn to think of our neighbour. But *not* to think about how to stop him from getting one up on us, or how to outflank him: no, that way none of us will ever save ourselves. What's more, life will never set itself to rights on its own. We, each of us, if only for three minutes a day, ought to shut up and listen out to hear if someone's in trouble, because that means *you're* in trouble too! –

in the way that all Marconis at sea observe radio silence and listen out, in the way that we get concerned about some distant people on the other side of the Earth . . . Or is all that just useless day-dreaming? Yet it's not much – just three minutes! And then, you see, you gradually turn into a human being . . .

I was sitting by the window. Snowdrifts were piling up all over the station square, and there wasn't a soul in it; the lamps were swinging back and forth on their wires, making black shadows leap across the snow. Then from out of a dark, dark street crawled a Volga taxi, with a checkerboard strip along its side. It circled around and stopped in the middle of the square: it could drive no further. A woman got out of the taxi – backwards for some reason – wearing a thick brown fur coat, a white headscarf and deerskin boots, and pulled out a suitcase after her. The taxi-driver smiled at her and said something, and she answered him – also with a cheerful remark, it seemed – and then she started walking towards the station, leaning over sideways from the weight of her suitcase, while he grinned as he watched her go. Once she turned round to shout something to him, and he waved his hand to her.

She was walking into the station right outside the window where I was sitting. She didn't see me, but was smiling to herself, or at what the taxi-driver had said. I suddenly felt a hammering in my temple and a trembling in my hands that were holding the glass.

9

'I notice you're always standing in my way, Ginger.'

'No – you're in *my* way.'

Klavka collapsed into a chair, unbuttoned her fur coat and pushed her headscarf down on to her shoulders. And then she smiled at me, her whole face lighting up. Walking to the station entrance had been enough to chill and redden her face.

'Give me a sip of something hot, whatever it is you're drinking.' I handed her a glass. Klavka drank it down and frowned. 'My God, he drinks black coffee without sugar. How can anyone do that and survive? Nyurka, haven't you got eyes in your head?'

The barmaid looked out from behind a glass display-case.

'What?'

'Oh, nothing. Just that there's this lad sitting in your café and you can't be bothered to lift your fat bottom off your chair. Have you seen that film *My Dear Man*? Go and see it, it's on at the Kosmos. Well, this villain here is even dearer to me. He's sitting here like a helpless orphan. You should at least take a look and see what he's like. He's a wondrous creature from the sea!'

Nyurka blinked at me.

'Nothing special.'

'You need eyes to see!' said Klavka fiercely. 'And at least half a portion of brains. Of course he's nothing special when he's wearing this mucky old jacket. But if he'd have come in his posh jacket, you'd have lain down on your back and not got up again.' Klavka winked at me. 'I wanted to do that once.'

Nyurka looked at me again, but said nothing.

'Why haven't you given him some beer, Nyurka?'

''Cos he didn't ask for any!'

Klavka simply burst out laughing: 'Oh, Nyurka, you'll never catch any mice! "Didn't ask for any"! A good man like this doesn't ask – you have to give it to him yourself. Come on now, feed him up a bit. And don't offer him your Russian salad, I can see from here it's been there since the day before yesterday. Got any of your chicken in aspic? I know how well you make it.'

Nyurka was stirred into action.

'I can slice him some smoked sturgeon. Or some nice salami.'

'Smoked sturgeon will do fine . . . Would you like some? Yes, he would, he would, slice it nice and thick. Then we'll settle the bill. Move yourself, Nyurka, look lively – you have to do things at the double in the fleet!'

'I'm not in the fleet, thank God.'

'*You're* not. But he is. Come on, let me do it!'

Klavka threw her fur coat on to the chair, took a tray from Nyurka and collected my glasses. She tipped the dregs of coffee into the sink, brought me a bottle of Riga beer, a plate of smoked sturgeon and some bread. Then she wrapped herself in her fur coat again and looked at me, resting her cheek on her fist.

'Well, how have you been living without me? Did you miss me just a little bit?'

'A bit – yes.'

'So I haven't lived in vain!'

I asked her: 'Where are you going, Klavka?'

'To Severonickel, to bury my father-in-law. Well, not exactly to bury him, they've already buried him without me, but for the wake on the ninth day.' She kicked her suitcase. 'They're relying heavily on me, I'm bringing no less than seven tins of crab.'

'Wait a moment,' I said, 'did you say – father-in-law? Have you got a husband?'

She blushed to the roots of her hair, and looked away.

'I had one. But he upped and went.'

'Did he leave you?'

'Yes.'

'Or did you leave him?'

'He left me.'

Klavka frowned and bit her lip. I was absolutely amazed to hear all this.

'How could he leave you?'

'I'm not made of pure gold, am I? It just happened that way. Of course, it would have been better if I'd left him. Then everything would have been cut and dried. As it is – God alone knows . . . He took offence and left. He did have some grounds for it, though.'

'So *that* was it.'

'There – I've let the cat out of the bag.'

'Are you hoping he'll come back?'

Without answering, Klavka twitched one shoulder and began looking out of the window.

'Where is he now?'

'I told you: he upped and went. He's at sea, second engineer on a DWT. I suppose he might come back . . . but it wouldn't be for long. People have told him such awful things about me – how could he ever come back for good?'

'When you went to sea, did you hope to see *him* too?'

Klavka blushed even more.

'Let's not talk about it. Anyway, he won't come back. He'd have to fall in love with me all over again. And I'm not the same woman I was, don't you see, Ginger? You've already found one of the skeletons in my cupboard.'

Klavka smiled, and from the side I could see her two gold teeth.

'How old are you?'

'Twenty-six.'

'Oh, what an old woman!'

'Still, it's not eighteen.'

So that's what you were worrying about, I thought; that's what you meant when you said to me on the *Fyodor*: "What sort of a future can we look forward to?" I'd never seen him, I knew nothing about him, but I suddenly felt a surge of anger towards him. What right had he to come between us, once he'd left her? And what was so wonderful about him, that Klavka should agonize over him and wait for him, and so there could never be anything between her and me?

'How long did you live with him?'

'Three years. Minus seven trips.'

I finished my beer and pushed the bottle aside.

'When are you coming back, Klavka?'

'When are you going to sea?'

'I'm taking a week off. The *Ocean* sails next Friday.'

'I won't be back before Saturday.'

I thought to myself: you've just decided that. If I'd said Sunday, you'd have said Monday. All right – so that's how it is. Seems there wouldn't have been much point in our meeting, anyway.

'The money we talked about – I left it at the Seamen's Hostel for you. Ask Sanyechka, the old woman who looks after the storeroom.'

'All right.'

She made it sound as if I'd asked her when I was going to get the money. OK, then – this meant there was no further link between us.

'Will you come and see me off?' she asked. 'Since I've run into you here.'

I picked up her suitcase.

''Bye, Nyurka!'

We went out on to the terrace. Here, too, the snow had collected in drifts and formed mounds on the parapet of the stone balustrade. Klavka used her mitten to sweep some snow off the parapet, jumped up and sat on it. I put down her suitcase at her feet. Below us the railway lines glittered;

beyond them was the slope leading down to the Fishing Port, where funnels and masts could be seen among the puffs of steam and the channel-lights reflected in the black water like long, many-coloured threads.

A little shunting engine, still partly covered in snow, was pulling a train of short, non-corridor carriages, and they stopped just below us. Hoar frost gleamed on their roofs and windows. Klavka looked at these carriages and shivered.

'Will they heat them, at least? Or maybe that's not my train yet?'

Dim lights were burning inside the carriages, showing up the frost patterns on the windows. God only knew whether they were heated or not. About thirty little people with suitcases and bundles started to board the train.

'That's your train, for Severonickel,' I said to Klavka. 'The carriages still have to be heated, the train's only just come out of the depot.'

I had nothing more to say to her. There was, though, still something I wanted to ask her.

'Back on the ship – was everything all right?'

Klavka understood.

'Why did you have to think of that?' She turned away. 'Maybe I should have had your baby after all . . .'

'What would you have done with him?'

'What does one do with children? I'd have raised him . . . Why do you laugh? Well, yes, I suppose my head is in a fog. Don't pay too much attention to what I say.' She looked at the carriages again and shuddered. 'Well, goodbye. Will you remember me all the same? Even though our love was short . . .'

'It was short and necessary.'

'Is that really so? There was something – and now it's over?'

She tried to smile sarcastically, but couldn't – her lips were trembling and the smile that came out was bitter, somehow pathetic. I remembered that long, empty corridor in the ship, where she had walked along with that same smile – slowly, like a drunken woman, her slippers shuffling along the carpet – and walked past me, while I didn't even call out to her. Just like now; I wouldn't call out to her. I was going to let her go as she was – confused, upset, on a cold journey to strangers, to a drunken binge and a hangover. They wouldn't welcome her, given the state of affairs between her and her husband . . . My God, there was a limit to what she could take – and I wasn't even offering her a shoulder. I can talk about loving our neighbour, but this person, who's closest of all to me, I won't help in any way. And *then* what am I? What great qualities in me can ever make up for this? Well, I'll tell you what I am. The third man, the gooseberry. Who has to go.

'No.' I shook my head. 'Don't be offended . . . I expect I said it wrong. You can't begin to know how much you did for me in those few short hours: it was probably enough to last me for the rest of my life. Well, it just so happened I didn't realize from the very start what you felt for me – and whose fault is that, if not mine?'

'Perhaps it's the fault of both of us . . .'

'Perhaps. I don't know about you, though, but I wouldn't want it to have been any different. After all, much worse might have happened – we might both have grown old without ever having met each other . . . No, it was all necessary! . . . There's your train, Klavka, take it and good luck to you. And if you ever feel bad, which God forbid, or if you feel empty, as you put it, then send for me and I'll come. You and I know how it can be: it may seem like there's not a gleam of light, no angel's going to appear, not even a seagull's going to come flying – but no, someone *does* come. I'll come running to you from anywhere, wherever I may be. You don't even have to write a letter – I'll hear you, I'll feel it.'

I wanted to take her hand. She pulled off her mittens, put them on her knees, and took my hands in both of hers and squeezed them, then let them go, looking down and past me. A fluffy curl had pushed its way out from under her headscarf. I looked at it, something seemed to squeeze my heart and I thought – I mustn't kiss her goodbye, or how would I survive the day?

'Thanks, Ginger . . . It's lovely just to hear you say that. No, I know you're not lying. It's just that I think . . .' And she stopped for a moment. 'What about you, though? Will an angel ever appear for you? Or will you always be standing all alone in the middle of a field? I'm terribly afraid for you too.'

'Now that you musn't be, Klavka. Why should I be alone? A person only has to think of others and not just of himself, and he's not lonely any more, however alone he may be – in the middle of a field or at sea. You're going away and we won't meet again – but even so I won't be without you. And will you really be alone in that damned Severonickel of yours – quite alone, without me?'

Klavka sighed and slid down from the parapet. Again she looked at the freezing carriages, but this time quite calmly, without shivering. That's it, I thought, now she can leave with a clear mind. I wouldn't want her to go with something still upsetting her or for her to pity me. Let her go with a light heart, and not run away from me as if I had the plague. Let her remember me kindly. And I'll remember her in the same way. I'll never forget how warm it was when we were together. Even though it wasn't for long.

'Look over there,' said Klavka. 'Has that taxi driven away yet?'

'Why do you want to know?'

'Let's take it. And go to Rosta, to my place.'

'Now what's this, Klavka?'

'Let's go, I said. Let you and me try living together.'

'What about the wake?' was all I could think of to say.

'Oh, to hell with them!' She drew her fingers over her eyes. 'They won't miss me. And you at least are a real, live man. Hell, I'll just do one more stupid thing in my life and then give up.'

'Klavka, why are you torturing me?'

'It's myself I'm torturing . . . Maybe it'll work out with you and me. Maybe it won't come to an end too soon. Perhaps you'd even fight for me? Except when that happens it's somehow always the woman who ends up with a black eye.'

So you've been through that too, I thought. How much more am I going to find out about you?

Klavka and I went down the icebound steps into the square. It was still pitch dark, with no sign of daybreak. I had the feeling it would never come, it had missed our part of the world altogether and gone somewhere else. But the taxi-driver was still waiting there in the square, running his engine to keep it warm. He was waiting for passengers from the Polar Arrow express, which arrived at eight.

Klavka was walking in front of me, along the path trodden by taxi-drivers to the station buffet. Suddenly she turned round to me and I ran to her. She pressed her cold cheek to mine.

'What's the matter?'

'Perhaps we shouldn't? It was good once, and we'd always have something to remember – but what if we go and mess it all up?'

'I don't know.'

'"I don't know, I don't know" – you make it all Klavka's responsibility! . . . Button yourself up, you wretched beacher!' Klavka dropped her mittens and fastened my quilted jacket up to the throat. The freezing wind squeezed tears from her eyes. 'I've been doing my best to entice you, and now *I'm* getting cold feet . . .'

'Go on – keep walking,' I said.

She nodded: 'That's right.' And off she went.

I might have told you how we arrived and came into that room, where I could remember almost nothing, and from which I'd been carried out after being beaten up, and how we spent our first day and what happened after that; but that would have been quite another story, in which Klavka would have been a different woman and I would have been different too. But however it may end, you'll remember us at that particular moment, because, as our First Mate from Volokolamsk used to say: 'Perhaps we're only really alive in the moments we're being good to each other.'

So let's say goodbye on the embankment, where I turned round for a last look at that whole panorama. Klavka was standing a little to one side, waiting for me, and looking down at the port too. We heard three farewell blasts on a hooter as a black trawler went astern out of her berth and into the middle of the harbour. She cut across the coloured threads, and her three blasts were answered by the dockyard, the harbourmaster and several large ships where night work was still going on.

I had no idea where those fishermen were going, or where the stars might be twinkling above them. I was saying goodbye to them, yet I wasn't: in a week's time I'd be sailing away like that, too – the country needs fish, after all.

And I didn't feel a bit bad about my jacket. It can stay there, in the Gulf Stream.